D0311691

This book sho·'
Lancashi·

Tremarnock Summer

EMMA BURSTALL studied English at
Cambridge University before becoming
a journalist and author. *Tremarnock*, the
first novel in her series set in a delightful
Cornish village, was published in 2015
and became a top 10 bestseller.

Also by Emma Burstall

Gym and Slimline
Never Close Your Eyes
The Darling Girls

Tremarnock Series

Tremarnock
The Cornish Guest House

Key

1. Jack's Cottage
2. The Victory Inn
3. Children's Play Park
4. Ebb Tide (Tony and Felipe's Place)
5. The Nook (Pat's Place)
6. Dove Cottage (Esme and Tabitha's Place)
7. Shell Cottage
8. Bag End (Liz and Robert's Place)
9. The Methodist Church
10. Copper Cottage

11. Dolly's Place
12. Dynnargh (Jean and Tom's Place)
13. The Stables
14. The Hole in the Wall Pub
15. The Fishmonger
16. The Marketplace
17. The Bakery
18. General Store
19. Seaspray Boutique
20. Gull Cottage (Jenny and John's Place)

With love to Emily, Tom and Isabella Arikian

Copyright, Designs and Patents Act of 1988.

9 7 5 3 1 2 4 6 8

A catalogue record for this book is available
from the British Library.

ISBN (HB): 9781784972530
ISBN (E): 9781784972523

Typesetting: Adrian McLaughlin
Map: Amber Anderson

Printed and bound in Great Britain by
CPI Group (UK) Ltd, Croydon CR0 4YY

Head of Zeus Ltd
First Floor East
5–8 Hardwick Street
London EC1R 4RG

WWW.HEADOFZEUS.COM

Emma Burstall

Tremarnock Summer

HEAD
of ZEUS

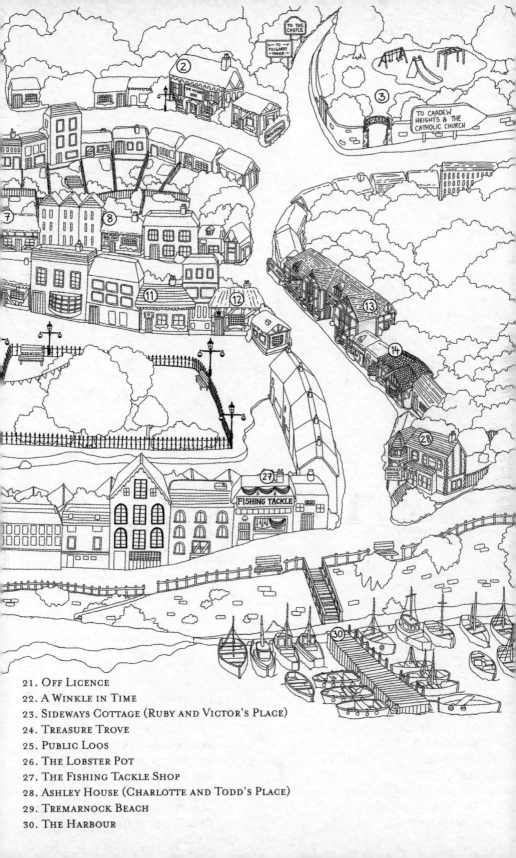

Chapter One

'IT'S FOR YOU.'

Bramble frowned. Her stepmother, Cassie, was bent double over the doormat, her not insubstantial backside blocking the hallway. Bramble was late, as usual, and she didn't like letters. They were usually bills, after all – mobile phone, credit card, store card. The only post she looked forward to was the clothes catalogues that regularly plopped through the letterbox with enticing discounts not to be ignored.

When Cassie rose, Bramble grabbed the letter, preparing to stuff it in her bag and read it on the bus on the way to work. Or this evening – or tomorrow, even...

'I wonder what it is.'

Something in Cassie's tone piqued Bramble's interest and she paused to cast an eye over the white envelope. It was thick and expensive-looking, with her name, Miss Bramble Challoner, and her address handwritten in black ink. Whoever penned it might have had calligraphy lessons, because the script was so neat and even. There was no stamp, just a blue mark saying 'Delivered by Royal Mail' and 'Postage Paid'. No clue then, but it didn't seem like a bill; it was too *personal*.

'Looks official,' Cassie commented unnecessarily, and Bramble felt a prickle of irritation.

'Yeah, well, it can wait till later.'

Cassie's face fell. Fifty-four years old and she still acted like a little girl sometimes, unable to disguise her feelings.

Bramble, softening, kissed her on the cheek and Cassie reluctantly moved aside as she headed for the exit.

'I'm staying at Matt's tonight. I'll give you a call, OK?'

'Don't forget your dad's birthday tomorrow!'

But Bramble was already halfway up the garden path, wobbling in her bright-red block heels across the uneven tiles. Tall and thin, with big blue eyes and fine, shoulder-length fair hair streaked with blonde, she looked a bit like a newborn deer, struggling to walk on Bambi legs, but there was no time to run inside for her trainers. If she didn't get a move on she'd miss the eight twenty-three a.m. and then there'd be fireworks.

The bus was packed, as usual, and she hung on to the metal rail as it lurched to and fro, cursing silently when the phone buzzed in her cavernous bag because she'd have to rootle inside, which wouldn't be easy with only one free hand.

It was Matt, wanting to discuss arrangements for the evening.

'It's the Premier League title decider,' he wheedled. 'Can't we catch your film another time?'

'No,' said Bramble firmly. 'It's had great reviews.'

More and more, she was finding that nights at his place did her head in, especially if there was football on. In fact, there always seemed to be some big match or other: rugby, soccer, cricket, snooker, darts even. When it came to sport, you name it, he'd watch all evening if she'd let him.

'I'll take Katie instead,' she warned, knowing that would shut him up. He wasn't that keen on going out but he was even less keen on her going out with someone else; he said he missed her.

His idea of bliss on earth was snuggling up on the sofa, one arm around her waist, the other clutching a can of lager, a bowl of popcorn balanced on their laps and the telly up full blast.

'What more could a man want?' he'd sigh contentedly above the din.

She had no right to complain, had she? Matt was handsome, loyal, solvent and he loved her. Lots of girls would give their eye teeth to be in her position. She ought to be grateful.

It wasn't until much later, when she was on her lunch break, that she remembered the letter and pulled it out of her bag while Katie went to the loo. They'd managed to find a seat in their favourite café, which served filled jacket potatoes as well as sandwiches and salads, all at a very reasonable price, and Bramble was willing Katie to get a move on so that they could return to their favourite subject: the boss, Judy. In a way it was just as well that she was such a cow because slagging her off helped wile away the monotonous hours.

The café was hot and crowded and the windows, which looked out on to the busy high street, were clouded with steam. It was a beautiful sunny summer's day and they were missing it. They should have bought sandwiches and gone to the municipal park to top up their tans.

Bramble ripped open the envelope and pulled out the letter, noticing the name and address on the right-hand side: 'Slater Brown Solicitors, Caxton Street, Westminster, London, SW1'.

Intrigued, she read on...

Dear Miss Challoner,

I regret to inform you that your grandfather, Arthur George Penrose, Lord Penrose, died on 10 June 2015. On behalf of the firm, I would like to offer my condolences for your loss...

She stopped for a moment. It seemed so strange to see the word 'grandfather', for she'd never met him and the little that she'd heard about him had been distinctly unfavourable. Why, she wondered, would they bother telling her? Lord Penrose hadn't exactly taken an interest in her or his daughter Mary, Bramble's mother. In any case, Bramble didn't consider Mary to be her real mum. That was Cassie, who'd brought her up since she was two years old.

Her eyes scanned down further.

Lord Penrose left a will dated 1 June 2010, under the terms of which myself and my partner in this firm, Henry Brown, were appointed as the executors and you are the sole residual beneficiary. This means that you inherit the entire estate after the payment of the costs of the estate administration, any debts and inheritance tax.

Lord Penrose's estate comprises the land, building and out-buildings of Polgarry Manor, Tremarnock, as well as its contents, and a sum of cash to the value of £670,000. One of our first tasks is to arrange for the assets in the estate to be valued so that we can work out the inheritance tax liability and how this might be settled. Once we have a clear indication of what this is we will write to you again.

If you would like to meet to discuss the estate in more detail, and indeed perhaps visit the manor, please let me know so that this can be arranged.

Yours, etc.

Bramble was so surprised that she had to re-read the letter several times to make sure that she wasn't imagining it. Perhaps it was a prank and she was secretly being filmed for a TV show. She glanced around furtively, half expecting a camera crew to leap out from under the table or behind the café counter, but no one came.

She stared at the half-eaten jacket potato on her plate and tried to collect her thoughts. Polgarry Manor? It sounded so grand. And £670,000 was an absolute fortune. The figure swam in front of her, making her dizzy.

'You all right?' Katie asked when she returned. 'You look like you've seen a ghost.'

Bramble slid the letter across the table and Katie sat down to read, her brown eyes growing wider by the second. She was shorter and curvier than Bramble, a bit of a man-magnet, with olive skin, a heart-shaped face and hair cut into a messy dark bob.

'Blimey!' she said at last, pushing back her chair so sharply that it tipped up, almost causing her to topple on to the customer behind, who spun around, scowling.

'Sorr-ee,' said Katie with an indifferent shrug, then she turned back to Bramble. 'A manor house? Cool! And all that dosh. You're gonna be rich!'

But Bramble could only manage half a smile.

'I'm scared,' she whispered. 'I feel all weird and sort of... like I'm looking down on myself from up there somewhere.' She pointed to the ceiling. 'I can't believe this is happening.'

Katie squeezed her arm. 'Don't worry, I'd be freaking out, too. Polgarry Manor?' She said the name slowly, as if testing it on her lips. 'It sounds sort of romantic – and a bit spooky, don't you think? I wonder what it's like.'

Bramble nodded, scarcely able to focus, and Katie peered at her through her dense, dark fringe.

'By the way, why have you never told me about Lord Penrose? You've kept that under your hat.'

'I never met him,' Bramble explained. 'He was an oddball, eccentric. He lived alone and had nothing to do with my mother after she was born; he completely disowned her. There didn't seem any point telling you. He's never been part of my life.'

Katie took a sip of Diet Coke.

'Maybe he regretted being so mean to your mum,' she said at last. 'Maybe this is his way of saying sorry. Anyway, who cares why the miserable old git's left the lot to you, since he has?'

Bramble was about to tell her off for being disrespectful to the dead, but she didn't get the chance.

'I can picture you as Lady Muck, bossing the servants around,' her friend added with a mischievous grin. 'And by the way, where the fuck's Tremarnock?'

The afternoon seemed interminable. As a call-centre sales agent for a mobile network, Bramble was stuck on the phone all day, but there was no opportunity to ring anyone for a chat, not with Judy breathing down her neck. Bramble didn't want to tell her about the letter, didn't want her to know, just in case it was all a wind-up and then her boss would have a field day; she'd laugh in Bramble's face.

At about half three, when she could stand it no longer, she told Judy that she was feeling unwell.

'What's the matter?' the other woman said, narrowing her eyes. 'You were perfectly all right earlier.'

'I feel shivery. I think I'm going to throw up,' Bramble replied, burping several times; it was a skill that she'd perfected at school and it had come in very handy down the years.

Alarmed, Judy said that she'd better go home immediately. 'Don't you dare vomit on the carpet.'

Relieved, Bramble grabbed her things and hurried from the office, nodding almost imperceptibly to Katie on the end of the row of desks as she left. Katie knew the score. She was familiar with the burping trick, though she herself generally favoured the toothpaste in the eye routine. Done properly, it looked remarkably like conjunctivitis, which, as everyone knew, was highly contagious.

Bramble caught the bus to Matt's and let herself in with her own key. His place was a small flat consisting of three rooms, just around the corner from the out-of-town industrial estate. He rented it from an older guy called Joe, who had his own carpet-fitting business. Joe must have done all right because he owned several properties in the sixties' block and drove an Audi convertible, which he'd park ostentatiously in front of the main entrance, half on the pavement, half off, when he came to check on his tenants.

When Matt first took possession, he and Bramble had thought the flat a palace, but it had soon started to feel cramped with all his clobber and a fair amount of hers, too. He'd begged her to move in with him but she'd resisted.

'I'm not ready for the commitment,' she'd insisted. 'It's too soon.'

'You're twenty-five and we've been together nearly ten years,' he'd replied grumpily. 'How long do you need?'

So she'd tried a new tack, reasoning that it made more sense for her to stay at her parents' while she helped save up for a deposit to buy somewhere of their own. This had temporarily mollified him, the only problem being that her plan wasn't working too well. Thriftiness wasn't her forte, and the more money she had, the more she seemed to spend. Just as well he didn't get to see her credit card bills; he'd be appalled.

She plonked down on the squishy black sofa on one side of the living room and took the phone from her bag. Matt wouldn't be home till after six and she wanted to speak to her dad first.

'Can you talk?' she asked when she heard his gruff, reassuring voice. She needed comforting right now because she was all at sixes and sevens. 'Are you alone?'

Bill was a cab driver and always answered when she rang, but she didn't want any of his customers overhearing.

'Just dropped someone off. On my way to Surbiton now. What's up, Sugarplum?'

He had a host of silly nicknames for her: Honeybun, Lamb Chop, Hoppity. Where did *that* come from?

He listened quietly while she told him about the letter, and when she'd finished, he let out a long sigh. 'Well, blow me! Never thought I'd hear that old bugger's name again.'

She wasn't entirely surprised. From the little that her dad had told her about Lord Penrose, it was clear that he loathed the man. Way back in the seventies, the story went, Bramble's grandmother, Alice, had visited the earl at his manor with her parents when she was about seventeen and he was considerably older. He'd taken advantage of Alice's youth and naïveté, and when the poor girl had found out that she was pregnant, he'd turned his back. Despite her parents' entreaties, she'd refused to have the child adopted, and Bramble's mother, Mary, had grown up with Alice in the suffocating, joyless Oxfordshire house of Alice's parents, forever made to feel ashamed of her very existence.

The moment she was old enough, she'd escaped to London and found herself a job and a place to live. Soon she'd met Bill, Bramble's dad, who'd been dazzled by her beauty, wit and upper-class otherness.

'Never seen anyone like her before in my life,' he told Bramble wistfully whenever she asked about her real mum. 'She was like something out of a fairytale.'

Kind, funny, down-to-earth Bill must have seemed like a breath of fresh air after the chilly isolation of Mary's upbringing, but sadly the marriage hadn't been a success. Bramble never heard Bill say a bad word about his first wife, but she could imagine that he'd had no idea what to do with the bewitching but highly damaged young woman he'd fallen in love with, no idea how to reach out to her.

'It was her nerves,' he used to say sadly when Bramble probed. 'She suffered dreadfully from 'em. Couldn't find peace, except in the bottle, and no good ever came of that.'

It must have been torture, watching his young wife drowning her sorrows in alcohol, while he struggled to raise their small daughter and earn enough to keep a roof over their heads. Mary's family wanted nothing more to do with her. He said he tried everything: throwing out the drink, hiding Mary's purse, even locking her in the house, but she was devious. One night she'd slipped out to join her boozing friends, fallen over the banisters at a party and suffered catastrophic injuries. She'd never regained consciousness and had died the following day.

Bill had been heartbroken and he said if it hadn't been

for Bramble, he might have chosen to end it all himself. They'd struggled on for a year on their own and then, thank goodness, Cassie had joined the office of the taxi firm where he worked.

'Fell in love with him the moment I set eyes on him,' she was wont to repeat to Bramble from time to time. 'It was that little-boy-lost look. Melted my heart, it did. And then when I met you, with your pigtails and your cheeky smile, well, that was me sold.'

Bramble could hear the noise of cars in the background, the odd hoot. It was still warm out and her dad probably had his window down. When she asked for advice, she could often guess more or less what he was going to say before he uttered a single word, but she wasn't prepared for what came next.

'We'll get that old place straight on the market. It's gone to rack and ruin, by all accounts. The sooner it's off your hands, the better.'

Bramble felt a stab of disappointment and wondered why, until it dawned on her that she'd already been mentally wafting around the property, running her hands through the floor-to-ceiling drapes, testing out the quaint old chairs and silver cutlery, trying out the dusty beds for size.

'Do you think it's true?' she asked. 'I mean, the letter could be a hoax.'

Her father growled, a low sound like a baited bear.

'It's legit all right, you mark my words. Just the sort of thing that man would do – spring a surprise like this to throw everyone into a flat spin. Evil, that's what he was. Malevolent.'

Bramble swallowed. She trusted her dad over anyone – he always had her best interests at heart – but right now she couldn't see his point of view.

'Shouldn't we at least go and visit the place? I mean, it's not every day you inherit a manor. We might even want to do it up and live there!'

Her father snorted. 'Not on your life. You take the money and run, my girl. Buy yourself a nice new house round here, one of them detached ones on Gloucester Road, maybe, with a carport and a decent bit of garden. Enough bedrooms so you and Matt can start a family when you're ready. After you're married, I mean,' he added hastily.

'Put the rest in the bank for a rainy day and don't tell no one, *no one...*' he repeated fiercely. 'You don't want to be one of them daft types who comes into some money and goes, "Wahay", and blows it all on foreign holidays for Uncle Tom Cobley and all. I don't know what that manor's worth, not a lot is my guess, but the cash'll go soon enough if you're not careful. You should be canny. Spend just what you need and not a penny more.'

He paused. 'We'll call that lawyer fella in the morning and tell him what we've decided. There'll be someone wants a gloomy old pile in the middle of nowhere, but not us, for sure. The sooner it's sold, the happier I'll be. That man caused nothing but trouble while he was breathing. I'm not having him casting a shadow over my girl now he's turned up his toes.'

When he'd rung off, Bramble leaned back and closed her eyes. For a few short hours she'd almost allowed herself to feel excited, to think that something was actually *happening* at last. She gave herself a shake. She was coming into money, for goodness' sake; rather a lot, in fact, more than she'd ever dreamed of. As her dad said, she and Matt could get married, buy a really nice house round here and settle down. What more could she wish for?

She found herself googling three- and four-bed houses for sale in the area on Matt's tablet and gazing at an array of master bedrooms, en-suite bathrooms, utility rooms. Cassie would kill for one of those. She said she'd always hated having to do the ironing in the front room.

Bramble was still eyeing up properties when Matt walked in, jangling his keys in one hand, the jacket of the pale-blue suit that they'd bought together at the designer outlet slung over his shoulder. Matt was of medium height and solidly built – 'dependable', Katie used to say – with a small nose, soft grey eyes and fair hair that was just beginning to recede at the sides. He was the general manager of a nearby gym, but he wasn't all that keen on using the facilities himself; he said he was more of an armchair athlete.

'Hello, gorgeous,' he said, strolling over to the sofa and giving Bramble a kiss. The sleeves of his white shirt were rolled up and the collar was undone – no tie. 'Good day?'

He didn't even have time to take off his suit or grab a glass of water before she was telling him all about the letter, which she produced from the bag beside her and thrust into his hands.

'My dad says I should sell the manor immediately, not even go and visit,' she said, watching impatiently while he sat down beside her to read. 'What do you think?'

Bramble and Matt had attended the same comprehensive school and had been going out together since Year Ten. With her striking looks, she'd already been receiving a lot of attention from the boys, but Matt was the only one who'd never used her hated nickname, Gawky.

'They only take the mick because it annoys you,' he'd whispered during one particularly dull maths lesson when they'd been sitting side by side. 'If you pretend not to care, they'll soon stop. Anyhow,' he'd continued, 'I think you're beautiful.'

They'd been to a film together that weekend, had a burger and a milkshake after, and the rest, as they say, is history.

He seemed to take an age to get to the bottom of the letter, and when he'd finished, he scratched his head slowly and stroked his chin.

'Your dad's right,' he said at last. 'What would we want with an old ruin anyway? Even if we had enough money to do it up, I can't think of anything worse than living in some draughty hall, miles from anywhere, with hundreds of empty rooms, creaking floorboards and creepy corridors. Ugh.' He shuddered. 'There are probably loads of spiders, too.' He hated spiders.

Bramble tipped her head to one side and a strand of hair fell across her face. She stuck out her bottom lip and puffed it away, only for it to settle back in the same position.

'It might not be creepy, it might be amazing,' she persisted. 'We should take a look, don't you think?'

Matt rubbed his palms up and down his sturdy thighs. Bramble had always liked his thighs; they made her feel safe.

'Why would we want to leave here? We've got everything we need.'

She thought of the familiar suburban streets that she'd tramped up and down since she was old enough to walk, the high street stores that she knew like the back of her hand, the cinema, the trains that could whiz you to London's Waterloo in thirty-six minutes on a really good day, the doctor's and the bowling alley. It was true, they didn't want for anything. Yet...

She stared at him with wide-open eyes, and at that moment it was as if the heavens parted and a bolt of lightning flashed through the ceiling into the little sitting room, landing on the dark-grey carpet right in front of her nose.

'Stop being an old stick-in-the-mud!' she cried. 'Where's your sense of adventure? Don't you see? This could be just what we've been waiting for!'

Chapter Two

One year later

SOME TWO HUNDRED and fifty miles away, on a remote Cornish peninsula, a woman called Liz was sitting under a big pink parasol while her toddler daughter tried to pick sand and pebbles off the beach and stuff them into her mouth.

'Don't do that,' Liz chided, pushing the little girl's pudgy hand away for the umpteenth time. 'Nasty. Yeeuch!'

She wiped the grit off the baby's palms with the corner of a towel, but a moment later Lowenna, who was not quite one, was reaching out again and the whole process had to be repeated.

'Why does she keep doing that?' laughed Liz's older daughter, Rosie, who was lying on her side on a turquoise towel nearby. 'She's so silly!'

'I don't know,' Liz sighed, 'but it's getting on my nerves. Come on, let's take her for a paddle.'

It was, in many ways, an idyllic spot. The small beach was flanked by rocky promontories that gave it a safe, sheltered feel. Behind was the sea wall, and beyond that, a row of gaily painted houses, shops and a pub, festooned with hanging baskets bursting with blooms. High above, set a little way back from the jagged cliff, you could just perceive the outline of a grand, grey-stone building, complete with decorative turrets, that cast a rather solemn eye over the frivolity below and seemed to say, 'Laugh now, by all means, but you wouldn't be so merry if you'd seen what I've seen these past three hundred years. Then, perhaps, you might feel melancholy, too.'

Lowenna was unsteady on her feet, having only just learned to walk, so Rosie held one hand and Liz the other as they picked their way slowly through numerous towels and bodies to the shoreline, taking care not to tread on anyone. On the third Thursday in July, when the schools had broken up and the summer season was in full swing, you expected to have to jostle for space with visitors on their annual break, and today was no exception.

The bright-blue sky overhead reflected on the surface of the sea, which was alive with children splashing and shouting and folk on paddleboards or in rubber dinghies, while further out, gaily coloured boats bobbed gently, like fairground ducks waiting to be hooked from the water. Lowenna's chocolate-brown eyes, just like her mother's, seemed to grow as big as her face as she gazed in wonder at the show, her head swivelling, owl-like, this way and that, so that she wouldn't miss a thing.

'Look, Lowie, sea,' Rosie said, bending down to run a hand through the white ripples. 'It's cold – brrr!'

Lowenna, who was wearing nothing but a cream bonnet and pink waterproof pants over a bulky nappy, copied her sister, crouching down on chunky thighs and allowing the tide to trickle between her fingers.

'Come on,' Rosie said when they'd had enough, 'let's go a bit further,' and she held the little girl's hand tightly as they waded out a short distance, being careful to avoid a group of rowdy boys to their left who were diving in and out of the waves after an orange ball.

Liz paused for a moment to watch as the girls went on ahead, the water up to the base of Lowenna's nappy, while for Rosie it was just calf high. Now fourteen, Rosie was in a cobalt-blue bikini – this was the first summer that she'd felt confident enough to wear one – and although she was small and thin for her age, her womanly curves had begun to take shape. She was growing up fast.

All of a sudden a rogue wave lapped up to Lowenna's chest, making her squeal in fright, and Rosie bent down and scooped her up, balancing her on one hip and rocking tenderly to and fro, just as she'd seen her mother do. Lowenna was lucky to have such a big sister, Liz thought; she hoped that they'd always be as close as they were now. She herself, an only child, had always felt the absence of a sibling.

It had been hot and sticky on the beach, but here the slight breeze and chilly water brought goosebumps to her arms and she felt less inclined to swim. Lowenna, though, was struggling to get down, so Liz took the plunge and immersed herself completely before reaching for the little girl's hands. Lowenna gasped as the pair bobbed up to their shoulders beneath the surface, unsure whether to laugh or cry, but was soon reassured by her mother's smile and began kicking wildly.

'She likes it!' Rosie cried, dipping down herself and popping up again just as quickly. 'She's a water baby, just like me!'

'She is,' Liz laughed, 'a proper little mermaid.'

When they'd had enough, they jogged back up the beach and grabbed their towels, making shivering noises as they rubbed themselves dry.

'Fancy an ice cream?' Liz asked when they'd settled back down, squinting in the sunlight. 'Run and get them for us, will you, Rosie? I'll give you the money.'

But Rosie wasn't keen. 'I have to go home and shower. I'm meeting some friends at the cinema.'

'Really?' It was the first Liz had heard of it. 'On a lovely day like today? Wouldn't you rather be outdoors?'

Rosie hesitated. 'Everyone'll be there…' Her voice trailed off and a dark line, like a pencil mark, appeared between her eyebrows.

'You don't have to be like everyone else,' Liz said gently.

'Tim's going – and Amelia.'

'Ah.'

Amelia had joined the class at the beginning of term. She was fun, pretty and very popular, it seemed, especially with Tim, who was Rosie's particular friend.

'We'll give you a lift to the ferry?' Liz offered, trying to ignore the niggle of anxiety that had lodged in her stomach. She'd always worried about her eldest daughter, who had mild cerebral palsy, but you couldn't shield your child from everything.

'It's OK,' said Rosie firmly. 'I'll get the bus.'

After that, Lowenna was whingey and unsettled, and Liz decided to pack up their things as well and take a short detour via the gift shop, Treasure Trove, to buy ice creams for just the two of them. She was thinking, as she often did, that it was a good job Rosie was so independent; her life wasn't easy and stubbornness helped to sustain her. Still, Liz did wish sometimes that she'd accept a little more support.

It was dark and poky inside the store and it took a moment or two for her eyes to adjust, but soon she could make out the imposing frame of Rick Kane behind the counter, chatting to his friend Audrey, who ran Seaspray Boutique, the clothes shop up the road.

Rick and Audrey, who were in their late fifties, had known each other since they were children, but there was no romance. Villagers used to wonder why, when they were both single and seemed to get on so well, until Audrey had confessed once in the pub that fond as she was of Rick, she couldn't stand his bushy beard and sideburns. Naturally, this had been all around the locality in the blink of an eye.

Having worked his way through a mind-boggling array of other attractive mature ladies, Rick had settled more recently on Liz's friend Esme, the potter. This had been something of a revelation, as Esme had never married – or seemed much interested in men, come to that. Art had been more her thing, and her collection of vintage teapots. Nor was she particularly glamorous, unlike her predecessors, favouring navy fishermen's smocks and droopy, flowing skirts over high heels and bling. Nevertheless, she and Rick had seemed to rub along all right for nearly a year until their big bust-up of a couple of months ago, and now they barely spoke. No one had managed to ascertain the cause of the rift, but the general consensus was that Rick had tried to 'go too far'. Unfortunately, the experience seemed to have robbed him of his mojo and everyone – apart from Esme – had been keen to cheer him up.

'Good day to you, and the little lady,' he said, breaking off his conversation with Audrey and managing a mournful smile. 'Been to the beach, have we?'

It must have been pretty obvious, as Liz's hair was still damp and she was wearing nothing but flip-flops and one of Robert's old white shirts over her soggy swimsuit, while Lowenna, bare-footed and sandy, was waving a red plastic bucket in one hand, a spade in the other.

Liz nodded. 'It's a gorgeous day. Have you had a swim yet?'

Rick used to be seen come rain or shine, winter or summer, plunging into the waves and thrashing to and fro in his strong crawl, sometimes for half an hour or more, but less so of late.

'Couldn't face it,' he replied gloomily. 'Too many emmets.'

'Emmets' was the local word for the hordes of tourists who came each summer, loved and hated in equal measure by the villagers, who relied on them for business but weren't so fond of their loud and sometimes inconsiderate ways.

Lowenna squealed tetchily, and Liz walked over to the giant freezer in the corner of the shop and picked out two lollies. Rick didn't want to take any money, but she insisted. He couldn't make much on his Cornish fudge and fairing biscuits, cheap souvenirs and postcards. In fact, it was a wonder he managed to stay solvent, especially in winter when hardly anyone ventured in, except for a chat.

'Where's our Rosie then?' he asked, putting the cash in the till.

Liz told him about the cinema trip and Rosie's FOMO, or Fear of Missing Out. She'd didn't mention Tim, though – or Amelia, come to that.

She was about to leave when Audrey tapped her on the arm, halting her in her tracks.

'Have you heard about Felipe's brother?' she said, lowering her voice confidentially.

Liz hadn't.

'He's left Rio and he's living with Felipe and Tony now. They're bringing him here this weekend. He's about fifteen, and a right tearaway by all accounts. His mother was at the end of her tether. Couldn't wait to see the back of him.'

Audrey sniffed, as if there was a bad smell, and raised her carefully plucked eyebrows expectantly.

'How nice!' said Liz, much to the older woman's disappointment. 'We can all practise our Portuguese!'

Tony, who lived some of the time in London and worked in PR, owned a cottage nearby, which he and his partner, Felipe, visited frequently. Liz was extremely fond of them both. She smiled to herself as she left the shop, thinking that a Brazilian bruiser in sleepy Tremarnock was going to be interesting. That would put the cat among the pigeons for sure.

Lowenna made contented sucking noises as they trundled up South Street, Liz pushing the buggy with one hand and holding on to her own ice cream in the other. The little girl would be a shocking mess by the time they reached home, but it didn't matter; her clothes could go straight in the wash after she'd settled down for a nap. They passed by Robert's restaurant, A Winkle in Time, on the other side of the cobbled street, and Liz took care not to catch the eye of customers still sitting at tables beneath the window, enjoying a late lunch. She and Lowenna must look like hillbillies and she didn't particularly want her husband to see them, let alone clients and staff; not till they'd scrubbed up.

Annie, the fitness trainer, was knocking on the door of Jenny Lambert's pink terrace house, Gull Cottage, and she turned and smiled at Lowenna, who brandished her ice cream proudly. Annie was small and pretty and her blonde hair was tied back in two girlish plaits.

'Mm. Nice lolly. Lucky Lowie!' she said in an excited baby voice as Jenny, who was normally in jeans and wellington boots, emerged in an old orange T-shirt, somewhat unbecoming purple Lycra leggings and bright-white trainers. They must have been brand new. She slammed the door behind her and Liz could hear Sally, her Jack Russell, yapping desperately inside.

'I've persuaded Jenny to come to my Mature Movers class,' Annie explained. She and her boyfriend, Nathan, the postman, had gone travelling earlier in the year, but after various escapades involving gippy tummies, mosquitoes and stolen wallets, they'd come home early, concluding that Tremarnock was the only place for them after all.

Jenny pulled a face. 'I can't pretend I'm looking forward to it. I was hopeless at sports at school. Walking's more my thing.' She laughed. 'And dreaming up a hundred and one things to do with a courgette.'

As well as helping her husband, John, run the village fishing-tackle shop on the seafront, Jenny was hub leader of the South East Cornwall Five Fishes Project, set up some months ago to provide hot meals for the poor and vulnerable using recycled food, mainly from shops and supermarkets.

Robert had offered to donate remains from A Winkle in Time, especially fresh fruit and vegetables that wouldn't pass muster in fancy dishes but that could easily be made into tasty, nutritious stews, tarts, crumbles and so forth, and soon Jenny had roped in Liz on Tuesday mornings as a volunteer chef, server and greeter. She, in turn, had recruited Robert's chief chef, Alex, sous-chef, Jesse, and waitress, Loveday, who was Robert's niece, on their days off, which made things a whole lot more fun. It had become quite a family affair.

Jenny, who was small, blonde and round, fiddled with the waistband of her leggings, as if they were digging into her tummy.

'Don't worry, the class is quite gentle,' Annie reassured her.

Then, glancing at Liz, she said, 'I'm starting a BuggyFit class for mums and babies in September. You should come along.'

'I'd love to. I need toning up.'

'You?' said Jenny incredulously. 'You're as thin as a rake!'

The foursome paused at the top of the hill while a large group of brightly dressed mums, dads and children sauntered by in the middle of the road, talking and laughing, flip-flops slapping as they went. Some of the kids were swinging masks, snorkels and fins, others had gaudy armbands and one small boy was carrying a bright-green inflatable crocodile that was almost as big as himself.

A car tooted impatiently and the crowd separated to allow it through.

'What's the hurry?' the small boy shouted cheekily from behind his crocodile, but the driver's windows were closed.

'They're renting the Old School House in Donkey Lane,' Jenny commented. 'The whole lot of them – must be a bit of a squash.'

'I hope they don't complain about Loveday and Jesse,' said Liz. 'They're having a do tomorrow night and we all know what *that* means.'

Much to everyone's relief, Loveday and Jesse had rekindled their relationship after a major crisis, and they were now sharing a rented flat next door to the Old School House, which seemed to have become Party Central.

One of the visiting children grabbed the crocodile off the boy, who screamed blue murder while his mother yelled back like a fishwife.

'Oh, I wouldn't worry about that,' Jenny replied, putting her fingers in her ears and wincing. 'This lot are so loud they won't hear a thing!'

★

As soon as she got back to Bag End, Liz dumped the bags, unbuckled Lowenna and carried her to the kitchen at the back of the cottage to peel off her filthy clothes and wash her face and hands. She didn't object, she was half-asleep already, and by the time Liz had taken her upstairs and changed her nappy, she was in that blissful, floppy, drugged-out state that babies and toddlers fall into when nothing, it seems, not even an earthquake, could rouse them. It was a shame when they grew out of it; you could get an amazing amount done during their comatose hours, even vacuuming.

Now, though, Liz was in no mood for housework. Rosie had already left – she must have been in a tremendous hurry – and Liz fancied collapsing herself, so she was irritated when the landline rang and half inclined to ignore it. Jenny, who should have been pounding away in the fitness class by now, sounded thoroughly stressed, having just received a text message informing her that a volunteer at Five Fishes had dropped out due to sickness, leaving a gap tomorrow, Friday.

'I know you normally only do Tuesdays. I'm sorry to ask, but could you step in and help me out of a hole?'

It would have been hard to refuse. 'That should be fine,' Liz reassured her, and she promised to check that Jean, the childminder, could take care of Lowenna.

'You're a doll.' Liz could hear the relief in Jenny's voice. 'I'll make sure I find someone else in plenty of time next week if our usual lady's still poorly.'

A quick call to Jean, who lived just up the road, soon settled matters, and after that Liz made herself a cup of tea and sat with her feet up on the sofa in their cosy front room, which looked straight on to Humble Hill. It was deliciously cool in here, and the air was filled with the scent of pink roses that she'd picked from a bush in the back garden and placed in a glass vase on the mantelpiece.

The house was quite compact, with low ceilings and thick walls, typical of the old fishermen's cottages around here, and she felt cocooned from the outside world. The only noises she could hear were the muffled voices of passers-by mingled with the cries of seagulls and the occasional low rumble of a car engine. She found her head lolling back against the cushion, her eyes closing. Even easy babies tended to wake with the larks and Lowenna was no exception. You had to catch up when you could...

They were both snoozing when Robert arrived home from the lunchtime shift. He strolled into the front room to find his wife flat out, a half-drunk mug of tea on the floor by her side. He was a tall, thin man with messy brown hair and a slightly harassed air. When he and Liz had first met she'd thought him odd and unfriendly, but love and marriage had smoothed away the rough edges.

He tiptoed over and brushed her forehead lightly with his lips.

'Hello, you,' he whispered, and she muttered something in her slumber.

'You're so beautiful,' he went on, sweeping a strand of hair off her face. She stirred slightly and the corners of her mouth tilted, as if she were having a nice dream.

'Liz?'

This time her eyelids fluttered open.

'You're awake, you little...' He pinched her arm, not too hard.

'Ow!' she squealed, shuffling over to make room for him. 'Don't stop, I was enjoying it!'

'I didn't think you could hear.'

She took his warm hand in hers and looked into his eyes – hazel flecked with amber. She'd always loved his eyes; she thought she could drown in them.

'You'd just got to the bit where you said I was beautiful, remember?'

He leaned over and whispered in her ear, 'Yes, Mrs Hart – and extraordinarily vain with it!'

Chapter Three

BACK IN LONDON, Cassie was standing in the bedroom doorway, clutching a pile of Bramble's ironed clothes so tightly to her bosom that it looked as if they'd have to be wrenched away.

'You can still change your mind, you know. You don't have to go.'

Bramble herself was sitting on the end of the bed with a blue canvas holdall, half-full and open, beside her, while another, zipped up and bulging, was on the floor at her feet.

'It's something I need to do,' she said gently, trying to ignore the tears pooling in the corners of her stepmother's eyes. 'You do understand, don't you? I have to give it a try.'

Cassie let out a small sob and Bill, standing behind, put a protective arm around her shoulders.

'Remember, you can always come back if you don't like it. There'll be no shame in it.' His eyes, too, were suspiciously glassy and there was a wobble in his voice that he couldn't disguise.

Bramble jumped up and flung her arms around both parents, so that they were huddled together like small animals clinging to each other for warmth and comfort.

'It's only Cornwall. It's not that far,' she said – uncertainly, for right now she felt as if she were emigrating to Australia. After all, she'd lived her whole life in Chessington and, bar the occasional week in Tenerife or Mallorca, had barely ventured outside the M25.

'They do things different there,' her father said ominously, knitting his unruly grey eyebrows. 'Instead of buses and cars, you'll see fields and sheep and...' He paused and rubbed his chin. '... and half-wits.'

Bramble laughed; she couldn't help it. 'Half-wits? What on earth do you mean?'

Her father nodded wisely. 'Inbreds. They go in for it; it's a known fact. There's not much choice, y'see.'

'Da-ad, I can't believe you said that.'

Bill shrugged. 'You can think what you like, but it's true. It's not for nothing they're described as wurzels with a piece of straw sticking out of their mouths. They're not quite all there, most of 'em.'

Bramble pursed her lips. There was no point arguing. Her father had tried every tactic known to man to persuade her to stay, but to no avail. The inbreeding theory was but the latest in a long litany of excuses as to why she shouldn't go. Chances were, he no more believed it than she did, but he was desperate.

'When are you coming to visit?' she said hopefully, but Bill only growled.

'Said I'd never set foot in that man's place, not after what he did, and I never will.'

'Nor me,' said Cassie, all choked up. 'Never.'

'But he's dead,' Bramble cried. 'And it's not his manor any more, it's mine!'

Bill broke away from the clinch and took a step back. 'He'll always be hanging round that place. There's no getting away. Like a bad smell, he'll linger on, and you'll sense his evil presence everywhere. That's why I wanted it off your hands. I didn't want you tainted...'

His voice cracked and he couldn't continue. Bramble hated to see him like this; it nearly broke her heart. She was almost inclined to cancel her plans, unpack her bags and stay here after all, but that wasn't the answer. For as long as she could remember she'd felt an itch, a sense that something wasn't quite right, and now, at last, life was about to change. Would she really throw away this opportunity because of a mean old man in his grave?

Matt arrived at seven p.m. and pecked her hello on the cheek, scarcely able to meet her eye. In all the long months that it had taken to complete the administration of the estate, she'd tried to convince him to come with her, but he'd dug in his heels and steadfastly refused. Flexible he was not.

'I like my job, my mates, my life,' he'd insisted. 'I don't want to live in Cornwall, miles from anywhere. I want to stay here with you.'

Bramble suspected he had been secretly banking on the fact that she wouldn't go on her own, that she'd be too scared, but he hadn't reckoned on Katie. Unlike him, she'd leaped at the chance of visiting the manor some months ago to check the place out, and after a certain amount of umming and aahing and more than a few heated discussions with her parents, she'd agreed to take his place. Matt had had to admit defeat, convinced that his girlfriend would return in a few months with her tail between her legs. He could do little to hide his hurt and resentment, however, and needless to say, Katie's name was mud.

Bill, Cassie, Bramble and Matt were a melancholy little foursome as they sat around the dark-brown table in the neat dining room at the front of the house, picking at the lamb casserole that Cassie had lovingly prepared earlier, lamb being one of Bramble's favourites. Matt had been part of the family for so long that it would have been extraordinary not to invite him, but no one had much of an appetite or seemed to know what to talk about. The subject of the manor was out of bounds, yet it loomed so large in their minds that any other topic seemed pointless.

'Have you remembered your toiletries?' Cassie asked, skewering a piece of carrot with the end of her fork and staring at it dolefully. 'I noticed you'd left a big pot of conditioner on the bathroom shelf.'

Small, pretty and ginger-haired, she was self-conscious of her curves and generally tried to cover them up with loose clothes in varying shades of beige, but this evening she'd donned the sparkly black Marks and Spencer frock reserved for special occasions. She'd also used the best porcelain crockery and silver-plated cutlery, and the crystal wine glasses that were normally kept in the glass display cabinet. Bramble wished that she hadn't; it only made her feel guiltier.

'The pot's almost empty,' she replied, trying to swallow a piece of meat that had stuck in her throat. 'I'll buy more when I get there.'

Bill looked up from his plate. 'Are there shops?' he asked doubtfully, as if Tremarnock were situated on the very edge of the world, about to topple off.

'Of course. There's one in the village, and a supermarket nearby. It's still England, you know. It's perfectly civilised.'

'Not much in the way of entertainment, though,' Matt growled; he couldn't resist it. After Bramble's brief recce, he'd professed astonishment at the lack of cinemas, theatres and bowling alleys.

'There are pubs, and there's supposed to be a really good restaurant,' Bramble insisted. 'Anyway, maybe you don't need much entertainment when you're surrounded by fields, cliffs and sea.'

Silence descended while everyone reflected on this observation. Bramble knew what they were thinking: that she'd never shown the slightest interest in nature, favouring retail therapy above all other pursuits, and nor did she much like beaches or swimming, come to that. Cassie used to joke that shopping malls were her natural habitat, but she didn't say it now; it was no use. Bramble's ancient yellow VW was parked outside and her bags were already in the hallway.

Bill and Cassie rose to clear the plates, and when they returned from the kitchen, Cassie was carrying her trademark homemade trifle, complete with chocolate sprinkles, glacé cherries and a sparkler on top. She'd always made it for Bramble's birthday parties and other special occasions: GCSE and A level results, her first job, passing her driving test.

'That looks a bit of all right,' Bill commented, setting down the bowls. 'Your stepmother's done us proud, as usual.'

It was what he always said, the same words for as long as Bramble could remember, but tonight there was no feeling in them; he could have been reading from a train timetable.

'I wish everyone would stop being so gloomy,' she blurted, biting back tears. 'I'm doing what I want. You should be happy for me.'

Cassie set down the trifle, pulled a tissue from the sleeve of her dress and blew her nose.

'We are happy for you, love, but we'll miss you like mad. Surely you can understand that?'

'I'll miss you, too, but I haven't died. The way everyone's behaving, you'd think it was my funeral.'

Matt helped to wash the dishes, then left early. He didn't linger. He and Bramble had agreed that they wouldn't have a protracted goodbye, so they hugged quickly at the front door and she promised to call soon. Tears filled her eyes again as she watched him walk slowly down the path, glancing back only once to give a half-hearted wave. He looked smaller, somehow, less robust, and it took all her self-control not to race down the street after him to say that she'd changed her mind, made a mistake, that she'd sell the manor straight away and use the cash to buy a place for them nearby.

And yet... it wasn't wrong, was it, to welcome a challenge? She was only just twenty-six, for goodness' sake, and had her whole life in front of her. It wasn't every day that you inherited a manor, and if she'd never lived there, she might look back in years to come and bitterly regret her lack of courage or imagination. No, she thought, closing the door and heading purposefully upstairs, she was doing the right thing, frightening as it seemed.

But she slept badly that night, tossing and turning in her little childhood room, too hot one minute, too cold the next, wishing that Matt were beside her, his strong arms keeping her safe. Once or twice she picked up her phone to call him, before reminding herself that it wouldn't be fair; she was the one who'd chosen to leave. Would she torture him now with hope that she might yet do an about-turn?

As morning light seeped through the pink curtains, illuminating the familiar pine shelf displaying her favourite childhood books, the white chest of drawers, the oval mirror where she'd first practised putting on make-up, the flowery rug, she wondered how it would feel to wake up in a strange place, surrounded by peculiar objects harking back to a bygone era. Would she leave behind her old self, too, like a snake shedding its skin, and emerge as a whole new person?

She threw back the curtains and looked out on to the wide street, lined with plane trees and mock-Tudor semis, cars parked neatly on identical front drives. Her own car, still gleaming from its recent wash, seemed to wink at her mysteriously. Only time would tell.

Packing wasn't her forte, and when Bill saw the slapdash way that she'd thrown everything in, he insisted on taking it all out again and doing it properly.

'You won't have room for Katie's stuff,' he warned. 'Or Katie, come to that.'

He eyed the wooden coat stand that had been squeezed in diagonally across the boxes and bags in the back, one end jutting through the gap between the front seats.

'Do you really need this?' He pulled it out, put it upright on the floor and scratched his head. 'Aren't there dozens in that windy old place already?'

'It's for my hats,' Bramble insisted, 'so they don't get crushed.'

'But you never wear hats.'

'I'm just waiting for the right occasion.'

'We'll have to dismantle it,' her father sighed, and he unscrewed the base of the stand and separated the post into two bits. 'It's easy enough to put back together. I'll show you how. Look.'

But Bramble was already scurrying back into the house to fetch the pile of hats sitting on her bed, one inside the other, still sporting their price tags. They were to go in last of all, on the very top.

'I've made you a picnic,' said Cassie, almost bumping into her in the hallway with a carrier bag stuffed with goodies. 'Ham sandwiches, crisps, lemonade, that sort of thing. It's a long drive.'

'Thanks, Ma,' said Bramble absent-mindedly. 'Put it by the car, will you? I'll shove it in later.'

By the time she set off – watching her parents in the mirror, dabbing their eyes and waving out of the window until she'd rounded the corner – it was after ten a.m. and Katie would be getting impatient. The regrets and anxieties of yesterday seemed to have lessened a little, the new day bringing with it fresh hope and a sense of giddy excitement. She'd been thinking about this moment for so long, planning it and trying to imagine how she'd feel. She couldn't believe that it had finally arrived.

Katie's home was only ten minutes away, at the end of a cul-de-sac leading to a field of urban allotments. She and Bramble had wreaked havoc there as children, when they'd found it tremendous fun to race their bikes, slalom-like, around the perimeter and through the gaps between enclosures, upsetting the gardeners, who'd shake their fists and threaten to tell their dads.

The pair had become firm friends on the very first day of the first term at secondary school, when they'd noticed that they were wearing the same black Mary Jane shoes and had decided that this was surely a sign of compatibility. And indeed it had proved to be so, because they'd barely been separated since. Matt used to joke – somewhat humourlessly, Bramble always thought – that she might as well be going out with Katie instead of him, they were so close.

'Double trouble,' he'd say when he saw them cackling like hyenas together. 'The gruesome twosome!'

Katie was peering anxiously out of the front window when Bramble drew up, but she vanished and reappeared in no time, hurtling down the path with her three younger sisters in hot pursuit.

'Where have you been? You're late!' she cried, opening Bramble's door and starting to pull her out, so that she nearly toppled, hands first, on to the pavement.

'Hold on!' Bramble said, regaining her balance. 'If I'm so late, where are your bags? I thought you'd be ready.'

Katie turned to her three smaller sisters, all pretty and dark-haired like herself, and clapped her hands imperiously. 'Chop chop.' They ran back into the house obediently and returned with a suitcase each; the cases were so heavy that they could hardly lift them.

'Here, I'll do that!' Katie's dad shouted as Bramble tried to heave one of the cases on to the back seat of the car. He'd followed the girls out and was staggering himself under the weight of two more canvas holdalls. 'Mind you don't hurt yourself.'

Of course Katie's mum, Lisa, insisted on fetching almost the entire contents of her kitchen cupboards stuffed into plastic carriers, which she somehow managed to squeeze into every last available nook and cranny, so that by the time she'd finished, Bramble wondered if she and Katie would be able to breathe.

'At least you won't go hungry tonight,' Lisa said with satisfaction when she'd finished, rubbing her hands together.

'You've got to be joking,' said Katie. 'We've got enough to last the entire summer!'

Her sisters flung themselves into her arms and the youngest, who was only eleven, burst into tears. When she'd finally stopped sobbing and Katie had managed to extricate herself and climb into the car, Katie was in such a state that she could hardly speak.

'Just drive,' she commanded Bramble, wiping her eyes and blowing her nose loudly. 'Hurry or I'll change my mind!'

Bramble put her foot on the accelerator – too hard – and they bucked away, toot-tooting and waving out of the window until they'd turned the corner.

'Bloody hell!' Bramble said, swallowing the lump in her throat. 'I never thought it would be so difficult. I hope we're doing the right thing.'

'Too late now,' Katie spluttered. 'But watch out for that cyclist or we won't be going anywhere.'

As London started to recede, the tears dried up and Bramble switched on some music to lift their spirits. The day was turning out hot and sunny, so they wound down the windows and enjoyed feeling the wind in their hair as they headed out, first on the motorway and then the A303, one of the main routes to the South West.

Katie wanted to stop at Stonehenge, but Bramble said it would make them too late.

'We don't want to arrive in the dark. We won't be able to find our way around.'

'We could always check into a B and B?' Katie suggested hopefully. 'Just for one night. We haven't seen the manor in the dark. It might be spooky.'

'Absolutely not,' said Bramble firmly. 'It's our new home now, and besides, we can't afford a B and B.'

She swallowed, thinking there wasn't much they would be able to afford, at least until they'd found jobs. To her dismay, inheritance tax had eaten up all the cash left by her grandfather, which had only made Matt and her dad more convinced that she should be shot of Polgarry as quickly as possible.

'What's the point of living in a bloody mansion if you've no money to run it?' they'd reasoned.

But Bramble reckoned that it wouldn't cost much to heat and light the place for just the two of them, surely? Neither had a huge appetite, and at least she wouldn't be tempted by clothes shops in such a remote place.

'Unwrap a sweetie for me, will you?' she said, indicating to the glove compartment, where she'd stowed a bag of chocolate éclairs. Being an optimist by nature, she'd just about managed to convince herself that something would turn up. It would have to.

They stopped for petrol and a pee, and stopped again to eat the picnic Cassie had packed, then they got stuck in heavy traffic outside Exeter and had to divert to a McDonald's for a further loo break. Once they'd crossed into Cornwall, the satnav took them on a crazy route, up steep, winding country lanes so narrow that there was only room for one car and they had to reverse into fields to let the other vehicles pass. By the time they spotted the first signs for Tremarnock, the journey had taken nearly eight hours, three hours more than anticipated.

'I'm looking forward to a glass of wine and a long, hot soak,' said Bramble, stretching her achy shoulders and neck.

'I hope there's hot water,' Katie replied gloomily. 'And not too many daddy-long-legs in the bath.'

At last they reached the narrow street lined with higgledy-piggledy cottages that led to the village centre, but instead of going straight ahead, they turned left up a twisting road lined with tall hedgerows that seemed to zigzag for miles, until finally they reached rusty iron gates that they recognised from their previous visit. The gates were open, surrounded by tall weeds and half-hanging off their supports, and you wouldn't think from the state of them that anyone had lived in the property for years. Bramble drove through, slowing to a snail's pace on the bumpy, potholed drive that was flanked on both sides by overgrown fields, and came to a halt just in front of the steps of the entrance to the manor.

Both girls were silent for a moment, taking in their new home, absorbing its grey walls and mock battlements, its sheer enormousness. In the fading summer light, Polgarry seemed to loom over them like a giant. Tired and discouraged suddenly, Bramble half-expected to see medieval knights peeping at them over the fake parapets, arrows aimed and cauldrons of boiling oil ready to be poured. Warm and welcoming, the place was not right now.

The central section of the manor, she knew, had been built in the late seventeen hundreds, while the two wide wings on either side were more modern, having been added in the late nineteenth century. There was the suggestion of a terraced garden sloping down to a low stone wall, but the trees and shrubs were overgrown, the steps broken and covered in weeds and moss. As Bramble switched off the engine and opened the door, a flock of rooks flew up from the slate roof and circled above them, making her shiver. It was different from how she'd remembered it here, more isolated and forbidding.

'Let's start unloading,' she said to Katie, trying to sound cheerful. Right now, the thought of a warm, clean, well-appointed home in one of the streets near her parents' house seemed tremendously appealing.

They staggered up the broken steps with their suitcases

and Bramble delved in her bag to find the heavy set of keys that had been sent to her by courier after the administration of the estate had been completed. Katie hung back while she fiddled with the lock, which appeared to be stuck.

Bramble swore as she attempted to twist the key this way and that. 'We'll have to try another door.'

Just then it creaked open and both girls jumped back. They were greeted by a slight elderly woman in a brown tweed skirt and a white blouse buttoned up to the neck. Her iron-grey hair was cut into a shapeless bob with a short fringe, and her small black eyes were partially obscured by a pair of rectangular, steel-rimmed spectacles.

'Miss Bramble?' she said in an Eastern European-sounding accent. 'I have been expecting you. Welcome to Polgarry Manor.' There was no hint of a smile.

Utterly thrown, Bramble didn't even think to ask who the strange woman was, but followed her, open-mouthed, into the wide, high marble hallway, which smelt of damp. In the centre was a large, round wooden table displaying a heavy bronze statuette of a naked youth playing a pipe, and around the edges were pieces of furniture protected by plastic sheets. The walls were decorated with gold-framed oil paintings of crusty-looking gentlemen on horseback and crinoline-clad ladies, and at the far end an imposing staircase, covered in a faded burgundy carpet, led to the galleried first floor.

Dust chased up Bramble's nostrils and she sneezed, while Katie, behind, gave a nervous giggle.

'It looks different in the evening,' she said in a small voice. 'I remember it being lighter and more, sort of, homely.'

'I have made up the beds in the Chinese Room and the Green Room,' the strange woman went on, ignoring Katie's comment and gazing at Bramble inscrutably. 'Of course, you are the mistress of the house, so you will decide which one you prefer for yourself.'

'Er, thank you,' Bramble said, feeling not at all like the mistress of anything. She was still holding her heavy suitcase, but the stranger made no move to help.

'There is a cold pie in the kitchen and some plums from the orchard,' the woman added coolly. 'If that is all you require, I shall go to my quarters. I normally retire early.'

She shot Bramble a look that made her feel to blame for causing so much trouble, turned on her heel and headed for the closed door on the left, her shoes tap-tapping on the cold marble.

Bramble took a deep breath and drew herself up. 'I'm – I'm sorry,' she stuttered. 'I hope you don't mind... er... who *are* you?'

The woman spun around, straight-backed and steely-faced.

'I am your housekeeper. My name is Maria, and I served Lord Penrose for thirty years.' Then, without further ado, she vanished through the door and closed it firmly behind her, leaving the girls still standing in the centre of the room, clutching their bags and gaping.

'Sheesh, she's scary!' Katie whispered at last. 'Where did she spring from? The morgue?'

'I haven't the faintest idea,' Bramble whispered back. 'There was no sign of her before, was there? I didn't know anyone else lived here. No one told *me*.'

Katie coughed and the noise echoed eerily around the empty space. The little light that was left was receding fast and shadows fell in the four corners of the room, from which protruded the stuffed heads of deer. Beside one of them was a fox mounted on a wooden shield, glass eyes staring and sharp teeth bared.

'He'll have to go,' she said firmly and Bramble nodded.

'He gives me the creeps.'

They decided to find their rooms and Katie went ahead, towards the stairs.

'Doesn't look like we'll get any help from that old battle-axe.'

It was just bravado, Bramble could tell, and she glanced left and right nervously as if Maria might materialise through the wall at any moment to tell them off. The hairs on the back of her neck stood on end and she had the strange sensation of being watched.

'I vote we share a room tonight,' she suggested.

'Good idea,' Katie agreed.

Chapter Four

THE GIRLS HADN'T even left London when Liz arrived at the community centre in the village of Polrethen, some three miles from Tremarnock. It was about nine thirty a.m., the lights were already on and she could see a figure scurrying about inside.

The building was tucked away in a side street, which was convenient, as some folk didn't want it known that they'd fallen on hard times; there was pride at stake. With ample room for parking outside, it wasn't far to carry the groceries, which Robert and his restaurant staff had bagged up the night before. Other volunteers, Liz knew, would have already collected supplies from the supermarkets and shops that donated on a regular basis, while the chefs would be starting to put together today's menu.

She passed underneath the green and yellow sign that said 'Polrethen Pop-up Kitchen' and underneath, in smaller letters, 'All welcome. No booking needed. Free three-course meal.' It was warm outside and hotter within, despite the open windows, so she was glad that she'd chosen to wear a simple strappy dress and sandals.

Mike, whom she'd got to know quite well as he volunteered with her on Tuesdays at the Methodist church hall in

Tremarnock, was hard at work putting out tables and chairs. A small, plump man with sandy hair and a beard, he worked part-time for a charity and was a devout Christian, though he never tried to foist his views on anyone else. He smiled and called hello, but didn't stop what he was doing to speak to her. The first guests would arrive at twelve and there was no time to spare.

There were usually six or seven volunteers for each session: a couple to collect the food and two or three to cook, while the rest acted as servers who would also sit down with the visitors and chat. That said, everyone tended to do a bit of everything; it was a case of all hands on deck. Guests ranged from homeless and unemployed people to elderly folk who simply wanted a bit of company and hot food. The volunteers worked hard to create a warm, welcoming atmosphere, aware that the community meal might be the highlight of the visitors' week.

Liz strolled into the kitchen where Jenny Lambert was putting on her apron and plonked two big bags of fruit and vegetables on the counter.

'Did you manage to do any of Annie's class yesterday?' Liz asked, removing five knobbly carrots, two wrinkled aubergines and an assortment of slightly overripe beef tomatoes from one of the carriers. The image of Jenny in her purple Lycra leggings and bright-white trainers would remain with her for some time.

'I missed most of it – thank goodness,' Jenny grinned. 'But unfortunately I had to promise Annie I'd go next week. I think she's a bit short on numbers.'

Jenny, who was in her late forties, came originally from Sussex and had two boys, one now at university and the other abroad on a gap year.

'They'll be perfect for our chilli con carne,' she commented, eyeing Liz's tomatoes. 'Someone picked up a ton of mince from the supermarket this morning. We'll chuck in the carrots, too. There's no rule that says you can't have carrots in a chilli, is there?'

'None that I know of. And look...' Liz delved into the other bag. 'I've got cucumbers, lettuce and spring onions. We can do a big salad to go with it.'

'Hi, Auntie!'

Liz glanced up to see Robert's niece, Loveday, sauntering in, followed by Jesse, who looked a little below par. Loveday sometimes called Liz 'Auntie' as a joke.

The girl was in black all over – black T-shirt, black miniskirt, black fishnet tights, black platform ankle boots. Her dyed black hair was shaved on one side and tied into a skew-whiff ponytail on the other. Two giant hooped earrings dangled from her lobes and a silver stud twinkled in her nose.

Jesse, on the other hand, was in ripped blue jeans and a tight green T-shirt that showed off his tanned, toned surfer's torso, and his blonde corkscrew curls had been bleached white by the summer sun. They were certainly a striking pair, though Loveday wouldn't have appeared out of place in a disco.

'Late night?' Liz asked wryly, noticing the smudged black kohl under the girl's eyes and Jesse's uncharacteristically sickly pallor.

'We meant to leave at midnight, didn't we, Jess?' Loveday said, and her boyfriend nodded glumly. 'Then we decided to have one more drink, and the next time we checked, it was five a.m.'

'Lord! I don't know how you do it,' Liz exclaimed, genuinely impressed, but Loveday shrugged as if there were nothing to it. She'd gone through a sensible phase of practical clothes and clean living after she and Jesse had split, but had come out the other side and appeared to be making up for lost time with a vengeance.

Jenny passed clean aprons to the new arrivals, and it was only when Loveday took hers with one hand that Liz noticed she was holding something small, black and furry in the crook of the other arm.

'What's that?' she asked, alarmed, and Jenny jumped back and shrieked, 'Rat!'

She spun around and grabbed a sharp knife from the counter behind, but Loveday reacted just in time to stop her, mid-lunge.

'It's a puppy!' she cried, backing off and gurgling with laughter in spite of herself, for Jenny's face was a picture. 'It's my friend's Chihuahua. I'm looking after it today 'cause she's got a dentist's appointment. She can't take it there.'

'Well, you can't bring it here either,' Jenny replied, scowling at the dog, which had woken up and was peering at her anxiously from the safety of its temporary mistress's arms. Jenny replaced the knife, but continued to maintain a safe distance.

'Aw, please!' Loveday wheedled. 'It's really good. It'll just sit on its little blanket in the corner. It won't move.'

'This is a kitchen. You must know about hygiene rules – you work in a restaurant, for heaven's sake!'

'It doesn't like being left on its own,' Loveday said resentfully. 'It gets depressed. But I suppose it'll be all right for a few hours.'

'Of course it will,' snapped Jenny, 'it's a dog.' She eyed it again, as if to be sure, and it bared its pointy little teeth and growled. 'Get it out of here as quickly as possible, before anyone catches sight of it.'

They were behind schedule now, as well as one person down as Jesse had volunteered to take the puppy back to the flat. As a general rule, Loveday disliked cooking and lived off toast and takeaways when her boyfriend wasn't around, but she was good at cakes, so Jenny gave her the task of baking four large lime-and-raspberry Victoria sponges for pudding, while she and Liz chopped veg and prepared sweetcorn fritters for starters.

It was a relief when Jesse returned some twenty minutes later and pitched in, too; a trained chef, he was much quicker than the others, and the chilli was soon bubbling merrily on the hob, giving off a delicious smell. Liz buttered four loaves of bread and arranged the slices on large plates, while Mike fetched jugs of water and the bowls of salad, and put them out on the tables along with colourful napkins and little bunches of fresh wildflowers in jam jars. By the time he'd finished, the room looked positively festive.

There was just time for a quick cuppa before the first guest, Stan, arrived promptly at midday. A former drug addict, he had a room up the road from Jesse and Loveday's old flat in Tremarnock and was dead keen on the Five Fishes project. In fact, he hardly missed a single meal. Liz liked him, not least because he'd managed to retain a sense of humour despite his difficulties. It was her task to meet and greet today, so she ushered him to one of the tables and settled down opposite.

'How are you doing?' she asked.

'Fine,' he grunted. 'Got any more of that caviar for me today?' he added with a toothless grin. 'Thought I'd have a spot with me champagne luncheon.'

Soon Mike strode past, carrying a platter of steaming food towards a huddle of elderly people on the other side, and Liz rose and made her way across the room. She could feel the temperature rising and brushed her fringe off her face with the back of an arm. The heat was on in the kitchen, too, where Jesse and Loveday were having a row over the sizzling fritters.

'You have to turn them carefully,' Jesse grumbled. 'Like this. See? Otherwise they break up.'

'Stop being so *bossy*,' Loveday snapped, and Jenny and Liz exchanged glances.

On returning to the dining room with a big plate of food, Liz was delighted to see Stan chatting with a middle-aged chap with a flushed face and blotchy skin and a slightly grumpy-looking woman in an orange woollen hat, which must have been rather hot on a day like today.

At one point, Stan got up and started playing Beatles' songs on the piano in the corner and Loveday, who was rather proud of her voice, came out to sing. Soon everyone was joining in, including Jesse, who seemed to have recovered from his lack of sleep and broke into a saucy, hip-gyrating dance that sent the ladies wild. The noise was so deafening that Jenny had to call a halt or the neighbours might complain, but by then even the grumpy woman was flush-cheeked and laughing. It was true what they said about good food and company; they really were a tonic.

By two thirty Liz was worn out, but the fact that the guests were leaving with smiles on their faces and full tummies gave her a warm glow of satisfaction. She would have scuttled off as soon as possible, but Mike cornered her and asked if she'd mind delivering a couple of bags of leftovers with him on the way home. He'd prefer to have backup, he said; not that he anticipated any trouble.

'It's a man who lives close to your place, in one of those old farm workers' cottages near Polgarry Manor. I used to see him in church from time to time. Nice fellow. Three kids, no wife. I enquired after him the other day and someone said he's got depression. He's in a bad way, really struggling. I thought I'd take some food and mention the community meals. We can drive in convoy. Sorry to ask, but you live nearest. I'd appreciate your help.'

Liz sighed inwardly. She was weary, it would add at least half an hour to her journey and she'd probably find the experience upsetting, but how could she refuse?

After calling Jean to let her know that she'd be late, she followed Mike in his red Vauxhall out of the village and up a series of winding country lanes overhung with trees. The roads climbed steeply for some time towards the cliffs, before flattening into a bumpy track surrounded by fields dotted with cows and sheep. They slowed to a snail's pace for a while behind a tractor and Liz wound down the window to breathe in the sweet scent of hedgerow flowers: frothy white cow parsley, purple vetch and red valerian. The sun was high and hoverflies swooped in and out of pale-green ferns and soft tendrils, while butterflies floated from one bloom to another. Nature, it seemed, was at its most rapturous; you could almost hear it singing.

At last the tractor veered off to the left and they picked up speed again, soon catching sight of Polgarry Manor, looming large and imposing, its crenellated towers blotting out the sky. Liz had always found the building daunting, not least because she'd heard the rumours about Lord Penrose, who'd hidden himself away there until he died.

She'd been told by Esme, who was something of an expert on the subject, that the old man had been quite a socialite in his youth, hosting fabulous parties for the rich, titled and famous that were written about in the gossip columns of national newspapers. Then something terrible had happened and the gaiety had ceased, the guests had stopped coming and he'd turned into a virtual hermit while his home had fallen to rack and ruin around him.

Mike had to slow to a crawl again, behind a cyclist this time, and Liz found herself remembering how Jenny had once spotted the elderly earl when she'd been out walking her dog. On her way back, she'd bumped into Liz and a group of others in the marketplace and told them, with great excitement, that he'd been dressed in an extraordinary, old-fashioned tweed shooting suit, complete with flat cap and plus fours, and carrying a sturdy walking stick, even though he'd been too frail to shuffle more than a few steps.

'He didn't smile at all,' she'd said, 'wouldn't even catch my eye.'

Audrey had called him 'downright nasty, by all accounts', while Jean had reminded them that local children nicknamed him 'Dracula'.

Despite the stories, Liz thought that right now, in the mellow light, the manor seemed quite affecting, a relic from a bygone era crumbling slowly and relentlessly into the landscape, one day to be reclaimed by its environment, so overgrown with grass, flowers and prickly bushes that you would forget it had ever been there, just like its strange inhabitant.

The cyclist stopped beside the rickety iron gate leading to the dilapidated driveway and took a drink of water from his plastic bottle. As she passed, Liz found herself speculating about the young woman from London who'd inherited the estate. There had been an article about her in the local newspaper explaining that she was Lord Penrose's only surviving relative, that she worked in a call centre and that having visited the manor last autumn, she had decided to move in there.

She'd sounded a little naïve, but it might have been a poorly written piece. When quizzed about the manor's shocking state of repair, she'd replied that she didn't mind, she'd been living with her mum and dad and it would be 'nice to have more space'. Anyway, the locals seemed to think that she'd arrive any day. Perhaps the cyclist was a friend.

The red Vauxhall took a sharp left along a gravelly dirt track and Liz hit a pothole so hard that she bounced up from the seat. It was a good job Robert wasn't around to complain about the suspension. The way was overgrown with trees that partially obscured the sun, and she began to wonder if they'd ever reach their destination.

The track narrowed even further, until at last they turned a bend and there, a little way ahead atop a slope, was a small, squat stone cottage surrounded by a wooden fence. Mike pulled up in the lay-by, leaving space for Liz to park beside him, and, carrying several bags of groceries between them, they walked towards the gate.

There was a rusty old bike on the path with a punctured tyre that Liz had to step around, and just outside the door was a green box overflowing with fly-infested rubbish: empty cans of food and plastic milk bottles, vegetable peelings, tins of pet food and sweet wrappers. Liz might have expected a bad smell, but – to her surprise – on either side of the door were two flowerbeds filled with fragrant sweet peas, busy Lizzies and jolly white daisies, and the earth around was freshly dug and watered. Someone must like gardening, she thought, but didn't take the same pride in the house. The thin beige curtains in the window to the right were closed, while those on the left appeared to have been tugged so hard that the pelmet had come off and was dangling sadly.

Mike put his bags on the step and rapped on the door with

the old iron knocker. Soon a child of about seven or eight appeared, a boy with shaggy brown hair, a pale face and big grey eyes.

'What do you want?' he asked suspiciously, only half-opening the door and peering around the edge. 'Me dad's not in.'

He was wearing blue shorts and a red T-shirt, and as Liz glanced down she noticed, behind him, another, much smaller boy of about two, with a grubby face and wary eyes just like his older brother's. He was dressed in nothing but a droopy nappy.

'We've brought some food,' Mike said, motioning to the bags at his feet and smiling reassuringly. 'We're from the community meal project in Polrethen. We make hot lunches for people and there's usually some left over. We thought you might like to try it?'

'You can't come in,' said the older boy, despite opening the door wider. 'You can leave it there.'

Liz put her own bags on the ground and stretched her fingers because the handles had been digging in.

'Is there anyone else we can speak to?' she asked softly. 'A big brother or sister maybe?'

'Shannon's here but she's asleep.'

Just then a skinny older girl appeared from the room on the right, rubbing her eyes. She must have been about fourteen or fifteen, with mousey hair that needed a good brush. She was wearing a white vest top and a denim miniskirt and her feet were bare.

'What do you want?' she asked abruptly, before bending down to pick up the toddler and balance him on her hip. He was quite a big lad and she was only small, with a pale, pinched face, thin little arms and protruding collarbones, but she made it seem relatively easy.

When Mike explained again why they were here, the girl bit her lip. 'You mean you cook for poor people like us?' She didn't turn them away, though. 'You can put everything in the kitchen,' she went on, moving aside to allow the visitors to pass and motioning to the older brother to give them a hand. 'Hurry up, they haven't got all day.'

There was a stale smell inside and Liz wrinkled her nose as she took in the torn pink wallpaper in the hallway, the dirty kitchen floor and the badly fitted units with some of the cupboard doors missing. The girl watched carefully as they plonked their carriers of Styrofoam containers on the wobbly pine table, and when Liz thanked the older boy for his help, he looked surprised, as if he wasn't used to compliments.

'Shall we put everything in the fridge?' she asked Shannon. 'It'll last a couple of days in there.'

'I can do it myself.'

Unfazed, Liz reached into her handbag, fished out a minia-ture packet of chocolate buttons and grinned at the toddler, who stretched out a greedy hand.

'Is it OK if I give them to him?'

The girl nodded, took the packet and set the boy down tenderly. Then she squatted to his height and opened the sweets before passing them across.

'There you go, Buster.' She didn't smile but her eyes were soft.

She loved him, Liz thought, but she was far too young to be playing mother. She ought to be out in the sunshine having fun.

Next, Liz produced a stick of rock for the older boy. They'd been sent several box-loads by a factory that had gone into overproduction and couldn't sell the stuff. It wasn't exactly healthy, but kids seemed to adore it.

'I could murder a cuppa,' she said, glancing at Mike.

He knew exactly what she was up to, and reached into a different bag to find a packet of teabags, some biscuits and a half-litre bottle of milk that he'd picked up earlier that morning. 'Ta da!'

Shannon grudgingly put on the kettle and filled three mugs, before leading the way into the room from which she'd first emerged. It was shadowy in there, so she walked over to the window and opened the thin beige curtains. Light filtered through the dirty glass, revealing a battered brown sofa, beside which lay two empty cups and a half-filled glass of water. There was also a small TV, perched precariously on an upturned box, but not much else save children's toys scattered across the floor: metal cars lined up in a row, a grubby-looking fluffy rabbit on its back, its plastic eyes staring vacantly, and bits of Lego.

'You can sit down if you want,' she said, nodding at the sofa, and Liz settled gingerly on the edge, afraid that the springs might collapse. Mike, meanwhile, opted for the floor.

'Where do you go to school, Shannon?' he asked casually, resting his arms on his knees, both hands circling his mug. 'It is Shannon, isn't it?'

She nodded. 'Marymount.'

'That's where my daughter goes,' Liz piped up, glad to find some common ground. 'She's called Rosie, Rosie Broome. She's just finished Year Eight. Do you know her?'

Shannon frowned. 'Is she the one with...?' She paused, uncertain how to go on, and Liz came to her rescue.

'With cerebral palsy, yes. She had a brain tumour, too, and she was very sick, but she's much better now. She likes school, though she's not so keen on some of the teachers. Do you like it?'

'S'all right. Waste of time, if you ask me.'

Mike took a sip of tea. 'Why's that then?'

'You don't learn nothing useful in them places. Geography, history, what good is that when you've got no food to eat and you can't pay the bills? They don't teach you how to wipe a kid's bum, do they, or stop it crying?'

Right on cue the toddler, Conor, who'd followed them into the room, dropped the now-empty packet of chocolate buttons on the floor and let out a high-pitched wail. Shannon bent over to pick him up. He was covered in chocolate, all around his mouth and on his hands, and she reached into a pocket of her denim skirt, fished out a crumpled tissue and tried to wipe his mouth clean while he twisted his head angrily to and fro.

'Where's me dad, Shannon?' Liz turned to look at the older boy, who was hovering by the door. 'Is he coming home?'

'Shut up, will you? Go outside and play,' Shannon snapped. But he didn't move.

'Me dad's always crying,' he went on uncertainly. 'He's dead sad, isn't he, Shannon? Ever since me mum went…'

Her eyes narrowed. 'Yeah, well, we're all sad, aren't we? But we've got to get on with it. Maybe he wouldn't be so miserable if he got himself a job instead of lying in bed all day or wandering around the place staring at sheep. It's selfish, that's what it is.'

'He's got depression, hasn't he?' Liz said kindly. 'It's an illness, you know, only it's not like having a broken leg because you can't see it.'

The girl curled her lip cynically. 'I wouldn't mind having depression, only I can't, can I? Who'd mind these two?'

'Biscuit?' Mike passed her the open packet and she took one, before sitting next to Liz, the toddler on her lap.

'Has he seen the doctor? Is he receiving treatment?' Liz enquired.

The girl sniffed. 'He's got pills. Don't seem to do any good, though.'

'You should encourage him to go back to his GP. We can speak to him if you like, or get someone from social services—'

'Don't you dare!' Shannon's eyes flashed dangerously. 'They've been up here before, poking their noses in and asking questions. We don't want them here. We're all right on our own.'

Liz quickly steered the subject in a safer direction. 'He gets benefits, right? Would he like some help with budgeting, do you think? There are organisations that can talk to him about managing money, so you don't run out of food and things...'

Her voice trailed off and she found herself thinking that Shannon was only a little older than Rosie, who was probably on the beach with her friends right now or hanging out at someone's house. She'd had more than her fair share of problems but was still able to enjoy many aspects of being a child.

'He spends money on stupid things,' Shannon muttered, staring at the wall. 'He can't help himself. He bought Liam a phone, some Samsung thing, but he couldn't pay the bills, and then Liam left it on the floor and Conor stood on it.' She gave a hollow laugh. 'Liam's too young for a phone; he can't look after it. It's only 'cause he said all his friends had one and my dad felt guilty.'

'I'm not too young,' cried the older boy. 'It wasn't my fault – it was him, with his big, clumsy feet.' He pointed at the toddler, who was fiddling with a bangle on Shannon's wrist.

'Budgeting is hard,' Liz persisted. 'Maybe your dad would appreciate some tips?'

But Shannon shook her head. 'He doesn't want help from no one. He hates it when people interfere. Just leave us be.'

Her mouth set in a thin, hard line and Liz sensed that it was time to stop probing. Still, she and Mike had brought enough for at least a couple of meals for the family. They'd need to talk between themselves before deciding what more, if anything, they could do.

As she rose, an idea popped into her head. 'Do you ever go into Tremarnock?'

She thought she might have seen Shannon once or twice by the harbour, though it could have been someone else. Quickly, she fished a piece of paper from her bag and wrote down her name, address and phone number before handing it across.

'This is where I live. It's not far from the seafront. Why don't you knock on my door one day when you're looking after your brothers? I've got a little girl called Lowenna who's nearly one. They might like playing together.'

Shannon didn't reply, but folded up the piece of paper and tucked it in her pocket.

'Tell your dad he can just heat up the chilli on the stove. He'll need to leave it bubbling for a few minutes,' Liz went on, smoothing the crumples from her dress. 'We can bring some more another time if you like.'

'Here, take these,' added Mike, rising and passing Shannon the packet of biscuits. 'I shouldn't have any more. My wife says I'm fat enough as it is.'

On the way out, he ruffled Liam's hair. 'You're a big boy now. You help your sister as much as you can.' Then he grinned at Conor. 'And you be a good boy, too. No more stamping on phones!'

Shannon and the two boys followed the visitors to the door, perhaps to be certain that they really were leaving, and as Liz stepped outside she noticed again the neat flowerbeds that she'd seen on the way in.

'Who does the gardening?' she asked, pointing at the brightly coloured blooms.

'That's me sister,' Liam replied proudly. 'She loves flowers. She grows 'em from tiny little seeds.'

'How clever!' Liz turned back to Shannon. 'You must have green fingers.'

'They're pink!' Liam cried in a 'durr, silly' kind of way.

'I mean she's really good with plants. Not everyone has the knack. I just need to look at a house plant and it seems to wither and die.'

Shannon shrugged, as if praise meant nothing to her, but just for a moment her eyes lit up and for the first time Liz thought that she could detect the merest hint of a smile.

Chapter Five

THE GIRLS' FIRST night at Polgarry Manor wasn't a great success. After phoning Matt to say that they'd arrived safely, Bramble was too scared to search for the kitchen, so she and Katie went to bed hungry. It then took them ages to drop off and Bramble woke frequently, alarmed by the unfamiliar creaks and groans of a strange house and missing Matt's strong arms around her.

If he were here, he'd get up to investigate the noises. He'd scout around in a masculine sort of way, checking corners and behind doors, before coming back to reassure her that all was well. But there was no Matt, only Katie beside her in the big double bed, and she was terrified, too. They huddled beneath the covers, whispering quietly, until they finally nodded off, only for some new sound to frighten the living daylights out of them all over again, so that by the time morning arrived they were exhausted and unable to get up.

The main topic of conversation in the wee small hours was what on earth to do about the housekeeper. She quite clearly considered herself a fixture at Polgarry and perhaps intended to live out the rest of her days here, but Bramble neither wanted nor could afford staff, least of all hatchet-faced Maria.

'You'll have to ring the solicitor and tell him you don't need her,' Katie said firmly. 'There's no way you can pay her, and anyway, we don't want her snooping around the place, frightening us out of our wits. Besides, she doesn't seem to do her job very well. Everything's a right mess.'

'It's true,' Bramble agreed. 'But I don't particularly want a row with her. Maybe she'll just leave of her own accord when she realises I've got no money.'

It was almost ten a.m. when they finally stirred, and Bramble lay there quietly for a while, her eyes still closed, until there was a rap on the door and Maria stalked in, uninvited.

'Good morning, Miss Bramble, Miss Katie,' she said, quite unperturbed, it seemed, by the girls' unconventional sleeping arrangement. She walked quickly over to the two giant windows, one at the end of the bed, the other several feet away on Bramble's side, and pulled the cords sharply to open the floor-length gold curtains. Instantly, showers of dust flew out, catching the sunlight and scattering around the room like talcum powder.

'Bless you!' Katie said when Bramble sneezed, and they both giggled; they couldn't help it. But Maria remained stony-faced.

'Your breakfast has been waiting for you since seven o'clock this morning in the dining room,' she said curtly. 'Will you be wanting it or shall I clear it away?'

'Er, sorry, we're c-coming,' Bramble stammered. She'd like to laze a while longer but wouldn't dare. If anyone was the boss in this extraordinary relic of a place, it seemed it most definitely wasn't her.

When Maria left, Katie put on a sort of East German accent and said, 'Ve have vays of making you eat,' before bursting into gales of laughter. Bramble told her to shut up, before dissolving herself.

Finally, after wiping the tears from her eyes, she leaped out of bed to peek at the view from the window, which she hadn't been able to observe last night in the gloom. Resting her hands on the wooden frame and taking a deep breath as she gazed out, she thought that she'd never seen so much empty space, nor anything quite so beautiful.

They were perched on a headland, looking out over an unkempt garden filled with overgrown shrubs and bushes and broken statues, and surrounded by a low, fragmented wall. Behind it, green fields dotted with purple, yellow and white flowers swept away to the cliff edge, beyond which, as far as the eye could see, stretched the turquoise ocean, sparkling like polished glass in the early-morning sunshine. Far off, a big grey ship was making its way lazily around the promontory, leaving a foamy path in its wake, while seagulls circled overhead, wheeling and crying. There wasn't a soul to be seen.

'Oh my God, it's amazing!' Bramble exclaimed. 'Come and see!'

She dashed to the other window, which looked out over a different aspect – perhaps once a more formal part of the garden, if you could call it that, for nature had run riot. Wide stone steps led down to a gravel path and then a large patch of land divided into two sections by rusty metal railings, with unkempt flowerbeds on either side. At the far end of the left-hand section lay the remains of a brick gazebo, now covered in ivy and missing its roof, while a broken sundial took pride of place in the middle of the garden on the right.

Unloved the grounds might be, but ugly they were not, for in amongst the weeds and chaos flourished rambling pink, red and white roses and a host of other flowers whose names Bramble didn't know, which tumbled over crumbling benches and raced up walls. On closer inspection, she realised that in the centre of the gazebo garden what she'd thought was mossy grass of a slightly different colour than the rest was, in fact, a rectangular pond covered in dark-green weeds, and presiding over it was a disused stone fountain shaped like a voluptuous mermaid who was missing her head.

The whole scene reminded Bramble of Sleeping Beauty's castle, which stood silent and unvisited for a hundred years until the prince arrived. There were parts of Polgarry's gardens that you would, no doubt, have trouble finding your way through, so thick and dense were they with growth, and Bramble wondered when they'd last seen the flash of shears' blades or the snip of some secateurs. Not for a very long time.

Katie joined her at the window and made a whistling sound. 'It's nicer in the sunshine. I hardly even looked out when we came before, did you?'

'We'll see if we can find a lawnmower,' Bramble said, more to herself than her friend. 'If not, we'll buy a new one.'

'It'll take more than a bit of mowing to tidy that lot up. It's like a jungle. I wouldn't know where to begin.'

But Bramble waved a hand dismissively. 'We'll do it gradually, not all in one go.'

After that, she swung around and surveyed the interior of the Chinese Room, which they picked last night as it seemed marginally less creepy than the other room. It was so called, no doubt, because of the silk wallpaper, painted duck-egg blue and decorated with tiny pink blossoms and exquisite birds, only it might have been there since Queen Victoria's reign, given its dirty, faded state.

Gold-framed oil paintings hung on the walls, depicting severe old ancestors with dead eyes and granite expressions. In one corner was a giant wooden wardrobe, and next to that, a dressing table with a bevelled mirror and glass heavily foxed with age. There were table lamps with oversized shades on either side of the bed, and now that it was light Bramble was able to see the dirt settled between the thick pleats. She wouldn't dare to close the royal-blue curtains around the four-poster bed, for fear of unleashing another shower of filth, and she resolved not to sleep here another night until she'd washed, dusted, polished and vacuumed the place clean.

'We'll make a list of things to do today while we have breakfast,' she continued. 'C'mon, we'd better hurry up and get dressed or Maria will be on the warpath.'

There was an eerie hush as they descended the giant wooden staircase, followed, it seemed, by the eyes of countless subjects in gloomy portraits on the walls, and when they reached the marble-floored hallway, they gazed around, unable to remember how on earth to find the dining room.

They half-expected Maria to emerge, apparition-like, and point them in the right direction, but no one came and there was nothing for it but to try the various doors and hope for the best. The first one led to a long corridor, at the end of which lay the square kitchen with small windows overlooking what might have been a kitchen garden, now overgrown with weeds and lined with broken greenhouses with cracked glass roofs and doors hanging off their hinges.

Inside the kitchen was a white porcelain sink, a black iron Aga and a cumbersome fridge that wouldn't look out of place in a museum. At least the place seemed clean; the black and white tiles on the floor were well-scrubbed. When Bramble peeped next door, she saw another double sink and wooden draining board, an extraordinarily ancient washing machine and what looked suspiciously like an instrument of torture.

'What's that?' she squeaked to Katie, who was right behind her, sticking close.

'I think it's a mangle for drying wet laundry. There was one like it at that stately home our mums used to take us to.'

Bramble eyed the metal contraption doubtfully. 'Do you think Maria still uses it?'

'Probably. Look!'

She glanced up to where her friend was pointing, and noticed a wooden pulley suspended from the ceiling from which hung several pairs of long-legged beige knickers. Her shoulders started to shake and she only just managed to stifle the snorts and gurgles.

'Quick, let's get out of here,' she said, stumbling for the exit with Katie hot on her heels.

Back in the hall, they chose another door, which led, this time, through a series of smaller rooms into a giant drawing room with French windows looking on to the terrace and, beyond, the metal railings that Bramble had seen from her bedroom. Sunlight streamed in, making her blink, and it took a moment or two for her eyes to adjust enough to register the grand piano at one end, the impressive marble fireplace, the faded chaise longue and two intricate tapestries, one depicting female figures bathing by a river, surrounded by rocks and trees, the other a white heron in a wooded landscape with buildings on the horizon and a large house, not unlike Polgarry, on the hill.

Above the fireplace hung a mirror, and to the right was a painting much like the others in style, only smaller, and Bramble went for a closer look. It was an oil painting depicting a stern young woman in profile against a featureless backdrop of broken brushstrokes in black, yellow and white. She was wearing a dark dress and had a loose bun on the top of her head from which a coil of chestnut hair, tinged with auburn, had escaped and was running down the side of her pale cheek.

'I wonder who she was,' Bramble commented, and speculated on the fact that she and this strange lady, like all the other crusty characters around the place, might in some way have been related.

Katie shrugged. 'Some second cousin four times removed? Her dress isn't particularly grand. She must have been a long way down the Penrose pecking order. Come on, we'd better hurry up.'

They hastened through another, smaller reception chamber into a big, square, wood-panelled space with a long rectangular table in the centre and windows looking out on to a lawn, now more of a meadow strewn with wildflowers. Maria was standing very upright in front of a heavy sideboard, on which Bramble could see two lidded, antique silver breakfast dishes, a toaster and a jug of orange juice, and the table was laid with silver cutlery, linen napkins and pots of jam.

'Will you require a cooked breakfast?' Maria asked crisply. 'The eggs and bacon have gone cold, but I can make more if you wish?'

Bramble's tummy rumbled at the prospect of hot food, but she shook her head.

'We'll just have toast and cereal,' she said, eyeing a jar of something that might be muesli. 'And some tea – if you don't mind?'

'As you wish,' Maria replied, before sweeping out, leaving the girls to tiptoe nervously about, pouring cereal and toasting bread in the wobbly old toaster, which popped up noisily, making them jump.

'We've got to stop being on edge,' Katie said crossly. 'We're not trespassers. This place is yours; you can do whatever you like.'

But still, they found themselves whispering as they ate, and they jumped again when Maria returned with a pot of tea.

'Shall I prepare luncheon at one? Lord Penrose always had luncheon at one and dinner at seven.'

'Yes,' they chorused without even looking at each other.

'I assume that you will wish me to continue with the usual menu?' Maria added. 'But if you would prefer to make changes...?'

'Oh no, just the usual please,' Bramble replied swiftly, before hesitating. 'That is... do you need some money? For the food, I mean...'

Her voice trailed off and she felt stupid and incompetent, wishing that she'd had lessons in how to behave with staff. She hadn't exactly needed skills like that back home.

'Lord Penrose made suitable provisions for your first few months,' Maria answered coolly. 'He paid my salary up until the first of February next year, as well as the heating and lighting bills, and I have enough money for food for the period, too. After that, it will be your responsibility.'

Bramble was astonished and would have liked to ask more, but the housekeeper vanished again, leaving her clueless. The idea that the old man had planned in some way for her arrival seemed quite extraordinary. What had made him assume that she would move to Polgarry at all? She might well have decided to get the place off her hands as quickly as possible.

Still, it was a tremendous relief to know that their basic needs would be covered for six months, even if it did mean putting up with Maria, and the girls toasted the unexpected good news with cups of tea. After that, they set about writing a shopping list of cleaning products, because they didn't fancy asking the housekeeper for whatever was in the cupboards, and as soon as they'd finished, they hopped in the car and headed for the supermarket, relieved to get away from their oppressive surroundings.

It didn't take them long to locate the nearest store, and after stocking up on bleach, polish and the like, they discussed checking out the local pub until they realised that it would make them late for 'luncheon'. Back at the manor, they eyed with some trepidation the fresh array of serving dishes on the dining room sideboard, both wishing that they had the courage to tell Maria they'd rather sort themselves out.

There was chicken in thick, unappetising-looking gravy, cabbage and overboiled carrots and potatoes, with sponge pudding for dessert. Bramble did her best to eat up, thinking that she should be grateful for not having had to prepare the meal, but yearning all the same for the good old days of filled jacket potatoes and sandwiches.

Afterwards, stuffed to the brim, they decided to postpone the spring clean until a little later and explore the grounds instead. Leaving by the front door, they took with them the big bunch of old iron keys that they'd been given. They skirted around the perimeter of the grounds before venturing into the garden that they'd seen from their bedroom, with the gazebo, pond and headless mermaid fountain.

Now, standing by the water, raking desultorily through the thick weeds with a stick and admiring the dragonflies buzzing across the surface with their bright-blue bodies and gossamer wings, Bramble suddenly felt exhausted, as if she could sleep for a week. The hot sun was beating down on her back and the bees were humming lazily in the scrubby lavender bushes behind.

'I bet the gardens were really lovely once,' she commented. 'You can imagine ladies in fancy gowns and big straw hats promenading with their parasols, can't you?'

Katie nodded. 'And children in funny costumes playing hide and seek, and gentlemen playing croquet on the lawn. It's a shame old Lord Penrose didn't look after the place. It must have been rather sad watching it crumble around his ears.'

Bramble peered into the murky water, looking for fish, but there were none. They'd probably been suffocated by the rampaging weeds. A robin on the rose bush opposite cocked its head at her inquisitively, but soon flew off to a gnarled tree branch a little way away, where it flapped its wings cheekily as if to say, 'Ha ha, you can't catch me!'

'I want to clear the pond out and do some pruning,' Bramble announced suddenly. 'That'll be our first project after the bedroom. It'll be nice to be able to use one section of the garden at least.'

Pushing open an iron gate that led to another walled area consumed by overgrowth, they soon found an orchard of plum and greengage trees laden with ripening fruit. They plucked a few sweet plums and ate them, wiping their sticky hands on the long grass, before venturing towards a large tumbledown shed in one corner and trying the door, which opened. It was dark inside and full of cobwebs, and it smelled musty. Most of the space was taken up with gardening tools and a ride-on lawnmower the size of a small tractor.

'I wonder if it works,' Bramble commented.

'Doubtful,' said Katie. 'Probably hasn't been used for years.'

'We could get it fixed? There must be someone round here who can do that sort of thing.'

'Another job to add to the list,' Katie added wryly.

Having closed the shed door, they wandered into the uncultivated fields beyond the manor gardens, where the grass reached almost up to their knees, before making their way towards a wooded area in the distance. It was hot and humid, and once they'd gained the shade at last, they paused for a moment to catch their breath, relieved to be out of the sun. After that, a rough path took them through a tangle of silver birch, ash and holly before they arrived at open sky once more. Ahead lay grass, rocks and, finally, a sheer drop and the ocean. Bramble gasped for the second time that day.

'I didn't realise the sea was so close. I thought we had quite a bit further to go. Isn't it beautiful?'

They stood for a while gazing at the cobalt-blue water, which seemed not to move at all until it drew close to the land, where it smashed against the granite rocks and broke into a million glittering shards. Katie glanced to her right and pointed to a small stone cottage nearby that appeared to be teetering on the edge of the precipice, waiting to drop off. There was only space for a little front garden surrounded by a low wall before the sheer drop. The place seemed cared for, with windswept white roses growing around the door, a stumpy palm tree by the path and carefully trimmed shrubs.

'What a weird spot for a house!' she said.

Bramble frowned. 'It looks as if someone lives there.'

She hadn't yet worked out quite where her estate began and ended, but knew that it stretched far and wide and included a number of cottages that she'd understood were derelict.

'I wouldn't fancy it, would you?' Katie went on. 'It must be wild in winter.'

Curious, they strolled closer to the building, noticing two easels side by side on the grass, one large and one much smaller, as if for a child. There was a bright-red ball in one of the flowerbeds and a pile of miniature yellow and green plastic gardening tools – a trowel, rake, bucket, hoe and a funny little wheelbarrow.

'I think you've got squatters,' Katie whispered. 'You'll have to turf them out.'

Bramble hadn't considered the possibility of strangers sharing this vast space with her; not that there wasn't enough room.

'They don't seem to be doing any harm. We'll leave it for another time. C'mon, let's go for a swim. I'm boiling!'

Peering over the cliff, they looked for a suitable spot to clamber down, but there wasn't a path in sight. However, their attention was soon drawn to a tempting-looking small pebbly inlet wedged between two granite projections. It was so secluded it would be perfect for skinny dipping, if they could only get there.

'It's very steep,' Bramble said doubtfully.

'We could scramble down,' Katie suggested. 'It's not so bad in some places. We can hang on to the bushes and slide some of the way on our bums.'

They were both in shorts and T-shirts and their arms and legs got scratched as they half-staggered, half-stumbled down the steep rocks. Before long, Bramble began to think that they might have made a mistake, because much as she fancied a swim, her whole body was hurting and she had no idea how they were going to clamber back up.

'I'm not sure if this is such a good idea,' she squeaked, hoping that Katie might suggest they turn around and do their best to retrace their steps before reaching the point of no return, but she was undeterred.

'We've started now; we might as well go on,' she pronounced, just before her backside hit something particularly sharp – 'Ow!' – and she slipped and slid several feet before landing in a crevice.

'Are you OK?' Bramble's courage had all but vanished.

'Not really,' Katie whimpered. 'I've hurt my elbow.'

Perched precariously on a narrow ledge and clutching on to a flimsy clump of samphire, Bramble felt her head start to reel. She wasn't at all sure that she could go either up or down. She might just have to sit here for ever.

Just then they heard a shout – 'Oi!' – and glancing up, Bramble caught sight of a large pair of muddy brown leather walking boots.

'What the hell do you think you're doing?' came a deep voice. 'You could get yourselves killed.'

'I – I think I'm stuck,' Bramble stammered. 'I can't move. And my friend's hurt.'

'I'm all right,' Katie called back bravely. 'Just.'

Bramble couldn't bring herself to look down; she thought she might faint.

'Wait there,' the voice cried, as if they were capable of doing anything else. 'I'll fetch some rope.'

Then the boots disappeared and the girls were alone again, hanging on for dear life, their only company a bunch of seagulls and a flock of red-billed choughs preening themselves ostentatiously on a peaky promontory. To keep up their spirits, Bramble started to sing Beyoncé's 'Love on Top', until Katie begged her not to because it was making her feel sick. Bramble was just beginning to think that perhaps the pair of boots had been a figment of her febrile imagination when she heard voices, this time belonging to a man and child.

'What are they doing, Daddy?' the child asked in a puzzled tone.

'I don't know,' came the reply, 'but they're bloody stupid.'

Bramble bristled and might have called something rude back, but she remembered that she was hardly in a position to upset any potential rescuers.

'Pass me the end,' the man commanded from above and she heard a thud followed by a few grunts.

'That's a figure-eight knot, see? Safe as houses. Won't budge. D'you remember how to do it?'

Soon a length of coarse rope snaked down the cliff beside Bramble and the man shouted at her to grab it and hang on tight.

'I'm going to pull you up. For Christ's sake, don't let go. It's tied to a tree but I'll be holding on as well. You won't drop unless you do something daft.'

There was nothing for it but to obey. Bramble seized the lifeline with both hands, and he shouted, 'Ready? One, two, three.'

Then, slowly, he began to heave her up the bank while she did her best to help, seeking out foot holes and taking care not to smash into the side. When at last she reached the top and flopped, gasping, on to her tummy, the first thing she noticed was the lovely safe, flat land covered in soft, springy grass. The second was a small boy with a mop of blonde hair shaking his head and waggling his finger at her. He couldn't have been more than seven or eight.

'My dad says you shouldn't have gone down there,' the boy said in a superior voice. 'It's too dangerous.'

Bramble, who was hot, thirsty, shaken and in no mood for a ticking-off from anyone, let alone a kid, shot him a dirty look.

'I'll have you know—' she started to say, but she was interrupted by the boy's father.

'Can she do it on her own, do you think, or will she need help?'

So focused had she been on the boy that for a moment Bramble didn't know what he meant.

'Your friend,' the man continued crossly. 'Can she come up on her own or is she too badly hurt?'

Bramble looked at him for the first time. He was tall and powerful, with a tanned face, short, closely cut dark-brown hair, a long, straight nose and wide cheekbones. His narrow-ish eyes were framed by dark brows and lashes but she couldn't see the colour because he was frowning, waiting for her answer.

'I, er, I'm not sure,' she replied truthfully. 'I think she's hurt her elbow.'

The man muttered something under his breath before turning to the boy.

'Stay here and don't touch the rope – it might burn. I'll go and get her.'

The boy nodded gravely and Bramble watched his father scramble over the edge, hanging on to the rope with both hands and lowering himself down. He seemed quite agile, as if he were in his natural element. Perhaps he went rock climbing as a hobby.

'Are you all right?' Bramble called after a time, because he had disappeared over a bulge in the cliff face and she couldn't see him any more.

There was silence for a moment; then, 'We're fine!' Katie cried valiantly, and Bramble sighed with relief. Her pleasure was short-lived, however, as she watched the man come into view again, heaving Katie up the steep escarpment on his back. She had her legs wrapped around his waist and her arms firmly around his neck, and his face was locked in concentration, veins swelling on his temples and beads of sweat on his forehead.

Bramble grabbed the rope and tried to tug, but it was too heavy. It must have been very hard work for him. What if Katie let go or he lost his grip?

The small boy, who was standing still and watching intently, seemed to sense her anxiety and whispered, 'Don't worry. My dad's very strong.'

But it did little to reassure Bramble, who remembered that when she was young, she'd truly believed her father could fly her to the moon and back. It had been a terrible shock when he'd slipped once on a tree root and twisted his ankle.

At last, when the man was within a few feet of the top, he paused.

'Can you climb over now?' he asked Katie, and Bramble and the boy rushed to help. She'd quite forgotten about Katie's bad elbow, though, and grabbed her by the arm, only for her to shriek in protest.

'Sorry.' Bramble tugged hard on the waist of her friend's shorts instead, and after one great heave, they were lying side by side in a heap on the grass, their eyes closed, heads swimming with shock and elation.

'Thank God,' said Bramble, listening to Katie's panting and conscious of her own pumping heart. 'That was scary.'

For a few moments, she quite forgot about the strange man who had come to their rescue, but gradually she became aware of a shadow across her face, and when she opened her eyes, he was standing right over her, his big frame blotting out the sun.

'What on earth were you doing?' he growled. 'That was incredibly stupid.' She felt herself shrink like the leaves of a touch-me-not flower.

He was wearing a crumpled grey T-shirt and faded jeans, now covered in mud and chalk.

'We were hot. We wanted a swim,' she said in a small voice, wishing that she didn't sound so foolish.

'If I hadn't been here, you might have fallen all the way and seriously injured yourselves,' he continued, his eyes flashing dangerously. 'Either that or you'd have got yourselves drowned.'

Sitting up slowly, she brushed the grass and stones off her arm and legs. A lump had appeared in her throat, her eyes were stinging and she realised that she hadn't felt quite like this since school, when she'd been dispatched to the head teacher's office for messing around with the Bunsen burner in a chemistry lesson and accidentally setting fire to another girl's fringe. Well, sort of accidentally – she'd been a very annoying girl – but Bramble had only meant to give her a bit of a fright. Afterwards, she'd received a telling-off that she'd never forgotten.

She was about to apologise for all the trouble they'd caused when a little voice reminded her that she wasn't at school any more and this man wasn't her head teacher. He might have saved them but he was extremely rude, and what's more, he was most probably trespassing on *her* land.

Mustering what dignity she could, she stood up and straightened her back and shoulders.

'Who are you exactly?' she said imperiously. 'I'm the new owner of Polgarry Manor.'

'Are you?' The man looked unimpressed. 'You should get yourself better acquainted with the area then before attempting any more daft escapades.'

Bramble's face flamed with anger and embarrassment.

'Lord Penrose was my grandfather and I'm his granddaughter, Bramble Challoner,' she announced, raising her chin and extending a hand. The stranger looked at it for a moment, as if he didn't know what to do with it, before taking it reluctantly and giving it a half-hearted shake.

'And this,' Bramble continued, attempting a grand lady gesture, 'is my friend, Katie Leonard.'

'Fergus Wall,' the man replied curtly. 'I suppose that's yours now, too.' He turned and pointed to the cottage. 'I live there.'

His brusque manner and seeming sense of entitlement irritated Bramble more than she could say, and she decided there and then that whatever arrangement he'd made with Lord Penrose would have to be reviewed forthwith.

'Thank you for bringing the rope,' she said airily, as if they could have managed perfectly well without him.

But the boy was having none of it. 'If my dad hadn't have come, you'd still be stuck. You'd have been there all night if it wasn't for him.'

There was no point arguing – it would only have made her look worse – so Bramble glanced the other way. Katie was sitting up at last, nursing her injured elbow, which was swollen and covered in red, raw scrapes.

'Is it broken, do you think?' Bramble asked. 'Can you walk back to the house?' She couldn't wait to get away.

'I think so... it's not too bad... I reckon it's just bruised.' Then Katie turned to Fergus. 'Thank you so much. You're a hero.'

'If it's not better by tomorrow, I'd get it checked out at the hospital,' he muttered, taking his son's hand, before turning and heading back to his cottage without so much as a goodbye.

'What a rude man!' Bramble exclaimed as they trudged home, arm in arm, through the woods and across the fields before reaching the safety of the manor once more. 'He didn't even offer to come with us, to make sure you were OK.'

'No, but he's quite fit,' Katie grinned. 'Don't you think? Gorgeous face and body, but his eyes are sad.'

Chapter Six

THAT EVENING TABITHA arrived at Bag End with her son, Oscar, clutching a small overnight case with a picture of Winnie the Pooh on the front. It was around six thirty and, to the little boy's enormous pleasure, his mother had informed him that he was to have a sleepover. A former nightclub singer, she was due to perform at the local pub, her first gig for many years. Robert had taken time off work especially and was to look after Oscar with Lowenna, while Liz and Tabitha went out. Oscar had been excited all day, constantly asking, 'Is it time now?', until Tabitha had grown irritated and told him not to mention it again or she might cancel the whole arrangement.

Finally, mother and son walked together from their home, Dove Cottage, just up the road, stopping for a brief chat with Pat, who had spotted them passing and leaned out of her little front window to say hello, almost upsetting her display of precious china knick-knacks on the ledge beneath. Pat was well into her eighties and had never been quite the same since she'd fallen victim to a scam the previous year and badly broken her arm. She was frailer now, and had had to give up flower arranging at the nearby Methodist church as it had become too much for her, but there was nothing wrong with her mind. Liz always said that she was as sharp as a tack; so much so, in fact, that you could cut yourself on her. Even now, very little escaped her beady gaze.

After they said goodbye, Oscar skipped ahead of his mother and went up on tiptoe to rap on Liz's door himself. He was only three, but if he'd been a little older he could have made his own way, because he knew the route perfectly well, having visited often enough. In fact, Bag End was almost his second home.

It hadn't always been so. He was just eighteen months old when he and his parents had arrived in Tremarnock, having left Manchester to start a new life down south. They'd soon become the talk of the village, because on the face of it they'd seemed like the perfect couple. Luke was handsome, charming and wealthy, Tabitha, young and glamorous, and they were pouring thousands of pounds into converting one of the village's most historic buildings into a super-chic boutique guest house called The Stables.

Right from the start, though, Liz had had her doubts about Luke, who'd seemed too good to be true, and Tabitha, who'd appeared withdrawn; but few had shared her suspicions, and for a time even Robert had fallen under Luke's spell. But in the end, Liz had been thoroughly vindicated when Luke had been unmasked not only as an evil fraudster who'd made his fortune by swindling old folk, including poor Pat, but also a vicious bully who had made his wife's life a living hell.

Thankfully, Luke was now locked up in prison, but this had unsettled Oscar, of course, who'd not only lost his father but had also had to cope with yet another move, from his spacious new home, which had had to be sold off, to a poky ground-floor flat with his mum, who was originally from Liverpool. The saving grace had been that the flat was near

Bag End and Liz had taken Tabitha under her wing. The pair were now firm friends, and in a way the two households had become like one big, happy family.

It was Liz who answered the door, with Lowenna balanced on her hip in a pair of pink and white spotty pyjamas. She'd just come out of the bath and her dark, silky hair was carefully combed, her pink cheeks gleaming like a mirror; you could practically see your face in them.

Liz ruffled Oscar's hair, and when she caught sight of Tabitha behind him, she gasped. 'You look stunning!'

Tabitha was wearing a knee-length, shiny silver halter-neck dress that clung in all the right places and showed off her creamy-brown arms and shoulders, while her glossy black hair fanned out around her like a cloud of cottonseed.

'I've done my best,' she replied modestly.

Lowenna struggled to get down and Liz set her carefully on her bottom on the floor in front of Oscar, who gave her a clumsy bear hug that almost sent her flying. Just like his mother, the little boy had big brown eyes and a mass of black wavy hair, which Tabitha refused to cut, meaning that he was sometimes mistaken for a girl.

'Come on in!' called a voice, and Robert appeared in the corridor behind Liz, rubbing his eyes and looking suspiciously as if he'd been enjoying an extended afternoon nap.

'I like your suitcase,' he said to Oscar, who promptly thrust the bag forwards.

'It's got Winnie the Pooh on,' he said proudly, and Lowenna gave it a curious look.

'I can see that,' Robert replied, trying to stifle a yawn. 'We're going to have lots of fun tonight. We've got a midnight feast.' He winked blearily. 'Don't tell your mum.'

After he'd scooped Lowenna from the floor, they

disappeared upstairs to show Oscar his bedroom while Liz and Tabitha strolled into the kitchen. It was a reasonably sized, wide white room with low ceilings and an old pine table in the middle, scored with marks through years of use.

'Tea, or something stronger?' Liz asked and Tabitha bit her lower lip.

'I'd better not have a drink now. I'm dead nervous. What if I balls it up? It's so long since I performed, I think I've lost my nerve.'

'Nonsense, you'll be great. And remember, you'll be surrounded by friends.'

'I know,' said Tabitha, frowning. 'But I've never been on stage on my own. I've always had a band.'

Liz turned to the counter behind and passed her friend a tiny parcel wrapped in pink tissue paper.

'What is it?'

'Open it.'

Tabitha tore off the sticky tape and inside was another sheet of white tissue paper, and inside that, a tiny gold charm depicting a seated figure with peaky ears and funny pointed shoes, his arms wrapped around his knees. It was similar in size to the ones on the bracelet that she was wearing now.

'It's a Cornish piskey,' Liz explained. 'When you're feeling nervous, you can stroke it and it's supposed to bring you good luck.'

Tabitha immediately took off the bracelet and attached the charm.

'Thank you,' she said, kissing her friend on the cheek. 'I feel braver already!'

When they went upstairs to say goodbye, Oscar was chasing Lowenna around the blow-up bed in Rosie's room, where he was to sleep, while Rosie sat with Robert on the end of her own bed, watching with a mixture of amusement and trepidation, in case one of them should fall.

To Liz's surprise, Rosie was in her daft pink and black leopard-print onesie, which must have been rather warm today.

'What time is Tim coming?' Liz asked, as the last thing she'd heard was that his mum was to drop him off for a couple of hours. Tim and Rosie usually went to one or the other's house at the weekend, or they'd meet up with friends, and Rosie always did her hair and put on make-up. She was becoming prettier by the day, people often commented.

She shrugged. 'He can't make it.'

'Oh, why?'

Rosie continued to watch the younger ones, avoiding Liz's gaze. 'I think he's got to tidy his room.'

It was a lie, and she knew that Liz knew.

'That's a shame. Why don't you go to his place instead? Robert could give you a lift – he can take the little ones; they'll enjoy it.'

'I'd rather stay in.'

Liz was as sure as she could be that Amelia was involved, and little flames of worry licked around her insides. She felt her daughter's wounds more keenly than if they were her own. Sometimes it seemed like a curse.

'Let's go shopping tomorrow. We can get you some new jeans – or a dress, if you prefer?'

Rosie smiled sadly. 'Thanks, Mum, but I've already got plans.'

There was nothing for it but to take their leave, and Liz and Tabitha set off down Humble Hill, stopping for a moment to admire the sumptuous display of pinks, anemones, lupins, delphiniums and purple foxgloves in Jean's garden. Liz was thinking all the while that she wished she could wave a magic wand and make Amelia disappear, but life wasn't like that, and in any case, it wasn't the girl's fault that she was pretty and fun and Tim was drawn to her like a moth to a flame.

They turned right into Fore Street and it wasn't long before they passed Tabitha's former home, which was standing cold, dark and empty, awaiting the arrival of its new owners. Tabitha looked the other way, not wishing to stir up unhappy memories.

A few doors down, they reached The Hole in the Wall pub, so named because it once had a spy hole that enabled smugglers to keep watch for customs men. The place had been doing a roaring trade since being taken over by its new landlord, Danny, and initially this had ruffled the feathers of Barbara, who ran the nearby Lobster Pot and had noticed a worrying dip in business. Fortunately, however, things had settled down once she'd realised that the two establishments appealed to completely different clienteles and her old customers had started to return. Now, she and Danny got on famously, even drinking in each other's hostelries occasionally and toasting each other's health, much to Liz's relief, as she hated conflict of any sort; she just wanted everyone to get on.

The doorway of Danny's pub was so low that anyone over about five feet five inches tall had to stoop to get in, which wasn't a problem for Liz, but Tabitha was careful to lower her head as they stepped over the threshold. It was dark inside and it took a moment or two for the women to notice the landlord, who was behind the wooden bar, wiping it down with a big blue cloth. He had grown up in Devon and appeared to have three main passions: business, rock and pop music and water sports, particularly surfing. In fact, it was the lure of the Cornish waves that had drawn him to the county in the first place.

Tall and slim, Danny had longish fair hair tied back in a ponytail, a neatly trimmed beard and a year-round tan, owing, no doubt, to the amount of time he spent in the fresh air. He'd often pop out during the day to get in a spot of surfing or windsailing, leaving the pub in the hands of his staff, who adored his laid-back, hipster-ish style, although they were well aware that there was a line they couldn't cross. Behind the easy-going exterior lay a strong sense of fair play coupled with a shrewd business brain that they'd ignore at their peril. He looked after his staff and believed in having a laugh, but there'd be trouble if someone failed to pull their weight and let the others do all the work.

He looked up when the women entered, and on catching sight of Tabitha his eyes widened and he swallowed repeatedly, making his Adam's apple bob. Liz was amused. She could sense sparks of static crackling off Tabitha, too, and was half-inclined to push them together. The whole village could tell that they fancied each other like crazy, but neither had made a move. Tabitha was, understandably, wary of men, having had such a bad experience, while Danny just seemed overawed, yet Liz was pretty sure that her friend wouldn't say no if he'd only take the plunge and ask her out.

There were various huddles of customers and you could hear the sounds of instruments being tuned and microphones being tested next door, as there were to be a number of different acts.

'Can I buy you a drink, Tabs?' Liz asked as they walked past a heavily pierced woman in a pink vest top and approached the bar. 'White wine?' She rested her elbows on the counter and leaned towards Danny. 'She's a bit nervous. I keep telling her she'll be great.'

Danny scratched his shoulder, trying to appear nonchalant,

and nodded several times too often. "Course she will. She'll be extraordinary. In a good way, I mean,' he added quickly. 'I mean, she's stunning.' His face fell. 'That is, her voice is stunning, not her looks.' His eyes widened in alarm. 'Of course, she *does* look great...'

Liz came to his rescue.

'What time will she be on?' she asked breezily, while Tabitha fiddled with her charm bracelet, twisting it round and round and being no help at all. 'I want to be able to see her properly.'

Danny took a deep breath and glanced at Tabitha, whose eyes fell to the floor. 'After the interval. I thought she'd prefer it.'

Just then one of his bar staff arrived with a cheery 'Hi, boss!' and Danny called 'Hi' back. He could communicate perfectly well with everyone else.

Tabitha went to get ready while Liz nursed a glass of white wine, and it wasn't long before she was joined by Tony, Felipe and a lanky youth of about fifteen with a startling Mohawk hairdo, shaved all over apart from a bright-green strip running down the centre of his scalp, and a silver stud in his nose. He appeared to favour the Loveday school of fashion because he was dressed all in black: black jeans, black leather jacket, black T-shirt, black trainers and black shades, which seemed a little unnecessary indoors.

The most unusual thing about him, though, was the large round holes in both earlobes lined with thick silver rings, like flesh plugs, off which hung substantial wooden crosses. Liz, who'd never seen anything quite like them before, was mesmerised.

'Darling!' Tony cried, embracing her. 'How are you? Meet Rafael, Felipe's brother! He's come to live with us for a while. Isn't that grand?' He leaned in close and whispered in her ear,

'He looks a bit intimidating but he's a softie really. Wouldn't hurt a fly.'

Rafael craned his neck awkwardly as if it were stiff, before grunting hello to Liz and running a hand through his Mohawk. He had an array of thick silver rings, like knuckledusters, on his fingers and thumbs, and the air of someone trying his best to look hard but not quite pulling it off. The baby-soft skin on his cheeks was a giveaway, as was the downy fluff on his upper lip.

'How long have you been in England?' she asked, hoping to put him at ease, and he replied in a thick accent that he'd arrived on Tuesday.

'My mother wants me to have British education, but I prefer the school of life.'

She couldn't tell if he were joking or not. Difficult to say.

'Would you like a drink?' she asked, wanting to be welcoming. 'I think my daughter's about your age. Her name's Rosie.'

Seizing the moment, Rafael told the bar girl that he'd like a Peroni beer, only for Tony to intercept.

'Absolutely no alcohol! We've told you about that before.'

Wrapping his arms across his chest, Rafael said something in Portuguese that Liz couldn't understand but that didn't sound too polite. Hoping that he wouldn't swear at her, too, she decided that it would be wise to leave Tony to organise the drinks and took a step back.

'It must be very different here,' she said, scrabbling around for a safe topic of conversation. 'I've never been to Brazil. I'd love to go.'

'Here is boring,' Rafael replied gloomily. 'It is all children, old people and dogs.'

Liz tried not to be offended. 'It's not as dull as you think.

There's plenty of trouble on a Saturday night. Sometimes the police get called.'

This seemed to perk him up, until Tony snapped at him to take off his sunglasses. The boy pulled a face before grudgingly putting them on his head, and Liz shot him a sympathetic smile. Tony could be a bit like a bull in a china shop sometimes, not having mastered the art of subtle persuasion, and he had virtually no experience of dealing with teenagers either.

Now that the glasses were off, she could see that Rafael was a handsome young man, similar in looks to his older brother, with big, puppyish brown eyes and olive skin. He'd be a hit with the Cornish girls, that was for sure.

Felipe explained that he and Rafael would be based in Tremarnock full-time from now on, while Tony, who worked in London, would join them as often as he could.

'We think it is a better environment for Rafael here,' said Felipe, 'and he has a place at Marymount Academy, starting in September.'

'You'll probably be in the year above Rosie then,' Liz commented. 'She loves it there. They have an excellent drama department, if that's your thing, and they do lots of sport.'

Rafael seemed unimpressed, so she tried a different tack.

'There's a legendary school disco at the end of the Christmas term.' She eyed him slyly. 'Everyone goes a bit mad, even the teachers.'

Instantly, the clouds lifted. 'That is good. I hope it is good music. I am experienced DJ. I can do really excellent rave.'

The room was filling up, the temperature rising and the noise increasing as more and more bodies squashed into what was quite a small area. It was certainly proving to be a popular event. Liz couldn't think of anything worse than performing in front of a huge crowd, but Tabitha, who used to sing in pubs and clubs all over Hull, Manchester and Leeds before she met Luke, was almost a pro, or had been.

Liz had never watched her live, but knew that she had a lovely voice because she'd heard her singing to herself around the village when she thought no one was listening. The sound always gladdened Liz's heart because it seemed to her to be a sign that her friend's scars were slowly healing.

'I can't abide pop!' A shrill voice nearby jogged her out of her reverie.

Turning, Liz saw Esme's long, pointy nose, followed by Rick's bushy beard. They were standing very close to one another, forced together by the crush of bodies, and behind them, towering over most of the other folk, was Audrey, in a low-cut citrus-orange top from her own clothes boutique.

'They might be all right,' Rick replied hopefully.

Esme gave him a withering look and twisted slightly so that her bony shoulders were wedged between them like a barrier. 'I very much doubt it.' She was wearing some unusual dangly earrings with turquoise ceramic beads and feathers. 'I only came to support Tabitha, but I shall probably have to block my ears.'

'You've got selective hearing anyway,' Audrey commented, smirking at Liz, who knew what she meant: Esme had a habit of blanking you if she couldn't be bothered to answer.

True to form, Esme pretended not to have caught the comment while Audrey motioned bossily to Rick to order her G and T.

'What'll you have?' he asked Esme hopefully.

'I'll buy my own,' she snapped, and Liz flinched on his behalf.

While he dutifully bought Audrey's drink, Liz went next door to hear the first act, a local group called Heat Haze whose self-recorded demos had led to their being taken on by a well-known record producer. They were inspired by the bands of the sixties, and when Esme came to join Liz, even she had to concede that they were rather good and was soon tapping her feet and jigging along to the music with the best of them.

Next up was Death Rattle, a group of brothers from Bude with long hair, bare chests and black leather trousers who wielded their electric guitars like weapons. After a while, Liz's head started to thump and, wanting a breath of fresh air, she wove her way back through the crowd towards the exit, spotting Jenny and John Lambert, as well as Ryan, the fishmonger, Nathan, the postman, fitness trainer Annie and Jean and her husband, Tom. Practically the whole of Tremarnock, it seemed, had turned out to cheer Tabitha on – apart, of course, from the team at A Winkle in Time, who were holding the fort in Robert's absence. You couldn't close the restaurant on its busiest night, however much you might wish to.

Outside felt deliciously cool and Liz walked a few metres along the dark cobbled street until she reached the seafront, where she perched on the wall, her legs pulled up beneath her, and gazed at the millions of different-coloured stars in the inky sky: white, yellow, orange, red and ice-blue. She could hear laughter coming from The Lobster Pot, where some folk were spilling out on to the road, as well as the distant, raucous voices of the band over the metallic twang of their electric guitars.

Zoning out for a few moments, she focused on the stillness of the warm, dense air around her, listening to the rattle, slap and swish of the incoming tide as it whooshed over pebbles and lapped up the wall, and inhaling the salty scent of rock, water, shell and seaweed. Just for a few moments, she seemed to sense a formidable power linking her to the tide, the moon and the stars, which swell and shrink, pulsing like a beating heart before burning themselves out.

Until she'd come to Tremarnock, she reflected, her life had been chaotic, a meaningless hurtle from one hour to the next, from one day to the other, hoping merely for the energy to keep going, to keep running, and for the strength to carry Rosie on her tired back. Now, however, the hours and days were so rich and full that it was a question, rather, of trying to stand still, to pause and savour each moment as if it were her last. It was a miracle how much had changed.

She might have remained like that for some time had she not been startled by a shout – 'Hey!' – followed by a gurgle of wild laughter and the sound of footsteps racing in her direction. Soon she was greeted by the sight of four teens, two boys and two girls, rushing towards her, and Barbara, landlady of the Lobster Pot, clopping after them in high heels, waving her fists.

Without thinking, Liz hopped off the wall and stood in the middle of the street. It would have been easy enough to push past, but on seeing her the teens stopped short, giving Barbara time to catch up. Liz now recognised the girl nearest to her as Shannon, whose home she had visited only yesterday with Mike.

'Oh!' Shannon said with a flash of recognition. 'I didn't know it was you.'

The girl behind snorted and pushed her so hard that she stumbled and almost fell.

'Fuck off!' Shannon said furiously before turning back to Liz. 'She's just being stupid.'

Liz smiled thinly. Shannon was swaying slightly and smelled

of alcohol, while behind her the two boys, with cigarettes in their hands, hung back and pulled up their hoods so that she couldn't see their faces properly.

'I will NOT have you behaving like that with my customers,' Barbara roared. She might have been short in height but there was nothing little about her voice. 'I'll have you arrested.'

Liz glanced at Shannon, who had a capital G for Guilt written all over her face, and then again at Barbara.

'What's happened?'

'They were nicking people's drinks,' Barbara hollered, her tanned bosom threatening to spill out of her tight white dress. 'They were glugging them back when they thought no one was looking, the little—'

She lunged forward and grabbed one of the boys by his hood, yanking it down.

'Don't think you can hide behind that, young man! I've half a mind to call your parents...'

Her voice trailed off and Liz cleared her throat.

'I know this girl,' she said, fixing on Shannon. 'She lives near the manor with her father and brothers. I can take care of this. I'll make sure she writes an apology.'

The landlady huffed. 'An apology won't bring back my customers who left in disgust when they saw what this lot was up to.' But her shoulders had relaxed somewhat and her cheeks weren't quite so flushed.

'That goes for you, too,' Liz said, staring at the boys, who had stubbed out their cigarettes and shoved their hands in the pockets of their tracksuit bottoms, then at the other girl, whose blonde head hung sheepishly.

'First thing tomorrow you come down here with a letter saying sorry, understand?'

The four of them nodded.

'And you can pay Barbara back now for the drinks you stole.'
The taller boy groaned. 'But we don't have no money. Look!'
He turned out his pockets as evidence.

'I have,' Shannon piped up, producing a tatty black purse
from the tasselled bag on her shoulder and fishing out a five-
pound note, which she passed to Barbara.

'I'm sorry,' she said. 'We was bang out of order.'

Barbara harrumphed, but turned and walked back to the
pub, shaking her head and muttering as she went.

Time was getting on and Liz was concerned about missing
Tabitha, so she asked the teens if they'd like to join her for a
soft drink.

'Nah.' Shannon kicked a pebble at her feet while the other
girl laughed nervously. 'We're going for a walk. It's a gorgeous
evening.'

'It's a gorgeous evening,' mimicked the tallest lad at the
back and his friend told him to shut up, but Liz ignored them.

'How are your brothers – and your dad?' she went on as
Shannon shifted uncomfortably.

'All right, I s'pose. Well, my dad's a waste of space, no
change there. He's at home with the boys,' she added quickly,
as if Liz might start asking awkward questions.

The shorter boy passed a fag to the other girl, who took
a puff. Neither she nor Shannon were exactly dressed for a
walk, in full make-up, teeny tops with spaghetti straps, skirts
that barely covered their knickers and stiletto shoes.

'I gave you my phone number and address, didn't I?' Liz
asked gently, and Shannon nodded. 'Do call sometime. I'd love
to see you and the boys.'

Liz watched as they sauntered off, fake-innocently, past the
jetty. As soon as they rounded the corner wild laughter broke
out, mingled with expletives and followed by the thud and

clatter of running feet. Liz wondered if they'd make for the cliffs and walk to Shannon's cottage across the fields, but it was a long way. Or maybe they'd double back and try to catch a bus. They'd be lucky, though, at this hour.

She tried to tell herself that Shannon wasn't her problem, but couldn't help worrying all the same. The truth was, though, that unless the girl chose to come to her for help, there was little more that she could do.

It wasn't easy to manoeuvre her way back into the pub as yet more folk had arrived, and Liz didn't even bother to try to get to the bar but forced her way through the throng towards the room where the musicians were performing. It was handy being small, because people tended not to notice what you were doing until you'd squeezed past.

It was the interval still and the noise of chatter had become almost deafening. She spotted Esme and Jenny Lambert, but they were too far off so she merely waved.

'What's coming up next?' she heard the tall, attractive young woman beside her ask her pretty, shorter companion.

'A female singer, I think. Then there's a boy band to finish.'

The shorter girl, who had a dark-brown bob, took a swig of her drink. 'I'm starving. D'you think they serve food?'

'Dunno. You should have eaten more of that dinner.'

The dark-haired girl pulled a face, her friend laughed and Liz wondered where they were staying. Their accents weren't local and she imagined that they must be holidaymakers. There again, plenty of folk from all over moved to Cornwall for the lifestyle; though they tended to be retirees seeking balmier weather and a quieter existence.

At that moment Danny appeared on stage with a

microphone. Like his staff, he was wearing jeans and a red T-shirt, and he looked high on the success of the night so far. He must have been making a fortune at the bar as the tills hadn't stopped ringing.

'Our next act,' he announced, 'is a hugely talented artist from Liverpool...'

There was a roar of approval and some folk chanted, 'Scouser, Scouser!' Danny smiled and raised a hand to quieten them.

'An artist from Liverpool,' he went on, 'who performed widely with her band, Juniper Sling, before taking the plunge recently to go solo.'

There was a low murmuring, the sound of people clearing their throats, a few coughs.

'This is her first gig for a while and we're honoured that she's chosen us as her guinea pigs.' He grinned again and Liz felt her heart flutter on Tabitha's behalf. She must be feeling so nervous right now. It wasn't just old hits that she'd be singing, it was her own compositions, some of which she'd been working on for months.

'She's got a stunning voice and she's feeling pretty anxious,' Danny continued, echoing Liz's thoughts, 'so I hope you'll give her a warm Cornish welcome.'

There were shouts of approval, followed by stamping feet.

'Ladies and gentlemen, please welcome... Tabitha!'

The crowd clapped enthusiastically and Liz reflected that it was probably just as well her friend had chosen to drop the surname Mallon. Luke was notorious around here, and the more she managed to distance herself, the better. Soon she arrived, Danny handed her the microphone and she made her way to centre stage, her silver dress shimmering in the artificial light.

'Thank you so much,' she said, flicking away her hair and blinking in the glare. 'It's great to be here.' She fiddled with her dress, pulling it down, but kept her brown eyes fixed on the crowd.

'Tremarnock has a very special place in my heart,' she went on steadily. 'Although I grew up in the north, this is my home now and I wouldn't want to be anywhere else.'

Her voice might have cracked very lightly but she disguised it well by clearing her throat.

'The people here are the kindest in the world—'

'Piss-heads, the lot of them!' someone shouted. 'Not a sober one among 'em!'

Everybody laughed.

Tabitha turned to the heckler and smiled. 'They like a drink, yeah, and they definitely eat too many pasties, but I don't hold that against them.'

More laughter.

'But seriously, I love living here and I'm really grateful to everyone for making me and my little boy so welcome. So I'd like to dedicate these songs tonight to Tremarnock, and to a very special person called Liz. She knows who she is.'

Tabitha's eyes scanned the crowd again and Liz, surprised, felt herself redden. She huddled close to her next-door neighbour, hoping to go unnoticed, but she was touched all the same. There was no time to dwell on her friend's kind words, however, because Tabitha turned to pick up the guitar behind and pull up a stool before sitting down, positioning the instrument on her lap and licking her lips, ready to begin. Then, after a quick introduction to the opening number, she struck her first chords.

It was a simple melody but haunting and lovely. Her voice was low and husky, and the music seemed to fill Liz's head and course through her veins. It spoke of love, suffering and broken dreams, but there was something else, too. The chorus, like watery sunlight filtering through a cloud, hinted at hope, while the final verse, so quiet that you had to strain your ears to catch the lyrics, surely offered relief and acceptance.

Tabitha held the last note for what seemed like an age and no one moved; you could have heard a pin drop. When she'd finished, she hung her head and the audience erupted in a cacophony of clapping and cheering.

'She's really good,' the blonde girl cried over the hubbub.

'Gorgeous voice,' her friend agreed. 'Haunting song.'

There was a brief pause before Tabitha started up again, and this time the theme was more joyful. Liz turned around and went on tiptoe for a moment, hoping to catch sight of someone she knew, and through a chink in the crowd she spotted Danny by the exit, leaning against the wall, his arms crossed, and gazing at Tabitha with such awe that she might have been a heavenly vision. He was certainly handsome, Liz thought, but he looked thinner. Perhaps it was lovesickness. He'd better make a move soon or he might waste away.

At last Tabitha rose from the stool and bowed to the audience, mouthing 'Thank you' over and over. She looked ecstatic, with good reason because the noise was deafening, and it was some minutes after she'd left the stage that they quietened down. There was to be one more act after another break, and Liz and Esme made their way to the ladies' before joining the queue at the bar for another drink.

'Where's Rick – and Audrey?' Liz asked, waving a ten-pound note at the bar staff, hoping one of them would spot her.

'No idea,' said Esme haughtily. 'We're not friends any more.'

'Really?' Liz pretended not to know.

'Carnal desires,' the older woman muttered darkly. 'He has no control.'

They decided to take their drinks outside, where they were soon joined by the two young women who had stood next to Liz earlier.

'It's so hot in there,' the tall blonde one complained to her friend, catching Liz's eye.

She was in her early or mid-twenties, Liz guessed, slender and willowy, with pale English skin, round blue eyes, an arched nose that was just a shade too big, a mouth just a fraction too large and a pronounced dimple in her chin. She was wearing a simple green sundress and flip-flops, and there were several nasty scratches on her slender arms and one on her shoulder that looked quite sore. She didn't go in for much make-up and her blonde hair, tied back in a ponytail, had darker roots sprouting through. She was certainly striking because of her height and slimness, but it was only after a close inspection that you realised she was actually quite gorgeous in a quirky kind of way. Her features were too uneven to be classically beautiful.

Her friend, meanwhile, was more conventionally pretty, smaller and curvy, with big brown eyes, a slightly upturned nose and a pointed chin. She, too, was casually dressed, in jeans and a white vest top, and she was fanning herself with a leaflet advertising tonight's event with one hand while the other, bandaged, arm was hanging at her side.

'Are you here on holiday?' Liz asked, sensing that the blonde girl wanted to chat.

'We've just moved to Polgarry Manor. Do you know it?'

The penny dropped and Liz's eyes grew. 'You're Lord Penrose's granddaughter? I heard you were coming but I wasn't sure when.'

Introductions rapidly followed and Liz was interested to hear about the girls' first day at the manor. She couldn't help thinking that it must be strange to have gone from a suburban semi to a rattling old mansion with so many rooms that you couldn't count them.

'It's a bit creepy, to be honest,' Katie said, as if reading Liz's mind. 'Everything's so old, and there's this weird housekeeper person called Maria. Do you know her?'

Liz shook her head. 'I know of her, but she rarely comes into the village. Years ago, people used to see her out with Lord Penrose occasionally, but not after he became infirm.'

She wanted to ask about Bramble's plans for the manor but was distracted by Danny, who had emerged from the pub and was leaning against the wall, lighting a cigarette. After inhaling deeply, he spotted Liz and Esme and walked over to say hello.

'Polgarry Manor? Wow! It's enormous, isn't it?' he said when Liz told him who the girls were. 'I've always wondered what it's like inside.'

Ryan the fishmonger had shuffled closer, with Nathan, the postman, and his girlfriend, Annie, and Liz beckoned them over, too.

'Come and visit,' Katie said to Danny, quick as a flash. 'I'll show you round.'

Danny looked pleased. 'I love old buildings.'

'It's absolutely stuffed with antiques. And cobwebs.' She pulled a face.

'Seen any ghosts?' He took a puff of his cigarette and grinned.

'Not yet, but we could do with some company, couldn't we, Bramble?' said Katie, flicking her brown bob coquettishly.

Raising her eyebrows, Bramble nodded, while Danny stubbed out his cigarette, picked up the butt and announced that it was time to get back to work. But Katie hadn't finished with him yet.

'Can I ask you something?' she enquired, tipping her head to one side before explaining that she badly needed a job. 'Have you got any vacancies? I was in a call centre before, but I used to work in a pub after I left school. I'll do anything – even temporary.'

She seemed awfully keen.

'Yeah, possibly,' he replied casually. 'I think two of my part-timers will be going back to university.'

Katie's eyes sparkled. 'I'll pop in for a chat. Tomorrow morning? About ten?'

He looked a little taken aback. 'So soon? I'll probably still be clearing up after tonight. Besides,' he added, glancing at her bandaged arm as if noticing it for the first time, 'aren't you a bit incapacitated at the moment?'

'It's only a bruise. It'll be fine in a day or two.'

Danny turned to Bramble. 'What about you? Are you looking for a job, too, or will you have enough on your plate being lady of the manor?' He grinned again.

'I do need a job, but I'll have to focus on the manor for a while. There's so much to do.'

'Have you got workers lined up?' Liz asked, assuming that she'd have an army of architects, builders and gardeners at the ready, but Bramble seemed embarrassed.

'I haven't got the cash at the moment, to be honest. Once I'd paid the death duties, there wasn't any left.'

'I'll do some gardening for you,' Ryan piped up in his strong Cornish accent; he'd been quiet up to now. 'I finish work by four; I could come on over after that. I don't want anything for it,' he added swiftly. 'Money, I mean. I like gardening. I'm pretty handy with the shears.'

It was a very generous offer and Liz couldn't help thinking that Bramble's allure might have something to do with it. He seemed quite captivated by Katie, too, come to that.

Bramble eyed him doubtfully, taking in the shaggy brown hair and dense black eyebrows that almost met in the middle. He wasn't unattractive, but there was a slight fishy pong about him, though his clothes were clean.

'That's very kind but I'm sure we can manage,' she said swiftly. 'Anyone for another drink?'

Ryan immediately insisted on buying the next round and disappeared inside with Danny while the next band struck up. They were very loud and soon Jenny emerged, looking a little flushed, followed by her husband, John. Hot on his heels were Tony and Felipe and Audrey and Rick, who gazed at Esme with puppy-dog eyes, which she ignored.

'Where's Rafael?' Liz asked Felipe, who'd clearly had a few. As far as she could tell, it was the first time he'd left the boy's side all evening.

'He stay here. He loves the music. We are going home.'

Tony frowned. 'Are you sure this is a good idea, darling? Don't you think he should come with us?'

'No, no,' Felipe insisted. 'He's a big boy now. We cannot make him cling to our apron tails any more.'

'Apron strings,' Tony said patiently, 'or coat tails, not apron tails.'

Felipe shrugged. 'Tails, strings, whatever.'

He stumbled slightly and Tony took his arm. 'We'd better get you home.'

They headed up South Street, Felipe swaying as he went, and Liz smiled inwardly. She'd bet that he wouldn't hear the end of it, which was a tad hypocritical as Tony wasn't averse to a tipple himself when he was in the mood.

'I think I'll be off now, too,' she told the others, before pushing her way back into the pub to say goodbye to Tabitha. The band was still playing but the crowd had thinned a little and it wouldn't be long now until the gig ended, surely? The place would be closing soon.

It was easy to spot her friend by her distinctive black hair and silver frock. She was perched on a high stool, leaning on the bar and holding a glass of white wine. She seemed deep in conversation and at first Liz couldn't tell whom she was talking to, until a tall man moved away, clearing the view, to reveal Danny standing very close to her, his head inclined.

Something in their body language told Liz that for once they weren't a bundle of nerves, and was it her imagination or were their fingers touching? She smiled to herself and crept quietly away, not wishing to spoil the moment.

Chapter Seven

IT HAD BEEN Katie's suggestion to summon the land agent and Bramble had leaped at the idea.

'Of course! Brilliant! Why didn't we think of it before?'

Now, as she watched the visitor from her first-floor bedroom, leaving his swish black Land Rover and picking his way gingerly through the weeds and up the broken steps to the manor's old oak door, she felt even more heartened. From his elegant frame in a tweed blazer and tan chinos to his silver-flecked hair, she couldn't help thinking that if she were going to go through the complicated and tedious process of selling off land, she'd rather be guided by someone whose looks would provide a bit of welcome distraction.

Maria answered the door and the man seemed quite relieved when Bramble hurtled down the stairs a moment later and introduced herself.

'I didn't think she could be you,' he said, turning swiftly from the grim-faced housekeeper and extending a hand to the younger woman. His hand was smooth and soft and Bramble noticed a gold ring on his pinkie finger.

'Piers Fenton-Wallis,' he continued, reaching into his breast pocket and passing her an embossed silver business card. 'Delighted to make your acquaintance.'

'I'm so glad you could come,' she gushed, searching involuntarily for the heart-shaped stud in her ear and twiddling it around. She was dressed in the short, navy, cotton shirtdress that she'd often worn for work. 'I'm rather hoping you can save me from destitution.'

He smiled, revealing a row of small, even teeth that seemed particularly white against his summer tan, or perhaps he was always brown. Now she thought about it, he seemed like the type to go on winter Caribbean holidays and ski trips every spring. He looked as if he knew how to have *fun*.

'Always pleased to help a damsel in distress.' His eyes swept around the marble-floored hallway, taking in the paintings, the furniture and the stuffed animal heads. 'My! This is a fine old place. I've never been inside before. An absolute jewel!'

Pleased, Bramble led him proudly into the drawing room with views of the overgrown garden, orchards and fields beyond. Maria, who had followed them, stood aloof and expectant, as if waiting to be dismissed, and seemed almost put out when Bramble requested a pot of coffee and three cups; 'Katie's joining us shortly,' she explained.

It was a week to the day since they'd arrived in Cornwall and Bramble was still uncomfortable with Maria and thought she'd never get used to issuing orders; she was always half-expecting the housekeeper to turn around and tell her where to go. Despite Maria's surly manner, however, Bramble couldn't quite pluck up the courage to fire her, and besides, Lord Penrose had paid her salary up until the end of January, so for the time being at least it seemed she would have to remain a fixture.

It wasn't long before Katie arrived, looking slightly the worse for wear. Buoyed by a highly satisfactory meeting with Danny after the gig, when he'd offered her an evening's work this coming Monday as a trial run for the job of barmaid, she'd insisted on returning to The Hole in the Wall last night. Fortunately, her bruised arm was healing nicely. Unfortunately, however, on this occasion the handsome manager had hardly had time to speak, and consequently she'd drunk rather too much wine and woken with a throbbing head. Bramble, on the other hand, who'd been the designated driver, was as fresh as a daisy.

With Katie beside her on the dusty velvet sofa, she started to explain to Piers that they badly needed to raise funds for renovations.

'There are holes in the roof which let the rain in,' she explained, pointing to a bucket that Maria had placed strategically in the corner of the room after discovering a new leak this very morning. There had been a thunderstorm in the middle of the night that had woken Bramble, though Katie had managed to snore through it. On the plus side, it had washed away yesterday's mugginess and the garden was looking beautifully lush and green, but water had leaked not only through the roof but also into the girls' bedroom via the ill-fitting window frames, which they'd had to plug with towels.

'And all the windows need replacing,' Bramble continued, 'and the whole place needs painting, plus a new kitchen, bathrooms and carpets.' She smiled ruefully. 'I could go on.'

Piers ran a hand through the fringe of his hair and nodded.

'I can see there's a lot to be done.' He reached into the brown leather briefcase at his feet and pulled out a clipboard and pen. 'But don't be discouraged. The land will be worth quite a lot, especially with planning permission. I'll need to do an initial site appraisal before we move on to a valuation. First, let me ask some questions.'

The interview – for that's what it felt like – seemed to go on for an awfully long time. Bramble didn't mind in the least, but she could sense Katie twitching with impatience and heard her sigh with relief when Maria finally appeared with a tray of coffee. She'd even remembered biscuits, an unusually generous touch, and Katie reached greedily for the plate and would have grabbed one for herself but she remembered her manners and passed them around first.

The visitor wanted to know not just about the size of the manor, the number of rooms and the layout of the grounds, but also quite a bit about Bramble herself and what she had done before coming to Cornwall.

'I had such a boring job,' she explained, crossing her bare legs and coiling the ends of her long blonde hair around a finger. 'I wasn't really going anywhere. That's partly why I decided to move here rather than sell the place. My dad and my stepmum, Cassie, were dead set against my keeping it. They said I should cash in and buy somewhere in London. To be honest, I thought I would until I saw it for myself.'

'Such potential,' Piers agreed, gazing up at the high ceiling with its intricate cornicing and out through the floor-length French windows. 'So unusual. It's not often something like this comes on the market. The Americans would go mad for it – so much history. And the Russians and Chinese maybe, too. A golf course...'

His eyes seemed to glaze over and his voice trailed off as he pondered the possibilities, before squiggling something on his piece of paper.

'But she's not selling,' Katie said grumpily. She'd almost polished off the biscuits and was keen to move the conversation on. 'So we don't need to think about that.'

Piers looked up from his clipboard. 'Of course not. I was

merely speculating. It's my job; I can't help it.' He raised an eyebrow, propped the clipboard down the side of the armchair and rested a foot on his knee. His brown brogues were very shiny and he was wearing bright-red socks with yellow dots that seemed to Bramble to hint at hidden depths, an interesting, racy streak.

'I don't want to turn it into some fancy place with designer this and designer that,' she said quickly. 'I mean, I like nice things, but I think I should keep the character of the manor, don't you? It'd be fantastic more or less as it is, but without the leaks and dodgy bathrooms. Unfortunately, the repairs will cost loads and I don't have any money – it's all gone on inheritance tax.'

Piers nodded reflectively. 'You plan to live here on your own, do you? That is, you and, um, your friend?' He glanced at Katie, whose name he had clearly forgotten already, before shifting his gaze back to Bramble. 'And the housekeeper, of course.'

Katie seemed quite miffed. 'We do,' she snapped. 'But we're not here to discuss our living arrangements.'

If he were put out he didn't show it, instead smiling again respectfully before fixing back on Bramble. He was so charming and earnest that she felt quite embarrassed by her friend's abruptness.

'My boyfriend... well, it's a bit complicated,' she explained, wondering how to describe the situation. 'He didn't fancy giving up his job or leaving Chessington, you see.'

This time the land agent raised both eyebrows. 'Really? I should have thought there'd be no contest.' He sounded quite amused. 'I mean, who wouldn't want to live in a Cornish manor with you? How exciting – and romantic!'

Bramble felt curiously validated, because here at last was

a man who thought the same way as her. Matt and her dad didn't seem to believe in excitement; in fact, they played it so safe that the words 'routine' and 'schedule' might have been invented for them. It occurred to her then, though it never quite had before, that in refusing to come it wasn't just Cornwall that Matt had rejected, it was her and that side of her personality that he'd seemed almost frightened of: her spirit of adventure.

At that moment her phone buzzed in her pocket and she was dismayed to see his name appear before her eyes, like a silent rebuke. She pressed the off button quickly. Perhaps she should finish with him, she thought guiltily. But they'd been together so long that even their names seemed indelibly linked: Matt 'n' Bramble, Bramble 'n' Matt, bread and butter, yin and yang… it was hard to imagine anything different. She'd have to mull it over, but not today, she decided, mentally consigning the issue to her ever-expanding 'to do' list.

Maria arrived to remove the coffee tray, and during the break in conversation Bramble examined the newcomer surreptitiously. He was of medium height and lean, with a bump on the bridge of his nose and lips that were a shade too thin. However, his arresting blue eyes, relaxed, easy manner and delightful smile were more than enough to distract her from any real or imagined physical fault, and the overall package, she concluded, was extremely pleasing.

'Shall we have a stroll round the estate?' he asked, rising at last. His beautifully tailored chinos fell into perfect creases. 'I don't suppose we can see everything today, but I'd like to get a sense of the lie of the land. I can come back and view it properly another day.' He cleared his throat and lowered his eyes deferentially. 'That is, if you wish me to act for you, of course.'

Bramble, who'd already made up her mind that she wasn't going to let him get away without a struggle, nodded vigorously.

'I think we'll make a really good team. I have to have somebody I feel comfortable with, who'll explain the process clearly as we go along. I'm not exactly used to this sort of thing; in fact, I haven't a clue. I need a lot of hand-holding...' Crimson spots blossomed on her cheeks when she realised what she'd said, but Piers put her at ease.

'It can seem daunting if you've never done anything like it before, but rest assured, we'll make everything as smooth and painless as possible.'

Relieved, Bramble rose and gestured towards the French doors. 'Let's go out this way. I'll show you the front afterwards.'

Katie yawned loudly and stretched her arms above her head. 'I don't think I'll come. I didn't sleep very well last night. You don't mind, do you, Bram?'

'A morning siesta?' Piers interjected. 'Good idea! I'm sure we'll cope alone.'

Katie smiled coolly before turning on her heel, and as soon as she'd disappeared Piers followed Bramble to the set of doors. The key was in the lock and turned quite easily, but the doors themselves were stuck tight so that she had to move back while he gave a firm push with his shoulder.

'That should do it,' he said, stepping aside while Bramble gave the final shove, which sent her tumbling ungracefully on to the crumbling terrace, where she landed with a thump on her hands and knees.

'Ouch!' she squealed as dozens of tiny, sharp stones dug into her flesh. The pain was quite intense but the shock was worse.

She might have paused like that for a moment, waiting for the dizziness to pass, but Piers grabbed her elbow and helped her up to standing.

'Are you hurt? I'm so sorry. I didn't expect it to fly open like that.'

He was most solicitous, squatting at her feet and examining her poor knees, which were sore and bleeding and had only just healed after the débâcle on the cliff. It could have been far worse, however. She could have fallen on glass or broken a bone.

'That must have really hurt,' he said, and he took her hands, one by one, and wiped them gently with his fingertips to remove the gravel. 'It was totally my fault. Let's go inside and get you properly cleaned up.'

But Bramble wouldn't hear of it. She was enjoying his company too much to let a few grazes spoil the occasion.

'I'm fine, honestly. It's only scratches.'

He took some convincing, but eventually brushed the gravel off his own trouser legs and agreed to continue their tour. Before setting off, they paused for a moment with their backs to the manor to admire the rolling landscape and he whistled through his teeth appreciatively.

'Wow! Stunning! It looks like a painting it's so perfect.'

Bramble couldn't help thinking that if Matt had been here, he'd hardly have noticed the scenery. He wasn't particularly observant, which was handy when it came to disguising new purchases but irritating in other ways. In fact, it seemed to her now that he possessed little or no aesthetic sense whatsoever. He even asked her which colour shirt to buy, what lamp to get for the flat or rug to choose, insisting that she was better at that sort of thing than him.

'It's even lovelier on the other side,' she enthused, ignoring her smarting knees. 'I can see the ocean from my bedroom window.'

'Clifftop views,' Piers murmured. 'Stunning seaside vista.'

'You sound like an estate agent. I suppose you are one!' she giggled, but he didn't seem to hear.

They strolled through the overgrown gardens, past the broken mermaid fountain and into the orchard while he asked more questions and jotted things down on his clipboard. It was another glorious day, warm and sunny, and bees buzzed lazily around the long-legged lavender bushes while birds chirruped in the gnarled branches of old trees. The sky was so blue, with not a cloud in sight, that it was hard to imagine there had ever been a thunderstorm, though the grass, still damp in places, told a different story and Bramble's feet, in flip-flops, were quite wet.

She pushed open the wooden gate that led from the orchard into the fields and waited a moment while Piers took off his tweed blazer and rolled up the sleeves of his checked shirt. He must have been far too hot in all that material and she almost suggested that he remove the tie as well, but she feared the idea being misconstrued.

He didn't appear to be in any hurry, so they made their way across the high grass to the wooded area that she'd explored with Katie, because she wanted him to admire the cliff where they'd had their unfortunate escapade and the ocean, which stretched as far as the eye could see. For some reason she wanted him to fall in love with the place, as she was beginning to.

'Have you always lived round here?' she asked when there was a lull in the conversation. The grass was high, thistles scratched her calves and her grazed knees were beginning to stiffen, but she didn't complain.

'I grew up in Dorset,' he explained, flicking a fly off his face. 'My parents own a dairy farm. I did a land agency course in Shropshire after school, then moved down here for my first job and I've been here ever since. I adore it; it's very much my home now.'

Encouraged by his openness, she decided to probe further.

'How long have you been here?'

'Ooh, fifteen years or so.'

She did a quick mental calculation. If he left college at twenty or twenty-one, that would make him thirty-five or -six. The older man.

'Is your, um, wife from Cornwall?'

It just popped out and she found herself reddening again, but he didn't seem offended.

'I'm not married.'

'Oh.'

By now they were almost through the shady wood and Bramble was relieved when the trees parted and she could once more see sky and clear blue ocean.

Piers whistled for the second time that day.

'Glorious! And so close to the house. Just a stone's throw really.'

He stopped to look back at the wood behind. 'You could chop it down and make a road. Is there access to the sea? A track down the cliff? You could have your own private beach.'

Bramble was surprised because she hadn't thought of it before.

'I'm not sure I'd want to get rid of the trees. I bet some of them have been here since the manor was built.'

'A private beach would add value,' he mused, ignoring her comment. 'Especially if you had a boat hut and jetty. You'd have to fence off the area properly, though. It's not at all clear at the moment where the estate begins and ends. You don't want any old Tom, Dick or Harry using your facilities.'

To be honest, the thought of strangers wandering on to her

land hadn't much worried Bramble, though it was true that she had taken exception to that man Fergus, but only because he'd been rude. Polgarry was so remote that few would make the journey unless they had specific business. She was about to point this out when Piers tapped her on the arm.

'Is that part of the estate? It looks inhabited.'

He was indicating the stone cottage on the edge of the cliff where Fergus lived with his son.

'There's a tenant,' she replied. 'With a little boy. I don't know about the mother.'

'What does he pay in rent?'

Bramble had no idea.

'Not nearly enough, I bet.' Piers tutted. 'I'll find out for you. The sooner I get my hands on the paperwork, the better.'

With so many pressing problems, one grumpy character living in a cottage that she didn't use seemed reasonably low on her list of priorities, especially now that she'd got over her annoyance. However, every penny counted, and if Fergus could be made to pay a bit more, it would be all to the good. She did feel a little sorry for the boy, though.

They decided to head in the other direction, and the further they walked, the more animated Piers seemed to become.

'I reckon one plot of, say, two acres with planning permission for a four-bed farmhouse would be worth about five hundred and fifty thousand pounds, more with a sea view. Obviously, this is just a ballpark figure. With this amount of land you could parcel up two or three plots, plough the cash into renovations and still have money to spare, plus ample grounds for other uses. Of course, the manor itself will be worth a great deal more after the upgrade, too.'

He stopped and rubbed his chin. 'You could be sitting on a goldmine here, you know.'

Bramble's eyes widened. 'Really? I'm amazed!'

The prospect of potential legal wrangles, major building works and multiple changes alarmed her somewhat when in truth she'd like more than anything just to be able to make Polgarry a bit cosier for her and Katie while they found their feet. This wasn't an option, however. Somehow or other the manor must start bringing in revenue, and Piers, it seemed, had all the answers. Bramble was grateful, she really was. With him at her side, she was sure that the task would be far less daunting.

The deep boom of a ship's horn far off in the bay dragged her from her thoughts and she suggested walking to the next ridge, where she hadn't yet been. The cliff climbed steeply for several hundred yards, and as the midday sun beat down on her back and neck she wished that she'd brought some water. She could hear Piers's breath coming in short, sharp bursts and his arms and legs were pumping hard.

Once they reached the peak, they stood for a few moments, enjoying the fabulous view of ocean and rugged landscape. The rough track continued down the other side before rising again steeply towards a craggy promontory a little distance away that was shaped like a giant fist hewn out of rock and sandstone. As she squinted in the sunlight, Bramble spied something right on the very end of the peninsula: the figure of a man, sitting very still, his legs hanging over the edge. He looked lost in thought and rather melancholy, with his hands lying motionless in his lap, his chin raised, scrutinising the horizon as if searching for something.

Piers spotted him, too; it would be hard not to. 'Who's that?'

'I think it's the bloke I told you about, the one who rents the cottage.'

'What's he doing there?'

Fergus was too far off to hear, but something made him turn his head and he stared at them for several seconds as if checking them out before slowly returning to his original position.

'You don't think he's about to jump, do you?' Bramble asked, alarmed, but Piers laughed.

'I reckon he's just contemplating Life, the Universe and Everything. He looks a bit odd, though, I'll give you that.'

She shivered, hoping the land agent was right. 'Let's go back. Katie will be wondering where we are.'

As they began to descend the way they'd come, she glanced over her shoulder and saw her peculiar tenant still fixed to his spot, staring at the water. He reminded her of the fable of King Canute trying to hold back the tide, except that in this case it might have been the movement of the earth and of time itself that he was trying to restrain.

Not looking where she was going, she skidded on some rubble and almost tripped.

'Careful,' said Piers, catching her by the arm. 'We don't want any more accidents.'

He didn't let go until she'd safely reached the bottom, by which time Fergus was no longer in view.

'I'll return on Monday or Tuesday next week,' Piers announced once they were on firm ground. 'I might have done a full site appraisal now, but I didn't fancy rubbing that chap up the wrong way.' He jerked his head to indicate where they'd come from.

The prospect of another morning – or day, even – with the handsome land agent filled Bramble with anticipation, and she couldn't help thinking that life was looking more interesting by the minute. Daydreaming all the way home about spins in his Land Rover, more country walks and perhaps even a candlelit dinner or two, she soon forgot all about Fergus and that strange encounter on the cliff.

Some time later, Liz was leaving the bakery with a packet of iced buns for tea when she noticed a slim, elegant man with silver-flecked hair entering the fishmonger's shop. He was a fairly unusual sight in the village, in an expensive-looking tweed blazer and shiny brown brogues, and she wondered who he was and the nature of his business.

She paused for a moment with Lowenna in her pushchair and eyed him through the window as he pointed to something on the fresh fish counter, behind which stood Ryan in his white overalls. He gave her a wave and she waved back, before being distracted by a group of noisy young people in bathing suits and carrying towels who were making their way from the beach. They were around fifteen or sixteen probably, a mix of boys and girls, some nut-brown, others paler-skinned with pink noses and shoulders.

She'd seen them before and knew they were part of the large group of families renting three cottages side by side. They looked as if they were having a wonderful holiday; it would be hard not to when the weather was so perfect.

A girl in a white bikini shouted, 'Race you home!', and all at once five or six youngsters hurtled past, laughing and waving their brightly coloured towels, while one remained behind, pleading with them to wait because she'd dropped her sunglasses. Liz stooped to pick them up and noticed Rafael lurking in the corner of the square, his hands in his pockets. She bet he'd like to be part of their crowd, but of course he didn't know them, or anyone else his age.

He was wearing similar black clothes to those she'd seen him in at the live music night, and he must have been rather hot. The only difference in his appearance today was that the strip of hair running along his scalp was blue now rather than green.

She was about to go and speak to him when he spotted an empty can of Coke at his feet and began kicking it disconsolately. He wasn't doing any harm, but a voice behind shouted, 'Oi!', and Audrey jogged past in a blue-and-white-striped T-shirt and white jeans. Liz watched as she drew up in front of Rafael, who stopped what he was doing and cowered against the wall behind. He was tall but Audrey was taller, and although her back was turned, it was clear from her body language that she was furious, shaking her artfully mussed pixie crop and trembling with rage.

'Don't you dare...' Liz heard, and, 'What on earth...?' and, 'Damage...'

The more she went on, the more Rafael seemed to diminish in size. Even the blue Mohawk started to wilt.

'What's going on?'

The elegant man in the suit came out of the fishmonger's carrying something wrapped in white paper and stood by Liz, staring at the curious scene.

When she explained what had happened, he raised an eyebrow. 'Ah!'

'She's on the warpath, as you see,' Liz whispered and the stranger tutted.

'I'm not surprised. The little hooligan could have hit someone or smashed a window.' He tucked the bag of fish under an arm and took a step forwards. 'D'you think she needs my help?'

'Oh no. Rafael's harmless.'

At last Audrey stopped shouting, and she marched towards Liz with a face like thunder. Liz would have liked to speak to Rafael, to explain that Audrey could be a bit over the top sometimes and it would blow over, but he was already sloping off in the other direction, head down, hands still firmly in pockets.

'It's not on,' snarled the older woman when she was close enough to be heard. She'd clearly made a rapid decision that the elegant man was one of them and it was therefore safe to proceed. 'That lad's a menace. Have you seen the way he skulks around, looking for trouble?'

'An unsavoury character,' the stranger agreed.

Liz did her best to pour oil on troubled waters. 'I had a nice chat with him the other day. I feel a bit sorry for him actually. He's got no friends here yet and nothing to do. It must be hard to adjust.'

'If he doesn't like it, he should jolly well go back to Brazil,' Audrey snapped. 'I can't imagine what possessed Felipe and Tony to bring him.'

Esme – in a clay-smeared pottery smock, billowing purple cheesecloth skirt and green Birkenstocks – left the bakery and came over to join the fray. When she heard about Rafael's doings, she seemed unperturbed.

'I rather admire his hair,' she chirped randomly. 'It's quite artistic, don't you think?'

Audrey gave her a withering look. 'I couldn't agree less. And that unmentionable hole in his ear...' She shuddered.

'I think we should all have them,' Liz joked. 'It's an ancient cultural practice, you know. The larger the hole, the greater your standing in the tribe.'

Audrey seemed to experience a severe sense of humour failure.

'Small studs are quite enough, and drop earrings for the evening. On women, that is. If the men round here start getting them, I shall be forced to move.'

Lowenna, who'd been as quiet as a mouse, yawned and closed her eyes. Liz had almost forgotten about her, but the last thing she needed was for her daughter to snooze now and then be up half the night wanting to play.

'I'd better get going,' she said, smiling briefly at the strange man whose name she still didn't know.

'Piers,' he said, almost on cue. 'Piers Fenton-Wallis. I work for GB Clark, land agents. I've been up at Polgarry Manor. I'm acting for Miss Challoner.'

Audrey's face lit up and Rafael was instantly forgotten.

'Are you? How interesting. Do tell me, what are her plans?'

Liz left them to it while she trundled Lowenna back up South Street, thinking that if anyone could winkle out the information, it was Audrey. She should have been a reporter, she had such a nose for news. She could sniff out a good story a mile off – and a handsome man, come to that. Piers Fenton-Wallis had better watch out.

It was quite a surprise to find Rosie at home, as she'd told Liz that she'd be going to Tim's to work on their website, U-R-Special, which they'd set up to help pupils with disabilities throughout Cornwall. Children could post their problems and the pair would get back to them with pertinent comments and useful links. It was all their own idea and had proved a great success, as there was nothing quite like it in the area. What's more, it had helped Tim with his stammer and had taken Rosie out of herself and given her confidence as well as a new circle of friends.

'Hey,' said Liz, pleased, when she found her eldest daughter in front of an open packet of biscuits at the kitchen table. 'I didn't expect to find you here. Fancy an iced bun? Good job I bought four.'

Rosie didn't reply.

'Tim busy again?' Liz persisted, plonking the iced buns on the table, and Rosie shook her head, indicating that she didn't want to speak.

It wasn't simply tiredness, Liz could tell. She knew her daughter back to front and inside out. She would have tried to get to the bottom of it, but Lowenna, who'd dropped off despite Liz's best efforts, woke up and squawked loudly from her pushchair in the hallway, demanding to be fetched.

'All right, all right,' said Liz, hurrying to find her. The little girl's face was red with rage and she was struggling so much that it was quite hard to free her from her restraints. 'Come on then.' Liz picked her up and planted a kiss on her hot, wet cheek. 'Rosie's home! Let's go and find her.'

At the mention of her big sister's name, Lowenna stopped crying and her brown eyes opened wide.

'Wo-wo!' she cried eagerly, bouncing up and down as if it would somehow speed her mother's progress.

Normally, Rosie would have rushed out to give her a cuddle, but not today. Instead she looked up listlessly from the table when they entered and barely smiled when Liz plopped the little girl on her lap. Lowenna snuggled happily into her big sister's arms and stuck her thumb in her mouth, while Rosie buried her face in her dark, silky hair.

'What is it?' Liz asked gently, pulling out a chair for herself and settling down. She pushed the packet of buns forward but they remained untouched.

'Nothing.' Rosie's bottom lip quivered.

'You can tell me,' Liz coaxed. 'I've got broad shoulders, you know.'

A big, fat tear rolled down the girl's cheek. 'Tim doesn't want to do the website with me any more.'

Liz started. 'Really? Why?' He'd been to their house only a few days ago and Liz had heard them talking about it. He'd certainly been less committed of late, but hadn't seemed to want to give it up altogether.

Lowenna was playing with the yellow watch on Rosie's wrist, fiddling with the plastic strap, which she unfastened and handed mechanically to her sister.

'Why?' Liz repeated. 'Maybe he just wants a break over the summer? You can go back to it in the autumn.'

Rosie sniffed and shook her head again. 'He said he hasn't got time. He wants to do more with Amelia now.'

That name again. Liz felt it like a needle in the arm, or a dagger in the heart.

'Wretched girl.' It came out as a snarl; she couldn't help it. 'What's so great about her? I don't get it.'

Rosie fixed her mother with a pair of watery greenish-grey eyes. 'She doesn't have a tricky arm or a wonky leg.'

Another jab of the knife.

'Well, I bet she's not as nice – or as brave,' Liz retorted, fury bubbling inside her. It was wrong to hate anyone, let alone a schoolgirl, but right now she thought that she could strangle Amelia with her own bare hands.

'She's a really good runner,' Rosie replied. 'She wins all the races at school. She's going to France next week with her family and they've invited Tim, too.'

Liz's shoulders drooped. How could you compete with that?

'Lucky Tim. Whereabouts in France?' she asked fake-brightly.

'La Rochelle.'

Of course Rosie would know. She'd have been thinking about it for days, ever since she'd heard the news, chewing it over and over and trying to swallow it down so that no one would see her pain.

'When did you find out?' Liz dreaded the answer because it would reveal how long her daughter had suffered in silence.

'Last week. Tim's going to her house tomorrow to talk about it.'

'They'll probably have a horrible time,' Liz said savagely. 'I've heard La Rochelle's packed in summer. I can't think why they'd want to go there when we've got such beautiful beaches on our doorstep.'

'They speak *French*,' Rosie replied as if her mother were stupid. 'And eat baguettes and have nicer weather.'

'We can go to France sometime if you want? We'll discuss it with Robert.'

It wasn't the point, of course, and Liz knew it. Another tear trickled down Rosie's cheek and plopped on to her sister's head, but Lowenna was busy chewing the watchstrap and didn't notice.

'Well, I think it's mean of Tim to stop the website like that. What about all your followers? It's not fair.'

'You don't understand,' said Rosie flatly. 'He's getting into other things now. He and Amelia have joined an athletics club.'

Liz took a deep breath. She felt so helpless. Tim was perfectly within his rights to move on, of course, but that didn't make it any easier. She thought back to when she was that age and had just started to take an interest in the opposite sex. She'd had a major crush on a boy in her class and had thought her heart would break when he'd begun going out with someone else. Rosie and Tim mightn't have been boyfriend and girlfriend officially, but Rosie had treasured their special bond and would miss him terribly. It was so hard.

'I'm sorry.' Liz moved around to the other side of the table to give her daughter a hug. 'I know you're upset, but I promise you'll get over it in time.'

Rosie buried her face in her mother's top. 'No one will ever want to go out with me, not with my stupid arm and glasses.'

'Oh yes they will,' Liz cried, looking quite fierce. 'You're clever, kind and utterly gorgeous. But trust me, men can be absolute fools, and if my experience is anything to go by, you're going to have to kiss a fair few frogs before you find your prince.'

Chapter Eight

AFTER THAT, THEY decided to go for fish and chips on the beach to cheer themselves up before calling in on Pat on the way home. The old woman had lived in and around Tremarnock all her life and married a fisherman, long since deceased. They'd had no children – 'they never came along' – but she'd grown up with younger brothers and sisters and adored little ones, especially Rosie, who called her 'Nan'.

Pat had babysat Rosie in the evenings when Liz had worked as a waitress at A Winkle in Time before her marriage. Money had been tight back then and the old woman had refused any payment, insisting that she liked the company. Liz was eternally grateful. She often did Pat's shopping and had dropped a bag of food at her house the day before but hadn't had time to stop. She'd thought then that Pat looked a bit off colour and Pat had also complained that she hadn't seen Rosie for a while.

'She's too busy now to bother with an old thing like me,' she'd said mournfully while Liz had plonked the carriers on the kitchen table. 'She's got better things to do.'

'I haven't seen much of her myself,' Liz had confessed, feeling guilty on behalf of them both. Pat didn't get many visitors these days and Liz had promised to return soon for a proper chat, but the old woman had merely shrugged.

'It's always the same with you young people. Your lives are so full. Rush, rush, rush. Never mind,' she'd added, shaking her snowy head in a long-suffering manner, 'I expect there'll be another time – if I don't die first.'

It took Pat a while to get to the front door and when she saw the three of them on the step, their hands and faces sticky with the salt water they'd used to wash off the tomato ketchup and vinegar, she gave a beautiful smile, flashing her false teeth.

'Are you coming in? Really? Oh good! I'll put the kettle on.'

She ushered them into her little front room and Lowenna, who was getting sleepy, sat quietly on her mother's lap while Rosie helped make the tea and arrange chocolate biscuits on a flowery porcelain plate.

'Well now,' said Pat, plonking down gratefully in her favourite armchair with a crocheted blanket on the back. Beside it was a little table on which she proudly displayed part of her precious china owl collection. 'What's the gossip?'

Liz racked her brains to come up with some juicy news and remembered Bramble, whom she'd met in the pub.

'She's brought her friend from London,' she explained, taking a sip of hot tea. 'They're both young and Bramble's got a lot of plans for the manor.'

Pat nibbled reflectively on the corner of a biscuit. 'She'll need a fortune to do up that place. It's in a right old state.'

'I'm not sure if she's got one, though. I bumped into her land agent this afternoon. Perhaps he'll have some bright ideas. I just hope she doesn't want to turn it into a theme park.'

Liz was only joking but Rosie, who'd been listening in silence, sat bolt upright. 'A theme park? Ooh!'

Pat was all set for a good grumble, until she remembered something more pressing.

'I say, I saw our Tabitha earlier on with that long-haired, beardy fellow from the pub.'

Liz's ears pricked up. 'Did you?'

'They walked past my window. Very cosy with each other, they seemed.' Pat shuffled forwards, as if someone might be eavesdropping. 'They stopped outside her flat and guess what? They had a smooch. A proper snog!'

'Not that you were spying!' Liz laughed. Pat would have had to crane her neck to see that far.

'Certainly not,' she huffed. 'Whatever gave you that idea? I was dusting my ornaments.'

Liz let it pass. 'I was beginning to wonder if it would ever happen. They seem ideal for each other, and Tabby so deserves some happiness after all she's been through.'

'Handsome fella he is, too. Wouldn't fancy that beard myself, though. Too prickly by half.'

Liz was about to reflect on the wisdom of this observation when she noticed Pat wince and shift slightly in her chair, as if she were in pain.

'Are you all right?'

'Just a bit of indigestion, that's all.'

But the old woman looked strained and the deep lines around her eyes and mouth had deepened into fissures.

'You've had a lot of indigestion recently. You should see the doctor about it.'

'Ach no.' Pat sounded quite fierce. 'I'm sick to death of doctors and hospitals. It'll pass; it always does.'

Rosie got up to fetch her another cushion and Pat tipped

her head on one side and eyed the girl beadily, as if seeing her properly for the first time.

'My! What have you been doing to yourself, young lady? You're that pale you wouldn't think it was the height of summer. Whatever's the matter?'

Liz swallowed. Pat might be old and frail but she didn't miss a trick, and she knew Rosie almost as well as Liz herself.

'I'm fine,' Rosie insisted. 'I don't like sunbathing.' She leaned forward and took two biscuits, as if she hadn't a care in the world, but it cut no ice with Pat.

'How's that young man of yours?' she asked slyly.

Rosie hesitated. 'Who?'

'Whatshisname. Tim. The one who does the computer thingy with you.'

'He's OK.' Rosie smiled bravely but couldn't keep it up, and soon her face started to crumple like a used tissue.

Liz put an arm around her shoulders and quickly filled Pat in. When she'd finished, the old woman picked up the mug beside her and took a slow, considered sip.

'More fool him,' she said, narrowing her eyes dangerously. 'He'll regret it, you mark my words, and when he realises what he's lost and comes running back, you give him a piece of your mind, my girl. No ifs and buts. I'd do it for you, only he'd be halfway to Hindustan before I could box his ears good and proper.'

The image of Pat hobbling after Tim in her flowery apron, fists raised, was too much for Rosie, who giggled despite herself. That set Liz off, too, and even Pat snorted, spraying bits of biscuit on to her lap, only it made the pain in her abdomen worse so she had to stop.

'You really should see the doctor,' Liz repeated, noticing her friend wince again and her hands start to tremble.

'I'll be all right in a minute.' Pat brushed the crumbs off her lap. 'I'm more concerned about that Tim, to be honest with you. I reckon we should send him a poison pen letter starting with, "You nasty little toad"!'

Liz was still smiling when they reached Bag End, and Rosie's mood had lightened, too.

'Shall we watch a movie after Lowie's gone to sleep?' she asked. Her sister's eyelids were drooping.

'Good idea,' Liz agreed. 'Run the bath for me, will you? We'd better get our skates on.' It was going to be a job to get Lowenna washed and into her pyjamas before she dropped off.

She was perched on one hip while Liz poured milk into a plastic bottle with the other hand when the doorbell rang, making them both start. Liz stuck the bottle in the microwave and turned it on before hurrying to answer, the little girl bouncing against her side.

'Coming!' she called, scooting down the hall and muttering under her breath about bad timing.

The sight of Esme in her slippers and dressing gown, her hair wrapped up in a towelling turban, was too much for Lowenna, who promptly screamed blue murder, and Liz, whose nerves were already a little frayed, was tempted to slam the door. But there was no mistaking the look of alarm on her friend's face, so she quickly ushered Esme in and asked what the matter was, whilst simultaneously rocking her daughter to and fro, whispering 'hush, hush, there, there' to try to halt the screeching.

Esme, who didn't seem in the least self-conscious about her appearance or aware of the racket, stood hands on hips, her eyes flashing.

'Haven't you heard?' she asked accusingly, as if Liz had

been guilty of idling her whole day away with no thought for anyone but herself.

'The public conveniences,' Esme went on, 'and Rick's shop? It's disgusting!'

'Hang on a mo,' Liz said, tearing back into the kitchen to fetch Lowenna's bottle, which she jammed in the baby's mouth to instant, soothing effect.

She was so quick that when she returned to her visitor a moment later Esme had hardly had to halt the flow.

'Graffiti,' she spluttered, 'on the lavatory walls, and some-one knocked over Rick's postcard stand and sent the whole lot flying.'

By now Rosie had come down, too, and was sitting on the bottom stair, listening intently.

Liz took a deep breath. She'd been imagining a tsunami-style flood at the very least, but Esme, whose wet hair was beginning to dribble down her face and on to the carpet, was expecting something more than a disapproving tut.

'Well?' she said, raising her eyebrows.

'Dreadful!' Liz muttered. 'Shocking. Do they know who did it?'

'We can make a jolly good guess.'

Esme drew herself up to her full height and took a step forwards. She looked quite intimidating.

'That Brazilian boy, Rafael.'

Liz could hardly believe her ears. 'But we saw him in the marketplace just a few hours ago when Audrey told him off! We watched him leave!'

'Precisely,' Esme muttered darkly. 'Audrey reckons he came back to seek revenge.'

It sounded like the plot of a film noir and Liz almost laughed. 'Oh, I don't think so,' she said reasonably, jiggling

Lowenna, who was making contented sucking noises while she slurped her milk. 'It was probably day trippers who'd come over on the foot ferry from Plymouth with their cans of lager. You know what they're like.'

But Esme wasn't having it. 'Trouble,' she said, shaking her head grimly. 'Audrey's right, the boy's trouble. We've got an enemy in our midst.'

And with that, she stalked out of the house with a haughty flick of her towelling turban, leaving Liz staring at the empty space left behind.

She could understand, she thought as she closed the door and carried Lowenna upstairs, why folk might jump to conclusions. After all, Rafael's appearance made him stand out and he'd had a dubious reputation before he'd even arrived. But Liz doubted very much that he was capable of vandalism, and Tony and Felipe were watching him like hawks. Besides, it was unfair to point the finger without any evidence, and the village was filled with strangers at this time of year, any one of whom could have committed the dreadful deeds. Give the boy a chance.

Three days later, while Piers was busy striding around the estate again, clipboard in hand, Bramble decided to tackle the mermaid garden with Katie so that they'd at least have somewhere to sit and sunbathe. It was the first of August and it had crossed her mind that Piers, too, might enjoy relaxing in the sunshine with her when he'd finished his work. She could even lay a rug on the lawn and fetch a bottle of wine.

She felt very businesslike in her shorts, gloves, brand-new straw hat and wellington boots as she strode into the open, clutching a black bin bag in one hand and a pair of secateurs in the other, but when she re-surveyed the tangle of tall, spiky grasses, overgrown bushes and weeds that blocked the path, she was almost tempted to turn around and walk right back again.

Katie was clearly thinking the same thing.

'D'you think we're being a bit overambitious?' she asked, eyeing Bramble's stumpy clippers doubtfully. She herself had a medium-sized pair of shears and, balanced on her shoulder, an aluminium stepladder that they'd found in the laundry room, alongside Maria's scary mangle.

'I s'pose we've got to start somewhere,' Bramble replied, then yelped when she scratched her shin on something sharp.

They'd decided to wear shorts and vest tops so that they'd get a tan while they worked. It had seemed like a cunning plan, killing two birds with one stone, so to speak, but it occurred to them now that they might have been better off in beekeeper outfits or prickle-proof burkas.

Katie set the stepladder down by an undisciplined purple bush, declaring that this was as good a place to begin as any. Bramble set to work trimming the weeds around the broken metal gate, standing back every now and then to admire her handiwork.

'It's better already!' she announced after precisely four minutes. 'Look!'

Katie swivelled around sharply, making the ladder wobble and nearly toppling off.

'Bloody hell! Don't distract me. I almost fell.'

'Sorry,' said Bramble, noticing that the branches Katie had lopped off were almost as big as the bush itself and there was no way they'd fit them in a single bin bag. Still, they could worry about that another day. Perhaps they'd have a giant bonfire. That would be fun! If only they knew the best way to build one – and light it, come to that, without requiring emergency services backup…

Bramble squatted down and resumed her pruning, stopping every now and again to take a swig of water from the bottle hanging from her belt, but after twenty minutes she'd hardly made a difference.

'I think this calls for more drastic action,' she declared, rising. 'I'll try out the lawnmower.'

Katie, who was taking a breather on the bottom step of the ladder, nodded disconsolately. She looked exhausted and the bush had barely shrunk, although there was a pile of debris alongside almost as tall as Katie herself.

'I'm just going to have a little lie-down,' she muttered, flopping on to the grass beside her and covering her face with her baseball cap. 'I mustn't exhaust myself before my shift.'

It was to be her trial later at The Hole in the Wall and she'd spent some time last night testing out her new crimpers, before deciding that the style didn't suit her, so she'd washed the crinkles out and started again with the straighteners. As that had just been a dummy run, the hair would have to be washed and styled again later. Bramble hoped that Danny would appreciate all the effort.

She strolled into the orchard, taking care to avoid the spiki-est plants as well as the swarms of bees around the lavender bushes. The far-off sound of lowing cattle in the fields beyond her own estate mingled with birdsong and chirruping crickets was strangely soporific, so that she, too, was tempted to find a sheltered spot and lie down for a snooze. She gave herself a mental shake. Today, at least, they'd accomplish what they'd set out to do, for up to now their progress had been pitifully slow. Indeed, after ten days there was little to indicate that Polgarry Manor even had new residents.

Katie had at least found Piers, a coup indeed, and they'd also cleaned their bedroom and bathroom and weeded the steps leading up to the front door, but that was about it. The rest of their time seemed to have been spent walking, swimming and popping into Tremarnock for ice creams and other essential supplies. In truth, it had felt more like a holiday, and a very nice one at that, but the house was crumbling around them and something had to be done.

Bramble picked a greengage from one of the trees – they were ripening extra-early in the unusually hot weather – ate it greedily and threw the stone high into the air, watching it spin gaily before landing on a sunny patch of long green grass nearby, then she opened the door of the large tumbledown shed. At her feet a warty toad blinked in the half-light before hopping into a dark corner and she had to stifle a scream. She wasn't that keen on toads or frogs, or creepy crawlies of any sort really, but she told herself not to be silly. After all, the whole place – manor, grounds and all – was probably teeming with them, as well as mice, rats and other unmentionables. She'd better get used to it.

The lawnmower couldn't have been used for years and was covered in dirt and cobwebs. She wiped the seat with a tissue from her pocket before climbing up gingerly, putting her hands on the steering wheel and checking the controls. By her right knee was a rusty key in what she supposed was the ignition, and there were two pedals at her feet and a gear stick by her left hand. She hadn't a clue how to operate the thing, but supposed that it must be pretty much like a car, only easier. So without further ado, she turned the key and, to her delight, the engine sprang into life with a throaty roar.

'Tally-ho!' Bramble giggled, then she yelled 'Aaargh!' as she put her foot on the clutch, swung into gear, hit the accelerator and the machine lurched sickeningly before surging forwards at an alarming rate and heading purposefully towards a heavily laden plum tree.

Bramble took her foot quickly off the gas and scrabbled around for the brake pedal, only to realise that there wasn't one. Doomed, it seemed, to ram into the trunk, causing goodness knew what damage to herself, mower and tree, she closed her eyes, muttered a silent prayer and hoped for the best.

'PUT YOUR FOOT ON THE CLUTCH! IT'S A BRAKE, TOO!' roared a voice from somewhere, and instinctively Bramble did as she was told. To her enormous relief, the mower ground to a juddering halt just inches from the offending obstacle.

'Bloody hell,' she muttered, and took a deep breath. 'That was close.' For a moment she couldn't move for shock. She was soon jolted out of her daze, however, by that voice again, this time right by her ear.

'WHAT THE HELL WERE YOU PLAYING AT?'

Bramble opened her eyes to find Fergus just a foot away, hands raised and looking for all the world as if he were about to kill her. Terrified, she was about to leg it as fast she could when it dawned on her that his gesture was, in fact, one of horror not murderous intent.

'I – I'm sorry,' she stammered, eyes lowered. 'I wanted to cut the lawn.'

She scanned the long, thick grass all around her and stretching way in front, through the gardens beyond and as far as the gravel path leading to the manor steps, and all of a sudden felt out of her depth and very silly. He must think her a fool, and what's more, this was the second time he'd had to save her bacon since she'd arrived; the scenario was becoming all too familiar.

Fergus – who was in muddy jeans and a crumpled checked shirt, rolled up at the sleeves – narrowed his eyes sceptically.

'Have you ever driven one of these things?' He clearly knew the answer, so she didn't bother to reply. 'They're bloody dangerous if you don't know what you're doing. You could have got yourself killed.'

'I thought it would be simple,' she said in a small voice. 'I didn't mean to go so fast.'

'Well, at least you're all right.'

To her relief, he sounded a bit gentler now, and when he stretched out a hand to help her down, she took it gratefully. His rough fingers closed around hers, holding securely until she was safely on the ground, and he didn't let go until she'd stopped wobbling and was able to stand on her own.

'Thank you,' she said, glancing up and quickly scanning his features. The arrogance that he'd displayed the other day on the cliff had gone, but this time she thought that she could detect something else in his narrow, dark eyes – some deep sadness, perhaps, as Katie had suggested. But she might have been imagining it.

Bramble would have stayed for a while to chat, perhaps to ask if he'd like a cool drink in the manor as a token of her gratitude, but they were interrupted by another voice, sharp and edgy.

'What's going on?'

Piers emerged from the field behind, clutching his trusty clipboard, in a crisp blue-and-white-checked shirt and navy chinos. When Bramble explained what had happened, he glanced from her to Fergus and back again and frowned.

'You should've asked me to help. I've driven dozens of those things.'

'It was stupid,' Bramble admitted. 'I don't think I'll do any more gardening today.'

Piers put a hand on her arm. 'Thank God you're all right.' Then he turned and looked squarely at Fergus. 'I'll take care of her now.'

Realising that he'd been dismissed, Fergus nodded before turning on his heel and making towards the gate leading to the fields. He didn't even say goodbye.

'Thanks again!' Bramble shouted after him, but there was no reply, and when she swung around, Piers was manoeuvring the mower back into its home.

'What a stroke of luck Fergus was here!' she called over the engine's roar, and Piers grunted something that she couldn't catch.

It was only then that it occurred to her she hadn't thought to ask what her strange tenant had been doing in the orchard in the first place. Perhaps, like her, he had a taste for juicy plums and ripe greengages.

Chapter Nine

KATIE HAD WOKEN from her brief snooze and was once more up the ladder, finishing the pruning. The good news was that the unruly purple bush was now neater and much reduced in size, the bad, that the debris piled beside it was considerably higher than the original plant itself, so that the garden looked, if possible, even worse than it had before.

On spotting Bramble and Piers, she descended the steps, and when Bramble told her about the adventure and Fergus's timely intervention, she didn't seem surprised.

'I saw him in the field from the top of the ladder. He offered to help, but when I said you'd gone to get the mower, he went off to find you.'

So he hadn't been scrumping fruit after all. Bramble was rather touched, but she didn't have long to mull it over because Piers suggested a swim and both girls leaped at the idea. They were hot, sticky and downcast, and a refreshing dip seemed like the perfect pick-me-up, especially with an attractive land agent to accompany them.

They abandoned their gardening tools and ran inside to get their togs, only to be met by a scowling Maria on the stairs.

'Luncheon is served. It is past one o'clock.'

Bramble kicked herself inwardly for forgetting to tell

the housekeeper not to bother. She could smell meat and overcooked vegetables, and the last thing she fancied right now was a hot, heavy meal. Then it occurred to her that Piers might be hungry, and what's more, he could eat some of the unwanted food, so she scooted outside again to ask and he accepted immediately.

'This is the life!' he said, settling down at the head of the table and waiting while Maria brought extra cutlery and a glass. 'I thought I'd be having sandwiches, not a slap-up meal.'

The dining room window was open and an unexpected breeze made the velvet curtains tremble, fanning Bramble's hot face. Maria stood at the door, arms crossed, somehow conveying displeasure despite her lack of expression, while they helped themselves to tomato soup from the giant china tureen, followed by dry chicken and an assortment of soggy peas and carrots.

Piers didn't seem to mind the fare and tucked in hungrily, talking animatedly between forkfuls about his morning's work and occasionally dabbing his lips with the linen napkin. He had excellent manners, Bramble noted. Cassie would approve. She was keen on etiquette and wouldn't stand for elbows on the table, far less speaking with your mouth full.

Thankfully, the fresh fruit salad for pudding was an improvement on the previous courses, with small, sweet strawberries from the kitchen garden and thick clotted cream from the nearby dairy. When he'd finished, Piers threw his napkin down and sighed contentedly.

'I can hardly move,' he said, pushing back his chair and stretching out his legs. 'I could do with a lie-down now!'

'What about our swim?' Bramble protested. 'Don't tell me you've gone off the idea?'

Katie groaned. 'I can't walk far, not after all that.'

'We'll take it in turns to go on Piers's back,' Bramble joked.

She'd had a large glass of wine with her meal, which Piers had poured. It must have made her loose-tongued.

He sprang up and stepped around to the back of her chair, ready to help her from her seat.

'Ladies!' he said theatrically. 'I can do better than that. I'll drive you to the stunning beach at Pethgowan. It's well worth the journey, I promise, and it'll give you time to digest your meal.'

Katie started to say that she didn't think she could come because she was due at The Hole in the Wall at five thirty and would need to change and get ready, but he was having none of it.

'I'll have you back by four fifteen at the latest,' he promised, moving around to the other chair to assist her, too. 'You'll adore the beach. It's one of Cornwall's finest.'

This time there were no more false starts and he opened the sunroof and windows of his Land Rover while Katie clambered into the back seat, letting Bramble ride up front. She felt like the queen, or a movie star perhaps, as they whizzed along narrow country lanes, her dark glasses on and her blonde hair streaming out behind her like a horse's tail.

Piers, beside her, seemed utterly relaxed at the wheel, and they listened to music as they gazed at the passing scenery. Several people on the road or in their front gardens stopped to stare, perhaps imaging they were visiting celebs or local aristos, and Bramble almost wished now that her mysterious grandfather had passed on his title as well as the manor. She quite fancied herself as Lady So and So or Countess Bramble; she could get used to it.

She smiled, thinking how far she'd come from Chessington and that dull office where she'd worked, until a nasty stab of conscience reminded her that she hadn't yet returned Matt's calls. He'd left several messages saying that he missed her, that he'd like to fix a weekend to come and visit and asking her to ring, but something had always seemed to get in the way. She'd do it tonight – or tomorrow perhaps. Soon, anyway, when she wasn't so busy.

'Nearly there!' Piers shouted over the music, and she felt a thrill of excitement when she realised that they'd almost reached the bottom of the hot, dusty road that snaked sharply down the cliff side. He stopped for a moment by a gap in the hedge to allow her to admire the view: a slim ribbon of white-gold sand surrounded by majestic precipices that seemed to rise out of the deep blue ocean like prehistoric amphibians.

'Beautiful!' she sighed, and he nodded, pleased.

'If there's no space in the car park, we'll find a slot up the street.'

Before she knew it, she and Katie were grabbing their straw hats and bags and tramping past caravan parks and bungalows with quaint names like 'Dunroamin' and 'Asyoulikeit' towards the pathway down to the beach. The world and his wife, it seemed, had had the same idea, and in some places desperate owners appeared to have abandoned their cars entirely, double-parking them on grass verges or blocking driveways.

Finally, they reached the sand and looked around. To their right was a bar, a wooden chalet pumping out pop music, with a wide deck where glamorous young holidaymakers perched on stools or were propped against the fence, glasses in hand. On the other side, children in brightly coloured bathing suits played with buckets and spades, while parents and grandparents huddled beneath parasols or lay flat out on crumpled towels like basking seals.

It was a lively scene, to be sure, but Bramble couldn't help feeling a little disappointed. The beach was so covered in hot, sticky bodies that she wondered if they'd find any room to lay their towels.

'Pretty cool, huh?' Piers grinned, taking her by the arm and guiding her through the swathe of people while Katie followed behind. 'They call it mini-Ibiza round here. There's music and dancing at night all through the summer. It's party central.'

Bramble loved a party as much as the next person, but as she tripped over bags and dodged flying Frisbees, she found herself pining for the peace and quiet of her estate. Still, they were here now and the sea beckoned, so as soon as they'd located a patch on which they could dump their stuff, she stripped down to her bikini, which she'd put on underneath her clothes before they left.

'Come on!' she told the others. 'Hurry up!'

Piers took a moment to climb into his swimmers – a pair of bright-pink trunks decorated with toucans – before folding his shirt and trousers in a neat pile and removing his sunglasses and Panama. He placed them carefully on the other things and ran a hand through his hair.

'Lovely!' he said, stretching his arms lazily above his head, though whether he meant the weather or Bramble, she couldn't quite tell, because his eyes ran up and down her tall, slim body, taking it all in. She, in turn, had a quick peek at the light sprinkling of dark hair on his chest – no silver there – and the nice flat abs, though she was careful not to linger.

They picked their way down towards the ocean, Piers leading the way and the girls following, and just before they reached the shore they were accosted by a short, dark, hairy man in a very tight pair of turquoise Speedos.

'I say, who have we got here?' he drawled, looking at Bramble and Katie with interest. He had a narrow, bulging forehead and remarkably thick eyebrows.

Piers slapped him on the back. 'Anatole, my good man! I thought we'd find you!'

Anatole, it seemed, was an old pal from agricultural college.

'Bramble has just moved into Polgarry Manor. She inherited it from her grandfather,' Piers explained, and the stranger looked impressed.

'Did she now? Lucky girl!'

He winked at Piers and grinned, revealing a row of small, babyish, square teeth. Bramble saw Katie scowl and hoped that she wouldn't make a scene. She could be dreadfully rude if she took against someone.

'Do you live round here?' Bramble enquired, keen to deflect attention.

'I'm in London mostly, but my folks have a little place in the village.'

'Little? It's a mansion!' Piers laughed. He fake-whispered to Bramble: 'Swimming pool, tennis court, croquet lawn, you name it.'

Anatole looked gratified. 'You must come over sometime, say hello to the folks.'

'We'd love to, wouldn't we?'

Bramble stared hard at Katie, who remained stubbornly silent, but Piers's friend seemed more interested in the mistress of Polgarry anyway.

'And what about you? Where do you hail from originally?' he asked, and when Bramble mentioned Chessington, he made a strange noise at the back of his throat like a snort, or was it a cough?

'Isn't there a theme park there?'

Bramble nodded.

'I went on a school trip once. Knee-deep in chavs.' He chortled. 'I remember gazing at the sea of fake Adidas track-suits. Never seen anything like it in my life!'

Bramble blushed, wishing that she hadn't mentioned Chessington at all. To be honest, it had never occurred to her that the people there looked inferior, and she felt suddenly self-conscious in her Primark bikini.

Uncertain how to respond, she shifted uncomfortably from one foot to another, but luckily Piers came to her rescue.

'Polgarry's stunning, an absolute jewel. Needs a lot of work, of course.'

Anatole raised one black eyebrow. His skin was very dark, too; he must have had some foreign blood in him.

'Oh, I'm sure you'll sort her out,' he laughed. Bramble wasn't quite sure what he meant. Then he turned to Katie. 'Are you from Chessington as well?'

'Born and bred,' she said curtly. 'But you can't be English. You're too small and swarthy.'

Bramble would have kicked her friend in the ankle – hard – but she was too far away. A flicker of irritation crossed Anatole's face, but he soon recovered.

'Well spotted! I'm Russian, actually, or my parents are. They came over as children.'

'Descended from Russian nobility,' Piers chipped in help-fully, 'but he won't tell you that; he's far too modest.'

Katie grinned nastily. 'Funny that. I am, too, sort of. Working-class nobility through and through. We go back generations. My dad's a chippie and my mum's a school dinner lady. She can make a mean roast dinner with meat and three veg and a pudding with custard for less than a pound a head. She's famous for it.'

Anatole's small black eyes lit up with glee. 'A dinner lady? Excellent! I need to meet her!' He rubbed his hands together before pausing thoughtfully, as if filing the information away in a safe place for some future use.

A slightly awkward silence followed and Piers was about to fill the gap when they were interrupted by a tall, languid-looking girl in a knitted white bikini who sauntered up and rested an arm casually on Anatole's furry shoulder.

'Hey, lover boy, what's new?'

She had a deep, sultry voice, almond eyes and sleek black hair that might have been brushed a hundred times the previous night like Cinderella's. Her olive skin gleamed like a mirror and even her lips were full and glossy, giving her a sort of polished sheen, like a well-groomed horse. Around her neck was a small gold chain with a tiny winking diamond in the centre and there was another in her tummy button. Bramble, who thought she was quite beautiful, smiled nervously, and Piers introduced the girl as Anatole's girlfriend, Sheba, with an equally exotic-sounding surname that Bramble couldn't catch.

'Fiancée,' Anatole corrected swiftly. 'We're getting married in Nice next summer.' He snaked an arm around Sheba's slender hips and pulled her closer. 'Her parents have a place there.'

'Of course they do,' muttered Katie, not at all subtly, and Sheba looked at her oddly.

'Let's swim!' Bramble said quickly, fearing that Katie might be about to explode and grabbing her arm. 'I'll race you to the orange buoy.'

The girls ran towards the water's edge, closely followed by Piers, and plunged, squealing, into the froth. After a few strokes Bramble grew used to the temperature and felt her body relax as she stretched out her limbs, ducking under every now and again and tasting the salt water on her tongue. She easily beat Katie to the buoy but was no match for Piers, who lunged as soon as he was close enough and hung on, waving and grinning, until Bramble drew near, then he stretched out a hand, which she took, and reeled her in like a fish.

Slippery seaweed trailed around the bottom of the buoy as well as the bobbing chain that anchored it to the seabed. Unable to get a grip, she would have drifted off had he not put an arm around her waist and held her tight. Feeling the brush of his smooth, ice-cold skin against hers made her shiver, but he didn't seem aware of her trembling. Soon Katie swam up and seized the other side of the float, making it lurch to and fro, while Piers clung fast.

'That was further than I thought,' she gasped, blowing water noisily from her nose.

Bramble peered behind her friend and spotted the small figures of Anatole, in turquoise, and Sheba, in her white bikini, by the ocean's edge. They hadn't come in then. To be fair, Sheba didn't look like much of a swimmer; the water would mess up her shiny mane.

Some smallish children floated up on a pink lilo and Piers checked if they needed help, but they said no, turned around and started sculling back. He didn't seem in any hurry to release Bramble and she stayed as still as she could, paddling gently, because she was enjoying the moment and didn't want it to end. Now and again his hand wandered higher or lower on her side and the pressure of his fingers seemed to increase. She did wonder if it were deliberate, but he might just have been making sure that she didn't float off.

'It's just perfect,' she sighed, tilting her head and gazing up at the powder-blue sky, dotted with clouds. A light aircraft buzzed lazily by, trailing an advertising banner in its wake, and some way off two swimmers in masks and snorkels popped up their heads and chatted for a while, treading water.

At last Piers shifted slightly, as if he'd had enough, and when she turned to look she noticed the beads of water on his lips and trickling down the front of his neck. They were so close that she could have brushed them away with her mouth, her tongue…

'I'm going back!' shouted Katie, who was out of sight on the other side of the marker.

Reluctantly, Bramble cast off and started heading back to the shore. All the way she was acutely conscious of Piers's presence beside her, his lithe body finning through the waves, the rhythmic strokes of his arms and legs, and she sensed an electric charge between them so hot that it almost hurt. Surely he was experiencing it, too?

Had she ever felt quite this way about Matt? She tried to remember. She'd fancied him like crazy at first, sure, but after a time wild lust had faded, to be replaced by a more cosy kind of familiarity. She could slob around in her baggy pyjamas in front of Matt, clip her toenails even, and he wouldn't bat an eyelid, but he'd never *intrigued* her like Piers, who came from a different world entirely.

When they reached the beach again, Anatole and Sheba had wandered off somewhere. Piers was all for going to find them but Katie wasn't keen.

'I really have to get back now,' she said. 'Sorry to spoil the fun.'

Plucking up her courage, Bramble asked Piers if he'd like to meet her at the pub that evening, 'to keep an eye on Katie', but he said that he was busy.

'I have an appointment with another client, unfortunately.'

He looked so sad that Bramble couldn't be too disappointed; he would have come if he could.

'No problem. There's always another night.'

As they drove home, Katie in the front this time, she and Piers made small talk while Bramble hardly said a word. She was in a reflective mood, thinking about Piers and what her feelings might mean. She didn't believe in fate, but it did seem as if he'd been put in her path for a reason, because wasn't he just ideal – to the manor born, so to speak?

Her imagination took flight and she could picture him living in Polgarry, helping her to restore the place to its former glory. Perhaps in time they'd even hear the sound of children's voices in the gardens or echoing around the ancient walls. They'd have gorgeous children, she just knew it, and they'd all talk just like him.

He'd introduce her to his upper-class friends, show her what was what, and with him at her side she wouldn't feel embarrassed with Anatole, Sheba or anyone else because she'd become one of them, cool and sophisticated. She might even ask Sheba for a few styling tips when they got to know each other better.

She hugged her arms around herself, lost in delicious images of the future, and didn't even notice when they swept through the rickety iron gates and drew up at the door to the manor. Mrs Fenton-Wallis. She mouthed the name silently. It had a certain ring to it.

Chapter Ten

'So, what do you think? Isn't he gorgeous? Do you like him? I *really* do!'

Bramble hadn't gone to the pub to support Katie on her first shift after all. Instead, she'd had a long soak in the peeling but now spotlessly clean bathroom that the girls had scrubbed when they'd first arrived at the manor. She'd put on a face pack and lain back in the foam, humming along to the radio, her mind filled with pictures of Piers driving that Land Rover, Piers pulling on his pink trunks, Piers stretching out his hand to reach hers by the buoy, slipping it around her waist ever so lightly and leaving it there...

Afterwards, unable to sleep, she'd sat up in bed flicking through old magazines that she'd brought with her from London and waiting for her friend to return. Before Katie had even had a chance to put down her bag or remove her shoes, Bramble was firing off questions like corks from a popgun.

'How old do you think he is? He's very well-spoken, isn't he? I could listen to him for hours!'

'Hang on a minute!' said Katie, perching on the end of the bed and taking off her canvas trainers with a groan. 'My feet hurt. I'm absolutely knackered!' She did, indeed, look exhausted, with a sweaty face and smudged mascara. 'It was so busy in there. I haven't stopped all evening.'

Bramble clicked her tongue impatiently. 'Never mind that. What's the verdict?'

Her friend leaned back, crossing one nicely tanned leg over the other, and despite her weariness her face lit up in a huge, mischievous smile. 'Yeah, he's absolutely yummy!'

Bramble took a deep breath and sighed contentedly. 'He is, isn't he? So tall and handsome.' There was a dreamy, faraway look in her eyes. 'I like his silvery hair, too, don't you? It makes him look soooo distinguished.'

Katie, who'd been lounging on her elbow, sat bolt upright and frowned, knocking Bramble's magazine off the bed and on to the floor, where it landed with a splat.

'What do you mean, silvery? He hasn't got any silver. His hair's fair.'

Bramble looked confused. 'Don't be silly.' Then she giggled. 'His chest hair's not grey, though, and his legs aren't particularly hairy. I kept wondering what colour it was underneath those pink trunks.'

The penny dropped and Katie's mouth fell open. 'I thought you were talking about Danny!'

'Danny? Wherever did you get that idea from?' Bramble lowered her voice. 'I think I'm falling for Piers, Katie. It's not just lust, honestly. I mean, I really fancy him, but there's something else. A strong feeling. I've never met anyone like him before – and I think he likes me, too. I think he's the man I want to marry!'

'Whaaat?' Katie peered at her friend through narrowed eyes. 'You can't say that! You've only just met him, and besides, you're with Matt.'

Bramble fidgeted; it wasn't what she wanted to hear.

'I've changed since I came here. Maybe I need something more.'

Katie crossed her arms and pursed her lips. 'You're making a big mistake. Matt's a pearl among men – kind, intelligent, good-looking, faithful – and he really, really loves you. He'd do anything for you.'

'He wouldn't come to Polgarry with me.'

Her friend paused for a moment to consider this statement. 'He's cautious,' she said at last. 'He didn't want to chuck in his job, only for you to say in three months' time you didn't like it here. I mean, it's not as if you're immune to changing your mind. Remember the snakeskin boots?'

Bramble grimaced. She'd once spent hours with Matt and Katie in a central London store trying on some overpriced boots, only to decide when they reached home that she'd made a terrible mistake. After some heated discussion and much angst, the three had trekked all the way back to the shop, where Bramble had promptly resolved to keep the boots after all.

'Being cautious can be a good thing,' Katie went on. 'It's not a crime, you know.'

'I think I prefer reckless to dull.'

'Matt's not remotely dull!'

'Well, you go out with him instead!'

Katie laughed. 'He wouldn't have me.' Then she sighed. 'Poor Matt, he'd be devastated if he heard you. You'd better hurry up and finish with him if that's what you really want to do.'

'I'll ring. I just haven't had time.'

Katie was aghast. 'You'll have to see him in person!'

She was right, of course, but the mere idea of a face-to-face filled Bramble with horror. He'd probably break down and she would, too. It would feel like chopping off her own arm as well as his leg or foot.

'I'll think about it,' she said defensively. 'Anyway, since when have you been Miss Perfect? You were going out with *three* boys at the same time before we came here, remember? It was like a carousel, a different one every night!'

'That was then. If I was Danny's girlfriend, I wouldn't even look at anyone else.'

Now it was Bramble's turn to be surprised. 'Bloody hell,' she said, relieved to be off the subject of Matt. 'I knew you liked him, I just didn't realise how much...'

'He's really lovely and funny.' Katie swallowed. 'I don't think he's going out with anyone; he hasn't mentioned it anyway. I'd be too embarrassed to ask.'

'What about that singer, Tabitha? He seems quite keen on her?'

'Hmm. I know what you mean.' Katie chewed a fingernail. 'But I don't think they're an item, at least not yet. The good thing is, he's asked me back for more shifts so I'll get to work on him.'

Bramble scrutinised her friend carefully. She had that look on her face, the one that said something was afoot. When it came to scheming, Katie was an expert. She could have pulled off the Gunpowder Plot.

'As only you know how,' Bramble observed wryly.

There was a kerfuffle going on in the marketplace the following morning when they went down to stock up on chocolate. (Maria didn't seem to go in much for goodies and they wouldn't have dared raid the kitchen cupboards, so they'd been keeping secret supplies in their bedroom.) The village was buzzing with locals and holidaymakers buying fresh bread, buns and pasties from the bakery, and milk and newspapers from the general store. Thanks to more glorious weather, most folk – in shorts and T-shirts, skimpy dresses and sunglasses – were going about their business with happy, relaxed expressions, but Katie and Bramble spotted a huddle of folk around the fishmonger's. At the centre of them was Ryan, the chap with the bushy eyebrows whom they'd met at the music event. He was talking to a police officer, who was taking notes, while beside him a very tall middle-aged woman with a pixie crop was waving her arms in agitation.

Liz trundled into the square pushing a buggy. She was with a pretty young girl in a white dress and pale-blue glasses; the girl must have been about thirteen or fourteen, and had thick fair hair and a noticeable limp. She and Liz stopped beside Bramble, who by now had twigged what all the fuss was about.

'The shop window's been smashed,' she explained to Liz, who pulled a face when she, too, noticed the large circular puncture in the glass, with cracks emanating outwards like a spider's web, as if somebody had thrown a cricket ball, or a rock perhaps.

'Oh Lord,' she said. 'I wonder how that happened.'

'Maybe it was an accident,' the girl in glasses suggested, but Liz looked doubtful.

'I don't think it would break like that on its own. It must have been hit with quite a lot of force.'

Two men strolled over to join them, one fairly short and round, the other younger, tall and handsome. With them was a swarthy teenage boy all in black, with a sticky-up streak of violet in the centre of his otherwise shaven head. Bramble and Katie had seen them on Tabitha's gig night, and now Liz introduced the men as Tony and Felipe, and the boy as Rafael,

Felipe's brother. The girl, she explained, was her daughter, Rosie.

Lowenna squeaked in her stroller and flapped her chubby arms, determined not to be left out, and Bramble bent down to say hello.

'She's gorgeous!' she said, kneeling in front of the toddler and taking her hand. She adored small children. 'How do you do!'

'She's my sister,' Rosie announced proudly, and to Bramble's surprise Rafael squatted, too, and blew a raspberry, which made Lowenna chuckle.

'Bad business,' Tony commented, shaking his head at the broken window, at which point the crowd started to break up and scatter in different directions, leaving only the policeman, Audrey and Ryan still talking.

The village had by no means recovered from the shock of the graffiti on the public loos, not to mention Rick's flying postcard stand, and gossip had been spreading about Rafael's possible involvement, despite the lack of evidence. So far, however, Tony and Felipe were unaware, so busy had they been settling Rafael in and trying to keep him entertained.

Liz was rather hoping that they'd leave, but Audrey spun around suddenly, and on catching sight of Rafael her eyes narrowed dangerously and she pointed an accusing finger. 'That's him!'

The policeman, a portly fellow in shiny black boots, stomped towards them and explained that he was Sergeant Kent from the nearby station.

'This Rafael, is it?' he asked, looking sternly at the teenager, who was squeezing Lowenna's ticklish knees, making her squeal.

'We're his guardians,' Tony replied stiffly, proffering a hand. 'He lives with us in the village. Can I help?'

Rafael, who either hadn't heard or was choosing not to, gripped Lowenna's knee again, making her roar with helpless laughter, and Tony gave him a nudge. Rafael caught Rosie's eye as he stood up and the corners of both their mouths twitched naughtily.

'Where were you last night and in the early hours of this morning?' Sergeant Kent enquired, and Rafael shrugged as if he didn't understand.

'Excuse me?'

The policeman repeated his question and this time Felipe answered.

'He was at home with us, weren't you, Rafa?'

The boy nodded. 'I was reading *filosofia*,' he said, straight-faced. 'Do you know Kant? Very interesting.'

The policeman looked confused and Rosie giggled – she couldn't help it – but Sergeant Kent soon composed himself.

'I don't have much time to read, sir. I'm too busy catching criminals.' He eyed the boy sternly. 'Do you know anything about this broken window here, or the graffiti in the public toilet?'

'Of course he doesn't,' snapped Tony. 'I told you, he was minding his own business with us at home last night. And we don't know anything about any graffiti.'

'Some people are awfully good at burying their heads in the sand.'

It was Audrey, who'd sidled up with a sour expression on her face. She towered over the policeman, who seemed to shrink in her lengthy shadow.

'And what's that supposed to mean?' growled Tony, fiddling with the collar of his pale-blue polo shirt as if it were too tight. He'd never greatly cared for Audrey.

She, in a pink kaftan over cropped white jeans, looked

positively smug. 'I don't suppose Rafael mentioned to you that he was kicking a can around the square last Friday, vandalising property?'

Liz let out an involuntary squeak. 'Oh, come on, Audrey. I was there, too. He didn't cause any damage.'

Audrey's lips puckered into a tight O.

'Kicking a can is hardly a criminal offence,' Tony interjected hotly, 'and it's got nothing whatsoever to do with this.' He indicated the shopfront behind. 'You'd better mind what you say or I'll sue you for slander, you old trout.'

Now Audrey's mouth dropped wide open. 'Well, I—' She looked all set to give as good as she got, but the policeman raised a hand.

'That's quite enough of that, thank you. I suggest you two go on your way and leave this to the experts.' He fixed on Rafael, who raised an impudent eyebrow. 'And you, young man, had better behave yourself. I shall, of course, be making further enquiries.'

And with that he turned on his heel. Audrey stalked after him, leaving the others momentarily lost for words.

It was Tony who finally broke the silence. 'The bloody gall of the woman!' His face and neck had turned quite red. 'Who does she think she is, casting aspersions like that? Outrageous!'

Felipe sighed miserably.

'You didn't break the window, did you?' Tony went on, turning to Rafael. 'You must tell us the truth.'

Rafael, who'd removed his dark glasses and put them on his head in order to bond with Lowenna, appeared deeply offended.

'How can you think such a bad thing? I am very sad.' Tears sprang up in his eyes and he slapped his chest to demonstrate his depth of feeling. 'Do you imagine I am that sort of person? I will return to Rio. I cannot stay here a minute more.'

It seemed likely that he, too, would stalk off, but Rosie, who'd been listening intently all this time, put a hand on his arm.

'Please don't go,' she said softly. 'Tony's upset; we all are. Audrey's being stupid. We know you didn't do it. Please stay.'

It was a surprising show of emotion, given that the pair had only just met, but it seemed to do the trick. Rafael appeared doubtful for a moment, checking Rosie's hand as if to be sure he hadn't imagined it, then he glanced at Tony and Felipe, who nodded, before placing his own hand on the strange girl's and patting it.

'Thank you,' he said solemnly, 'for believing in me. I think that we shall be good friends.'

Rosie flashed her funny, gappy smile. 'I'm learning Spanish at school but I can't speak Portuguese.'

'Portuguese is much better. I will teach you,' the boy replied gallantly, and Bramble, who'd been quiet up to now, clapped her hands.

'Can I have lessons, too? I've always wanted to go to Rio.'

'And me,' Katie added. 'You can't go by yourself!'

Now that spirits had risen somewhat, they were soon chatting about the merits of England versus Brazil, which seemed to come off rather better, thanks to Rafael's enthusiastic review. When Lowenna got fed up with pulling her hair out of the scrappy bunches that Rosie had given her this morning, Liz lifted her from the pushchair and Bramble asked for a cuddle. The little girl instantly fixed on her dangly starfish earrings, determined to yank them out.

'Ouch!' said Bramble, pulling her head away, before asking Liz if she could buy Lowenna a lolly.

'Let's all have one,' Tony cried, perking up at the prospect of food. 'We can eat them on the seafront. They're on me!'

They trooped into Rick's little shop and picked out what they wanted from the giant fridge-freezer. Tony went for a large chocolate cone, while Felipe, Bramble and Katie opted for ice cream tubs. Lowenna, meanwhile, had guessed what was coming and misbehaved dreadfully so that Liz had to wait with her outside while Rosie fetched her an ice pop, and orange lollies for herself and her mother.

'I couldn't subject poor Rick to the noise,' Liz told Bramble when she emerged. 'She'd give him a headache.'

The beach was already alive with activity, though few people had as yet braved the water, preferring to wait until later in the day when it had warmed up. A group of scuba divers beside a motorboat were donning wetsuits, while a brown and white Jack Russell sniffed around their feet before attempting to run off with a man's snorkel. Luckily, he spotted what was going on and managed to grab the dog before it got away. Its owner was nowhere to be seen.

The friends sat side by side on the sea wall, their feet dangling over the edge, and Tony was very interested in Polgarry Manor. Bramble explained about the leaks in the roof.

'I dread to think what it'll be like in winter. We'll have to wear wellington boots indoors!'

He suggested that she could perhaps turn it into a B and B to make some money. There was a call for one, he explained, especially now that The Stables had closed down.

'I can help with publicity if you like. It's what I do.'

Bramble wrinkled her nose. 'I don't think I want paying guests. I'd rather keep it as a private home.'

'That's all very well, darling, but how are you going to survive?' asked Tony, loosening some chocolate off the side of his cone and popping it in his mouth. 'It's a big old place, and I don't mean to be rude, but can you afford to maintain it?'

Bramble licked her lolly disconsolately and picked at a scab on her knee. 'Not really.'

'You'd have no trouble finding staff for a B and B,' Liz said, trying to be helpful. 'And what about opening up the gardens? People love stately homes, and you could charge a fee and serve tea and cakes. I bet you'd be mobbed. Why not have a grand inauguration one afternoon? I'd be happy to help. I wouldn't want you to pay me,' she added hastily. 'It would be a pleasure. I'm sure other locals would pitch in, too.'

'That's not a bad idea,' Bramble replied thoughtfully. 'But I'll have to do some work on the garden first. I can't afford to employ anyone.'

She frowned, recalling the pile of rubbish from Katie's purple bush and her own disastrous efforts with the lawn-mower, then Piers popped into her head and the clouds lifted. 'Something will come up, I'm sure.'

'Think positive – that's the spirit,' cried Tony, biting into what was left of his cone and swallowing it down in one satisfied gulp. 'I could fit my cottage into a corner of one of your wings and it still seems like bloody hard work. Anyway, it's not as bad as keeping an eye on this young ruffian.' He looked at Rafael fondly. 'He'll give me a heart attack one of these days. Gotta watch him constantly.'

Lowenna, who'd plonked herself on Bramble's lap while she ate her lolly, now wiggled on to her sister's, at which point Rafael rose, picked up the toddler and, to her great amusement, threw her in the air.

When he'd finished, he took her by a sticky hand.

'We play in the waves, yes?' He glanced at Rosie. 'Want to come?'

Soon she was following him lopsidedly down the steps and on to the beach, and the others watched as they removed their shoes and paddled by the water's edge. At last Bramble sighed, remembering what she was supposed to be doing.

'We'd better get a move on,' she said to Katie, smoothing her skirt and brushing the grit off her hands. 'We're hacking down more bushes, remember?'

Katie pulled a face. 'It's far too hot to work. Can't it wait till tomorrow?'

There was a brief pause while Bramble considered the suggestion.

'We might get sunstroke,' Katie wheedled, spotting a chink in her friend's armour.

'Or heat exhaustion,' Tony added helpfully.

'Oh, all right,' said Bramble at last. 'Let's award ourselves a break.'

Tony laughed. 'Always put off till tomorrow what you can do today, eh? I don't blame you! I have every intention of doing as little as I possibly can.'

'Lucky you!' smiled Liz, who was planning to call in on Pat again. When she explained that she was worried about the old woman, Felipe said he'd come, too, and bring Rafael 'to cheer her up'.

'Come on,' Bramble said to Katie, yanking her by the arm. 'We haven't bought any chocolate yet and it's the only reason we came!'

'Bye, darlings!' Tony called cheerfully as they headed off. 'Have fun – and don't do anything I wouldn't do!'

It took a while to persuade Lowenna off the beach and into her pushchair, then Liz, Rosie, Lowenna, Felipe and Rafael left Tony at the turning to Market Square before continuing up South Street, past Audrey's dress shop and on to Humble Hill. Rafael was noticeably silent after being told that he was to visit an old lady he'd never met, so Rosie tried to cheer him up.

'She's really nice and not at all stuffy. She's like my grannie,' she said. 'And she always has good biscuits!'

Liz was glad that her daughter seemed a little less glum than of late and hoped that Rafael, who wasn't much older, would help distract her from her recent heartbreak. He would have noticed her disabilities, of course, but he didn't seem fazed. Perhaps he knew someone with cerebral palsy in Rio; it wasn't uncommon, after all.

'Here we are,' Liz said, stopping outside The Nook and ringing the bell on the canary-yellow front door.

It took an age for Pat to answer, and Felipe suggested that she might not be in, but Liz knew better.

'She hardly ever goes out. She's so deaf, she probably hasn't heard.'

When the old woman finally appeared, it was immediately clear that something was wrong. She had a shawl wrapped around her shoulders and her face was damp and putty-coloured. Her snow-white hair, normally so neatly combed, was bedraggled and sticking to her forehead, and she seemed perplexed, almost as if she couldn't remember who they were.

'Oh, it's you,' she said at last. 'I thought it might be the postman. I'm not feeling too well, to be honest with you.'

She didn't ask them in as usual, or enquire about Rafael, whom she hadn't met. She didn't even seem to notice Lowenna, now gently snoring in her stroller, a thin streak of saliva dribbling from her slack mouth down her chin.

'What's the trouble?' asked Liz, stepping inside despite

the lack of invitation and taking Pat by the arm. 'You should have rung.'

Rosie lifted the pushchair inside with the assistance of Rafael and Felipe, while Liz helped Pat into the little front room, where she almost fell into her armchair, gripping the sides as if to keep herself from falling off.

'It's that blasted indigestion again,' she complained. 'I've taken some tablets but they don't seem to do much good. I was up half the night with it, and I've got this pain in my back.' She gestured to an area behind a shoulder. 'And here,' she went on, clutching her abdomen. 'I thought it was getting a bit better but it seems to have come back. I must have slept in a funny position.'

Rosie, trying to be useful, offered to get her a drink, but Pat shook her head wearily.

'Help yourself to anything you want, dear. You know where everything is. I'm sorry I'm so hopeless today.'

But Rosie didn't move. She was watching her mother, who was pulling at her bottom lip with two fingers and eyeing the old woman carefully.

'I'm going to call the doctor,' Liz said at last. Ignoring Pat's protests, she disappeared into the kitchen to use the phone. She was soon speaking to a woman from the NHS helpline who fired off a list of questions.

'Does she have any nausea, light-headedness, unusual fatigue...?'

Liz carried the phone next door to ask. 'Yes, all of them.'

'Shortness of breath? Palpitations?' the woman went on, tapping away on her computer.

Pat nodded. She hadn't mentioned those before.

'Pain, particularly in her arm, neck, jaw, shoulder, upper back, abdomen?'

Pat explained where it hurt, and when Liz had finished relaying the information, the helpline woman cleared her throat.

'I'm going to call an ambulance,' she said firmly. 'Keep her calm but don't try to move her.'

Feeling sick with anxiety, Liz pulled up a chair and sat by Pat, holding her hand while they waited. The old woman kept insisting that the ambulance wasn't necessary, that she'd feel better after a good night's rest, but even in her confused state she realised from her friend's expression that things might be bad.

Rosie knelt by her other side, looking so upset that Pat tried to comfort her.

'I'll be fine, lambkin,' she said, stroking the girl's head clumsily. It was so typical of her to think of others even at a time like this.

The minutes seemed to tick by painfully slowly and Liz tried to appear cheerful, but it wasn't easy.

'It's best to get checked out. You'll be home in a jiffy, and when you're better I'll take you out for lunch in the countryside, to a nice pub or something. We'll have a bitter shandy to celebrate your recovery.'

As she spoke, the sky clouded over, there was a rumble of thunder and the rain started to come down, lightly at first, then in thick sheets, splattering on the road outside and against the windowpanes. It was so sudden that it seemed like a sign; everyone felt it.

After a while, the tension started to get to Rafael, who needed a pee, so Rosie took him to the bathroom upstairs, while Felipe hovered by the window, looking out and trying to crack jokes to lighten the atmosphere. Liz did her best to explain them to Pat, but they were rather complicated and didn't translate well from Portuguese.

'I've heard better,' Pat grumbled, and Liz managed a small smile.

Felipe was rather sensitive and might have taken offence, but luckily the ambulance arrived in the nick of time, pulling up in the middle of the damp street as there was nowhere to park. Soon two paramedics, a man and a woman, entered the front room. They talked in oddly cheerful voices while they took Pat's blood pressure and pulse. Then they gave her aspirin and put a drip in her arm as the others looked on fearfully.

When they'd finished, the woman paramedic took Liz aside.

'She has the symptoms of a heart attack. They'll be able to tell you more in Cardiac.'

Liz's teeth chattered despite the heat in the room.

Felipe volunteered to go with Pat, and Liz said she'd join them at the hospital as soon as she could, thinking all the while that she couldn't quite believe this was happening, that it must be a dream – or a nightmare, more like. As they lifted Pat on to the carry chair she turned to Liz, who saw for the first time that the old woman's watery blue eyes were full of fear.

'You'll look after my plants for me?'

'I promise.'

'And let Emily know where I am?' Emily was Pat's favourite niece.

'Of course.'

'If anything should happen to me...'

A painful lump lodged in Liz's throat. 'It won't. You mustn't worry.'

Then she kissed the old woman on the forehead, waved to Felipe and went outside with Rosie and Rafael to watch the ambulance drive away, its tyres splashing through puddles and spraying water as it went. They didn't care that they were getting wet themselves; they hardly even noticed.

Once the ambulance had rounded the corner, Liz turned back to her companions.

'I should have called for an ambulance the other day, when we visited. I feel so bad…'

'It's not your fault,' said Rosie, giving her mother a hug, while Rafael stuck his hands in his pockets and hung back awkwardly.

A strange silence seemed to have settled on the house when they re-entered, as if the life had gone out of it. They checked that all the windows were locked and everything was in order before slamming the front door, relieved to get away.

'Will she be all right?' Rosie asked as they hurried home in the wet, and Liz took a deep breath. She wanted so much to be positive, but it was difficult.

'I don't know, darling. She's very old, you see. But she's in excellent hands. I'm afraid there's nothing we can do now but wait and pray.'

Chapter Eleven

WHILE LIZ WAS helping Pat, Bramble and Katie were on their way back to the manor, munching chocolate and discussing plans. They'd watched the sun vanish and the sky turn from bright blue to an ominous shade of grey, and soon big, fat raindrops started to splash on the windscreen.

'Bugger!' Bramble said as she passed through the rickety iron gates and screeched to a halt near the old oak door. 'I thought it was supposed to be glorious sunshine all day? It's going to bucket down.'

Right on cue, a flash of lightning lit up the manor's turrets like a laser beam, followed by a crack of deafening thunder, and the rain descended in thick sheets that smacked on the car roof and resonated like a tin drum roll.

'We'll have to wait till it eases,' Katie shouted, 'or we'll get soaked.'

Bramble peered up at the swirling blackness overhead. 'I don't think it's going to stop for a while. We'd better make a run for it.'

Clutching their cardigans over their heads, they dashed towards the main door, which opened, as if by magic, to allow them in.

'Thanks, Maria,' Bramble said, spying the housekeeper

behind the entrance and hurrying past her into the hallway. Bramble paused for a moment, watching the water sluice off her clothes and make puddles on the marble floor.

'It's disgusting out there,' she said apologetically. 'Sorry about the mess.'

But Maria, unreadable as ever, merely nodded before closing the door firmly behind them.

'Will that be all?' she asked, and Bramble was relieved when she turned her back and made for the kitchen with her short, determined strides. She was so disagreeable that it was no wonder she and Lord Penrose had got on well. They might have been made for each other.

The girls ran upstairs to peel off their sodden clothes, and took it in turns to have baths as the ancient boiler couldn't cope with more than one at a time. When they'd dressed again, in jeans, socks and warm sweatshirts, they sat on the end of their bed and debated what to do. They hadn't anticipated an indoorsy type of day at all.

'We could see a film?' Katie suggested. Her face and arms were pink and flushed from the hot water and she'd tied back her dark hair in a damp ponytail.

'I don't feel like going out again in this,' Bramble replied gloomily, staring through the window. 'Anyway, it'd take ages to get to the nearest cinema. We're in the middle of bloody nowhere, remember?'

For the first time since they'd arrived, the reality of their location really hit home. Back in Chessington, if the weather was bad and they were off work, the girls would pop to the shopping centre for a spot of retail therapy, drink skinny lattes in a cosy café, maybe wile away some time with a mani-pedi, before taking in a film, eating out at a restaurant, meeting up with Matt and friends in a pub or wine bar and perhaps heading into central London later to hit the clubs. The climate hardly mattered because there was so much to do. Here, though, the elements ruled, and there was nothing for it but to remain inside until the sky brightened.

'I think I hate the country,' Bramble muttered.

'We could always take up needlepoint?' Katie joked. 'Isn't that what grand ladies used to do on rainy days?'

Bramble scowled before giving herself a mental shake. 'I've got a better idea,' she declared, and she suggested that they sort through Lord Penrose's old belongings.

'I haven't even seen his rooms properly yet. I've been avoiding them, as if he's still alive, watching our every move like a bad-tempered ghost. This place won't feel like ours till we've filled it with our presence and our stuff. It's not as if there's anything else to do.'

Katie looked doubtful. 'I don't like the idea of touching his things. Can't Maria take care of it?'

Bramble shook her head firmly. 'He was my relative and it should be me who decides what to keep and what to throw away.'

The old man's rooms were in the west wing of the building, through a heavy oak door that normally stayed shut. So far, the girls had only poked their noses in and retreated quickly, spooked by the stale smell; the worn leather slippers positioned by the four-poster bed, as if their owner might emerge at any moment from beneath the covers to put them on; and the dusty garments hanging on wardrobe doors in the dressing room next door. This time, however, Bramble led the way in purposefully, drawing back her shoulders and trying to ignore the wobble in her knees.

'It's so cluttered,' said Katie, gazing at the various portraits, the stag's antlers, the stuffed birds in glass cases on assorted surfaces, the thick gold curtains and the tattered rug on the wooden floor. Despite the size of the room and its two large windows, it felt quite dark, owing not just to the dull weather but also to the murky-green walls, the gloomy drapes around the four-poster and the heavy mahogany furniture.

Bramble wandered into the adjoining room and scanned the dressing table, on which sat a silver hairbrush, two clothes brushes, a mirror, an ivory comb and various little bottles of cologne. Daring herself, she picked up the hairbrush, and she felt its rounded end before turning it over. She started when she noticed a few stray white hairs still clinging to the bristles. Had they been shed the last time her grandfather had brushed his hair before he died? She replaced the item quickly, feeling like an intruder in a man's world – for it was, indeed, a very masculine place. No hint of femininity, nothing pretty or flowery, no sense of a woman's touch.

The only surprise, perhaps, was an elegant spinet in one corner of the bedroom, with a book of classical music still propped against its rest. Lord Penrose had written his name on the front in small, squiggly letters, and when Bramble looked inside she saw that he'd made various annotations in the same hand: 'quicker' and 'two beat', and 'EGBB' beneath a particular chord. Bramble had only learned the piano for one year at primary school but she could tell that he must have been good. She wondered why he'd kept the instrument here rather than downstairs like the grand piano, which looked as if it hadn't been used in years. Perhaps he'd preferred to practise in private.

'Where do you want to start?'

She jumped. So lost had she been in thought that she'd forgotten all about Katie.

'Can you sort through his clothes and put the decent ones

in there?' Bramble pointed to a large leather suitcase on top of one of the wardrobes. The rest, she said, they'd take to the charity shop, try to sell or chuck away.

She, meanwhile, resolved to begin with his bedside drawers. Feeling a little guilty, she slid open the first; it contained nothing more than a pair of grubby spectacles and a packet of prescription pills. She took a deep breath and emptied them into a large wastepaper basket, along with a battered copy of *Birds of the British Isles* from the drawer beneath. There was no point hanging on to them. No one would wish to stay in the room until it had been cleared of the old earl's personal possessions.

The third drawer down contained a box of tissues and, underneath that, a sketchbook of the type used in art classes at school. Bramble opened the first page and discovered a rather appealing drawing of the view from the old man's bed. The lines were few but conveyed beautifully one carved pillar of the four-poster and the spread of smooth floorboards leading towards the window, which looked out over rolling fields and the sun rising, or setting perhaps, behind the rugged cliffs.

Intrigued, she flipped to the next page, where there was a quite different drawing: a fluffy cat, its head cocked slightly to one side, its back leg raised at an awkward angle as it lazily washed its furry outstretched paw. Behind it was the same carved pillar, and beneath that, a hint of eiderdown and a bulge – perhaps of someone's feet. She shivered, wondering if they had belonged to her grandfather and if a cat had once sat there while he sketched, propped up against some pillows perhaps, his book on his lap, lovingly re-creating the arch of his pet's back, the oval smoothness of its pads and its absurdly long whiskers.

There were other drawings, too: a vase of delicate

wildflowers; a cheeky sparrow perched on the windowsill, eyeing the observer inquisitively. Lord Penrose must have loved nature, and he could certainly draw, she thought, putting the sketchbook to one side and resolving to keep it in a safe place for further perusal. Music and art? Such interests didn't seem to fit with what she knew of his boorish personality. Perhaps he'd had further talents, too.

On top of the set of drawers was an empty glass and a water jug that had left a round stain. They were functional rather than attractive, and went in the bin as well. Bracing herself, she knelt down and peered under the bed. She was relieved to find nothing but dust, until she felt mouse droppings and removed her hand swiftly. Ugh. The whole bed would have to be pulled out so that she could vacuum underneath, but she'd need Katie's help with that.

Next, she walked over to the heavy chest of drawers against the wall, in the centre of which sat a mirror flanked by a stuffed pelican and an owl. Poor creatures. These, too, Bramble had no intention of keeping, so she lifted them carefully and carried them to the landing, where she set them on the floor. Someone, surely, would want them as weird collectors' objects; she'd have to find them a home later.

The bottom few drawers were full of jumpers that smelled of mothballs. One or two that looked quite smart and expensive she handed to Katie for the Oxfam shop, and the rest she flung beside the other rubbish, ready for recycling. Higher up were piles of silk handkerchiefs and cravats, which she put in another suitcase for items that she might be able to sell online. The trouble was that disposing of all this stuff would be a lengthy task in itself, and it was the same throughout the manor. If she thought about it for too long, she could get depressed.

Cupboard by cupboard, she told herself, room by room. She must just put one foot in front of the other and allow herself a sense of achievement for completing even the smallest job, otherwise she'd go mad.

The top two drawers, which were smaller, contained socks and underwear, which Bramble quickly binned. The pile of rubbish was now a mini-mountain, but not so big that she couldn't bag it all up and cart it to the dump. All that remained was a black leather wallet that had been carefully placed under the old man's pants. An ancient trick, Bramble thought, that every burglar must surely know.

Expecting to find cash, a few notes perhaps, maybe the earl's passport, she opened the wallet and felt inside. To her surprise there was no money, but in one of the sections were four black-and-white photographs, yellowed with age and crinkled at the edges as if they'd been regularly thumbed.

Intrigued, she sat cross-legged on the floor and looked at them. One was of Lord Penrose himself in middle age – she recognised him from other pictures around the place – standing in a dinner jacket on the front steps of Polgarry Manor and gazing, unsmiling, at the camera. To his right was another, younger, man with slicked-back hair and a silk scarf in his top pocket, and to his left, a woman in a long evening gown with flared sleeves, her hair arranged, Princess Anne-style, in a stiff updo. Beside her was a slim girl of sixteen or seventeen with wavy hair, wearing a light, calf-length dress. The photographer must have been standing quite far back, as it was difficult to make out the faces, but Bramble could tell that the girl was pretty, with big dark eyes and a slightly awkward demeanour.

The second photo was of the same foursome, but this time inside the house, sitting around the fire in the main reception room: Lord Penrose in the armchair, the man and woman side by side on the sofa and the girl perched on the arm. It was most likely the same evening as their clothes hadn't changed, though the adults looked more relaxed and the girl was posing with one slender leg in front of the other, her hands resting on her lap, her head tipped at an angle and an amused smile playing on her lips. Behind Lord Penrose, interestingly, stood the spinet that was now in his bedroom.

Eagerly, Bramble turned to the third photo, which was a close-up of the girl, showing just her head and shoulders. It was less formal than the other snaps and seemed to capture something that only the very best photographer can achieve: a moment in time that conveyed the very essence of the subject, a core part of his or her being.

The girl was throwing back her head and laughing gaily. It might have been spontaneous, yet the tilt of her head, the wide-open mouth and arch of her slender neck suggested a degree of self-awareness, as if she were already beginning to understand the power of her beauty. It could have been called 'The Spirit of Youth', a picture to make old men and women sigh, lamenting their lost years and withered prospects. Only the young laughed like that, when they thought that they could rule the world and their whole lives seemed to spread out before them like a sumptuous carpet.

Bramble stared at it for quite a while, wondering if she recognised the girl. She looked a little like Mary, Bramble's mother, but it couldn't be her because the clothes were too dated, and besides, Mary had never met Lord Penrose. What's more, the woman beside Bill in the wedding picture that Bramble had seen at home was fuller-figured, with a rounder face and that big, curly hair that was fashionable in the late eighties and early nineties. She wasn't smiling either.

She looked lost and a bit miserable, clinging to Bill as if for dear life. Bramble had never liked the picture and rarely dug it out of the album, preferring to imagine her mother as a wild, carefree young thing, the exotic creature too beautiful for this world who had stolen Bill's heart away.

A thought crossed her mind that was at once thrilling and a bit frightening. Could the young girl be Bramble's grandmother, Alice, on the very night that she and Lord Penrose had met and conceived Mary? It might be a fanciful notion, but there was something about that shot, at once intimate and also slightly obsessive, that seemed to suggest there was more going on than simply three friends and one younger person enjoying a sociable evening together. Was Alice, if that was who it was, teasing Lord Penrose, and was he at that very moment determining to have her?

The fourth photo was of a baby in an old-fashioned Silver Cross pram, but it was so far away that you couldn't see the face, only its woolly hat and the hint of a snub nose and downy cheek. Bramble was about to put the snap away when she felt something stuck behind it, another photograph. She eased it off with a finger and it soon dropped down – and she almost gasped in disbelief.

The picture was in colour this time and showed another baby, perhaps six months old, with wispy fair hair, blue eyes and a dimple in her chin. She was wearing a pink summer dress and propped up against some cushions on a tartan rug in the garden, one chubby arm raised as if in greeting, the other clutching a blue toy. She looked happy, this child, and well cared for, obviously loved. Bramble recognised her instantly, and the photograph, too, because there was an identical, larger one in a frame on a windowsill at her parents' house. This baby was herself.

A thousand questions raced through her brain, making it ache. Who had given Lord Penrose the picture? Bramble understood that there'd been no contact between him and her grandmother, Alice, after their brief encounter, and certainly none between him and Mary. Why had he kept the photo hidden away here in his underwear drawer for all these years along with the others, and what, if any, feelings did he have for Bramble, the granddaughter whom he'd never met or shown the slightest interest in?

She didn't hear the door to the bedroom open or Maria walk in, and it was only when the housekeeper spoke that Bramble realised she'd been watching.

'Ah, yes,' she said softly, gazing down at the baby picture. 'He said you took after his mother more than her side of the family. He said you were bonny.'

Her expression was unusually gentle and there was a mistiness in her eyes, or was Bramble imagining it?

'Did he?' She was astonished. 'I didn't think he knew anything about me.'

'Oh, he knew more than you realise. He cared about you very much.'

'He had a funny way of showing it. I'd hardly even heard of him until he died.'

Bramble realised as soon as she'd spoken that it had been the wrong thing to say, for Maria's eyes hardened and her face seemed to shut like a clam.

'That was not his choice,' she said icily. Then: 'Luncheon is served.'

Before Bramble had the chance to reply, she'd turned on her heel and left the room.

Bramble didn't mention the photos to Katie over lunch, partly because Maria might have overheard but also because she wanted time to process her discovery. It was possible, of course, that her grandfather might have tucked the snaps away because he didn't like them, but then why keep them at all? Why not burn the lot? Bramble was almost positive now that the pretty young girl in the first pictures was indeed her grandmother, and that the baby in the Silver Cross pram was Mary. This meant that there must have been some communication between Lord Penrose and her family, yet Bill had never suggested this to be the case and Bramble was certain that he wouldn't lie.

She wanted desperately to call her father, but he would be working now and this wasn't something to discuss in a hurry. There was a great deal more to do upstairs and so she resolved to contact him later.

She and Katie carted bags of rubbish down to the car bit by bit and piled them in, before returning to Lord Penrose's rooms to sort through more of his belongings. Most of the contents of his dressing table were disposed of, while the grooming set went in a suitcase with the items that might fetch something in an antiques shop or at auction. The tatty carpet was rolled up and carted to the car, too, along with the heavy curtains that gave Bramble the creeps. Then, together, the girls stripped the bed and gave the sheets to Maria to launder.

By about five p.m. the rooms had been emptied of virtually everything relating to their former inhabitant and all that was left to do was a thorough clean, which they set to with a vengeance. Wood and mirrors were polished to a gleam, windows washed, shelves dusted, drawers tipped out and thoroughly scrubbed. The girls even managed to push the heavy bed to one side so that Bramble could vacuum underneath.

'Do you know, I might paint the walls and move my stuff

in here,' she said at last, feeling a lightness of spirit as she gazed around at the empty surfaces, the bare floorboards, the wardrobes waiting to be filled.

But Katie wasn't keen. 'It's a long way away from where we're sleeping. I'd be scared on my own.'

Keen to reassure her, Bramble said that they'd redecorate her room, too, and make it really cosy. 'We can't sleep in the same bed for ever. People might talk.'

'What people? There's no one here but us and Maria.'

'Let's have a housewarming party! It's time we cheered the place up!'

At this, Katie's face brightened immediately. Bramble could guess what her friend was thinking. She was imagining Danny coming for dinner; Danny dancing with her on the terrace on a moonlit night, glass of champagne in hand; Danny following her upstairs at the end of the evening to her boudoir...

'Great idea,' she said, clapping her hands. 'The sooner, the better.' She eyed Bramble quizzically. 'Why don't you invite Matt? I bet he'd come for the weekend. He might even decide he likes the place now we've cleaned it up a bit.'

Bramble hesitated. It was true that he'd suggested visiting, but there again he wouldn't get on with Piers, who wasn't his type.

'Nah,' she said quickly. 'Matt usually works Saturdays. It'd be difficult for him to get the time off.'

After that, they agreed to go to the dump and then try to pick up some paint for the bedrooms on the way back if they could find anywhere open. It had stopped raining at last, and as they jumped back in the car it crossed Bramble's mind that they weren't going about things particularly logically, starting one job and moving on to the next before the first was remotely finished. Still, with a huge place like this it was difficult to know where to begin, and at least some progress was being made.

For a moment, she found herself wondering if her grandfather would have approved of their efforts so far, but she dismissed the idea immediately. He'd behaved appallingly towards her grandmother and mother, and the fact that he'd kept her baby photo in his wallet didn't mean a damned thing.

'Hey, Crumble, what's up?'

Crumble was another of Bill's pet names for his daughter, and his pleasure at hearing her voice on the end of the line was palpable.

Now, crashed on the end of Katie's bed, Bramble proceeded to give a blow-by-blow account of their exhausting, action-packed day, including the trip to the refuse centre and their good fortune in finding a late-night DIY discount store on the return journey.

'We got loads of paint,' she informed him proudly. 'All white. We wanted something nice and fresh.'

'Er, emulsion?' he asked, sounding apprehensive.

Bramble knelt down and examined the writing on the side of one of the tins, which the girls had heaved into the bedroom, ready to start work on Lord Penrose's room tomorrow.

'Gloss,' she replied, 'and undercoat. We bought paintbrushes, too, and rollers.'

'You can use gloss on the woodwork, love, the skirtings and doors and that, but you'll need emulsion for the walls.'

Bramble's skin prickled with irritation. 'Nobody told us.'

'Um, did you ask?'

'It's not a problem,' she replied haughtily. 'I've kept all the receipts. We can always swap it.'

Wisely, he decided to let it pass.

'What else is new?' he asked, changing the subject. 'Seen any of them pixies?'

'None.'

'Pining for the bright lights and the big smoke yet?'

'Not really.'

Bill sighed. 'I thought you'd be sick of fields and cows by now.'

There was a rustle in the background and a clink, as if he were fiddling with something, playing for time.

'Matt came over for supper last night,' he went on finally. 'He brought Cassie a lovely plant.'

His fake-nonchalance didn't fool Bramble for a second.

'That's nice,' she replied, feigning casualness herself.

'They've asked him to manage their main fitness centre now. It's a big job. They must think very highly of him.'

'They must,' she repeated, surprised that Matt hadn't told her. There again, he had been trying to get in touch...

'He said he hasn't heard from you for a few days,' Bill persisted, as if reading her mind.

She paused. 'I've been so busy—'

'Don't keep him dangling, love. It's not fair.'

She bristled. First Katie, now her dad. Quite frankly, it was none of their business.

'He's the one who chose not to come, remember?' she said.

'He didn't think you'd like it. He thought you were making a mistake.'

'Well, he was wrong.'

Bill coughed diplomatically before changing tack again, this time to Cassie's most recent and surprising hobby – belly-dancing.

'They're doing a performance on Saturday week at the old

concert hall. She'd love it if you'd come; it would really make her day.'

Bramble shuddered. It was Cassie's friend Sheila who'd signed the women up for a starter course some while ago, allegedly to build their core strength and improve their posture.

'Anyone can do it. It doesn't matter what size you are,' Cassie had declared as she'd headed off to her first class in black yoga pants and a baggy white T-shirt, clutching a spangly hip scarf.

At the time Bramble had been supportive, but she felt now that witnessing her stepmother in action might be a step too far.

'I can't...' she started to say, remembering the miserable hours she'd spent as a child on rickety chairs in draughty church halls watching Cassie in oratorios, and later in a gospel choir. It had felt like torture then, but at least the belly had been kept well hidden.

'I know it's a long way,' Bill wheedled, 'but it would mean such a lot to her. She misses you something dreadful. We both do.'

A groan rumbled at the back of Bramble's throat. She loved both of her parents more than anything; even thinking about them made her feel guilty. And she didn't really have an excuse, did she? She hadn't planned on returning to London so soon, but the weekend after next was free at the moment, and it was true, it would give Cassie so much joy.

'All right, I'll come,' she promised. 'But I'll have to drive back on Sunday morning. I've got a ridiculous amount to do here.'

'That's wonderful!' Bill chirped, his cup overflowing.

It was a shame, Bramble thought, that there'd be no time for her and Matt to see each other, but then again, Cassie's first public appearance with the Chessington Daughters of the

Silk Rose Belly-dance Troupe would hardly be the occasion for a heart-to-heart.

While her father chattered happily about how excited Cassie would be, what he'd make for supper and so on, Bramble walked over to the chest of drawers where she kept some of her clothes and pulled out the photos that she'd found in her grandfather's room. She was a little nervous about broaching the subject, but felt that she had a right to know the truth.

'Dad?' she said tentatively, before going on to explain her discovery. 'Am I right – is the girl in the pictures my grandmother? And how did he get the photos of my mother and me?'

Bill cleared his throat noisily and Bramble could imagine him at the other end of the line, his whiskery grey eyebrows knitting together like a couple of caterpillars.

'Look, love,' he said, 'I wasn't going to tell you but...' He sighed again. 'I guess you're old enough now...'

Bramble's heart pitter-pattered and, taking a deep breath, she straightened her shoulders, trying to tell herself that she was a woman now, and mistress of a manor no less. The past was over and done with, but unless you could unlock its secrets, it was difficult to understand the present or look to the future.

'Go on,' she said, sounding braver than she felt. 'I want to know.'

'You see Mary, your mum, she decided to get in touch with Lord Penrose after you were born,' Bill began.

This was news to Bramble.

'She wrote to him,' Bill continued, 'and sent him some photographs that Alice had given her. I guess the one of you, too.' He hesitated, as if gathering mental strength. 'I didn't see what she wrote, but she received a letter back from him not long after. Just a short note it was. She wouldn't show it to me. I – I don't know what she did with it,' he stammered, 'probably threw it away.'

There was another pause and Bramble waited expectantly.

'All I do know is, it upset your mum terribly. Inconsolable she was, for days. Drinking, crying, crying, drinking. That's all she did. From that moment her drinking got much worse than it had ever been, ten times worse. I didn't know what to do, how to help her. It wasn't long after that she died. I don't believe she would've if it hadn't been for *him*. Before that letter I could still talk to her, still get through to her just about, and she loved you...'

There was a catch in his voice and tears pricked in Bramble's eyes, too. She wished that she could burrow into her father's arms, where she'd always felt so safe, because she needed comforting right now.

'Whatever was in it sent her over the edge,' he explained, collecting himself a little. 'I didn't want to tell you. I didn't want to upset you or make you hate your grandfather any more than you already do. He was your own flesh and blood, after all, and it didn't seem right. But as far as I'm concerned, that man killed your mum as sure as if he'd held a knife to her chest and driven it in himself. He was wicked, inhuman. That's why I didn't want you to have anything to do with him or that godforsaken manor of his.'

Bramble's mind was racing. Her father's account was entirely plausible, but it didn't explain why the old earl had kept the photos in his underwear drawer. Bill, however, couldn't help.

'He was weird, twisted. Maybe it gave him satisfaction to take the pictures out and look at them and know that he'd wrecked Alice's and Mary's lives. Maybe that's what kept him going all those years.'

He made Lord Penrose sound like a monster, the devil incarnate, yet the description didn't seem to tally with the man who'd lovingly sketched the view from his bedroom window, the vase of flowers, the cat at his feet lazily washing its paws.

'I guess we'll never know the full truth,' Bramble said sadly, staring once more at the photos in her left hand. 'One more thing: do you know who took the close-up of Alice laughing?'

'He did,' her father replied savagely. 'Mary told me. With Alice's parents' camera. One of them servants must have taken the others. According to your mum, he asked Alice to pose for him. Like some filthy pervert...' Bill growled. 'The parents should never have allowed it. He was old enough to be her dad.'

The harsh words made Bramble shiver, yet there was one thing that slightly baffled her. The liaison was undoubtedly scandalous, given the age gap, and so the story went her grand-father had seduced the defenceless Alice before abandoning her. However, the young woman in the photographs seemed quite worldly for her years – playful, almost coquettish. Had there been a bit more to the brief relationship than history would have her believe? Had they, in fact, really rather liked one another, rather than the attraction being all one-way?

In any case, it wasn't something to raise with Bill, who wouldn't have examined the close-up as carefully as Bramble had; nor, for that matter, had he prowled around the earl's rooms, inhaling the same atmosphere that he once breathed, touching the objects that he once handled, absorbing some-thing of his habits and starting to form a sense of the real man.

She wound up the conversation, but despite being exhausted it took her a long time to get to sleep that night. She lay awake beside Katie, listening to the strange noises of grumbling pipes and creeping floorboards, the far-off hoot of an owl, the high-pitched howling of foxes. It seemed to her as if the ghosts of Alice and Lord Penrose were pacing about the manor, lurking in corners, occupying chairs, moving familiar objects around before replacing them in their original positions, whispering things – important things – that she so much wanted to understand.

Chapter Twelve

IT WAS AROUND six the following morning that Liz received the call from Pat's niece, Emily. Liz had been fast asleep beside Robert and it had taken her a few moments to work out where the noise was coming from.

'I – I'm so sorry to have to tell you,' Emily stammered when Liz picked up the receiver. Her stomach lurched. 'I got a call at about three a.m. from the hospital telling me to come quickly. She'd had another heart attack. They tried to get it started again but they couldn't. Pat's dead.'

The words plummeted like a bird from the sky and Liz's knees almost gave way. She was on the landing and staggered back into the bedroom, still clutching the phone, before plonking down beside her husband. He was sitting bolt upright, looking at her anxiously, but she shook her head, gesturing to him not to speak.

'Oh, God, I can't believe it,' she told Emily heavily. 'This is such a shock. I can't take it in.'

The two women had spoken late yesterday evening, just before Emily had left the hospital, having been told that Pat had suffered a heart attack but was in a stable condition and everything was under control.

'Rosie will be devastated,' Liz went on as the tears started to flow thick and fast. 'We're going to miss her so much. The village won't be the same without her.'

Emily, who was crying, too, took a moment to gather herself.

'You've been so good to her,' she started to say, but Liz stopped her.

'Don't – please. She's been like a grandmother to Rosie. We didn't know anyone when we came here. She was so kind…'

Images sprang to mind of Pat at her front window, looking out over her knick-knacks and waving at passers-by; Pat shuffling into the kitchen to fetch tea and chockie bickies; Pat cuddling Rosie in the big armchair in front of the TV that they used to share at Dove Cottage when Liz went to work at the restaurant. The old woman had been a mainstay in their lives for so long, always ready with a gentle word, some homespun advice, a piece of juicy gossip. How on earth were they going to manage without her?

'I've got to deal with some things here before I go home,' Emily said wearily. 'I haven't had much sleep, as you can imagine.'

Liz asked if she could help, imagining that there must be paperwork to fill in, effects to be gathered, whatever ghastly practical tasks had to be completed when someone passed away, but Emily said no, not at the moment.

'I'd like to talk to you about the funeral – when the time comes,' she added, and Liz shuddered. Funeral? Was this for real?

'Of course.' She was trying to compose herself while the very ground beneath her seemed to tremble. 'Look after yourself…'

But Emily, too upset for further discussion, had already gone.

Robert opened his arms wide and Liz melted in, allowing him to wrap her in a tight embrace.

'Poor Pat, poor darling,' he said, kissing the top of his wife's head, his body firm and still, absorbing the shudders that now racked her own.

He knew not to try to stop her tears; they needed to flow as surely as a wound must bleed before it can heal over.

'I never said goodbye,' Liz spluttered. 'It never crossed my mind that I wouldn't see her again.'

Robert did his best to comfort her. 'You did everything you could. She was very old...'

'But so funny and sharp,' Liz cried. 'So interested in everything and everybody – so very much *alive*.'

Age seemed irrelevant when you were still enjoying life and had something to give. What was it but a number, after all? Liz could think of people, old and young, who moaned and grumbled all day long and seemed to find no pleasure in anything. Pat, however, despite her aches and pains, had continued to embrace existence with gusto. It wasn't fair.

They didn't notice Rosie enter the room and hover for a moment, taking in the scene, before jumping on to the bed between Robert and her mother and curling like a small animal into their sides.

'Pat's dead, isn't she?' Rosie whispered, and when Liz said yes, her daughter burst into uncontrollable sobs and all that Robert could do was rock his girls gently to and fro.

When at last they could shed no more tears, Liz rose and walked to the window to draw back the curtains. She was amazed to see the sun already shining on the whitewashed cottages across the street, making them glint and sparkle. Normally, she loved the bright pink and red geraniums and blue lobelias that hung in baskets and peeped from window boxes, but they seemed like an outrage today, the cheerful seagulls and jolly red-and-white bunting an affront to decency.

Why was the world not in black mourning clothes? It should be, for Pat was gone.

Her eyes stung and her face felt tight with misery as she tramped slowly downstairs to switch on the kettle. Emily lived some miles away, and Liz supposed that it would be her job to tell the villagers what had happened. The outpouring of grief would be immense, because Pat had been adored – not least by Loveday, with whom she'd had a special bond. Tabitha, too, would be dreadfully upset, and Jean the childminder and her husband, Tom, Esme – everyone really, for the old woman had touched the lives of so many.

In all her years, Liz mused as she plopped teabags mindlessly into three mugs, Pat had barely stirred outside the narrow confines of Tremarnock. She'd never been abroad, never even been to London. She'd left school at fourteen and had worked in the grocery store until she'd retired. She'd hardly read any books and knew little of science or the arts; she couldn't even spell particularly well. Yet despite all this, locals valued her opinion and had always come to her for advice. In fact, she'd seemed, in her own unique way, to possess the wisdom of the world.

Bramble and Katie rose at about seven thirty a.m., and after a quick breakfast of cereal and toast in the dining room, they carried most of the tins of gloss back to the car and drove to the DIY store to swap them for emulsion. On returning, they dug out the oldest clothes they could find and set about dragging Lord Penrose's heavy furniture into the centre of his bedroom so that they could begin painting the walls and skirting boards.

Although neither girl knew much about decorating,

Bramble had at least helped her father do up the living room at home, so she was acquainted with turpentine and had been told how to spread the paint evenly across the walls. Katie, however, was clueless.

'How do you get it in the pot?' she asked, eyeing her roller doubtfully, and Bramble had to explain that you poured the emulsion into the tray first. It wasn't a great start.

Once they'd opened the windows wide to allow in some fresh air, they turned up the radio volume to lift their spirits. They started work side by side but kept bumping into each other, so Bramble suggested that it might be easier if Katie were to move to the opposite wall.

'This is simpler than I thought,' she chirped after about ten minutes, but when Bramble swivelled around, her heart sank.

'Look, I know this is only the first coat but you need to cover all the green,' she said, trying hard to be patient – and reminding herself somewhat of her father. 'Otherwise it'll look patchy.'

'Oh.' Katie bent down and dipped one corner of her roller in the gloopy tray.

'And you need to cover the whole roller,' Bramble went on bossily. 'Like I showed you, remember?'

Katie dutifully obliged, her tongue sticking out of the corner of her mouth in concentration, but a big splat fell on the wooden floor – 'Whoops!' – and she tried to wipe it off with a rag, only to smear it across a larger section.

Bramble turned back to her own work, thinking that however amateur the job might be, at least the room would be fresher and more liveable in than before. She couldn't have considered moving in otherwise.

By mid-morning they'd covered all the walls with the undercoat and started on the ceiling, taking it in turns to perch on the same ladder that Katie had used to chop down bushes in the garden. They were both ready for a break, so it was quite a relief when Bramble's mobile rang, and even more gratifying when she saw Piers's name flash up on the screen.

Quickly, she wiped her paint-covered hands on her jeans and pressed the answer button. It was noisy in the background, as if he were in his car, perhaps with the roof down, and she felt slightly wistful, wishing that she were beside him.

'Hey,' he said silkily, raising his voice so that she could hear him above the roar. 'Not been tempted to get that mower out again, I hope?'

'I've learned my lesson,' Bramble replied, smiling, before explaining that she was redecorating her grandfather's old bedroom, ready for her to move in.

'Are you now?' Piers sounded amused. 'You'll have to give me a guided tour when it's finished.'

He was flirting with her! Bramble smiled again. She could play that game, too.

'That depends,' she said, being deliberately mysterious.

Piers sounded interested. 'On what exactly?'

'On whether you behave...'

She glanced at Katie, who'd flopped on to the bed and was now lying there, eyes closed, limbs spread-eagled, looking for all the world as if she were ready for a nice long snooze.

'That's if we ever actually *do* finish. Which looks a bit doubtful at the moment.'

She thought that she could hear a voice in the background and a woman's laugh. She would have liked to ask who she was and where Piers was heading, but she didn't want to appear nosy. He could have been going anywhere, after all, and it was very good of him to call.

'Listen, I've got some information for you,' he shouted

over the roar of the engine. 'That artist fellow in the cottage –
he's not paying any rent. No wonder Lord Penrose was skint.
He was giving the place away!'

Bramble frowned. 'Are you sure?' It sounded highly
unlikely, but Piers confirmed that Fergus had indeed been
'freeloading', as he put it, for nearly five years.

'The earl was fully aware; it wasn't a mistake,' he went on.
'I've seen the contract, signed by them both, giving him permission to live there gratis. The good news is, now the earl's
dead the contract's null and void, so you've got every right to
demand proper rent or kick him out. I'll do it for you with
pleasure. I can go and see him first thing tomorrow if you like.'

Bramble hesitated. She wasn't running a charity and needed
every penny she could lay her hands on. There again, Fergus
had twice got her out of trouble and there was the little boy
to consider, too. Her tenant might be bad-tempered, but she
wasn't heartless. The cottage was his home, and she wouldn't
threaten to turf him out until he'd found somewhere else
to live.

'It's OK. I'll do it,' she replied, thinking that however kind
she tried to be, there was no getting away from the fact that
it wouldn't be a pleasant job.

'Are you sure?' Piers seemed doubtful. 'You don't want any
trouble.'

'I'll be fine,' Bramble insisted, sounding more confident
than she felt. 'He won't bite.'

The woman in the background said something and there
was another loud burst of laughter. Bramble thought that Piers
would probably hang up, but then he mentioned that he'd
found someone to fix the leaks in the manor roof.

'Remember Anatole?'

How could she forget? Those turquoise Speedos, that hairy

body – and the girlfriend, come to that. She listened closely while Piers explained that his friend was 'getting into property', buying places on the cheap and doing them up, and that he had a team of excellent builders.

'He doesn't normally do repairs – he's into the bigger picture – but because it's you, he said he'd be willing to help. If you're nice to him, he might even do some other jobs for you. Play your cards right and you could find him very useful.'

Bramble was immensely grateful, but had to remind Piers that she didn't have the money to pay anyone right now, not until she'd managed to sell some of her land. He, however, brushed her concerns away.

'Anatole's a reasonable chap. I should know; we've been friends for years. He'll be quite happy to wait for payment till your cash comes through. It's not as if he's short of a bob or two. I can't imagine why I didn't think of him before.'

It sounded like a very good offer and she *was* anxious to fix the leaks, but the prospect of spending money that she didn't yet have was scary.

'How long do you reckon it will it take to find buyers for the land?' she wanted to know. 'I mean, what progress have you made so far? Are we talking weeks or months?'

'Don't worry,' Piers reassured her. 'It's all in hand.' Then he announced that he had to go. 'More clients to see. No rest for the wicked.'

She was about to ask where the clients lived and what the job entailed, but he cut her short.

'Sorry, gotta fly. Anatole's guys will arrive soon. He'll give you a bell first. Byee!'

After that it required a great deal of energy to persuade Katie to get up and continue painting, and Bramble felt that it would be prudent not to mention the builders just now.

After all, Katie hadn't exactly been taken with Anatole. In fact, she'd positively taken against him.

When at last they'd completed the ceiling, Bramble agreed to call it a day and resume work in the morning, not least because Katie was doing another shift at The Hole in the Wall tonight and had already announced that she'd need time to get ready. A *lot* of time, Bramble mused wryly, remembering Danny. Hair, nails, make-up, outfit – they'd all require careful thought and extensive planning.

She set off on her own at about four p.m. for Fergus's cottage, leaving Katie to begin her preparations. It was the first time that Bramble had been out for hours, and the ground had completely dried after yesterday's thunderstorm and the air felt fresh and clean.

She had already resolved to try to avoid confrontation at all costs by putting Fergus fully in the picture about her tricky financial situation, something that she was sure he'd understand. Even so, her heart sank as she left the cover of the wood and the stone cottage came into view. The fact that it looked extra-homely today, with the door and windows flung wide open and a child's bike lying on its side on the path, only seemed to make matters worse.

A couple of hens and a very handsome red and black cockerel were pecking about on the lawn and a line of coloured washing spun merrily on a rotary airer. It would have been a picture of perfect domesticity were the house not perched so precariously on the edge of the cliff with just a small strip of garden between it and the roaring waves. As she walked tentatively towards the gate, Bramble found herself thinking that no *normal* person would choose to live in such an exposed spot; she wouldn't fancy it.

She called hello a few times at the door, and when there

was no reply she stepped inside. There was a faint smell of cooking and she peeked curiously into the square kitchen to her right, noticing a scrubbed wooden table in the centre, grey flagstones on the floor and an old cream Aga. No one was there, however, so she ventured into the living room on the opposite side, taking in the furniture: a squashy green sofa, one armchair, a chrome standard lamp and a small TV. It might have seemed sparse but for the fact that the walls were covered in bold abstract paintings.

As far as she could tell, most of the pictures related to the sea and boats, but her eye was caught by one large-ish portrait of a nude, sinewy woman with thick black hair, her body painted greenish-blue. She was reclining on a blue-grey surface and beside her, nestling in the crook of her arm, was an almost identical child, a mini-me. Their skin tones were so alike, their limbs so soft and fluid, that they seemed almost to blend into each other as well as the background, making it difficult to tell where one finished and the other began.

It was, in some ways, a beautiful image, yet both faces were devoid of features, as if eyes, noses and mouths had been washed away casually with a brush or cloth that had erased parts of the shoulders, too. Bramble got the strange impression that soon other bits would start to vanish, too, so that the figures would eventually blur into nothing more than a series of messy smudges, as if their creator had grown bored with his work and decided to destroy it.

She heard a noise and started guiltily, aware that she was trespassing. Stepping quickly into the hallway once more, she called out hello again, and this time a thud of feet told her that someone was running downstairs. Soon Fergus's son appeared, clutching a half-finished model in one hand and pieces of Lego in the other.

'What are you doing?' he asked, not impolitely. 'My daddy's in his studio.'

'Is he? I'm Bramble by the way,' she answered. 'I live in the manor.' She gestured in the general direction.

'I know. You and your friend got stuck on the cliff and we had to rescue you,' the little boy replied matter-of-factly, fixing a bit of Lego on to the side of his model.

Wincing slightly, Bramble was tempted to challenge the boy's interpretation of events but decided against it. Best not to engage in an argument unless you had truth firmly on your side.

'My name's Wilf,' said the lad, before thrusting out the Lego toy to show her. 'Look what I'm making. I've nearly finished.'

Bramble took the model and carefully turned it over in her hands. It was an aeroplane, or spaceship perhaps, with two little doors that opened at the side and a tiny man in a helmet sitting in the cockpit.

'You're very clever!'

Pleased, Wilf took the model back and proceeded to fish the little figure out of his seat.

'He's the pilot. He's called Ben. His hat comes off, but there's a hole in his head.' He pulled off the helmet to show her.

'Eeuw!' Bramble laughed. 'He's got no hair! He needs a wig!'

The boy considered this for a moment. 'Hang on! I might have some hair for him in my bedroom. I could run up and get it?'

Bramble was quite interested. In fact, she'd rather like to sit beside Wilf on his bedroom floor and construct a sister ship; she used to love Lego as a child. But she had a mission to accomplish, and the longer she delayed, the more daunting it would become.

'Actually, I'm in a bit of a hurry,' she said – a fib; she had nothing much to do for the rest of the day. 'I need to speak to your father. Can you show me where he is?'

She looked down the hallway through a half-open door at the end, expecting to see some evidence of a studio with Fergus inside, but there was only a cloakroom.

'All right,' said the boy cheerfully. 'It's not far.'

Without further ado, he slipped his hand into hers and led her purposefully past the cockerel and hens, out of a little gate in the bottom right-hand corner of the front garden and along a narrow track that led towards an area of dense, spiky bushes that were invisible from the house.

'What a handy path!' Bramble commented, noticing that the grass on either side was very tall and would have been difficult to get through.

'My daddy made it and I helped him. You can get to the studio along the cliff as well, but I'm not allowed that way.'

The track continued through the crop of spiky bushes, and as soon as they reached the other side Bramble spotted a low-lying, rectangular cabin with a dove-grey door and a wooden deck facing the ocean. It was a very peaceful setting and deliciously private.

'That's it!' Wilf pointed. 'That's his studio. Sometimes I do painting in there, too.'

'You go first,' Bramble said, suddenly remembering why she was here. 'D'you think he'll mind being disturbed?'

The boy paused, tipping his head to one side. 'We-ell, he doesn't like interruptions. But I s'pect he won't be too cross if you're really, really quick. I'm allowed in whenever I want,' he added rather smugly. 'I don't even have to knock.'

Not exactly heartened by this information, Bramble rapped tentatively on the wooden door. There was silence for a few moments, then she heard the thud of heavy feet and the door swung open.

'Wilf, why can't you—?'

On catching sight of Bramble, Fergus stopped mid-sentence and his expression turned from mild irritation to profound displeasure.

'I can't talk to you now,' he barked. 'Didn't my son tell you I'm working?'

It was perfectly obvious that he was speaking the truth, because from the top of his head right down to his T-shirt, jeans and tatty old trainers he was covered in splats of paint in different colours – orange, yellow, green, blue, black, red and white. There was even a blob on his nose, and Bramble couldn't help laughing despite herself.

'Aren't you supposed to get the paint on the canvas rather than on you?' she giggled. It just popped out. 'You look like a work of art! You should go on display!'

'I don't know what you mean,' said Fergus grumpily. He wiped his cheek with a forearm but it was covered in paint, too, a bright turquoise that blended with all the other colours into a sludgy brownish-blue.

This only made Bramble laugh more. 'It's all over your face now. You'll get it in your eyes.' And without thinking, she fished into the pocket of her shorts and stepped forward brandishing a bundle of tissues.

Understanding too late what was happening, Fergus tried to jerk his head away, but she'd already put a hand around the back to hold it firmly in place. There was nothing for it but to resign himself to his fate, so he closed his eyes, muttering 'absurd' and 'unnecessary' under his breath in a bid to salvage some dignity.

Bramble had to stand on tiptoes to get at some of the

offending blobs with clean bits of handkerchief, and after a while he stopped muttering and they both went quiet. In her case, this was to avoid jabbing him by mistake, but she soon forgot what she was doing and found her attention drawn to his unusual features – the dark eyebrows framing deep-set sockets; the bony section on the bridge of his nose; the high, prominent cheekbones that hinted, perhaps, at some Slavic influence; the surprisingly vulnerable lower lip with a small, pale scar in the middle.

He was naturally dark-skinned, and there was a stillness about him, not just in his expression but in his physical presence, too, a strength and intensity that made her think of rock and tree, earth, sky and ocean. She couldn't imagine him in a city because he seemed like part of the landscape he painted: beautiful in a way, yet damaged. To her surprise, she felt curious and wanted to know more.

At one point his eyes flickered open, perhaps to see if she'd nearly finished, and accidentally met her own. Startled, Bramble looked away quickly, but not before she'd registered their unexpected depth. He remained rooted to the spot after that, swallowing a few times as if to break the tension, and she became so engrossed that she was almost sorry when the tissue was all used up and there was no excuse to carry on. The worst of the paint was off anyway.

'There,' she said, making light of what had happened. 'That's most of it gone, you mucky pup!'

Wilf, who'd been watching the proceedings with interest, hopped up and down on the spot. 'He is, isn't he? Mucky Daddy, Mucky Pup!'

'Pipe down,' Fergus retorted, but the boy took absolutely no notice.

'You've got paint all over you. You're messy, messy, MESSY!'

he squealed in delight while his father looked on, exasperated, his authority having melted clean away.

When at last the boy stopped jeering and calmed down, Fergus whistled through his teeth.

'Thank God for that. I thought he'd never shut up.'

But was there a slight smile playing on his lips? Bramble wasn't sure. In any case, he seemed less angry now, and having had his afternoon well and truly disrupted, he decided to invite her in.

'The light was beautiful before you came,' he said reproachfully as he led her into a big rectangular room looking out over the ocean. 'It's gone now.'

Bramble gazed around with interest. She could see that he'd been working on a large canvas that was propped up on an easel in the centre of the studio. There was a dust sheet on the floor and in places, where it had ridden up, the wooden boards were splattered with thick, wet paint.

To the right was a long trestle table, on which were placed probably hundreds of little tubes of colour, every shade under the sun, along with plastic bottles of strange-looking liquids, old jam jars, tinfoil cartons, bits of rag and a large assortment of different-sized brushes. The display appeared at first to be extremely untidy, but then Bramble saw that there was a logic to it. The foil cartons, though crumpled and stained, were stacked together with those of a similar size, and the tubes of paint were lined up in rows, suggesting that the artist, if no one else, knew what he was doing.

Her eyes now slid to the end of the room where the glass doors were wide open, revealing glorious, unspoilt views, and then to the walls, leaning against which were numerous half-finished paintings that she longed to pore over and ask questions about. There was a scent of turpentine, and an atmosphere of industry and focus that she found appealing. She felt quite guilty for having disturbed it.

'Sit down,' Fergus said awkwardly, pointing to a paint-splashed stool beside the central canvas. When she looked at it doubtfully, he pulled up another, clean, one on which she settled gratefully.

'Do you want coffee?'

It wasn't the politest of requests but she accepted gladly, not least because it would delay the dreaded moment when she'd have to explain why she'd come.

'Lovely. Thanks. White, no sugar.'

'I'll have orange,' Wilf said, crouching happily by her side, still clutching the Lego toy.

Fergus strode next door to fill the kettle, and soon the boy was scuttling from one painting to another, explaining what was what.

'That's called "Sea Breeze",' he said, pointing to a misty-grey canvas with patches of yellowish-white sunlight glinting on the waves. 'And that's "Treasure Chest".' This time there was a hint of gold in the murky depths, a suggestion of rubies and other precious stones hiding behind rocks and beneath fronds of brownish-green seaweed.

'Does this one have a name?' Bramble asked, gesturing to the painting on the easel, which once more seemed to focus on the effects of light on water, clearly a favourite theme.

'I don't think so,' said Wilf, considering. 'Not yet anyway.'

The picture captured beautifully the view from the window at this particular moment in time as the sun, still high in the sky, seemed to flood the frame with hot, rich colour, turning the surface of the water below a glorious shade of orangey-red. Yet there was a sinister side, too, for not far beneath the waves the colour faded into swirling darkness, a chasm where light could not penetrate. The more Bramble stared, the more threatening it became; it made her shiver.

'Do you always paint the sea?' she asked when Fergus returned, carrying two mugs in one hand and a glass of juice in the other. 'I mean, do you ever pick other subjects?'

It seemed an innocent enough question, but he either didn't hear or chose to ignore her, passing her a mug of coffee and standing upright as he took a sip of his own.

She tried another tack. 'Have you lived in Cornwall all your life?'

He didn't move and there was no response, but fortunately Wilf came to the rescue.

'He went to art school in London,' he said brightly. 'It's where he met my mum—'

'That's enough,' Fergus interrupted, and the little boy's mouth clamped shut.

'I was born here,' the artist continued brusquely. 'I wouldn't be anywhere else.'

It was perfectly clear that he didn't wish to elaborate, so Bramble decided to move on.

'I'd never lived in the country before. I think it's going to take me a while to get used to it.'

Now that he was no longer the focus, Fergus seemed to relax a little and at last he sat down on the paint-covered stool beside her, his feet resting on the wooden rung beneath. Hunched like that over his mug, his shoulders wide, knees jutting, hands big and powerful, he reminded her rather of a giant statue hewn out of a slab of rock or marble, visually appealing but cold and impenetrable.

'How are you liking the manor?' he asked slowly, staring at the floor. She was about to reply when he glanced up through his dark eyebrows and lashes. 'Finished doing the garden yet?'

His expression hadn't altered one bit, but for some reason she had the uneasy feeling that he was laughing at her, and instinctively she raised her chin.

'Not yet. We've switched to decorating now.'

Fergus took another swig of his drink and nodded sagely. 'There are a lot of walls to cover. Hundreds, I shouldn't wonder. I should think you could do with a bit of help.'

It was hard to tell if this were just a statement of fact or some odd, inverted offer, but in any case she didn't want him involved, not after the way he'd barked at her by the cliff and in the orchard. He'd probably try to take over, and besides, she was about to tell him that he needed to get out or pay up, a task that she was dreading more as each minute ticked by.

She decided that now was the perfect moment. Bracing herself, she cleared her throat and then spoke in her most businesslike tone of voice.

'I want to talk to you about our arrangement.'

He looked at her steadily. 'Oh yes?'

'I... I thought it would be sensible to discuss it sooner rather than later.'

'I see.' He wasn't going to help her out, not one bit.

She opened her mouth, but to her dismay nothing emerged. Then Wilf, who'd been sitting cross-legged on the floor, slurping his juice, jumped up and wriggled on to his dad's lap, twining an arm around the back of his neck. There was hardly room for one man on the stool, let alone a man and boy, and Fergus had to hold tight to stop him slipping off. Then he bent and kissed the boy's soft hair ever so gently. He probably wasn't even aware that he was doing it.

The boy smiled contentedly, and after a time he dropped his arm while Fergus rested his chin on his son's head.

'What arrangement is that then?' he asked at last, picking up the conversation where they'd left off.

Bramble took a deep breath. 'Never mind. I can't remember what I was going to say anyway.'

Wilf looked so happy and secure, sitting there in his father's arms, that she hadn't the heart to bring bad news. She'd simply have to come up with an alternative money-making scheme.

As she hadn't quite finished her coffee, she decided to risk trying to find out a bit more about her tenant before she left. Hoping to put him at his ease, she started to tell him about Katie's job at The Hole in the Wall and its landlord, Danny.

'Do you know him?' she asked, but Fergus shook his head.

'I don't mix much with the locals.' He ruffled his son's hair. 'We're quite happy on our own, aren't we, Wilf?'

The boy nodded while fixing Bramble with his bright-blue eyes. 'Do *you* like being on your own?'

'Not much,' she admitted. 'I'll probably sit in the pub tonight and watch Katie. Either that or go to bed. I don't like being around Maria on my own. She's the housekeeper. She's very scary.'

To her astonishment Fergus laughed out loud. It was the first time that she'd heard him do it.

'Oh, she's all right really. Her bark's worse than her bite.'

But Bramble wasn't having any of it. 'She's like The Woman in Black, the way she lurks round corners and appears out of nowhere. I think she might be a witch in disguise.'

It was only after she'd finished speaking that she realised what he'd said a moment before.

'Do you know her?' she asked suddenly. 'Personally, I mean?'

'A little. Your grandfather was fond of her. She was very loyal.'

'And what about Lord Penrose? How well did you know him?'

His smile vanished and the shutters came down over his eyes. 'I'd rather not talk about it.'

Bramble could have kicked herself. She should have guessed by now that it would take more than a quick chat over coffee to draw Fergus out. Remembering her discussion with Katie about having a party in the manor, she decided to try something else.

'We haven't fixed a date yet, but it'd be great if you could come. And Wilf, of course.'

'I'm not into socialising. We lead a very quiet life here, which suits us just fine.'

Wilf, though, had other ideas. 'Please, Daddy! I like parties.'

Spotting an opening, Bramble waded in. 'He can bring a friend if he likes? There are so many rooms in the manor – it'll be brilliant for hide and seek!'

The boy immediately announced that he'd bring Loppy, his stuffed rabbit, and she was surprised that he'd choose a cuddly toy over a real person. There again, they did seem to lead an awfully isolated existence up here. It might do him good to be in company for a change.

Still, Fergus hadn't accepted the invitation yet.

'Do come,' Bramble urged. 'I'm a rubbish cook – I burn everything – but Katie's brilliant. She'll probably make fish pie. I might do Eton mess for pudding. It's quite difficult to ruin.' She paused. 'I did manage it once, though, when I added salt instead of sugar...'

'How can I resist an offer like that?' he said wryly.

It was Wilf who clinched the deal.

'Hurray!' he shouted, jumping up and doing a silly dance in front of them. 'Will there be games like pass the parcel?'

'I'll see what we can do,' Bramble promised.

It was early evening by the time she said goodbye, and Fergus and Wilf walked with her to the cottage and stood together by the gate, waving. As she headed back across the fields, it occurred to her that pass the parcel wasn't quite what Katie had had in mind when they discussed the gathering. It might interfere with her plans to seduce Danny. Come to think of it, it might interfere with Bramble's designs on Piers, too.

Putting Piers and Fergus together in the same room might not be the cleverest idea either, given that the land agent did rather seem to have taken against her unusual tenant. There again, she could always position the men at opposite ends of the dinner table, and it would surely be worth a few raised hackles if some drinks were to loosen Fergus's tongue.

Chapter Thirteen

BRAMBLE WOULD HAVE suggested sending out party invitations straight away, but when she and Katie heard about Pat, they decided to postpone it till after the funeral. Neither girl had known the old woman, but it was clear that she'd been much loved and would be sorely missed. Indeed, the whole village seemed to be in mourning.

On Friday evening, The Hole in the Wall was much quieter than usual and even Tony was distinctly subdued when he, Felipe and Rafael popped in for a drink at around eight.

'I never thought she'd *die*,' Bramble overheard Felipe say shakily. 'One minute she is here with us, then poof' – he clicked his fingers – 'she is gone in a puff of smoke.'

'That's life, isn't it?' Tony responded gloomily, while Rafael swigged his drink through a straw and stared into the middle distance. Then Tony puffed out his chest and boomed, '"Golden lads and girls all must, as chimney-sweepers, come to dust."'

He looked as if he might burst into tears, until he spotted Bramble sitting quietly in a corner, pretending to read a book.

'Come and join us!' he cried, beckoning her over. 'Heard the dreadful news? We all need cheering up.'

Pleased to have someone to talk to, Bramble moved her

drink to the men's table and mentioned that she'd called in on Fergus two days ago.

This seemed to brighten Tony no end. 'What do you make of him?' he asked, forgetting Pat for a moment and shuffling closer. 'Bit of an odd fellow, isn't he? I see him coming and going but he never stops for a chat. Doesn't seem to like company. Can't work him out at all.'

Rafael, who was sitting on Bramble's other side, fiddled with an earring and jiggled his leg up and down as she described the studio and paintings. Having never met the artist, it was hardly surprising that he hadn't the slightest interest. When he'd finished his drink, he stretched noisily and announced that he was tired and wanted to go home.

'Do you have your key?' Tony asked and, rising, the teenager patted the pocket of his black jeans and nodded.

As he strolled towards the exit, staring at his feet, he almost bumped into Audrey, with Rick in tow.

'Excuse *me*!' she snapped, glaring at the young man as he slunk past. When he failed to reply she hissed, 'Rude boy', and poked Rick with an impatient finger.

'Isn't he?' she demanded, and Rick nodded miserably. She hadn't yet noticed Tony and Felipe, and when their eyes finally met she pursed her glossy red lips and glanced the other way.

'Bitch,' Tony muttered under his breath, and Bramble thought it was just as well that Audrey hadn't heard. She looked so formidable – tall and broad-shouldered, in a startling red polka-dot top and big gold necklace – that she'd probably be a match for both Tony and Felipe put together. She did have awfully long red nails, too.

'Shh!' Bramble whispered, giggling with nerves. 'She'll have your guts for garters!'

'Just let her try,' Tony replied. 'Felipe did boxing at school, didn't you, darling?'

The Brazilian frowned. 'But I do not think I can punch a woman, even one who is a...' He grinned mischievously. 'How you say? She-zombie.'

'Devil,' Tony replied patiently. 'She-*devil*, though actually zombie's more graphic.'

Katie came out from behind the bar to collect some dirty glasses from the table next door and stopped for a brief chat. She was looking gorgeous, even in the pub's regulation red T-shirt and jeans, with silky dark hair that had been ironed dead straight and her favourite silver jewellery. On her feet were pale-tan wedge espadrilles that gave her extra height, and her carefully made-up face was glowing. The most startling thing about her, however, was her fake black eyelashes, which were so thick and lush they seemed to have a life of their own.

'We're all devastated,' Tony said sonorously when Katie mentioned Pat. 'Liz and poor little Rosie are beside themselves, and Esme's hardly left her flat. As for Loveday, she's barely stopped crying since she heard the news. She's practically drowning in tears.'

He didn't notice Katie turn and stare when Tabitha sashayed in and Danny hurried out from behind the bar to greet her. He pulled out a stool and settled down beside her, whispering something in her ear that made her smile. Bramble, though, saw it all, as well as the look on Katie's face as she watched them. After a few moments she tossed her hair and waltzed back to the bar as if she hadn't a care in the world, but Bramble knew better.

'Can I get either of you a drink?' she heard Katie ask sweetly, resting her slim arms on the counter and showing off her silver bangles to full advantage, but Bramble couldn't hear the response. Perhaps Tabitha and Danny hadn't heard either, because they hardly took their eyes off one another. Katie would have to up her game to be in with a chance; there was some serious competition.

The tête-à-tête was interrupted by the arrival of Ryan, the fishmonger, and two male friends talking in loud Cornish accents. Ryan's black hair was still damp from the shower and he was wearing a clean white shirt rolled up at the sleeves. Bramble had seen the way he'd acted around her and Katie at Tabitha's gig night, and Katie had given him no encouragement whatsoever. Now, though, she batted her extraordinary eyelashes provocatively.

Tabitha left after about half an hour, and once Felipe and Tony had gone too Bramble joined Katie and her new companion at the bar; it was so quiet that it didn't matter. Even Danny had moved to Audrey and Rick's table as there was no one to serve. Ryan wasn't the smartest person on the planet, but he seemed very kind, and every time Katie mentioned a task he offered to help. If she'd accepted all his proposals, he'd have had to give up his job to become her full-time assistant.

At one point he asked if she liked sea bass, and when she admitted that she'd never tried it he looked genuinely shocked and promised to drop some off at the manor tomorrow.

'No, honestly,' she said, but he wouldn't listen.

'Just season it with salt and pepper, then fry it in a little oil.' He smacked his lips. 'It's dead easy.'

If he was hoping she'd ask him to cook the fish for her, he was disappointed. She did, however, invite him to the dinner party, on a date yet to be fixed, at which his bushy black eyebrows shot up almost to meet his hairline and his face lit up in a delighted smile.

'That'd be smashin',' he grinned. 'I can make pretty much any night. I don't get out a lot, to be honest with you.'

Katie looked unimpressed, but her frown soon disappeared.

'Be sure not to drive,' she smiled sweetly. 'Get a taxi, because things could get messy!'

Bramble did wonder whether it was wise of her friend to encourage Ryan and she raised the issue as they drove home that night.

'He doesn't seem your type at all, and he's so gentle – you'll make mincemeat of him!' She glanced at Katie suspiciously. 'Have you given up on Danny then?'

Katie, sitting beside her in the passenger seat, stared out of the windscreen and gave a Mona Lisa smile. 'Wait and see.'

Liz had no desire to do her usual volunteering at the Methodist church hall when she woke the following Tuesday after another restless night. She'd done very little since Pat had died, preferring to stay at home and lick her wounds in private, and she was already dreading the funeral next week; there wouldn't be a dry eye in the house.

Lowenna, unused to spending so much time indoors, had been hard work, getting into mischief, making a big fuss at meal and bath times and generally running Liz ragged. It was as if she sensed that something was the matter, and even Rosie, normally so attentive, had been walking about with a long face and virtually ignoring her sister, which only made matters worse.

'Don't go today, darling,' Robert told Liz when he emerged from the shower, with damp hair and a soggy white towel around his waist, to find his wife sitting up in bed with her head on her knees. 'You're tired and upset. They'll understand. Pat was one of your dearest friends.'

But Liz wouldn't hear of it. 'People look forward to the community meal, and it's hard even with six or seven of us helping. Loveday's supposed to be coming but she won't be much use; she can't stop crying. I can't let the others down.'

Robert scratched his head and paced around the room. 'I'll come with you!' he said suddenly. 'We haven't got many bookings today. Alex can manage without me for once.'

'Would you? Could you?'

All at once the day seemed far less daunting, and Liz jumped up to hug her husband, making herself wet in the process. She knew that this was a big deal for him, as he took his business very seriously and hardly ever had an unscheduled day off. She really was grateful.

Lowenna perked up when her mother fetched the pushchair and wheeled her to Jean's house, Dynnargh, with Robert walking alongside. Jean, however, was in pieces, as to add to all her other woes someone had sneaked into her front garden on Friday night and stolen her precious flowerpots, as well as the prized metal statuette of a boy on a bicycle carrying a splendid array of blooms.

'Tom reckons it must have happened between eight thirty and ten,' she told Liz and Robert gloomily. 'Everything was fine when he did the watering, but when he went to put the bins out later, it was carnage.'

'Look at it!' she continued, waving her arms around wildly. 'It's stripped bare! I'm not so bothered about the pots, to be honest – we can always buy new ones of those – but we bought that statuette on holiday in Tenerife. We're not going back there any time soon. It's a crying shame.'

'Who could do such a thing?' Liz asked, glancing around at the devastation, but she soon regretted the question.

'Audrey reckons it's that boy, Rafael,' Jean replied, leaning in close. 'He was with Tony and Felipe that evening at The Hole in the Wall; she saw him in there. He got up and left for no reason, just like that, and went off on his own. First Pat and now this...' She let out a sob. 'It's too much, it really is.'

Liz's mind started to race. The graffiti, the broken window... there did appear to be a pattern. Someone was clearly intent on making trouble in the village, but Rafael? It seemed hard to believe.

'Did you call the police?' asked Robert, and Jean nodded.

'Don't s'pose they'll do anything, though. I mean, it's hardly a priority for them, is it? It wasn't worth much, that statuette, but it had great sentimental value.'

Jean's face, normally so round and smiley, suddenly darkened. 'I'd like to catch that villain red-handed. I'd grab him by the scruff of the neck and hold on tight till the coppers arrived. Proper punishment, that's what he needs, and a plane ticket back to Venezuela or wherever it is he comes from.'

Thinking how upset the rumours would make Tony and Felipe, Liz's heart sank. Then Jean added that they'd find out soon enough, because Rick's wheelie bin had also gone missing that same night and turned up on the beach yesterday morning, upside down with all the rubbish spilling everywhere.

'Dreadful mess it was,' she said fiercely. 'Audrey's properly on the warpath now. She won't let this drop.'

'Hold on to your hats!' Robert muttered gravely when he and Liz were out of earshot, and suddenly she felt rather relieved to be doing the community meal today after all. With any luck, it would mean they'd be well out of the way when

Audrey, Tony and Felipe came face-to-face again, though you'd probably be able to hear the fireworks in John O'Groats.

Liz and Robert popped into A Winkle in Time on the way to the church hall to fetch the leftovers from yesterday – some assorted vegetables and a mound of smoked haddock that Jesse had left out of the freezer by mistake.

'We could make fishcakes?' Robert suggested. 'Or fish pie?'

'Or kedgeree – with extra rice for you,' Liz joked. Her husband hated rice, as well as tomatoes and grapes, which was weird given that he ran a restaurant. There again, lots of things about him were a bit odd, including his dislike of heights and swimming, which others might mock but she found utterly endearing.

Loveday was late, as usual, and flung herself into her uncle's arms the moment she saw him, ignoring Jenny, Mike and Liz, who pretended to get on with their tasks in the kitchen. Loveday was wearing high, wobbly platforms, and Robert staggered slightly before righting himself.

'I haven't slept a wink,' she wailed, sobbing against his pale-blue shirt while he stood rather stiffly and patted her dark hair, which clearly hadn't seen a brush or comb for some time. She really was a mess.

Thank God for Jesse, Liz thought. He'd been a rock these past few days since Pat had died and she didn't know how Loveday would have coped without him. She still held herself responsible in some ways for the accident last year – which had led to the old woman breaking her arm badly, from which she'd never fully recovered – and it had been a hard job trying to persuade her that she was in no way to blame for the heart attack either.

When at last the tears had subsided, Loveday took a step or two back and stared at Robert as if she'd only just noticed him.

'What the hell are *you* doing here?'

Quite whose shirt it was that she thought she'd been soaking was unclear, and Robert was momentarily lost for words.

'He's helping us out this morning,' Liz quickly explained, fetching Loveday a chopping board and knife. 'We're all at sixes and sevens a bit because of Pat. We could do with an extra pair of hands.'

'I hope you're not going to boss me about like Jesse.' Loveday plonked her handbag, a bright-pink satchel, on the counter.

'He wouldn't dare – none of us would,' Jenny laughed. 'Now, put that away. You know it can't stay there.'

Other volunteers had already done the rounds of the supermarkets and there was a sizeable haul of slightly squashed fresh fruit – strawberries, raspberries and blueberries – which Jenny asked Loveday to make into a crumble. Meanwhile, Mike set up the tables and chairs next door while Liz and Jenny helped Robert prepare three individual fish pies, as there wasn't a dish big enough to feed everyone.

Although Robert wasn't a trained chef himself, he certainly knew how to cook, and in no time at all the pies were in the oven, waiting to be warmed up.

'I hope they like it,' he said, lowering his eyes, when Jenny expressed her admiration. He loathed being the centre of attention. 'Alex and Jesse are the real experts. They can turn anything into a feast.'

Soon it was midday and Liz was so busy talking to Stan, who'd arrived first as usual, that initially she didn't notice a boy of about seven or eight with shaggy brown hair hovering near the door, and beside him, a tall, thin man with a straggly beard carrying a heavy toddler. The man looked as if he'd like to be anywhere but here, his eyes darting nervously this way and that, the fist of his free hand clenching and unclenching as if he didn't know what to do with himself.

Liz had never seen him before, but she recognised the boys as Shannon's brothers whom she'd met at their rundown cottage. As she watched, the older one, Liam, grabbed the man by the arm and pulled him closer to where she was standing, as if fearing that at any minute he might bolt.

'Hello, Liam,' she smiled, coming over to greet them. 'How nice to see you!' She ruffled the younger boy, Conor's hair before turning to the man. 'And you must be their dad?'

As she held out her hand the man shrank back, so she dropped it, pretending that she hadn't noticed. 'Come and sit down! You've not been here before, right?'

Robert had clocked the strange trio from the kitchen, too, and approached to see if his wife needed support, but she gave a subtle signal that she wanted to do this on her own before leading the newcomers to an empty table.

The man was silent as she poured some water for them from the jug on the table, while Liam looked at him anxiously.

'My dad likes tea, not water, don't you, Dad?' he said at last. No response. 'With two sugars and...' He hesitated, as if he was unsure whether to go on. '... and milk.'

They didn't normally serve tea, but Liz decided to make an exception.

'I'll bring your starters at the same time. It's lentil and cheese slices today. I think you'll approve.'

They all looked as if they needed feeding up, and they weren't particularly clean either. Liam's navy T-shirt was stained, Conor's face was crying out for a good wipe and the man smelled, as if he hadn't had a bath or shower in ages. She half-thought that they might do a runner when her back was turned and was relieved when she returned with a laden tray to find them still there. The boys had already polished off a good deal of the bread and butter on the table and there were telltale smears around their mouths, while the man eyed the hot lentil slices greedily.

'Have one,' Liz coaxed, passing him the plate and noticing his dirty, torn fingernails. The sides of his thumbs were red raw where he'd picked at the skin until it bled.

He accepted without a murmur, tearing off a corner of food and passing it to the toddler, before gobbling up the rest himself. Liam, meanwhile, picked up his fork and took a rather cautious bite, but his eyes lit up once he'd tasted it and he crammed the rest in so fast that he almost choked. He was clearly ravenous.

Liz left them to it for a while and joined Robert, who was sitting between Stan and a middle-aged woman with grey dreadlocks in a grubby, crocheted orange poncho.

'Where do you live then?' Robert enquired, running a hand through his messy brown hair in that way he had, and Liz's heart melted. He wasn't good at small talk – in fact, it was his worst nightmare – but he was doing his very best.

Stan gave his address, but the woman in the orange poncho was too busy eating to reply, so Liz leaned forwards and mentioned that Robert had a restaurant in the village.

'He made the fish pie,' she said proudly. 'It's very tasty.'

She expected a nod at least, or perhaps a murmur of appreciation, but instead the woman stopped eating, pushed back her chair, dabbed her mouth on the hem of her dark skirt and cleared her throat before announcing imperiously, 'I beg to differ. It's rather bland, if you don't mind my saying, and it could do with a bit more salt and some tartar sauce.'

Robert's jaw dropped and Liz had to stifle a laugh. He was used to fussy customers but hadn't anticipated any here.

'Sorry about that,' he said, rallying. 'I'll bear it in mind for next time.' He glanced at Liz, who gave a surreptitious wink in return.

It was only during pudding that she felt able to approach Liam and his family again and start to probe – very tentatively, because she was afraid of scaring them off.

'How's Shannon?' she asked Liam, who was scraping the last vestiges of fruit crumble and custard from the bottom of his bowl.

'All right,' he replied, wiping his mouth with the back of a grubby hand.

'I live here in Tremarnock,' she went on. 'I've been looking out for you on the beach. I thought I might see you.'

The boy sat back comfortably and put his hands behind his head like an old fellow in the pub. 'Nah, we stay at home mostly. It's easier.'

'We're having a gorgeous summer, aren't we?' she continued, addressing the man now, who jiggled his leg nervously under the table and didn't say a word. 'I don't know your name?' Still he said nothing.

'It's Osiris,' the boy piped up. 'Osiris Turner.'

Liz smiled. 'That's unusual. Where does it come from?'

At last Osiris opened his mouth to speak.

'I...' he started. 'We...'

'Yes?' said Liz encouragingly, but he shook his head, unable to go on.

Liam waited a few moments, looking at his father hopefully, but it was no good.

'My dad wants to know if you've got any leftovers for us to take home,' he blurted, lowering his eyes at the same time and staring hard at the table.

Liz paused. It was perfectly obvious that they were in

desperate need, yet Mike had mentioned that he'd been up to their cottage only last Friday with a couple of bags of unused food. In fact, he'd been making a habit of it recently, and he'd checked that they were getting all the benefits they were entitled to, so what was going on?

Keen to establish the facts, she chatted with the boy about this and that – football, television programmes, video games (a favourite topic) – until she could steer the subject deftly on to his preferred foods.

'Did you enjoy the things I brought you that time?' she enquired, while Osiris stared vacantly into his empty teacup.

Liam looked shifty. 'They were all right.'

'Did Shannon heat you up some of that pasta with the red sauce?'

'Nah.' Liam kicked his legs back and forth under the table. 'Didn't fancy it.'

It took her a while, but little by little she winkled out the truth. Osiris, it seemed, had been selling the food they'd been given in order to fund a brand-new console for Liam, along with a pile of video games, and had made up the rest of the cash with benefits money.

'You promised you'd get me one, didn't you, Dad?' Liam said, leaning across the table and shaking his father's arm. 'Didn't you?' the boy repeated loudly.

This time the man muttered, 'Yes.'

Liam leaned back, pleased. 'You see?' he said proudly. 'He's like that, me dad. My sister went ballistic, but he always keeps his promises.'

Now Liz was beginning to understand their predicament. The cupboards were bare and Shannon, probably so disgusted with her father's profligacy, had forced him to come here to get a meal for himself and the boys.

'I'll see what we've got,' she said, rising. No one would argue with her decision.

When she returned a few minutes later with two large carrier bugs stuffed with groceries, the man seemed quite overcome.

'Thank you.' His hands shook as he took the bags from her. 'I'm grateful to you for your kindness.'

It was the first time that she'd properly heard his voice. She was about to help him to the door when he unexpectedly grabbed her arm. He was so quick that she didn't have time to pull away.

'Don't mention this to anyone, will you?' he pleaded, fixing her with watery brown eyes rimmed with deep, criss-crossing lines.

Liz hesitated. She knew exactly whom he meant, of course – social services, who might take the children away.

'You can't go buying expensive toys when you haven't enough to feed the children,' she said firmly.

The man swallowed. 'I know.'

'You might think you're being kind, but they need to eat and so do you. You've got to get your priorities right.'

'I will.'

'Promise me you won't do a silly thing like that again.'

She watched as he shuffled off with Liam, weighed down with a heavy carrier each, and when they'd left she headed over to Robert, who was helping to clear the tables.

'He's in a dreadful state, poor chap,' he said gravely, and his wife nodded.

'You should tell the authorities. Discuss it with Mike and Jenny. You can't have children going hungry in this day and age; it's a scandal.'

The suggestion made Liz shudder, although part of her thought that her husband was right.

'The man's sick for sure,' she replied. 'And he certainly doesn't know how to look after his kids properly. But he loves them and they love him, and separation would utterly devastate them.'

She remembered the gentle way that Shannon had picked up her little brother, Liam's concern about his dad, the neatly tended flowerbeds leading up to their front door.

'No,' she went on, pulling herself up to her full height and ignoring Robert's doubtful expression. 'There simply has to be another way.'

Chapter Fourteen

SATURDAY MORNING ARRIVED and leaving Cornwall was a terrible wrench for Bramble. As she looked out of her bedroom window she could see the sun glittering on the bright-blue ocean, and when Katie appeared in her fluorescent-pink bikini, clutching a magazine and towel, all set for a lazy day lounging in the garden, it felt like a double blow.

Bramble dragged her feet getting ready and ended up departing far later than intended, so that by the time she spotted signs for the M25 it was already three thirty p.m., and if she didn't put her foot down, she'd miss her father's 'light bite' before the dreaded belly-dancing display.

As soon as she pulled into the familiar Chessington street, lined with mock-Tudor semis, and stopped in front of her parents' house, Cassie dashed out, cheeks flushed and eyes shining. She must have been peering through the vertical cream blinds in the front window, keeping watch.

'It's been so long!' she cried, scarcely giving Bramble time to leave the car before enveloping her in a hug. Cassie's bosom was as soft as a pillow and she smelled of lavender perfume and hairspray. 'Let me take a peek. I'd forgotten what you look like!'

Being back in her old house felt strange to Bramble: easy

and comforting, yet somehow different, too, for although she had only been away for three weeks, so much had happened. Bill carried her small bag upstairs before retiring to the kitchen, where he could be heard clattering about, opening and closing cupboards, rattling pans and whizzing up ingredients in the blender. She was amused. So much for their simple supper, she thought. It sounded as if he were preparing a banquet.

She and Cassie sat side by side on the plush red sofa in the sitting room, sipping tea and catching up on news, but it wasn't long before Bill appeared again – with a white tea towel hung, waiter-style, on his arm – and summoned them with a flourish for their 'pre-performance meal'.

'Mesdames, your repast awaits,' he announced in a fake French accent, before ushering them into the dining room at the front of the house, where the table was laid with a lacy white cloth and Cassie's best cutlery and crystal wine glasses. Then he vanished again for a moment and returned with three large bowls of steaming seafood broth on a tray.

'What's this?' Cassie asked, eyeing the food that he put in front of her and sniffing suspiciously.

'Teriyaki prawns and broccoli noodles,' Bill said proudly. 'It's Japanese, doncha know. I thought we'd try something different for a change.'

After Maria's unappetising grub, Bramble would secretly have preferred Cassie's plain but delicious shepherd's pie or her tasty chicken hotpot, but she didn't let on.

'Yum,' she said, picking up a prawn and twizzling some brownish buckwheat noodles around her wooden chopsticks. 'What a treat!'

'Very unusual,' Cassie commented, rejecting her own chopsticks in favour of a spoon and fork, which Bill had thoughtfully placed alongside. 'I like prawns, but I'm not keen on that raw fish they're so fond of, are you? I'd rather have a nice bit of battered haddock and a bag of chips.'

Bill was so excited, jumping up and down to refill the women's glasses with water or white wine and bustling into the kitchen to check on pudding, that he scarcely ate any of the broth himself.

'I had a big lunch,' he insisted when Cassie pointed this out. 'But you eat up, love. You'll need plenty of energy for your dancing.'

Cassie dutifully obliged, though it was clearly a struggle, and Bramble hoped that her stepmother's supper wouldn't make an unfortunate reappearance during the course of the evening.

Pudding was a rather more traditional lemon meringue pie, which Bramble eagerly demolished before requesting seconds. Then Cassie went upstairs to get ready while father and daughter sat and talked. Bill wouldn't allow Bramble to help clear away; he said her time at home was too precious.

'We'll have plenty of opportunity to wash the dishes when you've gone.'

At around six, Sheila arrived in her car to collect Cassie, and half an hour later Bill and Bramble made their way up the road to the shabby 1960s-built concert hall. The performance wasn't until seven thirty p.m., but the tickets weren't numbered and he was anxious to get good seats. The last time Bramble was here, she'd been around twelve years old and had had to endure a particularly lengthy rendition of Elgar's *The Dream of Gerontius*. With luck, tonight's show would be rather more accessible.

The grubby white walls, linoleum floor and strip lighting, coupled with a faint smell of bleach, gave the hall the air of a down-at-heel doctor's surgery. The faded yellow curtains at the windows were only three quarters drawn, and a shaft of light from outside illuminated myriad particles of dust that seemed to dance before Bramble's eyes and scoot up her nose, making her want to sneeze.

To her surprise, Bill had so far tactfully avoided the subject of Matt, so it was a tremendous shock when she saw him stroll through the open doors and glance around the hall, already half-filled with the dancers' supportive friends and relatives and humming with enthusiastic chatter. She hadn't told him that she was coming, ostensibly because it was only to be a flying visit, though in truth she was anxious to avoid the dreaded heart-to-heart that Katie had insisted she must have.

'What's he doing here?' she asked, alarmed, before she could stop herself, and Bill stood up and waved.

'He asked to come,' he said, unable to disguise the reproof in his voice. 'He's very fond of Cassie, you know. He wanted to support her – and to see you, of course,' he added with a cough.

Matt's eyes lit up when they fell on Bramble, and her stomach fluttered. He looked very handsome, in a collarless pale-blue shirt and jeans, his fairish hair neat and freshly washed, his shoulders broad and solid. Forgetting all her doubts and reservations, she had an overwhelming urge to run over and fling her arms around him. In fact, she might have done just that, were it not for the fact that her phone pinged loudly in her handbag, distracting her attention, and she reached inside to check.

Her heart missed a beat when she saw that it was a text from Piers.

Hey, Countess! she read. How's the big smoke? I'll call you tomorrow when you're back.

His joky tone made her smile and the prospect of speaking to him again sent shivers up her spine. Quickly, she turned the phone to silent and managed to shove it in her bag just before Matt finished shuffling along the row of seats and settled down beside her.

It was hardly the moment for a passionate clinch, surrounded as they were by people, so he grabbed her hand instead and gave it a tight squeeze, not letting go even when a family – including Grandpa and Grannie, Dad, two smallish children and a noisy toddler – manoeuvred past and plonked on to the wooden chairs next door, dropping coats, bags, cartons of juice and packets of sweets as they went.

Despite the hubbub, she was acutely aware of his presence – his knees almost touching hers, their thighs pressed together – and she wondered what to do. She knew instinctively that he was expecting her to speak, but she had no idea what to say or how to express the confusing emotions swirling around her head, so instead she waited for him to open his mouth first.

'I've missed you, Bram,' he said at last, letting go of her hand, putting an arm around her shoulders and pulling her close.

'Me, too,' she replied, but her mouth was dry and she didn't melt into his side as usual.

Sensing her strangeness, he stiffened, too.

'Why didn't you tell me you were coming?' he asked, quite sharply now, staring straight ahead.

Bill, on Bramble's other side, was talking to his neighbour, but he would have been able to hear if he pricked up his ears.

'I – I only agreed at the last minute,' she stammered, scrabbling around for something, any excuse, to grasp on to. 'I'm just here for the performance. I didn't think you'd be interested in belly-dancing.'

It sounded lame and unconvincing, and she wasn't surprised when he put his hands in his lap, leaving a cold, empty space around her back where his arm had been.

'We need to talk,' he said heavily. 'After the show?'

'I can't,' she replied, quick as a flash; she was panicking. 'I promised my parents I'd spend the whole evening with them.'

Matt turned now and stared at her, willing her to meet his gaze. Reluctantly, she did, and she could see that his soft grey eyes were troubled and that hurt hung, screen-like, just behind the irises. Unable to bear it, she glanced away.

'I'll be back again soon,' she went on fake-cheerily. 'We can chat properly then. I'm sorry I'm in such a rush. Dad basically begged me to come for Cassie's sake, and you know what he's like. I couldn't refuse.'

Silence descended while Matt processed her words, so it was a relief when someone dragged the yellow curtains all the way across the windows and turned off the overhead lights. Gradually, the chattering around her ceased, but still she barely heard when a man in a dark suit got up on stage to introduce the troupe and explain a little about the history of belly-dancing. In fact, she wondered why the audience members were laughing, for the jokes passed her by completely.

At last the music commenced and about ten dancers appeared in a blaze of colour, swirling hips and flashing sequins, including Cassie, at one end, in a beaded bra top and peacock-blue harem pants with a matching chiffon scarf twined seductively around her head. Mostly, the women danced together, but from time to time one would take centre stage, shimmying sinuously into the spotlight, arms above her head and tummy rolling round and round, to rapturous applause and whoops of delight and amusement.

When it was Cassie's turn, Bill nudged Bramble in the ribs.

'Isn't she fantastic?' he whisper-shouted. 'I had no idea!'

She was, indeed, surprisingly fluid in her movements, and from the look on her face it was clear that she was enjoying every moment. Bramble nodded and smiled at her father and joined in the clapping, but she was only going through the motions. All the while her attention was really focused on Matt, sitting motionless and brooding beside her.

Thankfully, there was no opportunity for soul-searching during the interval, because Bill was too busy introducing Matt and Bramble to friends and neighbours, who seemed far more interested in hearing what she thought of the dancing than in Cornwall or Polgarry Manor. After about twenty minutes everyone resumed their seats for the second half, and she racked her brains for what to say when the performance finished.

The lights went off, the music struck up once more and she was just telling herself that this time she really must concentrate, for Cassie would surely want an in-depth analysis afterwards, when Matt touched her on the knee.

'I'm going,' he whispered hoarsely. 'Say well done to Cassie and tell her I'm sorry I couldn't congratulate her in person.'

Bramble's eyes widened. 'What? Why?'

But he shook his head and began to rise. 'Let me know when you're ready to speak.'

It sounded more like a rebuke than a request, and a familiar feeling of guilt washed over her, mingled with regret and sorrow.

'Won't you...?' she began, hating herself, but he was already shaking Bill's hand and pushing his way back along the row of seats towards the exit. She didn't blame him for leaving. She'd probably have done the same if he'd been as chilly and dishonest with her.

She watched him walk through the double doors and disappear from sight before turning her attention back to the troupe, who had been waiting in the wings. But she barely registered when Sheila stumbled on her veil and almost fell, or when Cassie twirled a set of flashing hoops around her tummy amidst frenzied drumming and gasps of admiration, the loudest of all from Bill.

All she could think of was the empty seat beside her and Matt heading home, unhappy, baffled and alone. It was only when she focused on Piers – his easy smile and languid, loose-limbed manner; the prospect of hearing his voice again – that she found she could blot out her boyfriend's image, temporarily at least, and focus on tomorrow.

Matt didn't try to contact her again that night, and Bramble returned to Polgarry early the following morning, determined to sort things out with him as soon as she'd marshalled her thoughts and, preferably, put them down on paper. She was aware, of course, that Pat's funeral was imminent, and although she and Katie didn't plan to attend, they'd already agreed between themselves to keep a respectful distance from the village and pubs until it was all over.

On Wednesday morning the Methodist church in Tremarnock was packed – so full, in fact, that some folk couldn't find seats and had to stand at the back. The sun beamed through the arched windows and poured on to the two magnificent bouquets of yellow, red and vibrant orange flowers in the transept, so that they seemed to be on fire, and Liz found herself thinking that Pat would surely have approved. She'd organised the flowers every week for years until she'd become too frail, and yellow and orange had always been her favourite colours. She'd never been one for subtlety – she'd liked a really good show – and she'd have adored the gaudy pink and yellow sprays on the ends of the pews, too. Liz fancied that she could hear her now, making comments.

'Just look at them. Aren't they as pretty as a picture? A feast for the eyes!'

She'd have grumbled if she'd known whom they were for, though.

'All that hard work, just for me! They shouldn't have gone to so much trouble. I'd have been just as happy with a bunch of roses from my garden!'

Robert and Rosie were beside Liz on the third row of pews from the front. At first Liz had thought they might have to bring Lowenna, inconvenient as it might be, but then Jenny Lambert had offered to ask if her daughter's friend was free for a couple of hours to babysit. She was a trained nanny and lived in the next-door village.

'We've known her since she was little. She's a lovely girl and totally reliable,' Jenny had reassured her, so Liz had invited the girl for a trial. It was lucky that Lowenna wasn't as clingy as some children and that the girl seemed so competent. Nevertheless, Liz had resolved to keep her mobile on vibrate throughout the ceremony just in case.

Sitting behind her were Loveday and Jesse, while Pat's niece, Emily, and her husband as well as assorted other family members occupied the first two rows. As she glanced around, she calculated that practically the whole of Tremarnock was there, as well as a handful of Pat's very elderly lady friends from nearby villages. She used to complain that they'd all popped their clogs and she was the only one of her peer group left, but it wasn't true and there were enough white heads and walking sticks to prove it.

Everyone was in colourful clothes, because Pat had insisted that she didn't want any black, and Liz herself was wearing a pale-cream dress decorated with pink flamingos, as the old woman had once told her that she liked it. Rosie, meanwhile, was in a blue-and-white-striped frock that she'd bought for a school disco, while Robert had on his favourite party shirt. Even Rafael, sitting with Tony and Felipe on the other side of the aisle, had abandoned his usual sombre garb and donned a white shirt. It was a little big and probably belonged to Felipe, but at least he'd made an effort, and his bright-blue Mohican looked freshly dyed.

Once Emily had told Liz that the funeral was to be two weeks after Pat's death, due to the fact that there was to be a post-mortem, Liz had knocked on doors and asked folk to circulate the date and time as widely as possible. Almost everyone had offered to bring food for the gathering in the church hall afterwards, but Emily had decided to employ a small firm of outside caterers, as she'd thought it would be easier. Pat had already given her a list of the hymns that she'd like as well as the readings. She hadn't been particularly religious but had been a regular member of the congregation nonetheless. She used to joke that she liked looking at the hats and joining in the singing. 'And the ladies make a good cuppa afterwards,' she'd told Liz confidentially. 'Bit stingy with the biscuits, mind.'

Apparently, there was to be a surprise during the service, too, a suggestion that Pat had made verbally to her niece during one of their chats.

'I wasn't all that thrilled with the idea, to be honest with you,' Emily had confessed to Liz. 'But it's what she wanted, so we must respect it.'

Liz's mind had boggled. What could it be? A special

rendition of '(There'll be Bluebirds Over) the White Cliffs of Dover'? A clip or two from *Battle of Britain*, Pat's favourite movie of all time, or perhaps they'd have to sit through the whole film?

Pat had only been young during the Second World War, but she'd seemed to remember every moment of it as if it were yesterday. She'd told Liz often enough that when bombs had started dropping on Cornwall, she'd slept in the cupboard under the stairs at home, which was why she'd always liked small, cosy spaces.

'I felt so safe in there,' she'd been wont to say. 'It was where my father kept his walking shoes and waxed jacket, and it smelled sort of earthy, like being in a tent. I was quite sorry when the bombing stopped and I had to go back to my old bedroom.'

Jean, in a red jacket, was just behind Liz, with a baby, one of her charges, on her knee, while two toddlers, between her and Tom, were busy colouring in the books on their laps. Because it was a weekday, Jean had had to bring them along, of course, or miss the funeral – and that was never going to happen. She smiled at Liz, who nodded back, hoping that the children would behave. Otherwise poor Jean would have to take them out and miss the service anyway.

Some way behind were Jenny Lambert and her husband, plus Barbara from The Lobster Pot and her son, Aiden. Behind them were the staff from Robert's restaurant: Alex, Callum, Jesse and Loveday, who was resting her head on Jesse's shoulder, a wodge of tissues pressed to her nose.

Soon Tabitha arrived, holding Oscar's hand, and Liz was pleased to see Danny follow shortly after and settle beside them, with Oscar sandwiched between. Tabitha looked, if possible, even more stunning than usual, in a simple turquoise top, her curly black hair pulled back in a chignon at the nape of her neck. Despite her grave expression, there was something almost luminous about her today that she couldn't quite disguise. Liz decided that it must be love.

She just had time to wave before the background music stopped, there was a hush and the pallbearers arrived, carrying Pat's coffin, which was smothered with white lilies and yellow chrysanthemums. Rosie gave a little sob and Liz took her hand. She, too, was trembling slightly and a chilly emptiness had crept into her bowels. She glanced at Robert, who gave a brave smile, no doubt thinking, like her, that it was hard to imagine dear Pat inside that cold wooden box, lying quiet and lifeless.

'"I am the resurrection and the life. He who believes in me will live, even though he dies,"' boomed the minister. '"For I am convinced that neither death nor life, neither angels nor demons, neither the present nor the future, nor any powers... will be able to separate us from the love of God..."'

He was a strange-looking fellow with a bald head, little round glasses, a stubby nose and big red cheeks. He sometimes made Rosie giggle, but she was silent now, like the rest of the congregation, while the coffin was set on its stand and he took his place at the pulpit to give the welcome and say the first prayer. After a rousing hymn, he then paid a warm tribute, remembering Pat's contribution to the church and to community life. She'd lived in Tremarnock for so long, he said, that she'd been an invaluable source of information when he'd arrived fifteen years ago to take over from his predecessor.

'She knew something about everybody, and some of the things she told me made my ears burn,' he joked. 'She could have written a novel about the goings-on here, and she was always so entertaining. But seriously, she hadn't really a bad word to say about anybody. Quite simply, she loved people and they loved her.'

Rosie hiccuped and Liz passed her a tissue from the packet in her handbag while Emily stood up to speak. Her tales were of Pat's kindness as an aunt, and the walks on which she used to take Emily and her siblings when they were young, pointing out the names of trees, flowers and birds and regaling them with stories of her youth. She would have loved children of her own, said Emily, but couldn't have them.

'Instead, she borrowed us as often as possible, and we always adored visiting her and Uncle Geoffrey at The Nook. Sometimes we'd go there just to get away from our mother, who didn't much like us sitting around, even in the holidays. Pat always gave us sweets, which were strictly rationed at home, and let us watch TV. It was like heaven in her house. She spoiled us rotten.'

Liz found herself smiling and weeping and smiling some more as the memories kept on coming. Perhaps the most moving eulogy, however, was from Elaine, whom Pat had known since school. She'd spoken often of Elaine in almost reverential terms – 'Elaine says this... Elaine says that...' – and in her mind's eye Liz had imagined a formidable character with a tight perm and self-righteous expression. When a tiny, bent lady in a jaunty fuchsia pillbox hat and matching cardigan shuffled forwards, using the ends of the pews for support, Liz had to do a rapid recalibration. She was even more surprised and moved when Elaine stood, with some difficulty, at the lectern and, in a remarkably clear voice which broke only once or twice, recounted tales of their escapades going right back to childhood, from the times when they used to play knock down ginger, enraging the neighbours, to teen flirtations and Pat's one-time obsession with Cary Grant.

'She was very popular with the lads,' Elaine remembered with a twinkle in her eye, 'and she wouldn't mind my telling you that when she was all dressed up for a dance, she'd have given the prettiest girl a run for her money. She looked like Rita Hayworth, with that auburn hair; everybody said so. But as soon as she set eyes on her Geoffrey, that was it. No other lad stood a chance after that, not even Mr Grant. She and Geoffrey fell in love the moment they met and didn't stop loving each other till the moment he died.'

Liz glanced at the order of service. On the cover was a recent photo of white-haired Pat in her front room, surrounded by her precious ornaments, while on the back was a smaller black-and-white picture of the younger woman in a pale dress with a full skirt and tiny waist, holding the hand of a dapper young man in a suit: Geoffrey.

Liz had never been able to imagine Pat as anything other than elderly really. She'd seemed to have been born eighty years old. But now, as Elaine's stories unfolded, she began to understand the process by which Pat had ripened into the warm, wise and fully rounded person that she'd been. These things didn't just happen by chance; you had to have embraced life with open arms, to have laughed, loved and wept aplenty. There'd never be another like her.

Liz could hear sniffing all around her, mingled with the occasional burst of affectionate chuckling. Emotions were so high that it was almost a relief when Elaine returned to her seat and Emily's husband got up to read a psalm. Another hymn followed, then prayers, and Liz was beginning to wonder if the 'surprise' had been scrapped at the last moment when the minister announced that there would now be a performance.

'I'm pleased to say that we have a very talented group of individuals here, some of whom you may recognise,' he said as Barbara's son, Aiden, and Alex moved to the front, along with a woman and two other men.

Aiden took the microphone – 'You might have guessed what's coming' – and Liz smiled at Rosie as the penny dropped, for Aiden and the others belonged to the same troupe of Morris dancers.

'As some of you will know, Pat was a big fan of ours,' Aiden went on, to murmurs of 'Yes' and a few laughs. 'She didn't want her funeral to be a miserable affair, and asked Emily if we could liven things up. Well, how could we refuse an offer like that? Livening things up is what we do!'

He and his friends disappeared into the minister's private vesting room behind the choir stalls and reappeared shortly after in their full regalia of tattered jackets, black top hats adorned with leaves and feathers, and pads on their shins from which bells dangled merrily. All apart from Alex, that is, who wasn't wearing a hat, probably on the grounds that it would squash his splendid Elvis-style quiff, though he did have a jolly red-and-white-spotted scarf around his neck and was wielding his accordion.

The minister moved the lectern out of the way, with help from one of the sidesmen, before announcing in a sonorous voice, 'Ladies and gentlemen, boys and girls, at the special request of our very special Pat may I present to you... the Tremarnock Wreckers!'

With that, Alex struck up on the accordion while Aiden and the others proceeded to jig, step, bash their sticks and wave their coloured handkerchiefs in a frenzy of noise and brightness. It was an unusual sight in a church, for sure, but no one could have objected because it seemed to encapsulate so much of Pat: her sense of fun, her vibrancy and her deep-rooted Cornish-ness.

When it had finished, the church erupted in loud clapping, cheering and stamping of feet, so that anyone outside must have wondered what on earth was going on. As Aiden and the rest returned to their seats, the minister stepped out into the transept once more and joked that they were a hard act to follow and he wasn't going to try.

'It therefore remains for me to ask for God's presence with those of us who mourn and to give thanks for Pat's life,' he said, signalling for hush and closing his hands in prayer.

Liz felt Rosie shiver again as they recited the Lord's Prayer and the priest began to commit Pat's body for cremation.

'Is this the end?' Rosie whispered, her voice cracking with emotion. 'Is this where we say goodbye?'

'It is,' Liz replied, pulling her close, for it was only Emily and her family who were to go with the coffin to the crematorium.

'Earth to earth, ashes to ashes, dust to dust...'

As the mourners filed out into the churchyard and watched solemnly while the hearse departed, Liz hugged her arms around her body. It was cloudy and humid, but she wasn't the only one who felt cold. Rosie had goosebumps and Robert's face was pinched and upset.

'Wait for me!' cried a familiar voice, and they turned to see Loveday pushing through the crowds towards them with Jesse close behind. She looked a mess again – red and blotchy, with black mascara smudged around her eyes – but no one cared.

'I still can't believe it!' she sobbed, flinging her arms around Robert and burying her face in his shoulder. He patted her back awkwardly.

'Come on,' Liz said gently. 'Pat would have hated all these tears. She'd have wanted us to laugh and remember the happy times.'

Loveday stopped crying and looked at Liz quite angrily. 'How am I supposed to laugh when I'm sad? It's the stupidest thing I've ever heard!'

Luckily, Jesse took his girlfriend by the hand and that seemed to calm her. He was remarkably smart for a change, in a clean blue shirt, navy tie and carefully pressed jeans.

'C'mon, babe, let's go inside and get a drink.'

Liz thought that this was the best idea she'd heard in a while. After so much emotional trauma they were all like overwound guitar strings, waiting to snap.

There was a queue leading into the church hall and they were still standing in line when Tony jogged up, looking terribly agitated.

'It's her again!' he spluttered, turning around and jabbing his finger in an unspecified direction. 'That woman! She should be locked up!'

'Who?' Liz asked, not understanding. She could see Felipe and Rafael hovering by the lychgate, a little way away from the other mourners.

'Audrey,' Tony spluttered. 'Now she's blaming Rafael for trashing Jean's garden and nicking her statue.'

Liz had been so caught up in the funeral arrangements that she'd quite forgotten about the mysterious theft, but now her eyes widened.

'He was at home when it happened, watching TV and minding his own business,' Tony went on. 'There's no way he'd do something like that. And anyway, what would he want with that naff statue? D'you know the one I mean? It's absolutely hideous.'

Liz nodded guiltily, for she'd never much cared for the boy on the bike, though she wouldn't have dreamed of saying so to Jean.

'Seems she's been telling everyone it was Rafael. She's been poisoning their minds. It's slander, libel.' He was shouting now and people turned to watch. 'I'll have her prosecuted and sent to prison! See how she likes *that*!'

The idea of Audrey in prison uniform was almost too much for Liz, who had to bite her cheek, but her smile soon faded when Tony's eyes pooled with tears.

'I've always loved it here,' he said, 'but I honestly don't think I can carry on living in a place where people are so narrow-minded that they believe the first bit of nonsense that's put in their heads. It's not a good atmosphere for Rafael to be in. We'll have to sell up.'

'You can't!' cried Loveday, who'd been listening in. 'If anyone should go, it should be her.'

'She's a dickhead,' Rosie announced, and for once Liz didn't bother to tell her off.

She offered to try to speak to Audrey, not really believing that she could any good, but Tony insisted he didn't want to involve anyone else anyway. Then Robert advised him to talk to the police.

'She can't go around destroying Rafael's good character. A ticking-off from the cops will shut her up.'

Tony looked doubtful but agreed in the end that it might be worth a try, and beckoned to Felipe and Rafael to join them. Liz gave them all a hug; she couldn't help it. Losing Pat was bad enough, and she couldn't bear it if they left Tremarnock, too. Tony had been around for years; he was part of the fabric of the place.

At last they strolled into the hall adjoining the church, sticking close together. Audrey was presiding over a different crowd on the other side of the room. She was so tall that Liz couldn't help noticing her glancing at Tony every now and again over the heads and shooting him dirty looks. At first he appeared most uncomfortable and Liz feared that he'd leave, but after a few glasses of red wine he seemed to forget his woes and start to relax.

Emily and her family arrived while the Methodist church choir were singing a medley of Pat's favourites, including 'My Way' and 'What a Wonderful World', accompanied by a cello, two squeaky violins, a flute, two clarinets and the piano. Then Rick gave a splendid rendition of Nat King Cole's 'Smile' in his booming baritone, while folk munched on ham, egg and cucumber sandwiches, little fairy cakes, jam tarts and miniature éclairs. The atmosphere was so cheery that Liz felt Pat would surely have enjoyed it, and it was only later, when Liz, Robert and Rosie walked home past The Nook, staring into its empty, darkened windows, that silence descended once more.

'Do you think she's up there now, looking down on us?' Rosie asked, glancing at the heavy sky, which seemed to presage rain.

'I'm sure she is,' Liz replied, taking her daughter's arm, 'and she'll be pleased we had such a jolly good knees-up. She told us not to cry, and of course we did a bit, but we laughed a lot, too, so hopefully she won't be too cross.'

As Robert put the key in the lock, she gave Rosie an extra-big squeeze, breathing in the light, flowery perfume that she'd put on especially for the occasion.

'You know, we owe it to Pat to get on with our lives and be happy, Sweet Pea,' she murmured. 'But my! We're going to miss her.'

Chapter Fifteen

BRAMBLE WAS STILL fast asleep with Katie snoring beside her when she heard loud male voices below, mingled with the occasional high-pitched interjection from Maria. It took a moment or two to focus before she remembered. Of course! It was Thursday morning and Anatole had arrived to start work on the roof.

She jumped up, while Katie rolled over and muttered something in her slumber. She was such a deep sleeper, that girl; once out for the count, almost nothing would wake her. Then Bramble pulled on the shorts and T-shirt she'd worn yesterday, checked her own sleep-soaked face in the mirror, made a snap decision that there was nothing to be done right now, grabbed an elastic band and hurried out of the room, yanking her knotty hair into a ponytail as she went.

Peering over the balustrade on the landing, she could see Anatole and three men standing facing Maria in the hallway below. The strangers were all in tatty jeans and T-shirts, while Anatole stood out in a smart pink polo shirt and pale chinos. You could tell just by looking at the group that they were having a disagreement, never mind the angry voices.

'I told you, Miss Bramble is expecting us,' Anatole barked, hands on hips.

Maria stood, arms crossed and ramrod straight, in front of the bronze statuette of a naked youth with a pipe, in a defiant stance that seemed to suggest if the men so much as tried to put a foot past her, she might just pick up the statue and smash them over the head with it.

'And I told *you* that Miss Bramble has not instructed me to allow you in,' she replied icily. 'She is sleeping and I will NOT disturb her.'

She sounded very loyal for once and really rather protective. Bramble felt strangely touched. Maria had always seemed to her like the silent enemy, the spy from her grandfather's ghostly camp. Now, though, with the not entirely welcome arrival of Anatole and his gang, it occurred to her that perhaps the doughty housekeeper wasn't such an adversary after all and that when the chips were down she could be just the person you needed on your side.

None of them had noticed Bramble at the top of the stairs and she was half-inclined to tiptoe back to her room and bury her head under the duvet, for in truth she wasn't entirely convinced that she should have agreed to employ the men at all. Anatole had texted her only yesterday to confirm that he would be starting work this morning, and she'd suggested – perfectly reasonably, she thought – that he might wish to view the job and discuss timescale and payment with her first, but he'd dismissed the idea out of hand.

Don't worry, he'd written. It's all arranged with Piers. My guys are the best.

Knowing that he and Piers were friends and that Piers thought so highly of him did reassure her, but still she was troubled by the prospect of engaging someone without so much as a site visit or a verbal estimate, let alone anything in writing. She could imagine her dad shaking his head and sucking in his teeth in that manner of his.

'Get it down in black and white,' he'd have said. 'That way there won't be any funny business.'

No doubt he'd also have advised her to obtain at least three quotes from other roofers, and written references too probably. He'd never buy anything, not even a dustpan and brush, without comparing prices and going out of his way to secure the best deal. There again, he was careful about everything, sometimes maddeningly so, and it wasn't as if he had experience of renovating an ancient manor or working with a land agent. Besides, she reasoned, he'd never met Piers and had no idea how impressive he was.

Rallying, she was just about to venture down when Katie popped into her head and made her pause again. She should at least have discussed this with Katie, but she would have put up fierce resistance, too, on the quite unreasonable grounds that she'd taken against Anatole. No, thought Bramble, straightening up, caution was all very well but sometimes you had to take the plunge. The roof was a mess and it would be good to get it fixed before the winter. Besides, she didn't want to offend Piers, who was going out of his way to help.

She cleared her throat loudly and they all turned to stare as she padded towards them in bare feet.

'It's all right, Maria,' she said, trying to sound professional. 'I can deal with this now.'

The housekeeper lowered her dark eyebrows, pursed her lips and didn't move.

'I've booked them in,' Bramble went on. 'They're going to mend the leaks in the roof.'

Still Maria remained glued to the spot.

'I know Anatole. He's, um, a friend,' Bramble continued, slightly desperate now. Her words seemed to do the trick, because at last the housekeeper gave a reluctant nod and started towards the door.

'Er, Maria?' Bramble called and she turned abruptly. 'Sorry I forgot to tell you about this – and thank you for your help.'

Was there the merest hint of a smile on the older woman's thin lips, an acknowledgement of Bramble's rare words of appreciation? It certainly seemed so, but the smile vanished as quickly as it had come.

'You must be careful these days,' she commented stiffly, opening the door that led to the kitchen. 'People can take advantage, you know...'

Once she'd gone, the atmosphere lightened considerably and Anatole exhaled loudly.

'What a witch!' he drawled, and the others snickered, revealing an assortment of stained, black and missing teeth.

The builders – all big, fairish fellows, with thick, muscly arms and weather-beaten faces – contrasted sharply with their much shorter, darker, well-groomed boss. One roofer had a long pink scar running across his cheek, another a shaved head and a broken nose, while the third had a pronounced squint that gave him a disconcertingly shifty air. A strong smell of cigarette smoke seemed to envelop them like a shroud.

'She's all right really,' Bramble said, surprised to hear herself defending the housekeeper, for she never had before. 'She worked for my grandfather for years.'

Anatole grimaced. 'She's like a bloody Rottweiler. You shouldn't have her front of house, you know; it's bad for your image. I'd keep her locked in the kitchen where she belongs.'

His misogynistic tone made Bramble cringe, and she didn't

like being told what to do in her own home either, but she decided to make no comment.

'Where are you going to begin?' she asked, feigning cheerfulness. 'I guess you'll want to tackle the worst part of the roof first?'

Anatole glanced questioningly at the man with the pink scar, who craned his thick neck as if to set the bones and muscles back in their proper place.

'Scaffolding goes up first, guv,' he said slowly, and Anatole rubbed his hands together, the backs of which were almost as dark and hairy as his arms.

'Of course, naturally. One step at a time, eh? Gotta get the structure in place.'

Bramble was about to offer tea or coffee to everyone before they started, but Anatole took a large set of keys from his pocket and jangled them from a finger.

'Righto. Gotta shoot.' He bent down to brush a speck of dust off his cream suede loafers.

Bramble started. 'Where are you going?' She'd imagined that he'd be helping his men, or supervising them at the very least. 'Aren't you staying here to watch what they do?'

'Oh no,' Anatole replied airily. 'I don't get my hands dirty. Gus here knows what's what, don't you, Gus?'

Anatole flashed his small, square teeth at the man with the scar, who gave a toothless grin in return.

'You can rely on us, guv. Don't you worry about a thing.' Then he eyed Bramble insolently. 'The young lady can show us where the trouble spots are, can't you, miss? I 'spect you notice where the rain comes pourin' down on them pretty little tootsies?' He pointed a nicotine-stained finger at her bare toes and chuckled at his own joke.

Bramble's cheeks flushed pink with annoyance and she

didn't reply but followed Anatole to his silver sports car, parked outside. The gravel hurt the soles of her feet but she scarcely noticed.

'When will you be back?' she said. 'To check on them, I mean.'

'I'll be in touch,' Anatole replied, pressing a button on one of his keys. The door swung open automatically and he lowered the sunglasses that had been on his head.

Bramble hesitated; it wasn't the answer that she'd been hoping for.

'Have they done a lot of work for you? Do you know them well?' she persisted, but he didn't seem to hear. 'How long will the job take? I mean, when will they finish?'

'Gus will give me a tinkle when he's done,' Anatole said at last, settling into his tan leather driving seat. 'He's a good man, solid. Feel free to ask him anything.'

For a moment Bramble contemplated cancelling the work right now, before they'd even begun. She could say that she needed more time to think; she could pretend that she'd spoken to her dad and that he'd recommended getting more estimates. It would be embarrassing, but she was the boss after all. The ball was in her court.

But the opportunity quickly passed. Anatole pulled the door firmly shut and lowered the window, resting one elbow nonchalantly on the frame.

'Must be off. Got a date with a prospective client on the golf course.' He rolled his eyes and grinned again. 'It's a hard life.'

Then she watched him accelerate down the drive before disappearing around a bend, leaving a cloud of smelly exhaust fumes in his wake.

When she turned back, Gus and his mates had reappeared

and begun unloading metal rods and brackets off the back of a truck, hurling them on the ground with a terrific crash and clang that set her teeth on edge. One of the rods caught the man with the broken nose on the shoulder and he let out a blood-curdling roar, along with a string of expletives. Bramble winced, because it must have hurt a lot, and offered him an ice pack or a plaster. The man, however, looked at her oddly, as if he didn't understand what she was on about, pulled a small bottle of what looked like spirits from his trouser pocket and took a large swig.

'This here's better 'n any plaster,' he said slowly, before wiping his mouth with the back of his hand and belching.

Bramble glanced over to where Gus was banging a very tall rod against the wall, sending bits of masonry flying. Presumably, when the scaffolding was in place they'd be shinning up and down like monkeys.

'Um, do you think you should drink that if you're going on the roof?' she asked in a small voice, but the man with the broken nose was already strolling over to the wall, dragging a thick wooden board behind him.

'Chuck us one of them long poles, Baz!' shouted Gus to his mate with the squint, who was standing on the back of the lorry, and a pole flew through the air and landed at his feet with a clatter, narrowly missing his toes. Even Katie, Bramble thought, couldn't sleep through this and would be down in a jiffy to find out what was going on.

She dreaded what her friend would say when she discovered that Anatole was involved, and dreaded even more the prospect of one of the workers getting hurt. If Anatole wasn't going to supervise then she'd better keep an eye on them herself.

As she strolled back inside she caught sight of Katie hurtling along the landing, still in her crumpled pyjamas and wearing an expression that suggested she wasn't impressed with the racket. For the time being at least, Bramble reflected gloomily, it seemed that her peace had been well and truly shattered.

Pat was no more, but life had to go on, and for Liz Tuesday morning came around once again alarmingly quickly. Determined to get herself back to the church hall, even though it had meant leaving Rosie still in bed, Liz had been relieved that it turned out to be a reasonably quiet session. She'd found herself worrying about her daughter, though, who'd already been upset by Tim's rejection; the death of the old woman whom she regarded as a surrogate grandmother had been a double blow.

Still, Rosie's moods were so changeable that it was hard sometimes to know how best to help. Liz had asked before leaving if she'd like to come with her, thinking that it might provide some welcome distraction, but Rosie had been grumpy and dismissive.

'No way!' she'd muttered from beneath her duvet. 'It's a waste of time. You're never going to solve people's problems by making a few meals. I don't know why you bother.'

Liz had shut her mouth, determined not to pick a fight. Rosie hadn't meant it – she'd just been out of sorts – but it had been hard not to retaliate when Liz, too, had been feeling so raw. It had taken a great deal of self-control to kiss her daughter on the cheek and remind her to make herself breakfast.

'I'll be back at two-ish,' she'd said with forced brightness. 'Let's take Lowie for a swim. It's another lovely day.'

Rosie had groused about something before turning away

and pulling the covers over her head. Fourteen was a difficult age, Liz had thought, and sometimes it seemed as if her daughter was her own worst enemy, determined to push away the very person who knew and loved her best.

Having fetched her coat and bag from the cloakroom, Liz was saying goodbye to Jenny while she locked the doors to the hall when Rosie rang to say that she'd arranged to go to Plymouth with a friend, that the mum was taking them and that they didn't know what time they'd be back. Liz was relieved in a way, as it meant that Rosie would be occupied, although she'd have liked a bit of company herself.

Instead of going straight home, she decided to take a detour to Shannon's house, calling Jean first to let her know that she'd be a little late for Lowenna. Liz would have visited Shannon earlier had it not been for poor Pat, but as she crawled through traffic – stuck behind caravans too big for the winding country lanes and waiting while two overheated motorists got out of their cars to have an argument – she wondered if she'd made a mistake.

Thankfully, the traffic started to ease further up the cliff, and as she approached the rusty entrance gate leading to Polgarry Manor she almost crashed into Bramble, driving too fast in her ancient VW. Both women jammed their feet on the brakes in the nick of time and Bramble leaped out.

'I'm so sorry,' she said, looking flushed. 'I wasn't thinking; I was a million miles away.'

She was so apologetic that Liz couldn't be annoyed for long, and she listened sympathetically while Bramble went on to explain that some workmen had arrived last Thursday to fix the manor roof.

'They're terribly thirsty. They've already had about ten cups of tea each, and we've run out of milk.' She made an anxious face. 'I hope they do a good job; they seem a bit slapdash, and the noise is unbelievable.'

Right on cue there was a loud bang that seemed to echo around the fields, sending flocks of startled birds flapping into the sky, followed by a cacophony of male shouts.

Liz put her hands over her ears and pulled a face. 'I see what you mean. Are they a local firm?'

'I don't know.' Bramble shrugged. 'They were recommended by my land agent, Piers.'

Liz nodded, remembering the suave chap with the silver-flecked hair whom she'd met coming out of the fishmonger's in the marketplace.

'They work for Piers's friend, who's a property developer,' Bramble added. 'Piers says they're very good.'

There was another deafening crash that made both women nearly jump out of their skins.

'You'll have to get earplugs,' Liz joked, her hair standing on end.

'And a tin helmet,' Bramble added ruefully.

They chatted for a few minutes more and Bramble said that she and Katie had decorated one of the bedrooms, which was looking lovely, but she wished that they'd made more progress with the garden.

'The weather's so amazing; it's a shame we can't really enjoy it. There's nowhere to sit where the grass isn't three feet high and covered in nettles.'

A thought flashed through Liz's mind and she decided to try it out, reasoning that the worst that could happen would be a straight 'no'. To her surprise and pleasure, however, Bramble listened with mounting interest and made enthusiastic noises.

'Well, if you think she'd be up for it… it could be a great idea.'

The sun was beating down on Liz's back and neck and she longed for a cool drink and a sea breeze, but she was all the more determined now to pay Shannon a visit before returning home. After the women parted, Liz continued up the lane, before turning sharply left and driving along the gravelly dirt track that led to the girl's house, taking care to avoid the large pothole that she'd fallen foul of previously, and parking her car at the bottom of the woody slope.

On reaching the top of the mound on which Shannon's cottage stood, she glanced around quickly, taking in the thin beige curtains at either window, one with a broken pelmet dangling sadly, and the same green box that she'd seen before, overflowing with rubbish. The sweet peas and busy Lizzies in the neatly kept flowerbeds were there, too, but aside from all this there was something very different about the place that made her skin prickle uneasily.

For a start, the rusty old bike was gone and the long grass had been roughly cut, perhaps with a pair of shears. Most significantly, however, her eyes soon fell on the long line of fine-looking terracotta pots leading up the path towards the closed front door, filled with masses of strangely familiar brightly coloured flowers that seemed to wink mischievously in the sunshine.

Liz's heart missed a beat and she scanned anxiously left and right. Soon her worst fears were confirmed for there, by the fence under a small fruit tree, not very well hidden, was Jean's statuette of the boy on the bicycle, complete with overflowing blooms in his front basket. He was only about three feet high but he must have weighed a bit, and Liz couldn't help wondering how on earth he'd been transported here, along with those heavy pots. They were far too heavy to drag up the hill single-handed.

Her first instinct was to scurry away somewhere private and give herself time to think, but it was already too late because Liam had spotted her out of the window and he appeared on the doorstep to say hello.

'Did you bring more of them biscuits?' he asked hopefully, and Liz reached mechanically into her handbag and fished out a packet.

'For you,' she smiled. 'Make sure you share them with your brother and sister.'

He grabbed them off her and ripped the packet open immediately, taking out the top biscuit and eyeing it reverentially before stuffing it in his mouth.

'Is Shannon here?' Liz asked and he mumbled 'Yes', indicating with his head towards the cottage behind.

She took a deep breath and stepped inside, wondering how on earth to handle this unexpected turn of events and praying for strength and inspiration.

'Shannon?' she called, and the girl soon appeared at the bottom of the stairs, balancing her heavy youngest brother, Conor, on a hip.

She was wearing a faded pink vest top with the same denim miniskirt that Liz had seen her in previously, and she was reminded of how pale and thin the girl was, with dark circles under her eyes and twig-like limbs that looked as if they might snap in the wind. Rosie was skinny, too, of course, but her hair shone and her big eyes flashed when she was joyful, whereas Shannon seemed worn out before she'd even really lived.

Most of the folk around here were tanned during such a long, hot summer, and even Rosie, so pale by nature, had a golden glow, while Lowenna's chubby arms and legs were nut-brown after spending many happy hours pottering around in the garden with Liz or on the beach. Shannon's skin, on the other hand, was almost blue it was so white, as if she rarely set foot in the sunshine. Perhaps, like some nocturnal creature, she stayed indoors all day, only venturing out after dark.

You would have thought she'd have wanted to set Conor down because he was so big, but instead she clung on to him as if needing him for ballast. Something in her expression, a mixture of defiance and fear, suggested to Liz that she'd already guessed what was in store.

'What do you want?' Shannon asked, shuffling the boy around to the front and refusing to meet Liz's gaze. 'We don't want no visitors. I told you we're all right.'

They were still standing in the narrow, dingy hallway and she clearly had no intention of inviting Liz in. Doing her best not to appear daunted, Liz pulled back her shoulders and tried desperately to formulate some sentences in her head.

'Well done for writing that nice letter to Barbara at The Lobster Pot,' she said, for the landlady had made a point of showing her the apology that she'd received the morning after Shannon and her friends had been messing around outside the pub, stealing people's drinks.

The girl – clearly expecting punishment, not praise – narrowed her eyes suspiciously and failed to reply.

'I've got a suggestion to make,' Liz went on falteringly, fearing that at any second her courage might fail. 'I don't know if it'll be your cup of tea but...'

At that moment Conor started struggling so that Shannon had to set him on the floor. She tried to grab his arm, but he toddled off on unsteady feet towards the sitting room before she could catch him.

'You'd better come in,' she said grudgingly over her shoulder, following the boy, and Liz offered up silent thanks.

She hadn't been turned away – yet – and there might still be hope, if she could only find the right words, the best solution.

Conor hunkered down beside a plastic toy train and pushed it across the grubby purple carpet, making driving noises, while Shannon knelt beside him. Liz, meanwhile, perched on the battered brown sofa, taking care to avoid the sunken side with broken springs. The half-closed beige curtains made the room gloomy and there were the remains of someone's sandwich on a plastic plate beside the TV.

'I know you like gardening,' Liz began, before going on to explain that Bramble, the new incumbent of Polgarry Manor, needed help with clearing up her mammoth grounds and she wondered if Shannon would consider getting involved.

'I don't think she'll be able to pay much, but it's an exciting project and there's masses to do. Bramble's young and really good fun; I think you'll like her. And it could be a great way of gaining experience and building your CV. I expect you could take the boys along with you, or I'd be happy to mind them for a few hours if you prefer. It would be no trouble. Lowenna would enjoy their company.'

She glanced at Shannon, who looked doubtful, though she hadn't rejected the proposal outright.

'Why don't you think about it?' Liz persisted, reflecting that at the very least it would get Shannon out of the house, and it would be a change of scenery for the boys, too. What's more, Bramble could certainly do with another pair of hands but had been reluctant to accept Liz's offer of assistance. Perhaps a vulnerable teenager who needed a break would be more acceptable.

'You could recommend some flowers for her beds,' Liz coaxed, sensing that she'd captured Shannon's interest, though she was trying hard not to show it. 'Maybe we could get some books out of the library about typical plants they might have used when the manor was built?'

'I don't know nothing about history,' Shannon responded uncertainly. 'All I know is what I like and what looks pretty.'

'Well, that's an excellent start.'

Conor trundled over to his pile of cars, lining them up in rows, and now that the atmosphere had thawed somewhat, Liz decided that it was time to broach the sensitive subject of Jean's possessions.

'Shannon?' she said, mustering all her strength, and the girl, sensing a change of tone, glanced up warily. 'Did you steal those flowerpots and that statue from Jean's garden?'

There was a sharp intake of breath and the air seemed to freeze over, but the question was out and there was nothing for it but to plough on.

'Jean's my friend and she bought that statue on holiday in Tenerife,' Liz continued steadily, wishing that she had Robert with her for moral support, for right now this felt like the most difficult thing that she'd ever had to do.

'I didn't steal nothing,' Shannon cried in a shrill voice that seemed to slice through the atmosphere like hot wire through ice. Her mouth was thin and hard, but she couldn't disguise her guilt; it was written all over her face.

'I don't know what you're talking about... You've got the wrong person... They were a present from my mate; he saw them in this shop, see...' she went on, piling excuse on excuse, each flimsier than a spider's negligée.

'She's really sad about it,' Liz continued, taking care not to raise her own voice. 'She doesn't mind so much about the pots – she can buy new ones of those – but the statue's of great sentimental value. It really means a lot to her. She's absolutely gutted.'

Shannon stared hard at her fingernails, which had been painted blue but the polish had chipped and the nails were broken. Liz feared that she might bolt at any moment or, worse, lash out with her fists, but instead her eyes started to fill with tears.

'What are you going to do?' she asked at last. 'You won't tell the police, will you? Please don't. They'll come up here and ask questions and say my dad can't look after us and they'll take the boys away.'

She sounded absolutely terrified, and despite everything Liz couldn't bear to crush her even further. Thinking on her feet, she came up with an idea that was bold and yet so startlingly obvious that it just might work.

'Listen carefully,' she said quietly, as if someone might be eavesdropping, 'here's what I propose. I won't breathe a word to anyone...'

Shannon's eyes lit up, but Liz quickly doused the flames with cold water. 'On one condition and one condition only,' she went on fiercely. 'And that is that you replace all the stolen items in Jean's garden, the statuette and every last pot and bloom. You go back and undo the damage you've caused and make everything look exactly as it was before.'

Shannon's face fell. 'How can I? Someone will see me. I'll get nicked.'

But Liz was having none of it. 'You managed to get them up here without being spotted; God knows how. You'll just have to use the same method to take them back.'

Shannon started to protest again, but Liz stood firm. 'No ifs and buts. It's the only way.'

At last the girl nodded. 'All right, I'll do it. I'll get Jerry to bring his van round. I'll make sure your friend's garden looks just as nice as it was before.'

Liz clasped her hands together on her lap. 'Good,' she said, but she wasn't done yet. 'I want you to be completely honest with me. Did you do that graffiti on the public toilets, too?'

Shannon flinched.

'The broken window in the marketplace?'

Her bottom lip quivered and she nodded her head.

'The wheelie bin on the beach? The postcard stand?'

'I'm sorry,' Shannon said at last. 'I know it was wrong...'

'It's got to stop,' Liz insisted, feeling a mixture of relief and anger. 'The whole village thinks another boy's responsible for everything. He's very upset, and it's not fair on him and his family.'

'I won't do it again, I swear,' Shannon blurted. 'You won't tell on me for that either, will you?'

Liz frowned, uncertain how to proceed.

'Please,' Shannon begged. 'I was with my mates. We were just larking around. We won't go near the place again.'

This time Liz didn't hold back. 'It was really stupid,' she barked. 'You caused that shopkeeper a lot of inconvenience, and the graffiti will have to be cleaned off by the council using taxpayers' money that might have been spent on something nice for the whole community. I bet you've used those loos sometimes yourself. If people keep vandalising them, they'll have to be closed, and then no one will have them any more. Actions have consequences, and you need to think before you do daft, destructive stuff. One of these days you'll land yourself in real trouble – the courts or prison even.'

She'd finished her lecture and her shoulders relaxed as she took a deep breath. Shannon, meanwhile, looked duly chastised.

'Are you going to tell?' she asked again, and Liz sighed.

'I don't want to, but to be honest I'm not sure what to do.

The fact remains that that poor boy, Rafael, who's only just arrived in England from Brazil, is being accused of something he knows nothing about. Now his uncles are saying they'll have to sell up and move because of the rumours, which is really sad because they love Tremarnock and it's been their home for years.'

The girl bit her lip and frowned, as if she were thinking very hard, which didn't come all that naturally. Then all of a sudden she sat bolt upright and clapped her hands.

'I know!' Conor looked up, surprised, before continuing with his game. 'I'll ring the shopkeeper and your friend Jean and the council, too, and I'll tell them it was me who did all those things. I won't give my name, but they'll hear my voice and they'll know it's not him.' She glanced at Liz. 'Has he got an accent?'

'A strong one, yes.'

'Perfect. So I'll sound completely different. No one really knows me there so they won't recognise my voice. I'll say I'm sorry and I'll swear it'll never happen again.'

Liz pondered the idea for a few moments. It wasn't a bad plan, but people might think Rafael had put someone up to it. There again, most folk were aware that he'd only just arrived and hardly knew a soul.

'It might just work,' she said, turning things over in her mind as she fished for the mobile phone in her bag. She was starting to scroll down her contacts list when a delicious notion popped into her head.

'Hang on a minute...' Instead of calling the council, Liz asked Shannon to ring Audrey. It was a bit naughty, but she couldn't resist. After writing down the numbers, she instructed the girl to act soon, warning her that unless she kept to her word, the police would have to be informed. When she'd finished, she fixed Shannon with a steely stare to make sure that the message had sunk in.

Liam wandered in from the garden, clutching the now almost empty packet of biscuits, and his little brother, noticing, raised his outstretched hands and set up a high-pitched wail. Liz rose, deciding that it was time to go, and promised to put Shannon in touch with Bramble about the gardening as soon as she'd fulfilled her mission.

'I've never met anyone like you before,' Shannon said, following Liz to the door. 'You seem so...' She wrinkled her brow. 'So *good*.'

Liz laughed. 'You should see me in the morning before I've had my first cup of tea. My husband says he doesn't dare speak to me! But seriously,' she went on, 'everything's going to be OK – so long as you keep your side of the bargain.'

Chapter Sixteen

LIZ FELT TEN feet tall when she left the cottage, but as she drove home through the dusty lanes, replaying the conversation with Shannon and wondering what Robert would say, her spirits started to fail. If she'd followed his advice after the last community meal and called the local authority, they'd have been able to deal with all this, but instead she was in it up to her neck. The more she thought about it, the more worried she became, so that by the time Robert returned from work at midnight she was a bundle of nerves.

'How come you're still awake?' he asked when he found the light on in their bedroom and his wife propped up against the pillows, pretending to read. He looked hot and tired but delighted to see her.

'I couldn't sleep,' she explained, her heart pitter-pattering as he kissed her on the forehead, sat down beside her and started to unbutton his shirt. 'I need to talk to you about something.'

Sensing her anxiety, he put his arm around her, but before she was halfway through recounting her story, he rose and started to pace the room, shaking his head.

'I can't believe you didn't discuss this with me,' he groaned when she'd finished. 'Don't you know it's breaking the law to cover up a crime? What if the girl messes up and the police find out it was you who persuaded her to do it? You'll be in even more trouble than her.'

Liz felt tears pricking in her eyes because she feared very much that it might be the truth.

'I couldn't shop her without giving her a chance to put everything right,' she argued. 'She's not a bad person; she's just a bit lost. She's crying out for love and guidance, and the boys would suffer if she got punished. It might break the family up.'

But Robert was having none of it. 'It was wrong to interfere,' he barked, staring down at his wife from his great height at the foot of the bed. 'You've probably made everything much worse for that family.'

He'd never shouted like that before – hardly ever raised his voice, in fact – and she feared that he might wake the children. A tear trickled down her cheek and plopped on to the open book on her lap.

'What can I do?' she asked, feeling stupid and scared. 'I should never have gone to her house.'

Robert knitted his dark brows and growled, but he couldn't keep it up for long. At last his shoulders relaxed a little and he took a deep breath.

'Oh, Liz, Liz,' he muttered more softly, settling down beside her once more and passing her a box of tissues. 'I know you meant well, but the whole thing could backfire horribly. I can't just stand by and let that happen.

'We'll drive to Shannon's place together first thing tomorrow and take her to the police station. At least then she'll have our support. She's young, so they'll probably be lenient. She might even get off with a caution or a small fine.'

Liz nodded, relieved that there might be a solution, but soon her mind was hurtling ahead again. 'What if she refuses to come with us? What if she tries to run away?'

Robert raised his palm. 'You can't solve all the problems of the world. You're not Mother Teresa, you know. If that happens, we'll go to the station on our own. I just hope for her sake that she'll have more sense.'

It was a warm night, one of those evenings when you can't bear to sleep under a duvet and even a sheet feels too much. The weather forecasters had predicted thunderstorms the following day and you could sense it in the thick atmosphere, the air of foreboding.

Liz dozed fitfully, and most people had left their bedroom windows open, desperate to catch the slightest breeze, but still no one heard a van pull up on Humble Hill and a small group of youngsters, laden with weighty items, tiptoeing in the direction of the cottage called Dynnargh. Perhaps it was the hour – around three thirty a.m. – or maybe it was the lulling swish of the distant waves creeping up and down the beach that muffled other sounds. In any case, only seagulls and the odd cat witnessed the miraculous trans-formation taking place in Jean's front garden, so that in the morning, when she went outside with her cup of tea to do a spot of watering, she rubbed her eyes, wondering if she were still dreaming.

Liz woke to the sound of a loud hammering on the front door and jumped in fright, instantly remembering yesterday's events, and when Robert called upstairs to say that Jean wanted to speak to her, she was tempted to pull the duvet over her head or climb out of a back window and dash for the hills.

But scarpering wasn't an option, so she braced herself and padded reluctantly downstairs, to be met in the hallway by an extremely overexcited Jean.

'Come out!' she cried, tugging on the sleeve of Liz's dressing gown. 'You have to come this instant!'

She sounded amazed rather than angry, but there was no time for questions because she was soon yanking Liz down the hill while Robert followed close behind. There was a slight chill in the air as it was still early, but Liz was in such a state of anxiety and confusion that she scarcely noticed.

'Look,' Jean said, coming to an abrupt halt outside her house. 'It's magic!'

Liz gazed at the garden and soon a warm glow, like melted chocolate, spread through her body from the tips of her toes to the top of her head, and she breathed in deeply, hoping to capture the feeling for ever. There, in front of her, in exactly the same position as before, was the metal statuette of the boy on the bicycle, his basket still brimming with colour and his face flashing, she could swear, a new, impish grin. Dotted around him were assorted summer flowers in terracotta pots and, to her great relief and pleasure, the display looked just as vibrant and jolly as before. In fact, nothing might ever have been stolen; everything was just as it had been. She'd never imagined in a million years that Shannon would act so quickly, or that she'd do such a great job.

'Are they all there?' Liz asked, feigning surprise. 'All the pots, every single one?' She glanced at Robert but he was staring steadfastly ahead, absorbing all the details.

'There's even more!' said Jean, swaying with excitement as she pointed to four big new containers that Liz hadn't taken in, bulging with pink, white and red geraniums. 'Whoever could have put them there? It's like a fairytale! I keep having to pinch myself to make sure I'm not imagining it.' She nudged Liz on the arm. 'You can see them, can't you? I've not gone mad?'

Liz laughed. 'They're there all right; you're perfectly sane. What did Tom say?'

'Same as me,' Jean replied breathlessly. 'He was flabbergasted. Said he needed a stiff drink to recover, but then he remembered what time it was.' She chuckled before turning serious. 'What do you think we should do? I mean, I can't decide whether to be angry or delighted! It's a complete mystery. Things like this don't happen in real life.'

Liz looked again at Robert, and this time he returned her gaze. He didn't utter a word but he didn't need to, because the smile in his eyes and at the corners of his mouth said it all. Swivelling back to face Jean, Liz replied that in her view she should just be grateful that the items had been returned intact and leave it at that. There was no need for further action.

'But I'll have to tell the police, surely? They're supposedly making enquiries about who took the stuff.'

Liz said that she thought Jean should just ask them to close the case.

'I mean, nothing's been damaged, and the thief – whoever he or she was – has even bought new pots and planted them up for you. It's their way of saying sorry, don't you think? You won't be bothered by them again.'

As she and Robert strolled home, hand in hand, she couldn't resist a small dig.

'Um, what was it you said exactly about everything backfiring horribly?'

He attempted to frown, but a bubble of laughter escaped, which he tried to disguise with a cough.

'You were lucky this time,' he admitted, giving her hand a squeeze, 'and it's turned out extraordinarily well. But please don't do any more crime-solving. There's only one Miss Marple, as far as I'm aware – and she's definitely not my wife!'

During the course of the day, there were other strange goings-on that had the whole village buzzing with gossip and speculation. First, as Liz wheeled Lowenna in her pushchair into the marketplace to buy fresh bread, Ryan, the fishmonger, came out from behind the counter and said that his cousin, who owned the shop, had received a call from a 'strange girl' who'd apologised for throwing a stone through the window and smashing the glass.

'She even said she'd pay back what it cost to repair the damage when she could get hold of the money. When my cousin asked who she was and why she'd done it, she hung up. Weird.'

Later that afternoon, after Liz left the beach, she made a point of going into Rick's shop, Treasure Trove, to buy ice creams. Lowenna was a little surprised, having just dropped off for a nap, but the sound of Rick's familiar voice soon restored her good mood, and when Liz thrust a lolly into her hand, she rose happily to the occasion.

'Strange thing,' Rick said, scratching his bushy grey beard thoughtfully. 'I got a call from some girl wanting to apologise for knocking over my postcard stand and nicking my wheelie bin. I'd forgotten all about it, to be honest with you. She sounded genuine, quite ashamed actually. I felt sorry for her, truth be told, 'cause she was quite upset and she didn't sound very old, not much more than a child. I said not to worry; worse things happen at sea. I didn't recognise her, but she sounded local, like. When I asked who she was, she put the phone down.'

Liz had never been much of an actress but she did her best to sound astonished: 'Well I never... how bizarre!'

Rick had already heard about Ryan's cousin and Jean's garden and, like everyone else, he was buzzing with theories. 'D'you think it's the same person? It must be! Too much of a coincidence.'

'No idea,' Liz said innocently. 'Maybe it's the Cornish piskies.'

After saying goodbye, she meandered up South Street, licking her ice cream contentedly. She couldn't help peering into Audrey's boutique to check if she were there, but her elderly mother was behind the till while Audrey herself was nowhere to be seen. Perhaps the mystery caller felt she'd done enough for the day and would complete her task tomorrow. At about five o'clock, however, when Liz was preparing supper, there was another loud hammering on the door and Esme burst in, smeared in clay and with strands of long grey hair dangling limply around her face, for it had started spitting with rain.

'Oh, my Lord!' she exclaimed and Liz, who had an inkling of what was coming, managed to raise her eyebrows in alarm.

'What is it?' She ushered her friend into the front room. 'Are you all right? Can I get you something?'

There was a flash of lightning, and in no time at all the sky turned black and the rain descended in thick sheets. Liz turned on one of the little lamps, creating a cosy glow, and Esme, still in her pottery smock, settled on the sofa before commencing her tale.

Audrey, it seemed, had left the shop early with a bit of a headache and had been putting her feet up at home.

'She thinks it's all the stress she's been under recently, what with Tony and Felipe – and Rafael...' said Esme, glancing at Liz, who gave a critical stare in return.

'Anyway,' Esme went on, undeterred, 'there she was, minding her own business, when the phone went and there was a strange voice, a girl's...'

She looked at Liz meaningfully. 'It must have been the same person who rang Rick and Ryan's cousin. Well, she sounded the same, youngish and definitely from round here somewhere.'

'What did she say?' Liz wanted to know, secretly hoping that Shannon hadn't messed up.

'She said Audrey was to stop' – Esme coughed awkwardly – '"shit-stirring". Pardon my French, but those were her exact words.' She shook her head. 'Appalling language.'

Liz looked suitably shocked.

'Anyway,' Esme continued, 'when Audrey asked who it was, she replied, "A friend of the truth. That's all you need to know." Then she insisted Rafael had nothing whatsoever to do with all the vandalism. She said Audrey was to "lay off" him and pick on someone as spiteful and mean as she was. Imagine that! Audrey was horrified, of course, and now her headache's ten times worse. I don't think she'll recover for days.'

Liz bit the inside of her cheek hard. It was all she could do not to laugh.

'Poor Audrey,' she spluttered, picking up a magazine from the floor by her feet and hiding behind it while Esme looked on, puzzled.

'Don't you think it's jolly sinister?' she persisted. 'I mean, perhaps we have a rampaging madman – or mad girl, rather – in our midst. Who is this mystery person? Who could it possibly be?'

Liz cleared her throat and finally managed to compose herself enough to speak. 'I don't know, but in my view whoever it is isn't mad at all. Quite the opposite. She's said sorry and she's returned Jean's flowers. As far as I'm concerned, we should draw a line under it now.'

Esme looked doubtful.

'Audrey will get over it,' Liz continued, 'and she was way out of order blaming Rafael. If you ask me, this girl's sprinkled a bit of fairy dust around the place and maybe, just maybe, things will start to get a bit better from now on.'

There was little talk in the village of anything else for days. Even the arrival of a B-list celebrity and his family, who were renting a big house on the seafront, failed to arouse much interest.

Bramble didn't know Audrey – or Jean or Rick, come to that – but she was kept up to date by Katie, who picked up all the gossip at The Hole in the Wall. When one of the students with a holiday job there quit, Danny asked Katie if she'd be interested in full-time work and she accepted immediately.

'I think he really likes me,' she told Bramble on the night that she heard. 'If only that Tabitha was out of the picture, I'd be home and dry.'

Bramble didn't like to point out that Tabitha seemed to be going precisely nowhere and that, as far as she could surmise, her relationship with Danny was very much on.

'Isn't there someone else you fancy?' she asked hopefully. 'Surely he's not the only one?'

Katie shook her head firmly. 'There are a few good-looking blokes around, sure, but no one's a patch on him. I told you, it's love. You can't just switch your feelings on and off, you know.'

Bramble was forced to agree for in truth, she was thinking

a great deal about Piers, too. The fact that he wasn't around much only seemed to whet her appetite. It was hardly surprising that she was seeing so little of him, because of course he had a busy job, and he assured her that his scheme for selling some of her land was coming along nicely.

'I've been putting out feelers and there's lots of interest,' he explained over the phone one afternoon when she was moving her stuff into her grandfather's freshly painted bedroom. It had taken a while to make a start because Katie had been dragging her feet, but finally, realising that Bramble was determined, she'd knuckled down and they were quite enjoying stacking clothes in Lord Penrose's old drawers and making the place feel homely.

'Great news!' Bramble replied, shifting the mobile from one ear to the other and tucking it under her chin. 'How soon d'you think we'll get a firm buyer? I could really do with the cash.'

She had begun to think about getting some paid work as well, but was holding out hope that with enough money from the land sale she might just be able to put the idea off until the manor was in a more habitable state and the dubious roofers had left.

'Don't fret,' Piers said airily. 'I'll let you know as soon as I have a bite.'

Bramble felt immensely relieved, because the workmen seemed to be spending ages fiddling around, drinking cups of tea and smoking, and as far as she could tell the roof was as leaky as ever. Presumably, Anatole would charge by the day, and it was obvious that they weren't going to finish any time soon.

One good piece of news was that, thanks to Liz, her young acquaintance, Shannon, had begun doing some work in the manor gardens, helped – or not helped, depending on your perspective – by her two brothers. In actual fact, the older one, Liam, was reasonably handy with a trowel and seemed to quite like wheeling the rubbish in the big barrow over to the compost heap at the back of the orchard. Conor, on the other hand, preferred to scrabble around in the earth with his toys, getting muckier as the day wore on. He didn't do any harm, though, and seemed to enjoy watching the others and feeling part of the proceedings.

Once or twice Liz popped along with her own toddler, Lowenna, to whom Bramble had taken a shine. This was a great success as both children enjoyed chasing each other around trees, eating picnics by the pond and examining ladybirds and butterflies.

Liz took the smallest children to the beach, too, while Shannon and Liam planted up the flowerbed nearest the back of the house, so that Bramble and Katie could look out from their drawing room on to a display of late-summer blooms colourful enough to gladden the stoniest heart.

It had been the warmest August that anyone could remember for a long time, punctuated by the odd clearing thunderstorm. Now, with September nigh, and with two weeks having elapsed since Pat's funeral and four weeks since she'd died, Bramble decided that if they didn't have their dinner party soon, the weather would turn and they wouldn't be coming out, glasses in hand, to admire the new flowerbed or dance on the terrace by moonlight as she'd imagined.

She suggested the date to Katie on Monday, and by Wednesday they'd had firm acceptances for that Saturday from everyone, including the elusive Fergus who admitted, when Bramble dropped off the written invitation at his cottage, that he'd say no if it weren't for Wilf.

'He's been going on and on ever since you mentioned it,'

Fergus grumbled. 'Seems to think it'll be like a kids' party. I keep telling him it'll be really boring, but he won't listen.'

'Don't worry,' Bramble replied breezily, for she was growing accustomed to her tenant's grumpy ways. 'I've asked someone called Liz along as well. She's got two children.'

She hoped, of course, that by Saturday Anatole's workmen would at least manage to fix the leak in the roof over the drawing room, though Gus explained that he was waiting on some special tiles from London, so for now there was only a temporary plastic cover.

'You can't just use any old tiles,' he said – rather patronisingly, Bramble thought. 'You need proper ones; good quality, like.' Then he winked at her through a haze of cigarette smoke. 'Don't you worry your pretty little head about it. We know what we're doing.'

Hearing voices, his mates joined them and announced that while they were hanging about they'd decided to do a spot of repointing, which was hot work, so they fancied some tea. It was only half an hour since Bramble had made the last cup, but they were already lighting up on the drive and it seemed rude to say no, so she dutifully bustled into the kitchen to put the kettle on. She didn't even think of asking Maria to do the job for her, fearing that she might have her head snapped off. Maria seemed appalled with the lot of them and was making herself even more scarce than usual, hiding in corners and shooting dirty looks whenever Gus or the others passed by.

She was having a running battle with them about the downstairs loo, which Bramble was trying to keep well out of. Someone kept putting his shaving things beside the washbasin, and three new toothbrushes and a tube of toothpaste appeared each morning in a plastic mug, only to be promptly removed by the housekeeper and plonked unceremoniously on the little table outside. Whenever Bramble passed again, the items had reappeared in the loo, soon to be fished out once more – and so it went on throughout the day, with never a word uttered.

Personally, Bramble didn't mind the roofers using her cloakroom for their ablutions, though they did seem to be making themselves very much at home. They'd also taken to washing and changing at the end of the day in the little bathroom at the top of the stairs, and it was probably only a matter of time before they commandeered one of the bedrooms. In fact, they were spending so many hours in the manor that she began to think they might just as well move in, belongings and all, and be done with it. She had a feeling it was what they were angling for anyway.

On the morning of the party, she and Katie drove to the supermarket to stock up on food and drink, before washing, chopping, steaming, baking and liquidising, until all three courses for the meal were ready and waiting in the fridge to be warmed up or served straight away.

Bramble insisted that Maria take the day off and go out, although she seemed most reluctant.

'There is nowhere I wish to visit,' she said in a surly voice.

Bramble warned her that she and Katie would be making a lot of mess in the kitchen, as well as moving furniture around in the drawing room and putting a loud music list together. This seemed to do the trick.

They didn't see Maria go, but guessed that she must have left very early because she wasn't around at breakfast, although she'd laid the table for them and left out cereal and juice.

'Thank God!' Katie said, and she glugged milk straight from the jug in an act of brazen rebelliousness. 'Now we can breathe again!'

Bramble was forced to admit that it did feel good to be

on their own for once – the roofers wouldn't be back till Monday – though she realised that perhaps she did feel a little warmer towards the housekeeper nowadays. Even so, it was a bit of a shock when Maria reappeared mid-afternoon in a knee-length, moss-green summer dress, wearing her usual inscrutable expression and carrying a bag of shopping.

'You do not have candles,' she announced, plonking the bag on the dining table, which the girls were about to lay. 'The earl always had candles at dinner and he insisted on white. He would not countenance any other colour.'

Without further ado, she removed her steel-rimmed glasses briefly to wipe them on a cloth from the pocket of her dress, reached for the four ornate solid-silver candlesticks on the sideboard behind her and produced a box of candles from the carrier, which she proceeded to unwrap.

'The candelabra are tarnished,' she said, turning them around in her hands, one by one, and examining them critically. 'They cannot go on display like that. I shall have to clean them.'

Katie made a face behind Maria's back, but Bramble pretended not to notice.

'Er, thank you,' she said, thinking that when the housekeeper made up her mind to do something, there was no way on God's earth that she or anyone else could make her change it.

After that, the girls laid the table. It felt strange taking the silver cutlery out of the drawer in the old mahogany sideboard, choosing the finest wine glasses that they could locate and folding the linen napkins, which were ironed and laid neatly in a drawer as if they'd been waiting all this time for the new arrivals. Although technically every item now belonged to Bramble, she couldn't quite absorb it, and felt almost guilty riffling through the cabinets to find what she needed.

At one point, Maria rematerialised with two newly gleaming candlesticks and told her off for using the wrong plates. There were a couple of porcelain dinner sets and Bramble picked the nearest, decorated with delicate flowers and a gold rim.

'These we use at Christmas only,' Maria said, taking the pile of side plates from Bramble and carefully replacing them in the cabinet. Then she removed some others and handed them across.

'Here are the ones for everyday entertaining.'

Bramble glanced at the crockery in her hands, with its faded Japanese-looking pattern in what must once have been a bright-blue, rust and gilt. There were numerous hairline cracks and little chips, but the items were still usable.

'They're so pretty,' she exclaimed. 'It's a shame they're damaged.'

'Yes,' Maria replied, gazing at them fondly. 'But I like to imagine that each flaw tells a story, like the wrinkles on a person's face. If everything were perfect, it would not be the sign of a good host.'

She vanished again and returned with the two remaining candelabra, complete with white candles, which she placed with the others along the length of the table. Then she rearranged the knives and forks, scolding Bramble for her sloppiness.

'The ends should be one inch from the edge of the table,' she tutted, nudging her mistress aside. 'And the dessert fork should be beneath the spoon, with the handle facing left. Like this, you see?'

Instead of taking offence, Bramble found herself watching with fascination as the older woman moved deftly about, positioning the water glasses just above the tip of the dinner knife, the wine glasses slightly to the right, lovingly refolding the napkins so that there was not a crease to be seen.

When everything was done, the three women stood back and admired their handiwork.

'It looks beautiful!' Bramble said, eyes shining, and she glanced at Maria, who gave a small, satisfied smile in return.

'Just as your grandfather would have wished,' she said, smoothing down the front of her skirt and readjusting the belt around her waist. 'Now that the most important tasks are done, I shall go and rest. I am tired, so you will have to finish the other jobs on your own.'

'Bloody cheek,' Katie whispered once the older woman was out of earshot. 'We didn't even ask for her help. And where the hell does she buy her clothes? That dress looks like something from the forties!'

'Probably is,' Bramble muttered. Then she said, 'Don't do that', because Katie was fiddling with Maria's table placement, setting the knives at odd angles, thinking that she was being funny.

Next the girls set about rearranging some of the furniture in the main reception room so that there was space on the parquet floor to dance, while those who so desired could spill out on to the terrace.

Katie had reluctantly conceded that they'd have to include Tabitha on the guest list, but her choice of outfit suggested she was determined not to let the competition get in her way. Now, at around six p.m., as she strolled into Bramble's new bedroom already fully robed and good to go, Bramble almost gasped.

'Are you *sure* you'll feel comfortable in that? Won't you be scared of popping out?'

Katie had picked the killer dress that she'd worn only once, some time ago, to a friend's twenty-first birthday in London. It was crimson and very tight fitting, hugging her curves and ending just above the knee. The most startling thing about it, however, was the gap that ran down the centre, from her neck almost to her tummy button, revealing a wide expanse of cleavage and bare flesh. It was only thanks to quantities of invisible lift-up tape that her assets didn't slip out altogether. Wondering how they stayed in place would inevitably be the main question on most people's minds.

Unfazed by Bramble's concern, Katie did a twirl, almost crashing to the ground when she caught a spiked heel in a floorboard.

'You'll have to be careful in those,' Bramble warned, thinking of the manor's multiple hazards indoors and out, especially after a few glasses of wine.

She herself was still in her pants and bra, unable to decide between her shimmery blue dress with the halter-neck or her faux-suede cream mini.

'Definitely the blue,' Katie said bossily. 'It's classier.'

Bramble slipped it on, along with a pair of high wedge sandals. She'd already painted her toenails pink, and Katie watched while her friend sat at her grandfather's antique dressing table and dabbed on grey-blue eyeshadow and lashings of mascara.

'How do I look?' she asked when she'd finished, running her fingers through her just-washed blonde hair.

'Gorgeous!' said Katie, reaching over to Bramble's make-up bag and passing her some pale-pink lipstick. 'You'll need some of this, too.'

Downstairs, Katie proposed opening a bottle of cava to get them in the mood, and while she fetched the drinks Bramble wandered into the drawing room. The French doors were wide open, allowing in a gentle breeze that fanned her face and arms. The sun was low in the sky and cast a rosy glow about the place that seemed to transform the faded rugs and curtains, the tattered sofas and the dusty paintings into priceless artefacts that could have graced the palaces of any French Bourbon or Russian Romanov.

So rich was the light that she felt like a princess in her shimmery gown as she stepped on to the terrace to gaze at Shannon's flowerbed, lovingly filled with pink anemones, purple phlox and orange helenium, and beyond it, the great swathe of garden and orchard that belonged to her. Tonight, of all nights, she almost had to pinch herself to believe it.

'Here you go,' said Katie, stepping out behind her and passing her a glass of ice-cold fizz. 'Chin chin!'

They chinked glasses, then stood there for a few more moments, side by side, listening to the distant lowing of cattle and the early-evening songs of birds, and breathing in the scent of baked earth and dried stone, of grass, tree, flower and salty Cornish air. Bramble could have stayed for ages, watching the majestic sun sink slowly below the horizon, but the throaty roar of a car on the driveway suggested the arrival of company.

'You go,' she told Katie, suddenly losing her nerve, for although they were hosting together, the responsibility seemed to weigh more heavily on Bramble's shoulders.

There was something else on her mind, too. Latterly, her grandfather may have been a recluse, but she knew that he'd once been famous for hosting glamorous parties and it seemed important that her very first event should go well. She felt that she owed it not so much to the guests or even to Lord Penrose but to Polgarry itself, as if it were a living creature. She wanted the place to feel happy, its ancient walls and rattling windows, its brick chimneys and creaking floors to be able to breathe easily. She wanted to release it from the strange gloom that had descended on it in latter years, for it to feel *free*.

Needing to do something while Katie went to the door, she plumped the shabby tasselled cushions and set straight the painting above the fireplace. It wasn't long, though, before her friend returned – alone.

'What's happened?' Bramble asked, alarmed, for Katie looked furious.

'She's there,' she hissed. 'Maria. She insisted on opening the door instead of me. She practically shoved me out of the way!'

Katie's face was a picture and Bramble almost laughed; she couldn't help it. Maria was absolutely determined to be part of the occasion, and you had to hand it to her, she was like a little terrier; she wouldn't let go.

They were interrupted by the arrival of the first guest, closely followed by Maria who announced in a loud voice, 'Mr Ryan Glossop!'

Bramble noticed that the housekeeper had changed since she'd last seen her, into a smart black A-line skirt and a white blouse buttoned up to the neck, and her grey hair had been freshly washed. Her expression was as stern as ever, but her dark eyes were glittering behind the steel-rimmed spectacles and her hands, resting on her lap, quivered slightly with nerves or excitement – or both.

Katie looked almost disappointed when she saw Ryan, who was neatly scrubbed and wearing a carefully pressed white shirt, rather tight pale-blue trousers and pointy black lace-ups, and carrying a bottle of something in his right hand. His eyes were out on stalks as he took in both his surroundings

EMMA BURSTALL

and Katie's revealing gown and he made a whistling sound. 'Wow! Massive!'

It could have been a double entendre, but somehow he didn't seem the type. In any case, Katie chose to ignore the ambiguity, intended or not, and clicked her tongue impatiently.

'It's a *manor*; of course it's huge,' she said, before taking the bottle off him and disappearing to put it in the fridge. She returned soon after with the glass of lager that he'd asked for.

Maria, meanwhile, retreated to the corner to observe the proceedings silently, and when the doorbell rang again, Bramble made a point of asking her to get it.

'Could you please help serve the meal, too?' she whispered when Katie wasn't listening. 'I'd really appreciate it.'

Tabitha, Danny, Liz and Robert arrived together. Robert was carrying an extremely wide-awake-looking Lowenna and explained that Rosie was staying with friends.

'Thankfully, I've got Alex and Jesse at the restaurant tonight or I wouldn't have been able to get away.'

They wandered around the drawing room, making admiring noises, and were soon joined by Tony and Felipe, who requested a guided tour. Bramble felt quite proud as she showed them around the best, most habitable bits of the manor, including her freshly painted bedroom.

'Darling, it's so grand!' Tony exclaimed, gazing out of the imposing windows with their magnificent views of fields and coastline, and back at the four-poster bed, the portraits and the stag's antlers – which Bramble had decided that she really rather liked and hung back on the wall – the spinet in the corner, the dressing room next door.

'Bit by bit, I'm starting to feel like it's really mine,' she replied, picking up a pair of shoes that she'd left by the bed and putting them back in a wardrobe. 'I'm not spooked any more – not much anyway.' She frowned. 'I just wish there wasn't so much to do.'

'Rome wasn't built in a day, you know,' Tony said kindly, while Robert, still carrying Lowenna on his hip, strolled over to the spinet and played a few notes. She struggled to get out of his arms and insisted on plonking the keys herself, making a horrible racket.

'Enough!' said Liz after a moment or two. 'She's hurting my ears. They'll hear us in Tremarnock!'

She looked extremely pretty in an off-the-shoulder black frock and heels, her dark hair pulled into a low bun at the nape of her neck and fastened with a sequined clip. She wore little make-up, but her chocolate-brown eyes seemed enormous – big enough to dwarf her small, oval face – and her silver earrings sparkled like stars.

Tabitha, meanwhile, who was much taller, was wearing simple, straight black trousers and a bronze-coloured vest top that looked almost jewel-like against her dark skin, while her curly black hair hung loose around her shoulders and fanned out around her like candyfloss.

Sometimes the two women touched or finished off each other's sentences. Bramble could tell that they were close, and she wondered if they'd met in the village or long before. They seemed to know each other very well. She also gathered that Robert adored Liz, and that Tony needed Felipe's quiet calm to counterbalance his own exuberance and volatility. It was fascinating how much you could pick up in a short space of time.

A good twenty minutes had passed, and when they went downstairs again Piers had arrived and was holding court in the drawing room with Katie. He looked very much at home, leaning against the fireplace with one arm propped on the mantelpiece, the other brandishing a glass of fizz. He was wearing an open-necked, red-and-blue-striped shirt tucked into tailored navy trousers, a black leather belt with a gold buckle and black loafers. The fringe of his silver-flecked hair was swept off his face and Bramble noticed the expensive-looking gold watch on his left wrist.

On seeing her, he strolled over and kissed her, quite deliberately, on the corner of the mouth and rested a hand lightly on her waist.

'You look glorious,' he whispered in her ear. 'A veritable goddess!'

Bramble smiled shyly and her face and body glowed. Then he turned to the others and shook hands or kissed on both cheeks, depending on their gender.

'Welcome all!' he said as if it were *his* party, and Bramble's heart pitter-pattered, for this, she reasoned, must surely be a signal of his intent.

For a moment Matt's face swam into her head and she felt that all-too-familiar stab of guilt, but she told herself that he wouldn't have enjoyed the party. In fact, she'd done him a favour by not asking him. What with Piers and Maria, not to mention the shabby grandeur of their surroundings, it wouldn't have been Matt's cup of tea at all. Besides, given her blatant and ongoing avoidance tactics and their disastrous reunion at Cassie's belly-dancing performance, he'd probably have refused to come anyway.

Maria started to pass around the smoked salmon and pâté canapés that Bramble and Katie had made, and when it came to Piers's turn, she whisked away the plate so fast that he nearly dropped the food on his clean trousers. Lowenna, meanwhile, was wriggling on Liz's lap, so Bramble took the little girl's hand and helped her toddle, with faltering steps, to the terrace, where they squatted down to examine the ants scurrying to and fro, the woodlice crawling over bits of dried twig and the butterflies fluttering their earthy wings and landing on bushes and flowers nearby.

They were inspecting a particularly large ant with something on its back when a rustling sound made Bramble look up and she saw Fergus strolling through the long grass towards them, with Wilf trotting by his side. Fergus looked very big, even bigger than usual, but there was something hesitant in his gait that made her heart go out to him; she wasn't sure why.

'Hello!' she said, rising, and her voice echoed in the stillness.

He didn't reply, but when he and Wilf were within a few feet the little boy raced up to hug her clumsily around the knees, before pulling back shyly, as if fearing that he'd overstepped the mark. She bent down and held out her arms to show that she wasn't offended.

'Hi, Wilf!' she said warmly as they embraced again. 'I thought you were never coming!'

Fergus muttered something about having to bring in the hens and fiddled awkwardly with a rolled-up sleeve of his white shirt, but once they stood face-to-face his hesitancy evaporated and he was himself again: cold, defiant and oddly angry.

'We won't be staying long,' he said then, as if she'd been about to raise an objection. 'We always come in this way. Your grandfather asked us to.'

Bramble's ears pricked up. She would have loved to enquire how often her strange tenant visited Lord Penrose and for what purpose, but they were joined by Piers, who took her arm and started to lead her indoors.

'Katie says it's time to eat. Everyone's famished.'

He glanced at Fergus and nodded at him haughtily. Bramble felt a flicker of embarrassment, because it was the sort of greeting that an upper-class gentleman might have once have given his chauffeur, or groom perhaps. If Fergus noticed, however, he chose not to react.

They were a strange crowd sitting around the elegant table, surrounded by crystal, silver and fine china. Lowenna was on Liz's knee, while Wilf settled beside his father, and it crossed Bramble's mind that it was unlikely Lord Penrose would have allowed infants at dinner – or any other meal, come to that. They'd surely have been banished to the nursery, if he even had one. Neither child appeared remotely sleepy, and it seemed possible they'd be with the adults all evening, even joining in the dancing later, if it ever got off the ground.

Bramble sat at the head of the table at one end, and although they hadn't prepared a seating plan, she was glad that Piers chose the chair beside her while Tony took the one opposite him. Beside Tony was Felipe, then Wilf, Fergus and Liz, while Katie took her place at the opposite end, nearest the door. To her right was Ryan, and beside him, Robert, then Tabitha, while Danny chose the spot between her and Piers.

The fact that Danny had positioned himself so far from Katie was obviously causing her some consternation, but she soon seemed to recover and must have been glad of Maria's assistance, for Piers was so attentive to Bramble that she was being no help at all.

At one point Bramble raised the subject of Anatole's workmen with Piers, explaining that she was a little concerned that they seemed to be taking a long time to finish the roof and had veered off temporarily on to another project.

'I'm not sure I can afford to have any repointing done yet,' she commented, realising that she didn't actually know what it was anyway, but Piers made light of her concerns.

'If they say it needs doing, it needs doing. You can rely on Anatole. I've known him for years.'

He gazed at her intently and she felt her legs turn to jelly, her stomach to mush. 'You really are very lovely,' he added, touching her fingers, which were twined around her crystal goblet. 'But I think you already know that.'

Tony, who must have been feeling a bit left out, leaned back and started talking to Fergus in a loud voice about 'that woman, Audrey'. As a result of her meddling and lies, Tony said, he and Felipe had been forced to consider selling up and leaving the village.

'People like her don't belong in a place like Tremarnock,' he boomed, his plump cheeks flushed from the wine. 'She doesn't understand the meaning of community spirit.'

Bramble, who'd finally managed to tear her eyes away from Piers for a moment, noticed that Fergus looked a little uncomfortable, perhaps because he had no idea whom Tony was talking about. After all, he rarely went into the village and the daily ins and outs of other people's lives were of no interest to him.

He said little in response, but later on she noticed that he and Wilf seemed to be hitting it off with Lowenna. Wilf started making silly faces at Lowenna, who roared with laughter, making Liz giggle, too. Then Fergus put his napkin on his head, which for some reason made the little girl laugh even more, and mayhem threatened to break out – until Wilf got down and tried to do a handstand by the window and Fergus had to tell him to calm down.

Meanwhile, Ryan was intent on chatting up Katie, who, with a few glasses of wine down her, was shamelessly flirting back. Every now and again she'd laugh loudly and flick her dark hair at Ryan before glancing in Danny's direction. Bramble guessed her game, but the truth was that Danny had eyes only for Tabitha and was unaware of the strenuous efforts being made on his behalf.

Bramble's gaze shifted back to Fergus and she was struck by how relaxed he seemed in the company of the children, like a different person. Had he once been less angry with the adult world, and if so, what had happened to make him shut himself away and hide up on the cliff? She supposed that it might have something to do with Wilf's mother, but she'd probably never know.

Katie rose to clear away the first course and Maria assisted. Piers had temporarily turned his attention to Felipe and so, seizing the moment, Bramble got up, too. As she passed Fergus, balancing a pile of dirty plates, she asked nonchalantly if he'd ever dined with Lord Penrose.

'Many times,' he replied, mid-laugh, for Lowenna was now scrambling on his lap and trying to put the napkin back on his head. 'He was a great raconteur.'

Desperately wanting to know more, Bramble would have loved to get him alone in a room and try to pump him for information, but Piers was right behind her, practically breathing down her neck.

'Let me take those,' he said, wrestling the plates off her. 'You go and sit down.'

The moment was over: Fergus was now preoccupied again with the little ones. Bramble settled down once more beside Tony, who took a sip of wine.

'Wonderful spread!' he said, dabbing his forehead with a handkerchief, for it was quite humid. 'We'll have to get you round for dinner at ours, if you don't think it's too much of a hovel compared with this!'

Pudding was Bramble's famous Eton mess (using sugar, not salt this time), as well as plum and greengage fool made with fruits from the orchard. By the time they'd finished, Lowenna had become tetchy, so Bramble took her and Liz to one of the bedrooms, where it was hoped that the little girl would settle.

On the way back, she poked her head into the kitchen, where Maria was washing dishes.

'Leave them – please,' she insisted. 'Katie and I will do them. I don't want you working this late.'

Maria glanced up from the sink and nodded. It was around ten thirty p.m. and she looked tired.

'Very well then.' She rubbed her hands dry on a towel. 'I'm glad that your party has been a success.'

The small smile that Bramble had noticed earlier reappeared briefly, but soon vanished.

'Miss Bramble?' the housekeeper went on with an urgency that hadn't been there before. 'That land agent...'

Bramble's eyes widened and she would have asked Maria what she meant, but the housekeeper shook her head as if she'd revealed too much already, and left the room. Bramble started to follow, until a loud crash from the dining room, followed by raised voices, sent her scurrying to investigate. Wilf, it seemed, who'd been running around the table, had caught one of the candelabra with his elbow and sent it flying. Luckily, the candles had blown out before hitting the floor and nothing was damaged, but still, the small boy had started sobbing.

Bramble took him into what she and Katie called the TV room, where he soon settled down. Lord Penrose had only old videos, no DVDs, and the choice was distinctly limited, so Wilf opted for a 1930s' Errol Flynn movie and pulled up his feet on the battered sofa to watch. He didn't seem to mind the stuffed weasel in a glass case, the dusty books on the shelves or the general air of decrepitude. It was very different from the small, neat front room in Chessington, with its comfy maroon-velvet three-piece and fluffy rug that you could sink your toes into, and Bramble was pretty certain that at his age she'd have run a mile.

The others took their drinks into the drawing room, where Katie put on some music. The doors were still open on to the terrace and the flickering candles cast strange shadows that made everyone appear mysterious and really rather beautiful. Katie's strategy with Danny had totally failed, because Tabitha was now snuggled into his side on the sofa, his arm around her shoulders, and both had dreamy, faraway looks on their faces as if they were wrapped in a fluffy cloud just big enough for the two of them.

Trying to make the best of things, Katie announced that everyone was to dance. When no one stirred, she grabbed Ryan's hand and forced him on to the floor.

'I've got two left feet,' he protested, but she was having none of it.

'I love dancing,' she declared, shimmying to the sounds of Adele. She was rather drunk and it would have been sensible to quit while she was ahead and take herself off to bed, but that was never going to happen. Bramble just hoped that her friend wouldn't make a fool of herself and burst into tears or, worse, pour a glass of wine over Tabitha's head.

Perched on the end of the coffee table near Piers, Bramble noticed him lean forwards, perhaps to ask her to dance, too, but a pitter-patter of rain on the stones outside stopped him in his tracks.

'The bucket!' she cried, dashing to the corner of the room where she'd put it earlier. She managed to position it in the right place on the floor under the leak just in time to catch the first fat drops of water, which soon started to turn into a steady trickle.

'I thought they'd fixed it – temporarily at least?' Katie slurred over the music.

Bramble frowned. 'Not yet, it seems.'

'What the hell have they been doing?' Katie went on, but Bramble merely smiled, not wishing to get into a debate in front of Piers about the pros and cons of Gus and his band of not-so-merry men.

Fergus, who had been talking to Felipe, walked over to where she was standing by the bucket and looked up at the ceiling.

'Oh dear. How long are the repairs going to take?'

Bramble's heart sank slightly; she wasn't sure why.

'The workmen didn't give a timescale,' she replied uneasily. 'They're doing other stuff while they wait for some special tiles to arrive.'

'Who are they?' her tenant asked now. He was frowning, and Bramble was aware of Piers watching from the other side of the room.

'The main one's called Gus, and there's a Baz, too. They're local, I think.'

She realised even as she spoke how limp this sounded, for the truth was, she knew nothing really about them, not even if they worked for Anatole full-time.

Fergus pulled a face. 'Gus Bottrell?'

'I don't know his surname.'

'Guy with a big scar on his face?' Fergus ran a finger across his cheek and Bramble nodded.

'What on earth made you choose him? He's worse than useless. He's a bloody cowboy.'

She recoiled, stung. 'They were highly recommended to me,' she said defensively. 'They're meant to be really—'

They were interrupted by Piers, who slipped an arm around her waist and whispered in her ear, 'You look as if you need rescuing.' Then he cleared his throat and bowed theatrically. 'Madam, I think the *painter* has taken up quite enough of your time. Will you do me the honour of giving me the next dance?'

Relieved, she took his hand and allowed him to whisk her to the other side of the room in a sort of waltz. Piers wasn't perfect at it and neither was she, but he moved with an ease and quickness that restored her confidence, and as the track changed to something slow and smoochy, she had no hesitation in melting into his arms, closing her eyes and breathing in the heady scent of his expensive aftershave.

At one point she glanced around and noticed that Fergus had moved – she couldn't see where – and when she checked again he was with Wilf by the door, speaking to a swaying Katie as if preparing to leave. Unintentionally, Bramble caught his eye over Katie's shoulder and she could have sworn that he shot her a reproving look. The gall of it, she thought, turning swiftly back to her dance partner and nuzzling quite deliberately into his neck. Fergus had no right to criticise her judgement, and what did he know about roofs and restoration anyway? She was glad that he'd had enough of the party. She didn't need him telling her what to do.

The track changed to something more upbeat, and Tony and Felipe took to the floor, along with Liz and Robert, who, like Ryan, wasn't a natural dancer and looked distinctly awkward. Katie, meanwhile, had crashed into a chair and appeared to have fallen asleep, while Ryan sat on the arm beside her, jiggling his leg up and down and gazing around the room forlornly as if unsure what he was supposed to do.

Bramble hardly even registered Liz and Robert leaving with Lowenna, soon followed by Felipe and Tony, who declared blearily that he'd had a 'tip-top evening', though he wouldn't be feeling quite so cheerful in the morning. When Katie stirred and mumbled something in her sleep, Ryan helped her upstairs, before heading off disconsolately on foot.

Left alone with Piers, Bramble suddenly felt shy. It had stopped raining but it was still wet outside, so she closed and locked the doors. Scanning the room, with all its empty glasses, she thought that it must be well after one a.m. and the clearing away would have to wait till tomorrow.

She was acutely aware of Piers watching while she snuffed out the candles on the mantelpiece, and when she turned around he took a few paces towards her, grabbed her in his arms and kissed her on the lips, before asking in a low, suggestive voice if he could see her new bedroom.

Half-drugged with sleep as she was, Bramble sighed with a mixture of happiness and guilt, because she already knew that she wasn't going to put up any resistance. This was just as she'd hoped, wasn't it? Just what she'd imagined when she and Katie had started planning the party, discussing who would come and what they'd eat. It was the real reason she hadn't wanted Matt here, wasn't it? She'd planned it all along.

She wrote a quick note to Maria, then led the way through the marble hallway and up the wood-panelled stairs to Lord Penrose's bedroom, where the blue shimmery dress soon found its way on to the spinet in the corner, the bra and pants on to the mantelpiece and the wedge sandals on to the floor beside the four-poster bed.

The only witness to the rest of the night's activities was a lonesome seagull that landed on the windowsill and cocked its head inquisitively before flapping off again; the only sound, the distant hooting of an owl and the scrabbling of a family of tiny brown mice that had made their home behind the wainscot.

Chapter Seventeen

KATIE LOOKED AND sounded like death the following morning, white-faced and extremely grumpy. The mention of breakfast made her gag, so Bramble went downstairs on her own, rather dreading seeing Maria – who, despite her relatively good humour last night, would undoubtedly have been dismayed to wake to a heap of dirty crockery and cutlery in the kitchen, a dining room that resembled a war zone and a rushed note from Bramble telling her to leave everything as she and Katie would do it later.

Although Maria was technically her employee, Bramble still couldn't cope with the idea of someone cleaning up after her. Besides, she felt sure that the housekeeper wouldn't approve of the fact that Piers had stayed over – and in the old earl's bedroom, to boot.

Bramble supposed it was fortunate, in a way, that Piers had risen at dawn and tiptoed out without waking her. He'd sent her a text later explaining that he had an appointment in Plymouth.

Thanks for last night, he'd written. I'll be in touch.

She'd found the text a little short; she'd have preferred a few reassuring kisses and something about how gorgeous she was. But she told herself that he must have been in a hurry.

As she padded across the hallway in bare feet, remembering last night, she realised that she felt uneasy on several counts, though she wasn't entirely sure why. After all, his performance had lived up to every expectation, hadn't it? His taut body and languorous touch, his devil-may-care smile in the moonlight, his air of adventure, the sense she'd had with him that nothing was out of bounds. He'd certainly done several things to her that she'd never experienced before. Yet despite all this, she'd felt strangely absent, as if she hadn't really been there at all and someone else pretending to be her had been there in her place. She brushed the thought away quickly, not wishing to dwell on it. She was probably just tired.

Maria was waiting for her at the dining room door, dressed in a calf-length beige skirt and pale-pink checked blouse, her arms crossed tightly over her chest and her expression just as sour and disapproving as Bramble had feared. All the softness of yesterday, it seemed, had melted clean away, though whether this was owing to the general chaos or to Piers's unexpected stopover, she couldn't tell.

'I have prepared breakfast for you in the morning room, Miss Bramble,' Maria said curtly, 'as there is no space elsewhere.'

'Sorry about the mess,' Bramble mumbled, cursing her complexion, for she could feel herself turning red under the housekeeper's gaze. 'Katie's still asleep, but we'll do the washing-up when she wakes.'

She scurried, head down, to the hexagonal room in the east wing of the manor, where the morning light was so bright that she rather wished she'd brought sunglasses. She and Katie had rarely been in here, because it seemed such a long way from the kitchen, and besides, who needed so many different living areas? If you used them all, you'd never be able to remember where you'd put your book or left your phone or shoes.

Still, Maria had gone to a lot of trouble to cart in the bread, cereal, jam pots and coffee jug, and Bramble did her best to look grateful.

'Thank you.' She settled down at the round walnut table and reached for the milk, orange juice and coffee. 'You're very kind.'

It was a long time since dinner last night and she was hungry; plus she had a slight headache herself and it would be good to have something to soak up the alcohol. It was hardly surprising that she felt groggy, given the quantity of wine she'd consumed, and she wasn't alone. In fact, the only sober people by the end of the evening had been Fergus and Liz, who was driving. Certainly, Robert, Tony and Felipe were extremely merry, Ryan was pie-eyed, Katie was utterly out of it and Piers was bewitchingly dangerous.

Surreptitiously, Bramble pulled a painkiller from the pocket of her shorts and downed it with a slug of juice before starting on the toast and honey. At least she wasn't as bad as Katie, who was probably throwing up at this very moment, and she had the Danny disappointment to cope with. As far as Bramble could tell, he'd hardly spoken to anyone, so wrapped up had he been in Tabitha. In fact, the pair might just as well have been alone on a desert island for all they'd contributed to the general gaiety of proceedings.

Bramble was tucking into her third slice of brown toast when the ancient corded Bakelite telephone rang on the desk in the corner, nearly making her jump out of her skin. She scarcely ever used the landline, and it took her a moment or two to work out where the noise was coming from. Rising to pick it up, she half-expected to find Piers at the other end, inviting her on some jolly jaunt after he'd finished his meeting, so it was a shock when a familiar London voice announced that it was Matt.

'How are you?' Bramble asked over-brightly; he was the very last person she wanted to speak to. In fact, the mere sound of his voice made her wish that the ground would swallow her up.

Matt didn't reply but paused for a moment instead, as if mustering courage.

'You've been avoiding my calls,' he said finally, very deadpan.

'No, I haven't,' Bramble protested, quick as a flash. 'You know I've been super-busy, that's all.'

'Did the party go well last night?'

She started. How did he know?

'It was all right. Quite dull actually,' she fibbed. 'I knew you wouldn't want to come.'

Matt sighed heavily. 'Don't, Bram. I'm not stupid.' He seemed to have the weight of the world on his shoulders. 'You weren't answering your mobile as usual, so I rang Katie. I don't give a damn about the party, though I would've come if you'd wanted me to. It's the lies I can't stand. At first, when you weren't getting back to me, I just thought you had a lot to do. Then when you came to London and you weren't even going to tell me, I tried so hard to give you the benefit of the doubt. But now I realise there's more to it. I can't believe it, but it's true...'

She could imagine his face, all screwed up with pain. He was a proud man, not given to emotional outbursts. He'd be finding this so hard.

'You could've told me you were having second thoughts, Bram,' he went on. 'You could have done me that courtesy at least. I've only ever had one proper girlfriend and that's you. I thought we were for keeps, together for ever and all that.' He sounded so hurt. 'Seems I was wrong.'

Bramble felt a tugging sensation in her guts and her eyes

filled with tears. She wasn't prepared for this, not at all, but she knew full well that she should have spoken to him sooner. She'd been a bitch.

'You refused to come to Cornwall with me,' she said querulously, hating the self-pity that had crept into her voice, the self-justification. 'How could it ever have worked with you there and me here?'

'I thought it was only temporary. I thought you'd get bored and want to come home. I would've waited for you. I would've joined you in the end, if you'd wanted to stay.' There was a catch in his voice and he seemed close to tears. 'You should've told me the truth. You should've said it was over.'

He paused to collect himself and she gripped the receiver so tightly that her knuckles turned white, waiting anxiously for what was coming next.

'There's someone else, isn't there? Tell me. I deserve to know.'

Bramble felt sick. She wanted so much to make it easier for herself, but she owed him more than that.

'Yes,' she said, screwing up her face and squeezing her eyes shut, 'there is.'

Matt made a strange noise, half-splutter, half-choke, and she prayed that he wouldn't break down completely because she didn't think that she could hold it together herself.

'Who is he?' he said at last, but Bramble couldn't bring herself to repeat his name. 'Just a local guy, someone who's helping me sell some land.'

'He's a lucky man,' Matt managed to respond. 'I hope he's worth it.'

She wished so much that she could make him feel better, but there were no words. Everyone back home assumed they'd get married one day and have kids. She'd thought so, too.

'I'm sorry,' she said, aware of how inadequate it sounded, and also how final. Was she doing the right thing? She drew back her shoulders. She'd been cheating on him in her head for weeks and finally, last night, she'd done it for real. There was no going back.

'At least I know,' Matt said at last. 'At least I won't be hanging on any more, like some stupid idiot.'

'I really am—' Bramble started to say, but there was a click and she realised that he'd gone.

After that, the toast tasted like charcoal in her mouth, the coffee bitter and cloying, and she pushed them away. Do to others what you would have them do to you, the saying went. Well, she'd hate Matt to treat her in the cruel manner that she'd treated him – but of course he never would.

Katie was no comfort whatsoever.

'You've made a big mistake,' she tutted from her bed when she heard what had happened. The curtains were still drawn and merely lifting her head off the pillow made her wince. 'You're going to regret it.'

It wasn't what Bramble wanted to hear, so she stormed off and refused to speak again for hours, festering alone in her room. Matt loomed so large in her mind that she feared she might go mad; the thought of him suffering made her feel wretched. She tried to focus on Piers instead, but it didn't help that he didn't call her back all that day.

'He's probably just tied up with work,' Katie said crossly when Bramble finally broke the silence later that afternoon. 'Maybe he's waiting to tell you he's had an offer of a million pounds for your land.'

'Don't be silly; it's not worth that much.' But she was

secretly pleased, for the thought of what Gus's bill would be when they'd finished made her feel sick.

Ryan turned up unexpectedly at about seven p.m. with a bunch of white roses for Katie and an invitation to the cinema. She was still in her pyjamas and didn't even ask him in, instead making him hover awkwardly at the door.

'I don't like sitting in cinemas and I'm not into dating at the moment; I'm focusing on other things,' she said haughtily while Bramble hid in the background. Poor Ryan looked crestfallen.

'You'd better keep these,' Katie added, handing the roses back, and he sloped off to his car with his tail between his legs. Bramble felt like running after him to give him a hug, but decided against it on the grounds that he might get the wrong impression and ask her out instead.

'You could have said it more nicely,' she scolded once the door was firmly shut.

But Katie was unrepentant. 'There's no way I'd *ever* go out with him. It would be meaner to string him along.'

Bramble didn't dare point out that it had been a very different story last night, when Katie had been batting her eyelashes and flirting with the fishmonger like mad. Now she was in such a bad mood that even the slightest criticism might spark World War Three.

When Piers did finally ring, at about five o'clock on Tuesday afternoon, Bramble was so relieved that she almost lost all composure and burst into tears.

'I thought something might have happened,' she said, watching Shannon out of an upstairs window, trug in hand, dead-heading a pink rosebush. She'd just gone back to school, but had promised that she'd come for an hour or two after lessons when she could. Piers laughed humourlessly.

'Sorry. It's been one meeting after another like you wouldn't believe.'

'You could have texted,' she scolded. 'How about supper tonight? The Lobster Pot in the village does good food.'

A change of scene would be welcome, and besides, she couldn't help feeling that he owed her. If anyone should take on the task of cheering her up and taking her mind off Matt, it was surely him.

'I can't,' he replied, before apologising again. 'I'll be in touch soon – at the end of the week. Promise.'

The end of the week? That was so far away! Disappointment washed over her, but she told herself that he must have his reasons.

'Any news about the land?' she asked, hoping to detain him a little longer. Besides, she really was keeping her fingers crossed for a cash injection, or at least the prospect of one.

'I, um...' He sounded slightly uncomfortable, or was she imagining it? 'Nothing yet.' Was he was holding something back? 'It takes time...'

'Of course,' she replied, trying to disguise the anxiety creeping into her bones. 'Just let me know as soon as you can.'

After he'd gone, she stood there for a few minutes, going over the conversation. He hadn't been particularly warm, which was peculiar given their intimacy on Saturday night. Had she done something wrong? If so, she couldn't imagine what. Over dinner he'd hardly taken his eyes off her, and he'd been extremely amorous later on and had seemed not at all dissatisfied with his experience either before, during or after. Quite the opposite, in fact.

Had something changed? But how, in such a short space of time? No, she told herself firmly, she was being silly and paranoid. He was stressed, super-busy and working extremely hard on her behalf. She must be patient. He'd no doubt call back soon sounding completely different, the gorgeous, dashing Piers again.

She could hear an engine starting up and peered out of a different window to see Gus and his men scrambling into their lorry. Gus spotted her from the passenger side, opened the door again and leaned out, flashing the large, lurid tattoo on his thick forearm.

'We're off for fish and chips,' he shouted merrily. 'Fancy anything? A battered sausage?' He made it sound faintly suggestive and she shook her head quickly. 'A nice juicy pasty? A pickled egg? You can pay us back later.'

Bramble retreated quickly, feeling rather tainted. They never worked beyond five. In fact they usually finished much earlier, and there was no sign of the new roof tiles yet. Piers, Gus – she wasn't having a good day. And if only she could stop brooding about Matt...

She'd been planning on making a start on the drawers in Lord Penrose's study downstairs, which was overflowing with papers and books that looked as if they hadn't been touched in years. It was time, she felt, to start opening up other parts of the house, to put her own stamp on them, but she wasn't in the mood now. Instead, she went to find Katie, having decided to accompany her to The Hole in the Wall. She'd be on duty but Bramble would be bound to bump into some locals there; she'd rather chat with them than stay here on her own.

Katie was lying on her bed again, staring at the ceiling. The windows were closed and the room smelled stuffy. She hadn't recovered from Saturday either. There had been little mention of Danny, despite the fact that she'd seen him at work, and she was clearly still upset that her best efforts at seduction had failed so miserably.

'Isn't it time to get ready?' Bramble asked, looking at her friend's blotchy face and greasy hair and thinking of all the hours that she'd once spent making herself beautiful for her bar shifts.

'In a minute.' Katie didn't move. 'I don't want to go to work today. In fact, I don't want to go there ever again. Maybe I'll call in sick.'

She'd only been doing the job for a few weeks and she needed the cash; they both did.

'You can't let them down,' Bramble said firmly. 'Get up and have a shower. You'll frighten away the customers if they see you in that state!'

'Shocking, the way she treated Ryan. What harm has he ever done anyone? He wouldn't hurt a fly. That girl needs to learn some manners.'

Esme's long nose twitched with annoyance and her small grey eyes flashed menacingly. She was sitting with Tabitha at Liz's kitchen table while Liz put the kettle on and handed beakers of diluted fruit juice to Oscar and Lowenna.

It had been a busy morning making lunches at the church hall, but fortunately Lowenna had slept after returning from Jean's house, giving Liz the chance to relax. She had been delighted when her friends had turned up at almost the same time for a chat and a cuppa; in fact, it had been perfect timing. Rosie was at a friend's and Robert had said he wouldn't make it home for supper, so there was no rush to prepare food.

'Biscuit?' asked Liz, handing the tin to Esme first, who looked as if she needed sweetening up.

She took a chocolate one before passing them to Tabitha.

'Did you hear what she did?' Esme went on, sinking her teeth into her food and crunching loudly.

Liz shook her head.

'He brought her a bunch of roses and she thrust them back at him. How rude is that? She could at least have taken them and thanked him graciously, even if she didn't want to go out with him. It's seriously dented his confidence – and he didn't have much in the first place.'

Liz poured boiling water into three mugs and stirred the teabags around.

'I wonder why Katie behaved so badly? Perhaps she was feeling terrible. She did seem to drink a lot that night.'

'That's no excuse,' snapped Esme, reaching for another biscuit. 'I know men are daft – look at Rick! But Ryan's a sensitive soul and she should have been gentler. I've half a mind to have a word with her and tell her how upset she's made him. He could hardly speak when I bought my fish this morning. He had tears in his eyes. I thought he was about to break down.'

Liz put three mugs on the table and sat down. She'd fetched a box of toys for Oscar and Lowenna, who were busy throwing them around and roaring with laughter. Tabitha, who'd been silent up to now, asked Esme how she knew about Katie's bad behaviour, and the older woman explained that Ryan had confided in Jesse, who'd told Loveday, who'd mentioned it to Barbara, who'd spilled the beans to Esme. Nothing was secret around here for long.

'It's odd, because she was flirting with Ryan at the party,' Tabitha commented. 'Flashing her boobs and batting her eyelashes. She was all over him like a rash.'

Liz took a sip of tea and nodded. 'That dress was something else.'

'I thought she was eyeing Danny up, too,' Tabitha went on slowly. 'Did you notice? He said it could have been embarrassing but he just ignored her. Apparently, she's been really frosty with him since and it's quite awkward in the pub. The others have commented as well.'

'Oh dear.' Liz *had* suspected that Katie was keen on Danny and had secretly never thought that she was serious about poor Ryan. But she hated bad feeling and didn't believe that deep down Katie was a mean person. Immature, a bit selfish and misguided, yes, but not deliberately cruel.

Fortunately, Tabitha wasn't a vindictive person either, and besides, she and Danny were clearly so crazy about each other that she really didn't need to worry. Esme, however, took a different view.

'Barbara says that girl isn't welcome in her pub any more,' she sniffed, brushing the crumbs off her lap. 'And I won't be inviting her to my next exhibition, that's for sure.' She waggled a finger at Tabitha. 'You watch her with your chap. I wouldn't let him out of my sight if I were you. Katie's a man-eater; I've seen her type before. She'll gobble him up for breakfast if you're not careful.'

By the time Esme had finished her rant, Tabitha was so alarmed that she asked Liz to mind Oscar for her while she hot-footed it to The Hole in the Wall to have a word with Danny. She wasn't quite sure what she'd say, but she wanted him to know that she wasn't happy about Katie and didn't trust her. At the very least, that might make him more wary of the other girl's charms.

He was in his flat upstairs, checking stock levels on his computer, and he looked up and grinned when Tabitha walked in.

'Hi, gorgeous!' he said. 'To what do I owe this unexpected pleasure?'

He was looking particularly handsome, in a close-fitting black T-shirt that showed off his muscles. His hair was tied back in a ponytail and his teeth flashed white against his brown face. It was quite dark in the room, owing to the low-beamed ceiling and small, leaded windows. The floor was uneven beneath the beige carpet, and there was an empty fireplace in the corner that must have been a blessing on cold winter nights before the central heating had been installed.

Tabitha pulled up a chair opposite and explained her conversation with Esme. For a moment it seemed that Danny might laugh, until he clocked his girlfriend's worried eyes, the anxious twisting of her lips. He knew her history and understood, deep down, how easily her fragile trust could be broken.

When she'd finished, he got up and knelt before her, smoothing away the furrows on her brow with his thumbs.

'I promise you,' he said warmly, 'that I'm not and never will be remotely interested in Katie. I offered her a job because she needed work and I needed a bar hand, simple as that. I'll happily fire her this evening if you want me to. She's been quite difficult these past few days, so I've got a very good excuse.'

'That won't be necessary.'

Danny looked up, and Tabitha turned and her mouth dropped open – for there, in the doorway, was Katie herself.

'I was planning to hand in my notice anyway,' she said, her chin jutting, arms crossed tightly over her chest. 'I don't like working here – in fact, I hate it – and I don't like Tremarnock either. I'm going back to London as soon as I can.'

And with that she stalked away, while Danny and Tabitha stared at each other, listening in silence to her angry footsteps on the wooden stairs and waiting until they were certain that she'd left before opening their mouths.

It was Danny who spoke first, exhaling loudly. 'Well! I didn't see that coming. I guess it makes things easier. Only problem is, I need a new barmaid now.'

'I can help out until you find one,' said Tabitha. 'If Liz doesn't mind looking after Oscar.'

She twisted a strand of her curly black hair round and round a forefinger. 'I'm glad she's going, though I feel a bit sorry for Bramble. I should think she'll be lonely in that leaky old manor with only the surly housekeeper for company. I wouldn't like it. I wonder what she'll decide to do now.'

Chapter Eighteen

BRAMBLE HAD DROPPED Katie off near the pub before heading to park the car. It was too early to go for a drink – she might be the only customer – so she decided to kill time and stroll along the seafront first.

The heatwave was finally over and a slight chill in the air suggested that autumn was just around the corner. Most folk had left the beach and the streets felt emptier than of late, but several people in shorts and warm sweaters were out exercising their dogs, nodding at each other and stopping for a moment to chat while their pets sniffed and growled or wagged their tails. The lights had just gone on in The Lobster Pot, for although it was only six thirty, the sky had already begun to darken, and the windows in the shops and cottages were shut tight to keep out the wind.

Meanwhile the tide, a fair way out, had left a wide stretch of sandy-coloured shingle covered in blobs of slimy seaweed and the odd length of crusty rope, perhaps from one of the boats bobbing out at sea. One hardy soul in red swimming trunks walked boldly down to the water, plunged in and swam vigorously towards an orange buoy. Bramble watched him getting smaller and smaller and shivered in her jeans and thin cotton top, wishing that she'd thought to bring a jumper.

Definitely no swimming today for her; she'd rather have a hot bath.

She wondered what the place would feel like when all the tourists had gone and felt a shudder of fear. So far she hadn't missed London, but perhaps the village would seem dull without the hordes of noisy, colourful holidaymakers to brighten things up. What if she went off the life here, as Matt had predicted that she surely would?

She was just reminding herself that at least she had Katie when her friend appeared, tapped her on the shoulder and pointed to the bench behind. 'You'd better sit down.'

Surprised, Bramble did as she was told, and listened in dismay as Katie explained that she'd packed in the job and wouldn't be going back.

'What?' stuttered Bramble, hoping that she'd misheard, but Katie's expression suggested otherwise. 'Why?'

The news was only just beginning to sink in when yet another bombshell made Bramble reel.

'I can't stay here any more. I miss home too much. I miss my family. I've tried, but I can't do it. I'm sorry, Bramble. Cornwall's not for me.'

She was so shocked that she couldn't speak for several minutes, and when the words finally came, they tumbled out in such a rush that she herself could hardly understand what she was saying.

'You can't... We've only been here one summer... Give it a bit longer... Just because Danny's not available... You'll meet someone else... What about *me*?'

She must have said 'please' at least ten times, and she would have got down on her hands and knees and begged if she thought it would do any good, but Katie looked at her sadly.

'It's no good, I won't change my mind. I'll stay a couple

more days to pack up and spend some time with you, but I need to be home by the weekend. It's my little sister's birthday on Sunday. I want to give her a surprise.'

'I – I don't think I can manage without you,' Bramble stammered. 'It's too big a project, too lonely...'

Katie seized her by the shoulders and stared earnestly into her eyes.

'Come with me. You can sell the manor and come home, too. It's such a big old place, it'll take years to get it how you want it, and that's always assuming you can make enough money from flogging the land to do the renovations. Come back to London; it's where you belong.'

Bramble shook her head. 'No.'

'Your mum and dad will be so happy,' Katie wheedled. 'And Matt...'

'I said that's finished. Over.'

'Are you sure?'

For a moment the thought of her old life with Matt danced tantalisingly before Bramble's eyes. She'd hated her job and had wanted some sort of change, an adventure, but picturing Sunday lunch with him at her parents' dining table, opening their presents together on Christmas morning, holding hands with him on the sofa in front of the telly – it gave her a lump in the throat.

But she'd dumped him and he'd never forgive her. And in any case, how could she leave Polgarry now, just when something about the place had started to seep into her very bones? She couldn't explain it, but she felt as if it had somehow become part of her, like a child, perhaps, that needed her love and protection. It would be treacherous to abandon it to whatever fate a new buyer might have in store – always assuming that she could find one.

She bit her lip. She could feel tears pricking in her eyes and it was all she could do not to crumple.

'I can't leave the manor. I have to see this through.'

'No!' Katie cried. 'You wanted to give it a go and you have. You've tried living here and you've got nothing to prove – you can hold your head up high. You're not a country girl; you're a Londoner through and through. You'll start to loathe Cornwall when the weather turns and there's nothing to do except stare at the bloody seagulls.'

She kicked viciously at the gravel beneath her feet, making the little stones fly, and Bramble, watching, sighed.

'You don't understand. Why would you?' she said slowly. 'Lord Penrose wasn't your grandfather. The manor's not part of your history. I'll miss you like crazy, but I can't make you stay.' A tear trickled down her cheek and plopped on to her khaki skirt, making a small, dark circle on the fabric. 'Will you come back and see me? You can bring your sisters, too.'

Katie took a deep breath.

'Of course!' she said eventually, giving Bramble a consoling squeeze that somehow just made her feel even more alone. 'They'll love it here – for a few nights,' Katie added quickly. 'Maybe when the weather improves in the spring.'

They were a sad pair as they made their way back to the manor in Bramble's yellow VW, squinting slightly as the reddening sun glowed bright and low in the sky. Neither had felt like going anywhere after their conversation, and besides, Bramble had some thinking to do. Now it seemed more urgent than ever to secure the funds from selling the land. Without Katie's help with painting and so on, not to mention her moral support, Bramble felt that she could achieve little.

She desperately needed a cash injection so that she could pay people to do the work for her.

Maria was surprised to see them home so early, as they'd told her they'd be out late and wouldn't be wanting supper.

'Do you wish me to prepare something now, Miss Bramble?' she asked coolly, and Bramble said no, they'd make themselves a sandwich if they were hungry.

Katie went to her room – it was obvious that she couldn't wait to start packing but felt too guilty to say it – so Bramble went into the morning room, closed the door and picked up the ancient corded telephone from the desk in the corner. She had to steel herself to tap in the number. To her surprise, Piers picked up immediately.

'Oh,' he said, sounding slightly shaken as if she'd caught him off guard. 'It's you. I wasn't expecting you to ring.'

Bramble noticed the uneasiness in his voice and felt her heart flutter. If it hadn't been for Katie, she wouldn't have pushed it, but she needed some sort of assurance, a proper update, so she pulled back her shoulders and began.

'Something's happened,' she said, drawing in her breath. 'Katie's just told me she's leaving, and I need to know roughly how long it'll take for the land to sell and the money to come through. I know you said things are in motion, but have you had any firm interest yet? What's the timescale?'

There was a pause during which she fancied she could almost hear his brain working, the little grey cells powering up.

'I, um...' He cleared his throat. 'I was going to tell you... I was getting the paperwork together.' He paused again. 'There's a slight problem, you see...'

Bramble's pulse started to race. This was too much after Katie's news. She needed something positive to hold on to. 'What problem? What's the matter?'

Piers coughed. 'There's a restrictive covenant in place preventing the sale of any land belonging to the estate.'

'What?' said Bramble, not understanding. 'How do you mean?'

'I didn't realise until I got a friend to examine the deeds properly with me on Sunday,' he went on. 'It seems your grandfather was determined to keep the estate intact and to ensure the land was only leased for agricultural purposes. There might be a way around it, but it's an extremely complex matter that will require time and...' He coughed again. 'Money.'

'How long?' Bramble asked. 'How much? What exactly are you saying?'

Piers hesitated. 'I'm saying,' he went on carefully, 'that you need a legal expert, someone familiar with this sort of thing. Until you get that advice, I'm afraid you're stuck. I must warn you that it is possible you might never be able to get the covenant lifted. It's not unknown...'

Bramble had been standing but she sank down now on to the chair by the desk and clutched the phone as if for dear life.

'Can't you handle it for me?' she asked desperately. 'Surely you don't need—'

'I'm sorry. I don't have the expertise.'

Bramble swallowed. Her mind was racing, her thoughts flying hither and thither. This changed absolutely everything. She'd pinned all her hopes on that cash; she'd reassured herself that it would be enough to upgrade Polgarry so that she could live comfortably enough and start to make it work for her in some way, though she hadn't yet fathomed how. Now she couldn't afford to do anything. She hardly had enough in the bank for a drink at the local pub, and soon the money Lord Penrose had put aside for bills, food and Maria's wages would be gone as well.

A thought occurred to her and she felt the panic rise even higher, right up to her throat. 'Gus!' she rasped. 'He's still working for me. How will I pay him?'

'Credit?' said Piers unhelpfully.

'I'm all maxed out,' Bramble wailed. 'Debts everywhere. He hasn't even fixed the roof,' she went on, thinking of the leaks, and winter coming. 'There's no way I can pay for those tiles now.'

'I expect you can owe it to him,' Piers offered. 'You'll be able to come to some kind of agreement.'

Bramble thought that she detected something in the background, a woman's voice, and almost jumped. Her nerves were ripped.

'Who's that?' she said sharply before she could stop herself.

'Just a friend,' Piers replied, murmuring softly before turning back to the phone.

'What about you and me?' Bramble said in a small voice. 'When will I see you again?' She hated how pathetic she sounded, but she couldn't help herself. She needed his support.

'I, um, I'm not sure.' He exhaled. 'Look, Bramble, you're a lovely girl and all that. It was nice on Saturday, but it was just a bit of fun, wasn't it? No hard feelings?'

Her stomach dropped into her feet.

'None at all,' she said, desperate to retain some shred of dignity, a tiny sliver, just to keep herself from seeping through the floorboards and turning into a puddle beneath the foundations. 'I – I'll see you around.'

The sun had sunk below the horizon and shadows loomed like gloomy spectres against the faded walls. Bramble stared out at the darkening land thinking what an irony it was that she'd once viewed those fields as full of promise, her passport to freedom, to a brave new life as the mistress of

Polgarry – perhaps with Piers, her handsome consort, at her side. Maybe even a brood of rosy-cheeked children running about the manor and playing hide and seek in the grounds. Fantasy-land. Instead, it seemed, she was yoked to that same land, those same fields, like a beast to a plough or Sisyphus to his rock, fated to drag them with her wherever she went, perhaps till the end of time.

How could she have misjudged Piers so badly? The shame, the sheer humiliation, was like a stab wound in the heart, the sense of loss a great weight of water weighing her down. She might have been thirty feet under. The fact that the veil had been lifted and she could now see him for what he really was might have afforded some comfort, but her dreams had been shattered and it only made her betrayal of Matt seem all the worse.

When all the light had faded, she tiptoed out of the room, anxious not to disturb Maria; she didn't know what she'd say. She thought of going to see Katie, but decided against it. She could hear her humming as she moved about upstairs, emptying things into her suitcase, filling her sponge bag. Mentally, she was already far away. It hadn't taken her long to detach.

Bramble climbed into her four-poster, knowing that she'd struggle to sleep. For some reason she pulled out Lord Penrose's old sketchbook, which she'd replaced in the bedside drawers. She found it comforting to flip through the pages and look again at his drawings of the cat, the cheeky sparrow, the vase of gorgeous flowers. He'd found such beauty and interest in the small things around him, the everyday sights that others might scarcely even register.

'What shall I do?' she said out loud, though whether to herself, the four walls or Lord Penrose's spirit, she wasn't sure.

The image of Fergus swam into her head. He was sitting, motionless, on the edge of the cliff, his feet hanging over the side, hands tucked into his trouser pockets and chin raised, scanning the horizon as if searching for something, the wind blowing his dark hair this way and that. It was the way she'd seen him when she'd been for that walk with Piers, when he'd said that he didn't like the cut of her strange tenant's jib.

Lord Penrose had obviously liked Fergus, trusted him enough to want to lend him the cottage rent-free, and Fergus had no time for Piers, Gus or his band of merry men, that much was clear. If only she'd thought to consult her tenant first, to ask his opinion, he might at least have saved her from her disastrous dealings with the lazy roofers.

But it was too late now. She shut the sketchbook and lay on her back, staring up into the darkness, willing the night to pass yet dreading the rising of the sun and the advent of the new day. In the past, she'd have phoned her parents, asked her dear dad for advice, but right now she couldn't even bear to do that, fearing his criticism, his disappointment and, worst of all, his pity. Instead, she closed her eyes and prayed for oblivion.

The hours were long and restless, and as the light seeped through a narrow chink in the curtains, rousing Bramble from her fitful slumber, she groaned out loud. The memories of yesterday felt like a fully packed trunk pressing down on her chest, compressing her lungs and making her ribs hurt so that she could scarcely draw breath.

Once again she scrabbled around for an answer, a lost child frightened of every noise and shadow. Common sense told her that she needed to pull herself together, that wallowing was useless and counterproductive, but she felt incapable of rational thought and every instinct screamed at her to pull the duvet over her head and make-believe that none of this had ever happened.

Nature had other ideas, however. A cock crowed, loud and insistent, in the distance and Bramble started, a sudden thought making her snap her eyes open in surprise. Fergus again. Of course! Never mind his advice; perhaps he'd fix the leaks in the roof for her, at least temporarily. He'd offered to help with the garden, after all, and he was extremely handy. Aside from his painting and looking after Wilf, he didn't seem to have much else to do.

She climbed out of bed, relieved to have some sort of plan, some reason to get up, however tenuous. Though she was groggy, she resolved to walk over there now, without disturbing Katie. She'd probably still be sleeping, and in any case, Bramble didn't think that she could cope with seeing her bags. Even if Fergus said no, she reasoned, a stroll would do her good and help to clear her head, and she could mentally prepare herself for the conversation that she'd have to have with Gus later in the day. She was dreading it.

The thought of Piers made her retch, so she tried to brush him from her mind and put one foot in front of the other, pulling on one item of clothing after another, hopefully in the right order. Survival, it seemed, was the name of the game now, just getting through each moment, each hour; she wasn't ready to give up as the world crumbled around her – not quite anyway.

Maria was hovering by the dining room as usual and Bramble told her abruptly that she'd eat breakfast later; she purposely chose not to meet her housekeeper's eye for fear that she'd expose the vulnerability, the deep sense of insecurity, loss and failure, rattling her very bones.

It was about a fifteen-minute walk to the cottage across the fields and she took her time; she wasn't in any hurry. The air was warmer again but the sky was overcast, and she felt sweat starting to prick on her back as she trekked through the stubbly wheat and tall grass, watching for scampering mice and voles, taking care not to stumble.

Fergus was in his garden, fixing the wire chicken run, while Wilf stood inside it, stroking one of the hens. His father remained squatting as Bramble approached, only stopping once to see who it was before resuming his task.

'Morning,' she said, and he growled something in reply without looking up again.

She hadn't heard from him since Saturday but hadn't expected to; he wasn't the type to send a thank-you note, and besides, he seemed to have left in a huff.

'We think a fox tried to get in last night,' Wilf piped up, moving closer to Bramble so that she could stroke the hen's silky feathers. It clucked obligingly, quite unperturbed by her presence.

'Luckily, they were all locked in the shed,' the boy went on, 'but Dad's trying to make the fence stronger so they don't get frightened when the foxes sniff around.'

'Good job.' Bramble noticed how deftly Fergus stretched the wire with his fingers and bent it into shape. There was a well-worn tan leather belt round his waist from which hung pockets containing various heavy tools, and his earthy trousers, crumpled fawn T-shirt and muddy boots acted like camouflage.

'I – I wondered if I could ask you something,' she began uncertainly, feeling the trace of courage that she'd managed to muster earlier trickle away.

Fergus didn't reply.

'I've found out I can't sell any land – not for now, at least – which means I can't pay Gus. I'll have to tell him to go, but the manor's roof isn't fixed yet, and with winter coming...'

She broke off because Fergus had risen and was stretching his back, arching his spine, his arms above his head, elbows bent.

'You mean that cowboy's not done the job?' he said slowly, bringing his arms down again and resting his hands on his hips. 'Can't say I'm surprised.'

He might just as well have crowed, 'I told you so.' Bramble felt a stab of irritation, but she was in no position to justify Gus – or anyone else for that matter, least of all herself.

'I wondered if you could maybe give me a hand,' she said timidly, examining her tenant's face for signs of anger. 'I – I hope you don't mind my asking. I'm in a bit of a mess...'

He fixed her with intense brown eyes that scarcely flickered. 'Can't that land agent friend of yours sort it? He knows everything, doesn't he?'

She blinked nervously, afraid that she'd give herself away.

'He's not working for me any more,' she said carefully, 'not now the land can't be sold for development.'

'Ah. Scarpered as soon as the pound signs vanished.'

Red spots blossomed on Bramble's face and neck and it was all she could do not to cry. She felt so stupid and childish, a fool stumbling in the dark. How wrong she'd been to imagine that she could just turn up in Cornwall without knowing anything about the county, its traditions or its people – without a clue about ancient buildings, restoration, land management or land managers, come to that! To imagine that she could make a new life for herself as the lady of the manor and that everything would fall into place... how naïve! How vain and arrogant!

Polgarry needed someone with far more nous than her to take it on, someone with sound business sense and plenty of cash, as well as friends in high places, including lawyers, gardeners, architects and project managers – and builders who actually knew what they were doing. She cursed herself for having thought that she could do it, or that Fergus would be willing and able to help in any way at all. Why on earth would he want to assist an idiot like her? If she were him, she'd run a mile.

'Katie's decided to go back to London,' she blurted, feeling tears spring to her eyes and swallowing furiously. 'She's had enough.'

Wilf, who'd been listening intently, popped the hen down and it scuttled off, bobbing its funny head.

'Never mind. We're still here,' he cried as if reading her thoughts. 'You won't be lonely 'cause you've got us!'

At that point she thought it best to leave before she broke down completely, but to her surprise, Fergus stopped her in her tracks.

'I suppose I could take a look at the roof. I could bring my ladder. I don't know if I can fix it but—'

'Would you? Could you? That would be wonderful! Even if you can just make it more or less watertight, at least for now. Maybe by next year I'll have a better plan.'

'I'm not making any promises,' he muttered, but to her relief he sounded marginally less hostile. 'I'll come over on Saturday. Around five-ish. While it's still light.'

'Thank you.' Bramble would have liked to hug him or at the very least shake his hand, but he crouched down by his coop again.

'See you on Saturday!' she said, giving Wilf a hug instead. 'Both of you, of course. I'll ask Maria to bake us a cake.'

Chapter Nineteen

NEWS TRAVELLED FAST in Tremarnock, and Liz had heard that Katie was leaving almost before Bramble herself. Of course, Tabitha had had to rush around to Liz's to tell her about the surprise resignation, and soon Liz had mentioned it to Jean, who'd passed it on to Felipe, Esme and Barbara.

'Good thing, too,' Esme had sniffed when she'd popped into Bag End to discuss the tidings from every possible angle. 'Ryan will be relieved. At least he won't be constantly reminded of that dreadful snub.'

'Bramble will miss her,' Liz had mused. 'It's an awfully big place to live in on your own with that grim housekeeper.'

'I thought you said Bramble was sweet on the land agent? Perhaps he'll move in with her?'

Liz had been slightly alarmed by the idea, not having considered it before. 'There's something about him... I don't know.'

A few days later, Tony had reported that he'd seen Bramble and Katie at Plymouth station when he'd been collecting a friend. He'd witnessed a tearful farewell between the girls at the station, then Bramble had left alone, looking young, lost and utterly dejected.

On Saturday afternoon, with this in mind, Liz decided to drive up to Polgarry with Lowenna in tow, thinking that

Bramble might be grateful for some company. The young woman came to the door as soon as the housekeeper announced their arrival and seemed delighted to see them both, but Liz almost left when she heard that Fergus was there.

'I can come back another day?' But Bramble wouldn't hear of it.

'He's up on the roof, examining the leaks,' she explained as they hovered in the hallway. 'He's going to try to patch them up for the winter.' She lowered her eyes. 'I've had to tell the workmen to leave.'

'Why's that? Weren't they any good?'

Bramble made a face. 'They were hopeless, but that's not why they're off.'

Lowenna seemed content looking around for a moment, so they remained where they were while Bramble gave details about the covenant and what it meant. 'So you see,' she said grimly, 'I can't afford to pay them any more.'

Liz wanted to know how they'd taken the news.

'They weren't at all happy, as you can imagine. They downed tools and two of them stalked off while the boss, Gus, ranted and raved that I'd have to find the cash to pay them quickly or he'd sue.'

Wilf joined them from another part of the manor and grinned at Lowenna, who was gazing in wonder at the glittering chandelier above, the bronze statuette of the naked youth playing a pipe in the centre of the table and the gold-framed oil paintings of gentlemen on horseback and crinoline-clad ladies.

'Can she stay and play?' he asked. Without waiting for an answer, he took the little girl's hand and led her into the drawing room. So intent was Liz on hearing Bramble's story that she scarcely noticed.

'So what will you do?' she asked, aghast.

Bramble shrugged. 'I managed to persuade Gus to give me a bit of time – three months. It was the most I could get.'

'Do you owe much?'

'Thousands – and they don't seem to have done anything. I knew they were bad news the moment I saw them.' She bit her lip. 'I should have listened to my gut instead of Piers, who's turned out to be a right shit.'

It was a relief to say the words out loud, like scratching a bad itch. Shit, shit, shitty shit, she thought. That felt better.

They joined Wilf and Lowenna in the main reception room and sat side by side on the sofa, from where they could hear Fergus on the roof, banging and scraping. At one point he popped his head through the hole, which seemed to have grown bigger since the night of the party, before pulling it out again quickly. It would have been funny if the women hadn't felt so glum.

'Goodness!' was all that Liz could muster. 'I hope he's careful.'

Sensing, perhaps, that they wanted to be alone, Wilf led Lowenna on to the crumbling terrace outside the open French doors, where they squatted side by side, examining bugs and interesting bits of stone and pebble. Liz noticed the dark circles under Bramble's eyes, the pinched nose and mouth, the worry lines on her forehead, and struggled to think how she could help.

'Tabitha's got a gig next month – the second Friday in October; perhaps you'd like to come?' she piped up, wondering if a little distraction might be welcome. 'It's in Callington, not far. I've offered to drive Tony and Felipe. There'll be plenty of room in the car.'

Bramble gave a small smile. She could hardly think beyond

today, let alone all the way to next month, but she thanked Liz and promised to let her know.

'Is she getting lots of opportunities? She's very good.'

'Not really. In fact, this is her first event since The Hole in the Wall. I guess it'll take time; it's such an overcrowded field.'

There was an awkward pause, so it was a relief when Maria appeared, carrying a silver tray laden with teacups and saucers, a teapot, milk and the most delicious-looking fruitcake that Liz had ever seen.

She sniffed appreciatively. 'Mmm! Is it homemade?'

'I baked it this morning,' Maria replied stiffly. 'It was one of Lord Penrose's favourites. I trust the children will enjoy it, too.'

Bramble's hand shook as she picked up the teapot, and the housekeeper hesitated, a question playing on her lips that she seemed only just able to suppress. Liz had always found Maria cold and terrifying, but now she fancied that she detected something new in her eye, a gentleness she hadn't noticed before, and it occurred to her that the formidable foreigner might actually care for her mistress. It was quite a revelation.

Her presence, however, appeared to unsettle Bramble more than comfort her, and she almost dropped the cup and saucer as she passed it to Liz.

'That'll be all, thank you,' she said a little sharply, and Maria discreetly withdrew, closing the door behind her.

The tinkle of china, and perhaps the smell of cake, soon brought Fergus in, and he sat opposite the women, stretching out his long legs.

'I think I've got some tiles that'll do for now,' he commented after taking a slurp of tea. The delicate porcelain cup seemed too small for his hands; it could have been a thimble. 'They won't look great, but they're the right size and weight. They'll keep you dry for a winter or two in any case.'

Liz was full of admiration. 'Do you mean to say you just happened to have them knocking around at home? You're amazing!'

Fergus scratched his nose as if he were embarrassed. 'There's a builders' yard over Liskeard way. It's where I get my paint boards. They've got all sorts of stuff, but you have to keep dropping in. If you don't nab what you want as soon as it arrives, it's gone.'

He must have been giving the roof some thought then since Bramble had been to the cottage, working out what was needed and how he'd go about it. She was touched.

'You must tell me how much the tiles cost,' she said, but he seemed almost offended.

'Ach, they were practically giving them away.'

Wilf and Lowenna trotted in – lured, no doubt, by the cake, too – and to Bramble's amazement, Maria popped her head around the door to ask if they'd like something to drink.

Liz mentioned Katie's sudden departure, but Bramble was reluctant to talk about it, so they changed the subject quickly.

'Rosie's having a little gathering at our house tonight with Rafael and a few other friends,' said Liz. 'She and Rafael seem to have struck up a bit of a friendship. I said I'd barbecue some burgers and hot dogs. There were originally six coming but now it's eight or ten.' She rolled her eyes. 'The number's growing all the time.'

Maria arrived with plastic cups of juice for the children, which they downed in a few short gulps. When they'd finished, Fergus rose, stretching, and said he'd return to the cottage and bring the tiles back in his van.

'Wouldn't you rather leave it for today?' Bramble suggested. 'It's getting rather late.'

'I may as well make a start now. The sooner you're water-tight, the better. You'll help me, won't you, Wilf?'

The boy made a face because he wanted to carry on playing with Lowenna, but Liz said they had to go to the supermarket.

'She'll probably make an awful fuss. She loathes shops with a passion.'

Bramble had a flash of inspiration. 'Why don't I look after the children while you get on with your jobs? I can take them for a walk.'

It seemed to her to be an excellent solution. She loved the little ones and it wasn't as if they didn't know her, but Fergus looked unsure.

'We won't go far,' Bramble promised. 'I won't take my eyes off them for a second.'

'Lowenna would love it – thank you,' Liz said warmly. 'I'll give you some spare nappies just in case.'

Wilf gazed at his father with big blue eyes. 'I can go, can't I, Dad?'

How could anyone resist?

But Fergus frowned. 'I don't think—'

'Please?' Wilf's bottom lip quivered.

'All right then,' his father sighed. 'But keep close to Bramble. Do as she says and don't go running off.'

While Fergus strode back to his cottage, Bramble and Wilf went with Liz to her car to fetch the pushchair and Lowenna climbed in obligingly. The walking party waved Liz off, then Bramble took Wilf by the hand, pushing the stroller purposefully with the other in the direction of the coast.

'Let's go to the sea! We can paddle in the waves and look for shells and you can bring some back for your dad to put on his bedside table.'

She decided to take the road from the manor in the opposite

direction to Fergus's cottage because she knew that the cliff sloped more gently there down to the shore. There was also a proper track and a small, secluded beach – if you could call it that. Really it was just a triangle-shaped area of sand surrounded by rocks. You wouldn't want to stay long because there was hardly room to lay out a towel for sunbathing, but it was perfect for small children: beautifully quiet, and the rocks would be covered in interesting mussels, seaweed and barnacles.

They passed by a couple of farm sheds and a rather ugly modern bungalow, which was owned by a Plymouth family and normally rented out, although the previous tenants had recently left and there were no signs of the new ones yet. A battered red Ford chugged past, its exhaust puffing out smoke and making dubious noises.

Wilf wrinkled his nose. 'Pooh! That stinks.'

'It does,' Bramble laughed. 'I think it needs to go to the garage.'

When they reached the second bend in the road, she pushed the stroller behind a bush, where it couldn't easily be seen, unbuckled Lowenna and slung her on a hip.

'Come on,' she said, taking Wilf's hand again. 'It'll be easier to walk down this bit. It's not too far.'

The path was narrow, rocky and uneven and she had to watch her footing so that she wouldn't stumble. On either side were tall scrubby bushes and gnarled trees, their knobbly roots sometimes extending across the track so that they had to clamber over. The sky was grey, the air heavy and Bramble hugged Lowenna's sticky little body tight to make sure she wouldn't wriggle out of her grasp. Wilf spotted a grasshopper on a leaf and stopped to admire it, but it soon sprang away, while Lowenna held out a hand and tore little bits off leaves as they brushed by.

When they rounded the final corner and saw the tiny beach and the grey-blue ocean stretching out in front of them, Bramble sighed with relief. The route had been slightly further than she'd remembered and she hoped that she hadn't bitten off more than she could chew; it would be quite an effort to carry Lowenna back up the hill. Still, they were here now and she was determined to enjoy it.

'Let's take off our shoes,' she suggested, setting Lowenna down on the gritty sand. 'I bet the sea feels cold.'

Stooping so as to be closer to Lowenna's height, she led the little girl to the water's edge, where the waves lapped over her tiny pink toes, making her squeal with shock and pleasure. Wilf, however, hung back.

'Come on!' Bramble called. 'It's fun.' A slightly bigger wave whooshed up Lowenna's thighs and she hopped back, giggling. 'We should have brought our swimming things.'

Still Wilf refused, and she wondered what had got into him.

'Are you afraid of the water? You don't need to be.' She turned to him, extending an arm. 'Look, you can hold on to me. I won't let you go.'

''Ook!' Lowenna coaxed, but Wilf shook his head obstinately.

'What's the matter, darling?' Bramble said, confused. He seemed to be engaged in an internal struggle. She took a few steps in his direction, but Lowenna's legs were shorter so they didn't get far.

'My dad says I'm not allowed to go in the water without him.' He wiped his nose with the back of his hand.

Bramble stared at the little boy in amazement. 'Why on earth not? That's ridiculous! I'm sure he won't mind as I'm here.'

Wilf kicked the stones at his feet. 'He doesn't like—'

'Oh, go on. It's not scary!' She turned once again to the water, pulling Lowenna up by both hands just in time to stop a choppy wave from soaking her through.

'More! More!' the little girl shouted, and this time Bramble spun her round in a circle until she was dizzy. She kept hold of her when she landed to stop her toppling over.

'You can roll up your shorts – you won't get wet,' Bramble shouted over her shoulder to Wilf, thinking that perhaps Fergus was worried he might spoil his clothes, though it seemed unlikely. The boy appeared to dither for a moment, but remained on the spot.

She was still looking at him when a much larger, more powerful wave that seemed to come from nowhere rushed almost up to her waist and right over Lowenna's head. It happened so quickly that the little girl didn't respond after it withdrew, staring with wide, startled brown eyes, her wet, dark hair clinging, seal-like, to her face as Bramble hurriedly scooped her up.

After a pause that seemed to last for ages, Lowenna opened her mouth and emitted a piercing shriek – 'Eeee!' – that made Bramble's teeth rattle and her bones shake. It was loud enough to wake the dead. She hugged Liz's daughter to her chest, shielding her head with a hand and intending to scramble to the shore, but before she got the chance another wave knocked her right off balance. Instinctively, she grabbed Lowenna by the waist and raised her up above her shoulders, so that she wouldn't be drenched again, before landing awkwardly on her bottom, scraping her leg on the sharp stones beneath. She tried to struggle up, but could feel herself toppling sideways, as if in slow motion, taking Lowenna with her right beneath the swell once more.

They both gasped as the wave receded, and again Bramble

fought to stand up, but the shingle beneath her seemed to slip away as she scrabbled desperately to find a foothold. Before long she was being pulled further out to sea, beyond where the sand shelved and there was any hope of staying upright, even on tiptoes.

Lowenna had gone quiet again, and Bramble kicked hard with her legs and tried to push the toddler to the shore. No sooner had she gained a few inches, however, than another freezing wave bowled them forwards and then dragged them further back. She felt as if they were being sucked into a funnel and swirled around like concrete in a mixer.

There were a few seconds more when she thought that she was still in with a chance, but as the water continued to churn around and over, squeezing the breath from her lungs, the dreaded word 'riptide' flashed into her mind and it finally dawned on her that she was in real trouble. She'd heard about riptide tragedies, but they only happened to unfortunate souls who ignored safety warnings, didn't they? Gripped with blind fear, she started to thrash helplessly, but her legs felt weak and her arms were growing tired with holding up Lowenna. She wasn't sure how much longer she could do it.

'Help!' she cried, realising even as she did so that it was hopeless as there was no one about, not even Wilf, for she could no longer see him on the shore. Perhaps he'd been too frightened to watch what was going on; he wouldn't have been able to do anything in any case.

She felt the water, a centrifugal force, pulling her down, down, and raised her chin, gasping for air and swallowing mouthfuls of salty seawater. Lowenna, too, spluttered and writhed before going limp, and Bramble screamed at her not to give up but to keep breathing, to hang in there. She had no idea if the child understood, and could only pray that her survival instinct – or a miracle – would save her, for she herself no longer could.

'Bramble!'

A distant voice pierced her consciousness, or was it just the seagulls? She couldn't tell.

'Bramble! Listen!'

It was louder and more insistent this time, definitely a human sound. Weak as she was, she managed to raise her head far enough above the tide to spot two figures, a man and boy, waving at her madly, and a little way behind them, the towering figure of Fergus.

The boy was Wilf, for sure, but the man beside him? She thought she must be seeing things, that she'd gone mad... but there was no time to reflect. Time was running out, and he and Wilf were still gesticulating wildly. At first she couldn't understand what they were doing; she thought that their arms were flailing in panic. Then it occurred to her that they were pointing to the right, urging her to swim in that direction, parallel to the shore.

'I can't!' she managed to yell, before another wave like a wall of water slapped her in the face, shooting up her nose and into her mouth, leaving her choking and breathless.

Some slight movement and a faint moaning came from Lowenna, signalling that she was still alive, and a sudden surge of energy charged through Bramble like lightning; this might be their last opportunity. She'd taken life-saving classes at school, hadn't she? Quickly, she flipped the child on to her back, cupped a hand beneath her chin, leaving her nose and mouth free, and, kicking with all her might and sculling with the other arm, she mustered just enough strength to tow her charge a metre or two to the right, out of the raging current and into slightly calmer waters.

As soon as she sensed that they were clear of the whirlpool, all her power seemed to dissolve and she could merely float, exhausted and shivering, staring up at the blank sky. She could feel the force of the current slowly, slowly drawing her back in, but there was nothing that she could do; she had no resources left.

She didn't see the strange man fling off his shirt and shoes and wade into the churning water towards them. She hardly felt it when he gripped her beneath the arms and hauled her and Lowenna through the torrent on to dry land, depositing them like beached whales on the shore. All she knew, or thought she knew, was that they were safe.

'Lowie!' Was that Wilf's cry?

'Thank God, oh thank God,' Fergus's cracked voice echoed back.

She coughed painfully, spewing out vomit and salty water that burned her throat. Overhead a helicopter roared. Had it been there earlier? She wasn't sure. Lots of voices around her now, men in fluorescent jackets with thick Cornish accents, like clotted cream.

'Could have been fatal...'

'Aye.'

'I was in the shop when I got the call... feared the worst.'

'Folk won't listen...'

Before long she was being wrapped in a foil blanket and winched up like a rag doll, shaking, choking and helpless.

'Lowenna!' she yelled, spitting brine. Down below she could see the lifeboat, the men standing around, someone attending to her mystery rescuer.

'She's all right, she's going to be OK,' came a disembodied male voice from inside the helicopter itself.

He placed a mask over her mouth and she guzzled fresh,

clean oxygen so pure and beautiful that she couldn't get enough of it; she wanted to cry.

She closed her eyes and could see water in every direction, above, around and below, ice-cold and terrifying. She was struggling to make sense of what had happened but understood only that she'd stared death in the face and had almost taken Liz's little daughter with her. A groan, the sound of a wounded beast, seemed to come from deep within and the man patted her arm gently.

'It's all right, love. It's over.'

'I'm so stupid!' she wailed, but no one could hear.

Her limbs were heavy and she was sinking way, way down. She was tired, so tired; she could sleep for a week, a month – for ever perhaps.

Lowenna was safe. Liz would never speak to her again, and probably Fergus, too. The strange man? She couldn't think about him. She was back in her warm bed in Chessington, her father holding her hand, Cassie stroking her hair. 'All right, Crumble?' She was a child again, cocooned.

Lord Penrose, Piers, the manor, Gus – it was all a nightmare; it had never even happened. Nothing mattered any more, only that she had to rest for a long, long time.

Her eyelids fluttered; her mind was thick and dense, like treacle.

Blackness engulfed her.

Chapter Twenty

HOURS PASSED, THE sun set and rose in the early-autumn sky and folk generally continued with their normal activities, going to bed, getting up with the light, eating breakfast, dressing, unaware of the drama that had taken place near a tiny Cornish fishing village called Tremarnock, in a remote corner of the UK which most had never visited or even heard of.

For a few, however, nothing would ever be quite the same again. When Bramble woke from her long sleep, she found herself tucked under crisp white sheets in a strange bed and unfamiliar surroundings. She wiggled her hands and feet, to check that she wasn't dreaming, before moving her head slowly and stiffly to the left, and the first thing that met her eyes was the face of her father, Bill, then that of his beloved wife, Cassie, who was gazing at her with deep concern.

'Where am I?' Bramble mumbled, semi-conscious.

Cassie pulled up the covers under her stepdaughter's chin and kissed her forehead. She smelled of the same lavender perfume she always wore, sweet and faintly dusty, and her gold necklace, shaped like a lucky horseshoe, grazed Bramble's cheek.

'You're in hospital, love,' her father said gently. The sound of his voice, deep and gravelly, brought a lump to her throat and she started to cry.

'It's all right. You've had a big shock, but there's no permanent damage. We jumped in the car the moment we heard. We've been here most of the night. You've been out for hours, but the doctors say sleep's the best healer. You'll be right as rain before long, you wait and see.'

A nurse in a pale-blue uniform with an efficient smile came to check Bramble's temperature and pulse, and Bill and Cassie stood back respectfully until she'd finished, watching her every move. When she'd gone, they resumed their places beside the bed, Bill on a plastic chair and Cassie perched on the covers, holding Bramble's hand.

'I expect you're hungry?' she said. 'Shall I ask for a cup of sweet tea and something to eat?'

Bramble's stomach growled and for a moment she wondered what the noise was. She would have said yes, but a sudden thought stopped her in her tracks.

'Lowenna?' she cried, struggling to rise and finding that she didn't have the strength.

Bill tutted. 'Lie down now. You must rest. She's OK, she's doing just fine.'

Exhausted, Bramble flopped back on the pillows and closed her eyes again.

'Where is she?' she mumbled, licking her dry lips. She needed all the details, to be certain that they were telling the truth and weren't trying to shield her from anything. Every last scrap of information.

'The poor little lamb's got mild hypothermia and her breathing's not quite right,' Bill explained. 'She'll be here for a while yet, but they're confident she'll pull through. You were both lucky they got you out of the water in time. When we got the call...' His voice cracked and Cassie took over.

'We didn't know what to expect. It was such a relief when

we saw you lying there, looking just like our Bramble.' A tear trickled down her cheek, and she wiped it away with a sleeve. 'That drive was the worst of my life; I thought we'd never arrive. But it's over now, thank heavens.'

She let out a sob and Bill put an arm around her shoulders and gave a reassuring squeeze. Now that Bramble had come to properly, more memories from yesterday started to flood back and her body trembled beneath the covers.

'I should never have...' she groaned, but Cassie put a finger to her lips.

'Hush now. It wasn't your fault; it could have happened to anyone.'

She wiped Bramble's damp nose with a soft tissue, just as she had when she was a little girl. 'You mustn't blame yourself—'

'But I do.' Bramble batted the tissue away. 'I shouldn't have taken the children there, not at that time of day with no one else around. It was stupid and reckless.'

Bill's dear, kind eyes were fixed on hers and his expression was one of such love and compassion that she wanted to break down completely; she didn't deserve his sympathy, or anyone else's, not one bit. She remembered holding Lowenna's small hand in her own and leading her, so trusting, into the treacherous waves. The little girl nearly drowned, her precious life cut cruelly short. Bramble would bear the guilt until the end of time.

And Wilf! What of him? She groaned in pain. She'd tried to coax him into the water, too, against his father's wishes. The boy had more sense than her. Her head pounded, as if it were being squeezed in a press, and her thoughts were black and mangled. If only she'd never woken, it would have been so much easier...

'How did I get here?' she asked, still trying to piece the fragments together, one by one.

Bill cleared his throat. 'The little boy you were with – Wilf, I think he's called? – he raced up the cliff and back to the manor. Luckily, Matt arrived at the same time as Fergus pulled up in his van. Fergus rang the coastguard while Matt and Wilf ran to find you. Matt was a real hero. Risked his life to get you out. Lifeboat would have been too late.'

Matt? Bramble quivered and her brain ached with shock and confusion. As she'd drifted in and out of sleep, she'd thought that she could recall her ex-boyfriend's comforting, sturdy figure by the water's edge, waving at her with all his might, but surely she'd been dreaming?

'Why was he here?' she asked hoarsely, struggling to understand.

Bill took her hand. 'I'm not sure, love. I think—'

They were interrupted by a different nurse wheeling a trolley. She stopped at the end of the bed and handed Cassie a cup of tea and two biscuits for the patient. Now Bill helped Bramble to sit, propping her against the pillows, and raised the cup to her lips. The liquid – warm, sweet and delicious – trickled down her throat and into her empty tummy.

'Another sip?' he asked, speaking to her as if she were a baby.

Bramble nodded, grateful. She wasn't sure that she'd be able to hold the cup herself, and besides, she needed to be babied right now.

'Matt?' she asked again between gulps, but her father shook his head.

'Finish your tea first,' he smiled. 'There, that'll put hairs on your chest. Here, have a bit of biscuit, too.'

Too feeble to resist, Bramble nibbled reluctantly on a corner as her mind darted this way and that. The idea that Matt had turned up was fantastic, yet her father and stepmother seemed real enough, and the food in her mouth, too.

Its sweet taste brought back the fruitcake that she'd eaten with Liz and Fergus only yesterday. It seemed like another life. She wished so much that she could wind back the clock and take Lowenna and Wilf for a walk in the orchard rather than down to the sea. She wished that she'd never offered to look after them at all.

'Does Maria know where I am?' she asked now, thinking that the older woman would wonder what had happened.

Bill handed the cup and saucer to his wife.

'That housekeeper of yours? She does. Fergus told me he'd spoken to her when he came here to see you.'

She started again. Fergus had been here, by her bed, while she'd been sleeping? She'd believed that her tenant would want nothing more to do with her. It seemed odd to think of him conversing with her dad and stepmother while she, Bramble, had been lying there unconscious.

'Did he, did he say anything – about the accident, I mean?' she asked anxiously, avoiding her parents' gazes.

'He, um—'

'He seemed very concerned about you,' Cassie replied quickly. 'He was glad to hear you were doing OK. He said his little boy had a big shock, but he's proud of him for acting so quickly and getting help. He said the coast's treacherous round here and people don't realise.' She shivered. 'People drown every year, no matter how many warnings they put in place. The sea's so unpredictable; it can change in a heartbeat. He said Matt's a strong swimmer, but sometimes no one can save you, not even the lifeboat men.'

Bramble grabbed Cassie's soft, plump arm and squeezed. 'You've got to tell me what Matt was doing here.'

'We're not sure, sweetheart. Honest. He's staying somewhere in the village—'

'He's in Tremarnock? Now?' She couldn't compute it.

Bill nodded. 'Says he'll pop in for a quick visit tomorrow –
if you're well enough, that is.'

For a moment, Bramble's heart lifted at the prospect of
seeing his kind, handsome face again, of feeling his solid,
reassuring presence. Then she remembered their final conversation. What was she thinking? He'd probably come here to
insult her. She deserved it.

'Of course he must visit,' she murmured, determined
to put him first for once. 'I need to thank him for saving
our lives.'

'Bramble, love...'

She recognised the tone and knew what her father was
going to say; she could hear the words before he'd uttered a
single one. He was going to tell her that moving to Cornwall
had been a terrible mistake, as he'd known all along that it
would be. He might clothe it in slightly different language,
but what he'd really mean was that Polgarry Manor was
jinxed, that she'd had a narrow escape and that she might
not be so lucky next time. She should cut her losses and come
back to Chessington before it was too late, pick up where
she'd left off.

She felt tears spring to her eyes again. Perhaps Bill was
right; maybe this accident had been a sign, a massive red light
warning her to quit while she still could. After all, she had
no money, and no friends – for even if Fergus forgave her,
which was by no means certain, not one single other person
in Tremarnock would trust her now. This could be God's
way of telling her that it was time to admit defeat. The Piers
débâcle had been but the entrée while the near-drowning

was the main course. If she had any sense, she wouldn't stick around for dessert.

'Don't – please,' Bramble told her father. 'I know what's coming. I'll think about it – OK?'

Bill took a deep breath and nodded, but he wouldn't give up, she was sure of it.

It was late afternoon by the time she was allowed to go home, and Bill and Cassie drove her in their black Skoda, which smelled of polish and was always immaculately clean. Bramble sat in the back, with Cassie's tartan rug over her knees, and was almost surprised as they passed the familiar lanes and fields to find that nothing had changed, for her own world had been turned upside down.

'My! It's gigantic!' Cassie commented as they approached Polgarry, and Bramble felt a stab of sadness, for she'd longed to show her parents the manor, to win them over and make them fall in love with its crumbling stones and quirky turrets, its rambling gardens and faded, tumbledown splendour. Yet now this felt almost like a goodbye. Soon, perhaps, she'd be handing over the keys, turning her back on the place for ever and heading once more to London. The beginning of the end, that's how it seemed to her, and her parents sensed it, too.

'It must cost a fortune to heat and light,' Cassie tutted, 'and I'll bet the cleaning's a nightmare.'

'There's not even a carport,' Bill sniffed, drawing to a halt and applying the handbrake. 'Our house might be compact, but at least the Skoda's under cover. Places like this weren't built for modern living. Inconvenient, that's what they are. That's why they don't make 'em like this any more.'

'I don't s'pose the lords and ladies worried about inconvenience, because they weren't the ones who had to run up and down all those stairs,' Cassie said, unfastening her seat belt, pulling down the mirror and patting her gingery hair. 'They had servants to do it for them.'

'Speak of the devil,' Bill muttered, and Bramble turned to find out what he meant.

For once she was almost relieved to see Maria at the door, wearing her usual severe expression. She, at least, had never uttered a word against Polgarry. Indeed, she seemed as much a part of it as the stones themselves.

'Is that the housekeeper you told us about?' Cassie asked in a small voice. 'She looks very fierce.'

Bill moved around to the side of the car to help Bramble out, and she took his arm as they made their way slowly towards the grand entrance where Maria was waiting.

'I trust you are feeling better, Miss Bramble?' she said, moving aside to let them pass. 'Will you require dinner for three tonight?'

Bramble thanked the housekeeper but said they'd rather have a light supper. 'Just sandwiches perhaps? Don't go to any trouble.'

She wanted to show her parents everything, every nook and cranny of the place that she'd come to call home, and she was about to lead them into the drawing room when her legs gave way beneath her and she stumbled slightly, losing hold of her father's arm. Cassie wasn't quick enough, but Maria grabbed Bramble before she fell, stooping to pull her upright so that she could take the weight with her shoulders. She staggered slightly as they rose but was stronger than she appeared.

'You are not well. You must go to bed,' she said firmly, leaning forwards a little to keep Bramble stable, and Bill supported his daughter by the other arm as they helped her upstairs.

Once undressed, she lay back against the cool pillows and sighed. It was a relief to be in her own room again, surrounded by her familiar things and looking out at the rolling Cornish fields instead of drab brick walls and concrete car parks. The air smelled sweet, thanks to the vase of delicate yellow and white freesias on her side table; Maria must have put them there.

She herself was standing by the door and seemed in no hurry to leave.

'I will bring you my chicken soup; it will build up your strength,' she said in a tone that suggested she'd brook no objection.

'Chicken soup!' Cassie exclaimed when she'd retreated. 'Now there's something I've never made myself. I used to buy you Lucozade when you were poorly. Do you remember? I don't think chicken soup's a particularly English thing, do you? Well, I suppose Heinz Cream of Chicken's quite popular, but I prefer the Cream of Tomato variety, always have.' She frowned. 'I never thought to give you chicken soup when you were ill. Maybe I should have.'

Bramble was too tired to reply, and Bill was too occupied with strolling around the room, taking in the antlers on the wall, the spinet, Lord Penrose's dressing table and the heavy mahogany wardrobes.

'Bit cumbersome,' he commented, standing in front of some thick, mirrored doors and scratching his head. 'Wouldn't you prefer built-in? I would. With a nice sliding front. It'd look neater and take up less space.'

His daughter suddenly experienced a strong urge to be alone.

'Can you show our guests to Katie's old bedroom, please?' she asked Maria when she returned with a tray of soup – complete with a solid silver spoon engraved with the initials AP for Arthur Penrose, a linen napkin and some milk in a crystal tumbler – which she set down carefully on the bed. Cassie's eyes were on stalks.

'Of course.' Maria beckoned Bill and Cassie out and closed the door gently behind them. She seemed to sense that her mistress needed peace and quiet. Perhaps she, too, found the parents irritating.

Bramble ate half her soup and drank a little milk, then placed the tray on the floor beside her. She must have dropped off to sleep, because when she opened her eyes again the big silver moon was gazing at her through the window, shining right in her face as if to say, 'Wake up, wake up, it's time to play!'

Reaching for her mobile phone, she discovered that it was after midnight. She must have been unconscious for hours! She would have closed her eyes and tried to doze again, but her brain slipped into overdrive as snippets of the previous day's conversations came back and Matt surged into her mind. What had he said to her in the water? She couldn't remember. But she did recall his strong arms dragging her out. He'd seemed ferocious in his determination, like a man possessed, but then hadn't he always been so in a crisis? One hundred per cent dependable, as Katie had always said.

The rest of the house's occupants had no doubt gone to bed, but Bramble was now wide awake. She reached for a sweater and padded silently into the bathroom, before tiptoeing downstairs to the kitchen, where she made herself a cup of tea. No matter if she was up for the rest of the night; she'd already had plenty of rest.

She carried her mug into the shabby TV room and sat on the squashy old sofa that Wilf had used when he'd seen the Robin Hood film. She was about to look for something to watch herself when a creak made her jump, and Maria popped her head around the door and asked if she was all right. She was in a plain dressing gown and her grey hair, normally iron-straight, was all messed up.

'I couldn't sleep,' Bramble explained, her heart still pitter-pattering. 'Did I wake you? I'm sorry.'

Instead of going back to bed, Maria waited, her glasses glinting in the semi-darkness, as if she had something to say. Bramble had never invited her to sit before, but for some reason she did so now, and the older woman acquiesced, perching slightly awkwardly on the edge of the sofa and staring at the small hands resting on her lap.

'You know...' she began in a low voice, as if someone might overhear, 'you know that things between your grandfather and grandmother were not as they seemed; it was not as people thought.'

Bramble started. 'What do you mean?'

'I mean,' Maria began slowly, 'I know you think, like everybody else, that Lord Penrose abandoned your grand-mother when she fell pregnant, but that was not at all the case. He loved her; he wanted to marry her. But she wouldn't have him; she said that he was too old for her. Her parents tried to persuade her but she flatly refused – she was a headstrong young woman – so once they'd finished bullying her, to no avail, they put it about that he'd behaved disgracefully.

'They were furious, you see. They only found out about the baby when your grandmother was six months gone, and by then it was too late. They wanted revenge, but it wasn't enough just to ruin their daughter's life; they had to harm

Lord Penrose, too. They lashed out, and in the end I think they even began to believe their own lies. He offered marriage, money, everything, but they wouldn't accept. They wanted to punish him for their shame and disappointment, and my God they succeeded.' She took a deep breath. 'They almost broke him.'

Bramble's pulse was racing. She'd wanted so much to learn about her grandfather, but Maria had always seemed so closed, so reluctant to give anything away. All that Bramble had managed to glean so far was that Lord Penrose apparently 'cared' about her, the granddaughter whom he'd never met. Now, it seemed, there was far more to the story.

'Did he have any contact with Alice after that – or his daughter, my mother?' she asked.

Maria shrugged. 'A little. The occasional note, the odd photograph. Perhaps Alice regretted her actions, I don't know. But it was very dangerous to correspond; her parents could never find out. When she died, Mary, your mother, wrote sometimes, too, but she was a troubled girl – such a terrible upbringing.' She sighed again. 'Lord Penrose would have given anything to help her, but she half-believed all the nonsense that had been peddled about him, and in any case, she was beyond rescuing, poor girl. She was doomed from the start.'

Bramble felt a lump in her throat, like a boiled sweet that wouldn't go down. 'Did my mother send him the photograph of me as a baby?'

Maria nodded. 'He treasured it, just like the others.'

'It's so sad. So many blighted lives, such a waste.' Bramble paused. 'I'm glad you've told me, but why now, Maria? Why didn't you tell me when I first came to see the manor, just after he'd died?'

Maria was still staring at her hands, but her black eyes

seemed to glisten in the moonlight that shone through a gap in the velvet curtains.

'I loved your grandfather,' she began. 'Not in the romantic sense, you understand, but because he was a good man, a kind man. I never knew him before he met Alice. I only came to work for him after she'd gone. By then he'd stopped laughing, stopped entertaining; he'd already become a recluse. But I heard the stories about the famous parties, the fun, and I could see the sadness in his eyes. I always hoped that he'd eventually meet someone new and find happiness at last, but it was not to be.'

She hadn't answered Bramble's question, and Bramble could tell that there was more to come.

'There were only two people who seemed to bring him any joy,' Maria went on, crossing her arms over her chest as if she were cold. 'The first was you.'

Bramble started. 'Really? Even though he didn't know me?'

'He knew *about* you. He knew your father was a good man and that he'd married a kind woman after your mother died. He knew they brought you up well and that you were a...' She hesitated, as if wondering which words to choose. '... a spirited young woman with, er, with potential.'

Bramble wasn't sure if this was a compliment or not, but let it pass.

'He also knew that you were bored with your job and craved adventure.'

'How on earth did he know that?'

'He had his ways,' Maria explained darkly.

'You mean he spied on me?' Bramble was astonished.

'Not exactly. Well, from time to time he hired someone to find out a little information. He only wanted to know how you were getting on and that you were all right.'

'That's still spying,' Bramble huffed. It made her shiver to think that Lord Penrose had been keeping an eye on her, discovering things that perhaps she'd rather he hadn't known. Had she been snooped on at work? At Matt's flat? At lunchtime in the café with Katie? There was a law against that, surely?

'Why did he bother if we were never going to meet anyway?'

'Because he wanted you to have the manor, but he needed to be sure that you could cope with the responsibility. He loved Polgarry, you see. He wanted to preserve it for future generations, but at the same time he knew that he'd failed at the task himself, that he'd neglected it badly, and that only the right person would be able to bring it back to life.'

Bramble narrowed her eyes. 'And what made him think I was the right person? I haven't exactly done a great job up to now.'

The housekeeper had been sitting very upright, staring into the darkness, but now she lowered her chin in acquiescence. 'That is true; you have made many mistakes. But all is not lost. You cannot allow a few setbacks to put you off. You must try harder – for your grandfather's sake.'

Now Bramble understood, and she was angry. 'A few setbacks?' she stuttered. 'Is that how you'd describe what's happened to me? I've split up with my long-term boyfriend, my land agent turned out to be a snake, Katie's gone, I'm up to my neck in debt, the manor's falling apart and I narrowly avoided drowning myself and my friend's little daughter.'

The housekeeper pursed her lips.

'Do you honestly expect me to give up everything just to keep this old manor going, because it's what Lord Penrose wanted, a man my mother and father hated and whom I never even met?'

Still Maria remained silent.

'He might have been good to you,' Bramble went on, aware that her face and neck were on fire, 'but as far as I'm concerned, he's given me nothing but trouble and unhappiness. And another thing,' she blurted, 'I didn't dare tell you before now, but you're going to have to leave when his money runs out in a few weeks. I haven't got anything in the bank; there's nothing up my sleeve.'

To her surprise, Maria simply shrugged. 'For me that is not such a problem. I am old now, past retirement age, and I have enough put by to last until I die. But you, you are young and vital. The estate's survival depends on you.'

Bramble felt suddenly very small, alone, overburdened and frightened. 'Don't leave me!' she wanted to say. 'I didn't mean it! I'll find the money somehow. I can't do this without you!'

She opened her mouth to speak, but the housekeeper had already risen and was re-fastening the cord on her gown.

'I am very tired now. I bid you goodnight. I would only ask that you think very carefully before you give up on your inheritance. It is for Lord Penrose that I say this, not for myself, but it is also for you. You see, despite your youth and your errors, I believe that if you abandon Polgarry, you will live to regret it.'

And with that, she departed, leaving Bramble staring at the empty space she'd left behind. Was the housekeeper right, or was she talking nonsense? And if Bramble were to stay at Polgarry after all, how on earth was she supposed to survive?

It was only when she rose, thinking she might go back to bed for a while, that she realised she hadn't asked Maria about the other person who had brought her strange, unhappy grandfather joy.

★

At Bag End, Liz was wide awake, too. Robert had insisted on taking over from her at the hospital so that she could get some rest, but whenever she closed her eyes, her mind was filled with nightmarish images of Lowenna in the churning water, choking and gasping, fighting for her very life, so that it was preferable to keep active, to try to distract herself.

After pouring boiling water from the kettle into a mug, she carried yet more tea that she probably wouldn't drink into the dimly lit sitting room and settled in an armchair, her feet pulled up beneath her. The television was on, but no matter how hard she tried to focus, nothing seemed to penetrate; it was as if she were imprisoned in an isolation chamber, the walls of which were transparent, yet no intelligible sight or sound could filter through. She wanted so much to break free, to receive warmth and comfort from the outside world, but couldn't. Even Robert had failed to ease her anxiety. She felt frozen with shock and fear.

Lowenna would recover; the doctors had told her so. As young as she was, they were confident that her little body would survive what had happened and that her brain, thank God, had been unaffected. But Liz knew what it was to experience the terror of nearly losing a child. Rosie's tumour had brought her close to death, and although she was stable now, there was always an underlying niggle at the back of Liz's mind, a dread that her eldest daughter would relapse.

Was there some curse on the family that meant the worst *would* happen? Had she been wrong to imagine when she met Robert, and after Rosie recovered, that their turn for happiness had finally arrived? Liz reached for the remote and turned up the volume, telling herself not to be stupid; there was no reason not to believe the doctors who'd assured her that Lowenna was on the mend, and yet... The roar of strange voices hurt her brain, and she was still unable to make out what they were saying. She snapped the set off again. Better to sit in silence than be assaulted by white noise.

Picturing Lowenna lying in that strange bed made Liz long to be beside her, to cuddle and reassure her if she woke. She should never have agreed to come home; almost drunk with exhaustion as she was, she'd have had more peace if she'd remained with her daughter all night. She was half-inclined to call a taxi and hurry to the hospital right now.

Tabitha had informed her that Bramble was already back home, but Liz had chosen not to make further enquiries. In fact, she could hardly bear to hear the young woman's name. She couldn't believe now that she'd entrusted Bramble with her daughter, and shuddered to remember how casually she'd handed her Lowenna's pushchair, her bag of nappies and the precious child herself, and how she, Liz, had breezed off to the supermarket feeling lucky that she wouldn't have to drag her youngest with her after all.

Never again. From now on she didn't think she'd let Lowenna leave her side. She'd forever be anxious, watching for signs of danger, and it was all Bramble's fault. She'd been reckless and immature, and it could have ended so very differently. Liz didn't ever want to see her again.

She was still sitting there, half-dozing in the armchair, when Rosie came limping downstairs as fast as she could in her school uniform. Dawn had broken and light now filtered through the half-closed curtains. It was Monday morning and Liz had quite forgotten.

Traumatised as she was, it gladdened her heart to see the fresh face of her eldest and her clear, bright eyes. She must be looking forward to the coming week, which was a blessing indeed after her previous unhappiness with Tim.

Liz suspected that Rafael was playing no small part in this, for Rosie had been sticking by his side since the start of term. She was no doubt enjoying introducing him to the other pupils, showing him what was what, and it would be increasing her kudos also, particularly among the girls.

'Are you all right, Mum?' Rosie asked, concerned, when she clocked her mother's strained expression.

Liz nodded. 'I'm tired, that's all. I didn't sleep much.'

Rosie went into the kitchen to make breakfast and Liz trailed after her, relieved at last to have some diversion.

'Robert said he'd be home around ten. I'll probably be at the hospital when you get back later, but I'll give you a ring.'

After Rosie had gone, Liz dressed and wandered around the house, wondering what to do with herself and praying that her husband would hurry. She was glad when the doorbell rang half an hour later and Tabitha was waiting on the step.

'I just dropped Oscar off,' she explained as Liz moved aside to allow her in. 'He didn't want me to go, but as soon as he spotted a friend he was all right.'

Liz made coffee, which they drank at the kitchen table, and Tabitha tried to tell her that Bramble had fought furiously to save Lowenna from the waves.

'I called in on Fergus on my way back from school,' she explained. 'He's an odd, gloomy bloke, but he seemed almost pleased to see me. It must get lonely up there on the cliff. He's had a massive shock, too. So has his son. He said he could see Bramble and Lowenna in the water as he followed the other man, Matt, down the hillside. Bramble was holding Lowenna above the waves, even when she was being sucked under herself.'

Tabitha reached out across the table and put a hand on Liz's.

'I completely understand why you're furious with her. I would be, too, if it had been Oscar. But—'

'Don't,' said Liz, pulling away. 'Can we change the subject – please?'

Tabitha agreed, and chatted for a few minutes about her forthcoming gig, but she could tell that Liz wasn't listening. At last Robert arrived, looking white and exhausted but bearing the news that Lowenna was awake and had eaten a good breakfast.

'I'm going to try to get a couple of hours' sleep,' he informed the women, running a hand through his messy brown fringe. 'Then I intend to call in on Matt at the B and B where he's staying. He told me he's planning to go back to London tonight and I want to thank him again. No words or gifts could repay him for what he did, but I'll do my best to persuade him to come for a free meal. It's the very least I can do.'

Liz nodded and said, 'Good idea.'

Tabitha said that she, too, had to get on with her day.

'Fergus said he was going to go to Polgarry Manor later to finish fixing the roof,' she commented, but Liz gave her a fierce look.

'Don't mention that place to me. I hate Bramble. I'm sorry but I can't help it; it's just the way things are. I don't want to think about her or speak to her again as long as I live.'

Chapter Twenty-One

IF IT HADN'T been for Matt, Bramble would have spent all day in her pyjamas, lounging around in bed, fussed over by Cassie, Bill and Maria, and trying her best not to dwell on either yesterday or tomorrow. As it was, she forced herself to take a shower and get dressed. She was shocked by the reflection that stared back from the bathroom mirror. The skin on her face, pale at the best of times, appeared bleached, like a sheet left to dry in the hot sun, her round blue eyes had shrunk to slits, while the arch in her nose and dimple in her chin seemed more prominent than ever.

'Did he say what time he was coming?' she asked Cassie when she strolled into the bedroom.

'Why don't you ring and ask?'

It was the obvious thing to do, but Bramble couldn't bring herself to speak to him on the phone, for she had no idea where to begin or what to say. Should she thank him for saving her life or apologise for her cruel treatment of him? Or perhaps she should make small talk first and ask about his parents and job? She could only hope that when she saw him face-to-face the right words would come, though truth and eloquence didn't seem enough; she'd need a touch of magic.

He arrived at around midday. Alone in the reception room, she could hear his footsteps through the open window crunching on the gravel, and she guessed that he would have made his own way. He preferred walking to hanging around for the bus or train, though he'd had to put up with it when she'd worn high heels. 'Nothing wrong with Shanks's pony,' he used to joke, eyeing her ankle snappers with disapproval. 'Cheapest form of transport.'

When the footsteps stopped for a moment, she pictured him pausing to take in the grand entrance, its battered stone steps leading up to the old oak door, the vast windows and decorative turrets. What would he make of it? That it was just as dilapidated and forbidding as he'd envisaged, or would he be pleasantly surprised by the soft-grey stone, crumbling gardens and pleasing symmetry?

Feeling suddenly sick with anxiety, she got up from the sofa where she'd been sitting and paced around, her ears pricked up, waiting for the creak of the door that would signal his arrival.

Maria spoke first, her words echoing in the marble stillness, followed by a breathless Cassie.

'Matt! Come in, for heaven's sake! Did you walk all the way? Goodness! You must be worn out!'

Her welcoming tones brought some comfort, until the sound of Matt's voice set Bramble's nerves jangling once more.

'I came across the fields. One of the locals pointed me in the right direction. It's not so far. Nice countryside. I was early, so I had a bit of a wander round the estate.'

She couldn't catch Cassie's reply, but soon Matt himself entered, pausing for a few seconds while Bramble's heart pitter-pattered so loudly in her chest that she feared he might hear. Her eyes scanned up and down quickly, taking him in.

She recognised the blue jeans, black trainers and olive-green polo shirt that his mum had bought him for one of his birthdays. Otherwise, though, it was the differences that stood out.

Before, she might have described him as a little shy in strange company or surroundings, but today he seemed self-assured, with his shoulders pulled back, his chin raised and his grey eyes fixed on her unwaveringly. She felt exposed and afraid and licked her lips nervously.

'Hello,' she ventured, half-expecting a tirade of abuse, but instead he took a few steps forward and kissed her lightly on the cheek. She was so taken aback that she let out a small cry – 'Oh!'

'How are you feeling?' he asked, ignoring her surprise.

'Better, th-thank you,' she stuttered, trying to gather herself and gesturing to the sofa, where he sat down. She was about to settle beside him when she had second thoughts, and she swayed awkwardly before plumping for the armchair opposite. Maria had already retired discreetly and Cassie was nowhere to be seen.

'I'm incredibly grateful—' Bramble started to say, but Matt raised a hand.

'Don't. I'm not looking for gratitude. That's not why I came. I happened to be in the right place at the right time, that's all.'

He was sitting up very straight, his legs wide apart, in that way that men have – filling the space available to him, confident of his place in the world. Bramble had envisaged doing most of the talking, but it seemed that he wanted it the other way around.

'I hadn't planned to come,' he went on, his voice sounding strong and resolute, as if he'd rehearsed his lines. 'I only decided at the last minute. I couldn't stand the way we left it, you see.' He cleared his throat. 'Not after all those years together. It didn't seem right.'

'I'm sorry—' Bramble began, but again he interrupted.

'Hear me out. Please.' He leaned forward, resting his elbows on his knees and clasping his hands together.

'I wanted to tell you that I don't regret a minute of our ten years together. Not one second. We were very young when we started dating, too young maybe, but most of it was good, wasn't it?'

He glanced up at her, his eyes focused and earnest, and she nodded miserably.

'I hate how it ended,' he continued, staring quickly at the floor again. 'I was furious with you, really angry and upset. But I've had time to think things over and I guess what I wanted to say is – no hard feelings, Bram.' He swallowed. 'I'd rather hold on to the good memories, because there were plenty of them, weren't there?'

Bramble felt tears pricking and the hands in her lap trembled. He sounded so big-hearted, generous and wise, far more so than her, and she wished, not for the first time in the last few days, that she could rewind the clock and do things differently.

'There were many, many good times, Matt,' she said with feeling, 'and I bitterly regret cheating on you. For what it's worth, things didn't work out with the other guy. He wasn't who I thought he was.' She gave a small laugh. 'Divine justice maybe.'

Matt's left cheek twitched but he didn't respond, and it was a relief when Maria reappeared with a tray of coffee to interrupt the silence. For a short while the former lovers made small talk about the manor, Matt's promotion at work, mutual London friends and so on, but the conversation felt forced and artificial.

At last, having finished his coffee, Matt rose and stretched his arms above his head.

'I'd best be off. My train goes at five fifteen and I need to collect my bag from the village.'

'Let me drive you?' Bramble asked, desperate to do something for him, but he shook his head.

'I fancy the exercise, to be honest with you. I'll be cooped up for hours on the journey.'

For a moment, his gaze swept around the room, taking in the oil paintings, the chandelier, the view from the French windows of gardens, orchard and fields beyond.

'I can see why you fell in the love with the place.'

She was taken aback. 'It's very different from Chessington.'

He gave a wry smile. 'It's a big project, a lot of work, but it's beautiful and I wish you well.'

She walked with him to the door, and when it came to saying goodbye she found herself hesitating, hoping to delay. After all those years together it would seem unnatural just to shake hands or peck him on the cheek, so she leaned forwards and hugged him clumsily instead.

'Thank you for everything,' she said, feeling her eyes fill with tears again.

'Don't,' he said thickly, pushing her away.

He turned his back and she watched him walking purposefully in the direction from which he'd come, his shoulders square, head held high and arms swinging rhythmically. At last his sturdy frame shrank to nothing more than a small, dark outline before disappearing completely, and she heard a dull thump in her head like the final closing of a much-loved book.

★

She couldn't bring herself to tell her parents what had passed between her and Matt, and they were tactful enough not to press. Fortunately, the accident gave her the perfect excuse to shut herself away in her bedroom for hours on end and pretend to rest. By the weekend, however, she was looking so much better that she could no longer feign sickness, and Bill raised the subject once more of her leaving Cornwall.

'Cassie and I have to get back to London. We can't take any more time off work,' he explained. 'We'll help you pack your things; it won't take long. I'll call a few estate agents about selling the manor. So long as they've got keys, I don't see why they need us here to show them round. The sooner you're home, the happier we'll be.'

Bramble had to use all her powers of persuasion to convince her parents that now wasn't the right time for her to depart. She'd rather see the estate agents in person, she insisted, and there were various loose ends to tie up before she could quit Cornwall for good. In truth, the conversation with Maria, followed by Matt's unexpected visit, had changed her perspective. She'd had plenty of time to go over things in her mind and was no longer convinced that she was ready to throw in the towel just yet, but she had to get Bill and Cassie off her back before she could make a final decision.

Part of her thought that she'd be mad not to take their advice and she'd miss them like crazy when they were no longer here. The other part, however, kept remembering the news about Lord Penrose and his deep love for her mother, as well as Matt's courage and honesty, which seemed to have cast things in a new light. Perhaps her work here wasn't quite finished; maybe there was something that she needed to accomplish first, though she wasn't sure what.

For a few moments on Saturday afternoon she allowed

herself to feel almost happy when Fergus turned up in his van with Wilf and told her that he intended to spend the day working on the roof. The mere fact they were here meant that her tenant must, on some level, have forgiven her for her stupidity, but her relief soon faded when he didn't enquire how she was, didn't even mention the rescue. In fact, he seemed determined to avoid the issue at all costs.

Bramble herself couldn't let things lie without conveying her heartfelt remorse. As they stood at the bottom of the aluminium ladder outside the main entrance to the manor, she started to say how bad she felt about the danger in which she'd put Wilf and everyone else, but Fergus raised a hand and shook his head, commanding her to stop.

'He's going to stay here and pass me the tools,' he mumbled, deliberately changing the subject.

Bramble bit her lip. Before the accident she would, of course, have offered to entertain the boy while his dad was busy, but not now. She was quite sure that Fergus wouldn't want her anywhere near his son, and who could blame him?

Wilf, seemingly oblivious to any tension, announced that he was thirsty and trotted off to the kitchen to find a drink; he was very much at home here.

'I – I do understand,' Bramble stammered, watching him go, 'that you don't trust me with him.' She hesitated, uncertain whether to continue yet unable to stop herself. 'He was nervous of the sea, which is why he didn't go in. I tried to persuade him but he wouldn't go anywhere near.' She lowered her eyes. 'He was right to be afraid. He's just a child but he had more sense than me.'

Fergus sighed deeply. He was holding on to the bottom of the ladder, poised to climb, one muddy, booted foot on the first rung.

'Bramble,' he began, and something in his voice made her turn to face him. 'I need to tell you something,' he went on, staring resolutely at the wall, and her stomach lurched; she didn't know why.

'My wife' – he swallowed – 'Julia. And our daughter, Felicity...'

He had a daughter? Bramble was dumbfounded. It was the first she'd heard of it. She had a million questions but could tell that Fergus hadn't finished.

He squeezed his eyes shut, as if whatever he was about to say caused him physical pain.

'She was just five,' he whispered. Why was he speaking in the past tense?

'They drowned at sea. They were in an inflatable dinghy. I was watching them on the beach. Wilf was only little, a baby.'

An image flashed before Bramble's eyes: a sunny day, a mother and daughter, cute as anything in a colourful boat while an adoring husband and baby looked on, oblivious to the horror that was about to unfold. She took a step towards Fergus, wanting to reach out and comfort him, but he shrank away.

'I tried to save them,' he went on in strangled tones. 'There were other people, too – strangers – trying to help, but the tide was too strong; it sucked them right out. I couldn't reach them. I swam so far, but I couldn't get there quickly enough. By the time the lifeboat arrived it was too late.'

He stared at her now, his face white, his eyes hollow, and all at once she imagined that she understood him completely: his loneliness, his gruff melancholy, the walks on the cliffs, the endless paintings of the ocean. She thought that she could see into his poor, broken soul and wished that she had the power to heal it for him.

'One minute we were happy,' he continued, his voice still cracking. 'We were getting on with our lives, thinking we were so lucky. Then it all went, just like that.' He snapped a finger and thumb in the air, making her blink.

'We were on holiday in Ireland.' He laughed bitterly. 'Some holiday. Your grandfather had seen my paintings and liked them and... well, to cut a long story short, when he found out what had happened he offered me the cottage. He must have felt sorry for me, I guess. He understood why I needed to be alone.'

Bramble's mind was racing. Another revelation about Lord Penrose and further confirmation of his humanity. How she wished now that they'd met!

Fergus seemed to read her thoughts. 'He was a good man. You would have liked him. It was reassuring for me to be near the sea; I suppose it made me feel closer to Julia and Felicity in some way. But I could never let Wilf near the water without me. You do understand, don't you? I have this terror...'

Bramble nodded dumbly, feeling even more of a monster than she had previously for trying to coax the little boy in against his father's wishes.

'I'm so sorry,' she whispered again. 'I wish I could—'

Without warning, Fergus grabbed her arm and squeezed so tight that it almost hurt.

'You mustn't blame yourself,' he said passionately. 'There was no warning; it wasn't rough or windy.' He sighed again. 'The sea claims countless victims. Lives are snuffed out in a heartbeat. That's just the way it is and always will be. She's insatiable, the ocean; she can never get her fill. She's beautiful but deadly. You can't ever trust her. People round here learn to be careful, respectful, but you're a Londoner – you weren't to know.'

He let go of Bramble's arm, which fell to her side, and she rubbed it with the other hand to stop the smarting.

'Seeing you in there with Lowenna, fighting for your life, brought back so many memories,' he continued, shaking his head again. 'I felt powerless. I couldn't move. If Matt hadn't been there, you'd have died, for sure, and I'd just have stood there, paralysed with fear. I can't go through that again. I thought it was comforting to watch the waves every day; to feel the rhythm, the ebb and flow; to try to absorb the majesty, the capriciousness. I thought I'd feel closer to Julia and Felicity, but now...' He wrapped his arms around his body. 'Now I know for sure it's beaten me and I need to get away – either that or I'll go under, too.'

Bramble felt an iciness creep through her body, freezing her to the core. 'What do you mean?' Her voice sounded loud and shrill. He was one of the few friends she had left.

'I'm going to take Wilf to the mountains – Spain, I think, or maybe Italy. We need a change of scenery, a fresh start. You can rent the cottage to someone else, charge them a fortune.' He gave a half-smile that she was unable to return. 'It'll help with Maria's wages – and your food bill. You'll be grateful when I'm gone.'

As tears sprang to Bramble's eyes, it occurred to her that only now did she feel she really knew this man to whom she'd lived so closely and whose little boy she'd learned to love. And she realised that she did love Wilf, with his big blue eyes, his old soul and his sweet nature. Maybe she even loved Fergus just a little, too.

'Won't you reconsider?' she pleaded. 'Wilf's happy here. He won't like the strange language and the foreign food...' She was clutching at straws. 'He won't want to leave Polgarry – or *me*,' she added, feeling herself redden.

Fergus gave a sad smile. 'He'll miss you, sure, but kids are adaptable; he'll soon get used to it.'

It was true, and she could tell that it was hopeless. Fergus turned back to the ladder and started to mount the steps purposefully, making a clanging noise with his heavy boots as he went.

'I'll finish the roof before we leave. It won't take long.'

She would have scrabbled around for some other reasons for him to remain – she'd have begged, if she felt that it would work – but she could see Wilf hurrying across the gravel towards her, slopping juice from a tumbler as he went.

'Maria says we can have a jar of her homemade strawberry jam to take home,' he hollered. 'I just tasted some; it's delicious!'

As he drew closer, she spotted the evidence around his mouth and there was a red blob on his cheek, too, which made her smile despite everything.

'You should try the greengage one next. I like it even more,' she replied fake-cheerfully. 'I'll ask Maria to make some of her jam tarts. We can have them later with a cup of tea.'

She walked quickly to the kitchen with Wilf's empty glass, fearing that if she waited, she might break down. First Matt, then Piers and Katie, Liz, and now Fergus, too. One by one, it seemed, everyone was turning their back on her, and somehow her tenant's imminent departure seemed like the final straw.

She tried to tell herself she'd soon forget him, but memories of their encounters flooded back: the way he'd rescued her and Katie from the cliff, protected her from the rampaging lawnmower and warned her, albeit obliquely, about Piers, Gus and his gang. The fact that he was fixing her roof now, not because he had to but because she needed him. All these things *mattered*.

Somehow, she reflected, he'd been there, looking out for her, right from the moment she'd arrived at Polgarry, yet she'd never properly registered it. How could she have been so blind? She wanted to break through his prickly defences and tell him that she couldn't manage at the manor without him, but it was too late now. Maybe it was for the best. After all, she'd brought him nothing but trouble. She poked a finger into the corner of each eye and told herself that self-pity would be of no avail, but still, she wanted to curl up in a ball in a corner somewhere and sob her heart out.

To her surprise, Cassie was in the kitchen with Maria, leafing through a well-thumbed recipe book. They looked up briefly when Bramble entered but didn't seem to notice her unhappiness, so engrossed were they in what they were doing. They seemed remarkably relaxed in each other's company, and Maria even smiled a little when Cassie commented that her own pastry wasn't as light as the housekeeper's.

'I have a special way of making it that guarantees lightness,' Maria replied. 'I can show you if you would like?'

Cassie leapt at the chance. 'Bill does love his pastry, especially meat pies. He's fond of a Cornish pasty, too. Not those supermarket ones, mind; only handmade, from a proper bakery.'

Bramble quickly left, pondering on the fact that in all the weeks she'd been here, Maria had never once spoken to her in such a pleasant, relaxed tone, had rarely even met her eye. She'd always found the housekeeper cold, but it occurred to her now that perhaps she herself could have been friendlier, too. After all, it must have been strange for Maria to have to get used to a new boss after all these years, and particularly one so young and silly. She must have wondered how long her new employer would stick around.

Bill had taken it upon himself to fix the rattling window in Bramble's bedroom, and while everyone else was busy she cast around for some distraction. Of course, there was the garden to attend to – especially now that Shannon was back at school and wasn't able to come as often – and there were many drawers and cupboards still to go through in different parts of the manor. However, those tasks were so huge and daunting that Bramble didn't know where to begin, and besides, there didn't seem much point.

'Cooee!'

Tabitha's voice calling through the open door raised her spirits momentarily, until she remembered how close her new friend was to Liz and Lowenna and how the women must have been talking. With faltering steps Bramble made her way to greet the visitor, but as soon as she saw Tabitha's warm smile and gentle brown eyes she knew that she needn't have worried.

'How are you feeling?' Tabitha wanted to know as they wandered into the reception room, where the sun was shining brightly through the open French doors. They could hear Fergus banging on the roof, but the hole was now sealed so that they could no longer see daylight. Settling on the sofa, Tabitha explained that the whole of Tremarnock was talking about the rescue and that Matt had become something of a hero.

Bramble nodded. 'He was incredibly brave.'

She wanted so much to tell Tabitha of their final conversation and of Fergus's imminent departure, but how could she explain the mass of emotions that she was experiencing right now? It seemed easier to focus elsewhere.

'What are the villagers saying about me?' she asked, lowering her eyes to the floor. 'Will anyone ever speak to me again?'

Tabitha seemed surprised. 'Of course! Everyone knows it was a freak accident; it could have happened to anyone. You did everything you possibly could.'

Bramble sighed. 'I shouldn't have been anywhere near the water with the children—'

'You were paddling, Bramble. There's no crime against that. We're just glad you're safe.'

Bramble felt somewhat reassured, but still, a bigger question remained unasked.

'How's Liz?' she ventured timidly. 'Has she mentioned me?'

This time a shadow crossed the other woman's face.

'She's very upset,' Tabitha said gently. 'It's natural, after everything she's been through with Rosie. Seeing Lowenna all wired up to machines in the hospital brought back so many memories. It was like her worst nightmare come true yet again.'

'I wish I could make it up to her,' Bramble sighed. 'Should I write to her? Send flowers, a present for Lowenna? What would be the best thing?'

Tabitha's pause spoke volumes.

'I think,' she said slowly, 'that you shouldn't do anything at all right now. Liz is the kindest, most understanding person in the world, but this has shaken her up big time. I hate to see her angry and upset and I want you two to be friends, but she's very raw. You're just going to have to be patient.'

Bramble pulled her knees under her chin so that she was scrunched up, like a little ball. Tabitha was trying to be tactful, but it was obvious from what she'd said that Liz was spitting mad, and the knowledge hurt.

'I was hoping to come to your gig next month with Liz,

Felipe and Tony,' she said in a small voice, remembering Liz's kindness in coming to cheer her up after Katie had left. 'I don't suppose she'll be going now, either.'

'It's been cancelled anyway. Something to do with a double-booking. I was pretty disappointed, to be honest.'

Bramble tried to comfort Tabitha by suggesting that there would be other venues, other occasions, but she was unconvinced.

'I'm not sure I've got it in me to perform any more. I can't bear touting myself around; I'm just not pushy enough. You've got to be so tough in this business.'

'But you're so good!' Bramble said, and then a thought came from nowhere that seemed all of a sudden to be the best idea that she'd ever had.

'We can have the gig here, at the manor! We can ask other bands along, too, if you like?'

Tabitha frowned. 'It would be much too much for you. These things take masses of organisation, and anyway, it's the wrong time of year. It would have to be in the garden and it'll be winter soon.'

'We'll hire a big tent,' Bramble persisted, refusing to be deterred. 'And I don't mind using bits of the manor, too. It's not as if there's anything very valuable here.'

Some of the profits could be donated to the air ambulance or lifeboat people, she went on, or the hospital – or maybe all three.

'It'll be my way of saying thank you for helping me. We might attract more visitors if it's in aid of charity, too.'

'But we'd need money to get the ball rolling and neither of us have got any,' Tabitha pointed out. 'Concerts cost thousands to put on. There's lighting, security, sound systems, not to mention portable loos, waiters and waitresses to serve drinks and so on. I doubt there'd be any cash left to donate after all that. In fact, we'd be lucky if we even managed to cover costs.'

But Bramble hardly heard her. 'We'll get sponsors. I'm sure local firms will want to be involved.' She looked at her friend seriously. 'I realise it's a big undertaking, but I don't feel like I've done anything worthwhile since I arrived here. I've just made one mistake after another. Polgarry needs to be opened up to the public; I'm sure it's what my grandfather would have wanted. People should be able to see and enjoy it, and I'd like to help you, too.'

She could tell that the other woman was tempted but was probably worried that it might be disloyal to Liz to say yes.

'I'm not sure—' she started to say, but Bramble interrupted.

'I know Liz won't want to come, but I imagine she'll be happy if you raise money for the services that helped save Lowenna? We'll have a meeting about it on Monday,' she continued, 'just you and me, and get some initial ideas together. I'll do a bit of research beforehand, and maybe you can think of people who might want to help and bands to approach. I think we should keep it local, but we want the best Cornwall has to offer. With enough notice, I'm sure lots of musicians will want to take part.'

At last Tabitha rose, explaining that she had to collect Oscar from his friend's, but there was a spring in her step as she exited the manor and climbed into her old red Fiesta.

'See you soon,' she shouted as she slammed the door. 'I'm quite coming round to the idea, you know. This could be a *Good Thing*!'

Bramble was in her own little world as she walked slowly back into the manor, oblivious to the sights, smells and sounds around her. She was thinking how weird it was that just when she was at her most unhappy, she'd come up with the idea of putting on a big event. Was she mad? Perhaps. But on the other hand, this could be a fantastic way of giving something back to the community, and perhaps of showing her remorse to some of those she'd injured, too. It would also breathe new life into the old manor, and deep down she was convinced that this was what Lord Penrose would have wished for.

Not a soul would guess that this would be her swansong, her final goodbye to Polgarry and the Cornish life that she'd envisaged for herself. Somehow or other she'd cobble together enough money to put on a fantastic, memorable event that she hoped people would talk about for months to come. After that, the old place would have to go on the market and wait for someone with more funds and vision than her to take it on. This was her decision; the answer had come.

'Bramble, love?' Cassie called from the kitchen. 'Is that you?'

Bramble woke from her daydream. Goodness knew how long she'd been standing in the hallway.

'Come and taste this pastry. I did it with Maria. It's as light as a feather!'

Bramble smiled. At this rate the housekeeper would be spending weekends with them in Chessington, visiting local garden centres with Cassie and getting to know the neighbours. Perhaps she'd even quit Cornwall herself and move in with them. You never knew. After all, stranger things had happened since Bramble had first set foot in Polgarry Manor.

Chapter Twenty-Two

AUTUMN BROUGHT THE morning valley mists rolling across the fields and hillsides and turned the trees around Tremarnock to red, orange and gold. The temperature was still warmer than elsewhere in England, but as the mercury slowly dipped, the woolly sweaters and fleeces started to come out and only the hardiest souls still ventured into the sea to swim, Rick Kane among them.

Thankfully, the long, hot summer seemed to have finally cured him of his chronic lovesickness and he no longer looked like a mournful basset hound whenever the name 'Esme' was uttered in his presence. Indeed, having finally returned to online dating after a break of several months, he was now stepping out with a red-blooded widow from Liskeard who favoured high heels and revealing tops and seemed eminently more suitable. The villages were pleased to see a smile back on Rick's whiskery face, and Esme was greatly relieved, too, as she could now stand beside him without fear of his wandering hands. All in all, things had worked out rather well.

Rafael had settled in at his new school, and Tim, perhaps envious of Rosie's handsome new friend, seemed to have rather lost interest in Amelia and had begun sending frequent messages to Rosie again on social media. While not averse to the attention, she felt that she'd moved on over the holidays and now preferred spending time in bigger groups rather than hanging out with one person. As a result, the messages frequently went unanswered.

Lowenna was fit again and seemed remarkably unscathed by her ordeal. The only significant repercussion was that she now refused to go anywhere near the sea, which didn't matter so much with winter coming on; but Liz and Robert hoped that her fear, though understandable, would pass in time. Doctors had suggested taking her to the swimming pool at first to get her used to the water again and Liz had resolved to sign her up for toddler classes in January.

Tabitha and Danny were making plans to move in together and had already looked at several properties in Tremarnock; Audrey had largely healed her rift with Tony, Felipe and Rafael after booking a holiday in Portugal and realising that it would be foolish not to tap the Brazilians for free language lessons; and Ryan had rallied after Katie's departure and found himself a nice girlfriend from Plymouth.

Meanwhile, since Cassie and Bill had returned to London Bramble had been so busy mugging up on how to organise a music festival in an extremely short space of time that she'd hardly left the grounds of Polgarry. In other circumstances she might have found this frustrating, but as it was the self-imposed confinement had suited her just fine as it meant that there'd been no opportunity to bump into Liz. Keeping busy meant less time to reflect on Matt, too.

Fergus had finished the roof, and as far as Bramble could tell he'd done an excellent job that should last for several years. She was eternally grateful. He'd also broken the news to Wilf that they'd be emigrating to Spain as soon as he'd found the right accommodation. Some time later, the boy had escaped from under his father's watchful eye and raced across the fields to tell Bramble. He'd been very upset, saying that he didn't want to go, that he hated Spain – though he'd never actually been – and that he'd run away and live with Bramble instead. Though she was heartbroken, she'd done her best to cheer him up and persuade him that, contrary to his beliefs, moving would be a marvellous adventure.

'You can come back in the holidays and impress me with your Spanish. You'll have fantastic weather there and make lots of new friends. I'll be jealous!'

'You can come, too!' Wilf had said hopefully, and she'd laughed.

'Who'd look after the manor and eat up Maria's delicious jam tarts? And someone's got to be here to stop the garden turning into a jungle.'

Tabitha had told Liz about the concert, of course, and Liz had agreed, for her friend's sake, that it was a good idea, but had vowed not to get involved herself in any way. Although this had saddened Tabitha, who knew that in other circumstances Liz would have loved to throw her weight behind the project, it had at least meant that she herself could spend time at Polgarry without feeling guilty or having to conceal what she was doing.

She and Bramble had already made enormous strides. Tony, who loved a party, had suggested using crowdfunding, a new method of raising many small amounts of money from a large number of people via the Internet, and had shown them how to set up a web page announcing details of the festival. Clearly, there was an appetite for watching bands in muddy fields, because to their delight within three weeks they'd raised twenty thousand pounds from more than two hundred supporters, which was enough to get started, and the money was still rolling in. In return for their cash, donors had been promised tickets and sponsorship opportunities.

The villagers, excited by the prospect of a rip-roaring night out, had also begun to feel they had an investment in the event, and many had offered their services either at a reduced price or for free. Felipe was helping with the artwork for posters, promotional leaflets, mail drops and so on, while Jenny and John Lambert, among others, had promised to man the gates, with Rick, Audrey, Jean, Tom and whoever else they could muster.

'I don't suppose I shall like the music much,' Audrey had sniffed when Jenny had approached her with the plan, 'but I'm happy to support Tabitha, and it's nice to think of Polgarry being open to the public after all these years.'

Meanwhile, Ryan and Nathan, the postman, had taken on car park duties and persuaded a group of their friends to act as security guards, and Barbara, an arch organiser, had offered to run the main bar, complete with local craft beers and cider, and also to coordinate food, which would be provided by a selection of local eateries, including Tremarnock's famous fish and chip shop and the nearby pizza place on the beach.

Of course, much advice had to be sought, equipment secured and licences bought, all of which was complicated and took a great deal of time, but no one seemed to mind. Tremarnock had never done anything quite like this before and there was a real will to muck in and make it a success.

The only gaping absences were Liz and Robert, who, out of loyalty to his wife, had agreed not to become involved either. It was quite awkward for them both, as locals seemed to talk of little else, and of course Robert's staff, including Jesse and Loveday, had been unable to resist participating in the plans, although so far they'd been tactful enough not to mention them in front of the boss.

Bramble had spoken on the phone many times to Katie, who'd often promised to visit without ever actually getting round to it, but now that the date of the concert – 3 December – was fixed firmly in the diary, she'd finally taken the plunge and booked her train ticket.

'I can't believe you're doing this, Bram!' she said admiringly one evening. 'Who'd have thought it? How many did you say are going?'

'About a thousand,' Bramble replied, feeling slightly sick, for she couldn't quite believe it either.

'Wow! And it's so soon – only three weeks away!'

'Don't remind me,' Bramble groaned.

They discussed potential outfits for a while, and Katie said that she'd be wearing her new pink woollen hat with the rabbit-fur pom-pom.

'I won't get attacked by animal rights people, will I?'

'Foxes more like,' Bramble joked. 'And maybe the odd badger or stoat.'

Katie's next comment caught her right off guard.

'I met Matt for a drink last night.'

'Oh yes?'

'He seems well.'

'Good.' Bramble didn't want to sound too interested.

'He's started seeing someone – a girl from work.'

'What?' She gathered herself quickly. 'That's nice.'

'She's called Lois. Works at reception. Did you ever meet her?'

A vision of the girl danced before Bramble's eyes. She was all boobs and blonde hair, as far as she could remember.

'I'm pleased for him,' she lied.

When they hung up, she found herself googling Lois's photo on the gym's website before reminding herself that she had no right. Matt wasn't part of her life any more, and what's more, he deserved all the happiness he could find, though she was a bit surprised that he'd gone for someone quite so *obvious*.

The festival, originally planned for the evening, was now to start in the afternoon and feature an eclectic mix of music including folk, funk, reggae, jazz and pop. Esme had suggested erecting a separate covered stage for drama, art, poetry and comedy performances, but Bramble had felt that would be too much. She had, however, agreed to a 'pottery tent' where Esme and her friends would give demonstrations, charging a small fee for people to make their own creations, which could be collected from their studio, fired and ready, at a later date.

Tremarnock Art Club would also run a stall, where children could try their hands at still-life painting, and Nathan's girlfriend, Annie, had offered to lay on yoga classes. In return for advertising, a local hire firm was to lend an indoor bouncy castle, a baby gym and, for the slightly older children, a giant ball pond and slide. Bramble intended to put them in the main reception area and the television room, having decided to keep the upstairs out of bounds.

As word spread, she'd sensed the excitement in the air, even from high up on her solitary estate. Chaps from local delivery firms who were dropping off equipment would tell her about the chatter in pubs and the posters in shop windows and on lampposts all around the area, so that she could be in no doubt that this was happening. Tony, too, had organised interviews for her with local TV and radio stations, which Bramble had reluctantly accepted, knowing that they needed all the publicity they could get, and she was aware of the interest the interviews had generated.

Reporters, who'd come to the manor with their sound people and camera crews, had jumped on the story of the ordinary young woman from London who'd inherited a mansion, nearly drowned at sea and was now raising funds for the charities that had helped save her. She'd tried her best to downplay her role in organising the event, highlighting all the hard work that the villagers were putting in, but still her story had seemed to capture the public imagination and tickets were selling like hot cakes.

One afternoon in mid-November, when the sky was grey and the wind rattled through the gaps in the manor windows, she was sitting on the floor with her back to the ancient radiator in the drawing room, trying to keep warm and going through the concert programme for the umpteenth time, looking for gaps or omissions. Tabitha had just left to collect Oscar from school, and Bramble was contemplating yet another evening on her own with just the TV for company. She was growing used to it now; she had no money to spend in the Tremarnock pubs, and anyway, she was frightened of seeing Liz.

She had on jeans, thick socks and an oversized cable-knit sweater that had once belonged to Bill – she'd sequestered it years ago because she liked the dark-green colour – yet still she felt chilled. She wondered how she'd cope in the depths of winter, until she remembered that she'd be leaving Cornwall after the concert, so that was one less thing to worry about.

A loud rat-a-tat-tat made her start. At first she wasn't sure where the rapping came from, but then, as she glanced over to the French windows, she spotted the familiar tall figure of Fergus hovering on the crumbling terrace. He was wearing a thick, dark overcoat and carrying something bulky under his arm, wrapped in plastic and tape.

'Can I come in?' he seemed to mouth, for she couldn't hear his voice clearly.

She laid the concert itinerary on the floor, jumped up – almost knocking over the half-drunk cup of coffee that she'd been nursing – and went to the door.

'Are you all right?' she asked, fearing that something was amiss.

'I've brought you something,' he replied gruffly, shifting from one foot to another as if he wasn't sure what to do with his body. 'Here.'

He thrust the package that he'd been carrying into her hands, and for a moment she just stared at it, nonplussed.

'What is it?' she said doubtfully. It was quite large, square and flat, a bit unwieldy but reasonably light, and covered in layers and layers of wrapping.

'It's a present,' he replied, 'for you.'

'For me? Why? Sorry,' she said, suddenly remembering her manners, for he was still standing outside in the cold. 'Come in! How nice! Can I open it now?'

They sat side by side on the sofa, her with the present on her lap, him in his big waxed overcoat. Keen to be hospitable, she offered him a drink, but he refused.

'I'm not staying.'

In the past she'd have thought him rude, but not now that she knew his story and the suffering he'd endured. In fact, she thought that she could forgive him anything.

'Where's Wilf?' she asked, and Fergus replied that he'd gone to a friend's house after school. Bramble was pleased, for the boy didn't seem to have many mates.

'Well, go on,' Fergus urged, nodding at the parcel. 'It might be a bit difficult to get into, I'm afraid.'

There was, indeed, a mountain of sticky tape, and beneath

the plastic, several layers of newspaper and bubble wrap. A knife or a pair of scissors would have been handy, but none were to hand and Bramble didn't want to have to get up to fetch them. As she tore off the layers, one by one, she found her curiosity mounting, for she had absolutely no idea what was inside. Then all of a sudden it occurred to her that it might be a goodbye gift, and she was tempted to stop right there, as though that might delay his leaving; but he was waiting expectantly and she must go on.

At last she reached the bottom layer and discovered a canvas, surrounded by a wooden frame, and quickly turned it to the correct side to find out what was on it. At first she couldn't make out a subject at all and, tilting her head to one side to see if it made a difference, she frowned uncertainly.

'Is it one of yours?' she asked, thinking that she recognised the bold abstract lines and bright colours, and he nodded.

Pleased that she'd got this right, at least, she tipped her head the other way, to no avail. 'It's, um, it's very—'

'It's the wrong way round,' Fergus interrupted, and when she glanced up she saw little crinkles on either side of his eyes and realised that he was smiling.

'Oh,' she said, feeling silly. 'Of course.'

He helped turn the canvas around, and now it was easy to see that the image was of a person, a girl in denim shorts and a white T-shirt, with long, slim limbs and blonde hair. She was outdoors, in a field or an orchard perhaps, surrounded by old, gnarled trees. The grass was very green, the sun was shining and the trees were laden with fruit – ripe greengages and reddish-purple plums. It must have been the height of summer.

The girl was leaning against one of the trees, her right leg drawn up, her bare foot resting on the bark, and she seemed reflective – not sad but confused perhaps, as if she wasn't sure what to do next, which way to go.

'It's beautiful,' Bramble said, meaning it. 'I love the quietness, the lushness. There's a mystery about it, too.' She looked at Fergus quizzically.

'It's you,' he said, pre-empting her next question. 'I wanted to paint you the moment I saw you in the orchard. Before then, in fact, but that was when I decided I'd definitely do it.'

'That time you saved me from the runaway lawnmower?' She was amazed. 'I thought you disliked me. I thought you'd decided I was the stupidest person alive.'

'Young and irresponsible, yes. Stupid, never.'

As his deep-set eyes met hers, they seemed to turn from black to brown to sea-green, and all at once something that Maria had said came back to her and her heart leaped. Fergus! Of course! He was the other person who had brought Lord Penrose joy. He'd loved the artist well enough to lend him the cottage for free and to leave the French doors open so that he and Wilf could let themselves in…

'Thank you,' she said quietly, trying to conceal her excitement. 'I'll treasure it always.'

He didn't smile but seemed relieved, as if he'd feared a different reaction. 'I was going to keep it, but I thought it was right you should have it. Call it a record of your earliest days at Polgarry and a memento of our brief time together.'

His words reminded her of the harsh truth, and instantly the spell was broken.

'I don't want you to go,' she said simply. 'I can't cope here on my own.'

'Of course you can.' He sounded quite angry. 'You'll make a success of this, I know. I can see you hosting all sorts of events in the future. Polgarry will probably become famous, a thriving hub of music and creativity. You'll be the toast of Tremarnock, the whole of the South West.'

She shook her head. 'This place is falling down around me, you know that. A few festivals aren't going to keep the manor warm and dry. Besides, I don't...'

She stopped speaking because she became aware that he was sitting very close to her, so close that their shoulders and knees were almost touching and she could hear the rise and fall of his breath. He was leaning inwards, his dark, troubled face turned towards her, and all of a sudden she was mesmerised by the small, pale scar in the centre of his lower lip. If she touched it with her finger, felt its rough edges, she might just be able to smooth them away.

Fergus must have guessed what she was thinking, for he reached up and brushed her cheek. In one swift movement she took the painting from him and propped it behind her, and before she knew it her hands were clasped behind his head and she was pulling his mouth on to hers. She was willing them to a place where there were no worries, where she could forget all about Matt, forget that she was selling Polgarry and would shortly be returning to the house that she'd longed to leave behind. A world where she would take care of Fergus and they could both be safe and happy. This was surely her destiny; it was what her grandfather would have wanted.

Lost in make-believe, it took her a moment or two to realise that he was unlacing her fingers and loosening her hands around his head.

'Fergus, I—'

'Don't,' he said, pulling back.

'Why?'

'I can't. I'm sorry...'

He rose abruptly and a cold hand gripped her intestines and squeezed tight.

'Stay here with me,' she pleaded. 'You and Wilf. You can paint and I'll get a job. We won't need much; we'll manage somehow. I can make you better...'

'You don't understand,' he said, shaking his head. 'I can never love another woman. That side of my life's over, finished. My heart broke when Julia and Felicity died. The only things that matter to me now are Wilf and my work. Nothing more. They're what I get up for every morning and what I go to sleep thinking of.

'I can't ever give you what you want. I felt sorry for you; I apologise if you feel I misled you. You're young, with your whole life in front of you. You deserve the best. Go and find someone your age. Go back to Matt.'

At the mention of his name, a sense of rage, self-pity, shame and powerlessness washed over her. All her hopes and dreams, it seemed, had come to nothing, all her plans turned to dust.

'You can take your painting back. I don't want it.' She hated herself for hurting him, yet wished to cause maximum damage nonetheless.

Fergus's shoulders drooped. 'Do you mean it?'

'I've got too many paintings already, and it won't fit with the others; it's too modern.'

He sighed, long and deep. 'Very well.' Then he bent down, picked up his work and tucked it back under his arm. The paper that he'd wrapped it in was still strewn all around but he didn't bother to pick it up.

She watched, dumbly, as he took several strides across the room and hesitated at the French doors.

'We're leaving on Friday.'

So soon? She'd thought that he might at least wait until after the festival, after Christmas even.

'I'll drop by in the next couple of days to say goodbye to Wilf then,' she said shakily. 'I expect you've already told Maria your plans?'

Fergus nodded.

'So that's all settled.'

'Yes.'

It took him a moment or two to wrestle with the lock on the French doors, which eventually flew open, letting in a blast of chilly air. She didn't move; she wasn't going to humiliate herself further.

He turned and looked at her before he left, willing her to understand, to meet him halfway at least, but she pretended not to notice. She bent down on her hands and knees to gather up the strewn newspaper, and it was only after he'd disappeared that her tears fell thick and fast, turning the newsprint to unsightly splodges of black, white and grey.

Chapter Twenty-Three

SHE COULDN'T WATCH them go. They left early, just after the sun had risen, and she'd already told Wilf that she wouldn't be there to wave them off.

'I can't spare the time. Sorry, darling, but I've too much work to do,' she'd lied, kissing him on the top of his head. 'Send me a postcard when you arrive.'

She'd been aware that Maria had been busy for the past few days making sandwiches, biscuits and pastries for their journey, but she hadn't commented. In fact, she and the housekeeper had barely exchanged more than a few words for what seemed like an age. Bramble had guessed that Maria was waiting to find out about her employer's long-term plans, for since the conversation in the television room they hadn't discussed the property or the housekeeper's position again. Maria had taken only a passing interest in the festival and had spent most of her time cooking, pottering in the kitchen garden or resting in her room. Perhaps she missed Cassie; she certainly seemed to have a better relationship with her than with her boss.

As Bramble lay in her four-poster, picturing Wilf and Fergus piling the last things in their van and locking up the cottage for the final time, she wondered if she'd ever felt so bleak and desolate. The thought of giving herself to Fergus, of dedicating her life to healing his wounds, had seemed for one wild moment to be the answer to all her problems, but she was certain now that true happiness was beyond her. The only thing keeping her from jumping in the car right this minute and driving back to London was her determination to see the festival through to the end. Then and only then would she be able to say that she'd done something worthwhile here, that she'd left her mark.

Knowing that Tabitha wouldn't come till the afternoon, Bramble could so easily have pulled the covers over her head and stayed where she was. However, keeping busy seemed preferable to brooding, so she allocated herself the unenviable task of going through Lord Penrose's study, something that she'd been putting off for weeks.

The study was situated in the east wing of the manor, near the morning room, and the door was usually kept firmly shut. She'd only ever been in once or twice and had left again quickly, because it was so dusty and oppressive, stacked from floor to ceiling with shelves groaning with files, crumbling old books that appeared not to have been touched for years, strange objects that might have been collected on foreign travels or given as gifts perhaps, and other sundry items. If there had ever been anything valuable in there, it had long since been given away or sold, leaving only tat and mess, items that no one in their right mind could possibly want.

On one wall, beneath the leaded glass window, was an ugly pedestal desk, Victorian perhaps, with four drawers on either side with decorative brass handles and a studded, battered green leather surface. Bramble had once peeked in the drawers and closed them again quickly, for they were stuffed with crumpled letters and bits of paper, cracked fountain pens that had leaked black ink, staples, broken rubbers and stray drawing pins.

She had gleaned, from the debris, that Lord Penrose must rarely have ventured in here himself, at least in his later years, and she doubted that she'd find anything noteworthy. However, before leaving Cornwall for good she felt duty-bound to go through his personal papers, saving anything that she fancied as a keepsake and throwing out the rest.

Armed with a roll of black bin bags, she settled on the worn leather-bound chair and pulled open the top right-hand drawer. Inside she found a pocket diary, dated 1961, with her grandfather's signature on the first page. He couldn't have used the diary for long, however, as the only entries were in January and February, and even these told her little, save that in those days at least he did have a social life: 'Dinner with Margery and Raymond, eight p.m.'; 'Burns Night – Henry and Maud, seven thirty'. She chucked the diary away.

The papers in the other drawers meant nothing to her, just jottings; lists of items, perhaps to take on holiday; scribbles to the bank manager that had never been sent; the beginnings of letters – 'My dear Anne...'; the odd postcard from a friend. These, too, went into a bin bag. She was beginning to think that she could empty the whole desk without bothering to check when she noticed for the first time a small brass ring, set flush into the leather surface so discreetly that most people would miss it.

Curious, she extracted the ring with a little finger and was surprised to find that it turned into a miniature handle, which when pulled opened the lid to a hidden compartment, almost as wide and deep as the upper part of the desk itself. Inside was a square parcel, clumsily wrapped in dusty brown paper, and on the front, in capital letters, was a name, written once again in Lord Penrose's hand, and beneath it the words 'Fragile. Handle With Care'.

Bramble stared at the name and a tingle ran up and down her spine, for there was no mistaking it: 'BRAMBLE CHALLONER'. She felt suddenly as if Lord Penrose had risen from his grave and handed her the package himself.

Her fingers trembled as she tentatively removed the wrapping, remembering Fergus's present of only a few days before. She wasn't sure whether to expect a gift or a curse. Inside the brown paper there appeared to be a bundle of dirty, yellowing fabric. Feeling slightly disappointed, and wondering if this was her grandfather's idea of a joke, she picked up the material.

Underneath lay a small oil painting within a narrow gilt frame. The image was of fruit in a blue bowl, resting on a white linen tablecloth beside a simple blue-and-white teapot. The paint was slightly damaged in places, but something about the work pleased her immensely. Perhaps it was the primitive vitality of the shapes or the intense, undiluted colours. She was no expert, but could see that it was nothing like the rather dull, static portraits that hung around Polgarry; it oozed individuality and panache.

Glancing down, she saw that in the bottom right-hand corner was a signature written in swirly black letters. The surname rang a bell, and for a moment she felt excited, but then she reminded herself that it was probably a copy. If so, though, why would Lord Penrose have hidden it here? And why give it to her? It was a mystery indeed.

Jumping up, she quickly scanned the books on the shelves around her, frustrated that the titles appeared to have been put there randomly, with no logic. It was clear that her grandfather had once had a taste for novels that were now mostly long forgotten, as well as books on birds and wildlife, but as she cast her eye along the rows she finally alighted on a small collection about art – the Renaissance, impressionism, surrealism and so on. Among them was an encyclopaedia of famous painters through the ages, listed in alphabetical order. Feeling strangely light-headed, she knelt down, opened the book and flicked through until she found the page about a French painter of the late nineteenth century, a post-impressionist who bore the same moniker as her artist.

His subject matter was wide and varied: portraits, landscapes, cityscapes, still lifes and, in later years, spiritual and mythological themes executed in a different, even more exuberant style. As she gazed at the numerous images, starting with his earliest works and moving through his life, her focus fell on a picture from 1864: 'Still Life with Teapot'. It was the same as her picture!

Her head swam and for a moment she thought she might faint. Turning back to the page in front of her, she read, 'His work was influential to many modern artists... bold, colourful design... only became popular after his death...' The words barely registered. What to do? Keep calm, said a voice inside her. Get a grip and take this step by step.

Fired, suddenly, with new-found energy, she jumped up, carefully rewrapped the painting in its rags and paper, put it back in the hidden compartment and laid the encyclopaedia on top. Then she forced herself to walk, not run, into the morning room where she picked up the corded phone.

When at last she'd found the number, she dialled with shaking fingers and a woman's clipped voice said the name of a well-known auction house, then, 'Good morning.'

Bramble drew back her shoulders and took a deep breath.

'I – I'd like to speak to an art expert,' she stammered. 'Someone who knows about old paintings. I've found... well, it might be nothing, of course. It's difficult to describe on the phone. What I'm trying to say is… I need to talk to someone as soon as possible.'

'QUIET, Lowenna! Stop screaming, will you? I'm being as quick as I can. I don't know what's got into you.'

Rosie glanced up from the kitchen table, where she was nibbling on the end of a peanut butter sandwich, and gave her mother a funny look.

'You're in a bad mood,' she commented as Liz lifted her youngest daughter out of the high chair and plonked her impatiently on the floor. 'What's the matter?'

Liz scowled. It was the day of the festival and she *was* feeling grumpy, though of course the event had nothing whatsoever to do with it. Rosie was going – as was the whole of Tremarnock, apparently. In fact, it seemed that no one could talk about anything else and Liz was sick to death of it. Didn't people realise that a stupid concert wasn't everyone's cup of tea?

Lowenna, dismayed by her mother's uncharacteristically rough handling and tone of voice, started bawling.

'Oh, for goodness' sake, what is it *now*?'

'I'm going to get changed,' Rosie said, pushing back her chair and rising quickly. She bent down and scooped up her little sister. 'Come on, Lowie, come with Rosie. Mummy's being naughty. Mummy must be very tired.'

Lowenna eyed her mother reproachfully over Rosie's shoulder.

Left alone amidst the debris of her daughters' late breakfast, Liz felt a mixture of anger and guilt. She knew that she'd been foul ever since she got out of bed and it was no surprise that her family was avoiding her. Even Robert had left for the restaurant earlier than usual, claiming that he had a mound of 'admin stuff' to get through, but she was pretty certain that her sour face and prickly manner were the real reason. In fact, if she were honest, she hadn't felt herself for ages. She could no longer legitimately claim delayed shock from Lowenna's accident at sea, however, because it had happened almost three months ago and everyone else had managed to move on.

As she crashed about, putting cups and plates into the dishwasher and sweeping crumbs off the floor, she found herself wondering what the festival crowd would be like, and how Tabitha was feeling and what she'd wear. Liz hated the fact that she wouldn't be there to support her friend, and she'd have quite liked to experience the atmosphere, too. If only Bramble wasn't going to be about, but of course the event wouldn't be happening without her.

Tony, Felipe, Jean, Tom and Esme – everyone had tried to persuade Liz to join them. Even Shannon had popped in unexpectedly with her brothers last weekend and asked why she wasn't going.

'It's going to be a right laugh,' she'd said, eyes shining. 'Most of my mates can't afford tickets, but Bramble gave me four, one each for me and my dad and two extra. That was kind, wasn't it?'

'Well, you have given her lots of help in her garden,' Liz had replied tartly. 'I hope she'll buy you a few drinks and something to eat as well.'

Shannon had looked at her oddly. 'She did *pay* me for the work, even if it was only a little. She's not rich, you know.'

Liz had pursed her lips and remained silent. Shannon had benefited in more ways than one from the association with Bramble, as Liz had hoped she would, but it hadn't been

Bramble's idea, and besides, she had gained, too. There was no call for hero worship.

Liz could hear Lowenna laughing with her sister upstairs and was tempted to see what they were up to, but realised that she'd only spoil their fun. It was a long time, she reflected, getting out the antibacterial spray and scrubbing the surfaces hard with a blue cloth, since she'd felt quite so bitter and out of sorts, and she didn't like the sensation. It wasn't something vague or general that was getting to her either; she wasn't upset about the state of the world or the bad weather. She didn't have PMS, and she and Robert hadn't argued. No, her resentment was directed at just one person: Bramble. Try as she might – and as pointless as it seemed to keep going over and over the accident – she couldn't seem to get the woman, or her bloody festival, out of her head.

She went into the sitting room and picked up the newspaper, but hardly a word sank in. Robert would be back for a couple of hours around four and they'd agreed to go for a stroll, but other than that she'd be alone with Lowenna all evening with the windows closed, trying her best not to hear the music booming down from the clifftop, to see the manor lit up in all its austere glory against the velvety black sky, to imagine Tabitha's soulful voice filtering through the rapt audience and melting hearts.

She hoped, for Tabitha's sake, that the event would be a wild success, that word of her talent would spread far and wide and that they'd manage to raise heaps of money for the wonderful rescue services. As for Bramble, however, she could only wish that one day, when she had children of her own, she might finally understand something of the pain that she'd put Liz through by risking Lowenna's life. Then perhaps she'd grasp why they could never be friends again.

Rosie sauntered down with her sister about an hour later, dressed in black jeans and a sequined top that left a sizeable strip of bare tummy.

'You'll freeze in that,' Liz snapped. She cast an eye over her daughter's silvery eyeshadow and heavily mascaraed lashes. 'And you're wearing an awful lot of make-up.'

Rosie pouted. 'Mu-um, it's a party. And I'll be in a tent most of the time and I'll have a coat with me.' She fiddled self-consciously with her top, pulling at the hem. 'Do I look all right?'

Liz wanted to kick herself. Rosie wasn't the most confident person, and she needed encouragement, not criticism. Besides, she was beautiful.

'You look absolutely gorgeous,' she commented, managing a small smile, almost for the first time that day. 'You'll raise gasps wherever you go.'

A group of friends, including Rafael in head-to-toe black, arrived at about one o'clock to pick Rosie up, and at two thirty, when Lowenna woke from her nap, Liz decided to take her to the play park. It wasn't raining but the sky was gloomy, the air felt slightly damp and all the colours had leeched away, turning houses, grass and hills into an indeterminate brownish-grey. There was virtually no one about; perhaps they were all getting changed and heading for Polgarry already. Even Lowenna seemed to sense that she was missing out. She normally loved the play park, but today as Liz pushed her on the swing she grizzled to get down and she only went on the little slide once before grumbling.

The wind whistled around Liz's ankles and she had an insane urge to cry. She might have indulged herself, but someone tapped her on the shoulder, making her spin around.

'Hey! Fancy seeing you!'

It was Robert, back early from the restaurant, towering over her in his dark-green jacket, his brown hair tousled and his navy scarf flying. Normally, she'd have gone up on tiptoe to give him a kiss, but not today.

'She's in a foul mood,' she said, gesturing to Lowenna, who was grizzling at the foot of the slide. 'I don't know what's got into her.'

Robert didn't reply, but instead strode over to where his small daughter was crouching and scooped her up, tickling her in the ribs and making her laugh straight away. This only made Liz crosser.

'Typical,' she muttered. 'She's all sweetness and light the minute *you* turn up.'

Robert coughed. 'Um, are you a teeny-weeny bit out of sorts, perhaps? Maybe she can sense it?'

'Rubbish!'

He looked at his wife askance. 'Anything to do with the music festival, by any chance?'

'Absolutely not!' Liz snapped back.

But he wasn't giving up that easily.

'You know, you could always pop up there with Lowenna for an hour or two, just to spend a bit of money and show some support, I mean. It's for a very good cause and you'll know practically everyone. You might even find you enjoy it.'

The heat rushed to Liz's face and her cheeks lit up in fury.

'There's no way I'm going anywhere near that woman. She practically drowned our daughter, remember? I can't believe you even suggested it.'

Upset by her mother's tone of voice again, Lowenna started whimpering, so Robert walked her over to the roundabout and popped her on, while Liz trailed miserably behind.

'Wouldn't Pat have enjoyed all the excitement?' he said,

giving his daughter a push. 'Not the loud music maybe, but the young people and the general hullabaloo.'

His comment seemed innocent enough, but Liz knew what he was up to, and sure enough, at the mention of the old woman's name she felt a stab of longing so sharp and fierce that it almost took her breath away. Since Pat had died, she'd tried hard not to dwell on her own grief but to think of the full and happy life her friend had led. Right now, though, she realised that more than anything else in the world she wanted to be back in The Nook, sitting beside Pat in her cosy front room with cups of tea in their hands and a plate of chocolate biscuits on the table beside them.

Pat would have understood. She'd have listened patiently to Liz and talked things through. Pat had adored Lowenna, and although she'd had no children herself, she'd have shared Liz's shock and horror after the accident, and no doubt would have railed against Bramble for taking two small children on her own to a beach with no lifeguards, when the weather was iffy and the sea was unpredictable at the best of times.

But would she have banished Bramble from her life for ever? Liz watched Lowenna going round and round, giggling at her father's funny faces. He had forgiven Bramble, and Pat would have, too. After all, she'd been deeply wronged once by Loveday and she'd given the girl a very hard time, but in the end she'd conceded that the harm hadn't been intended and they'd made up and become even closer than before.

Something that Liz had once read in a newspaper article came to mind. It must have struck her quite forcibly or she wouldn't have remembered it: 'Resentment is like taking poison and waiting for the other person to die.' Was she wallowing in a pool of bitterness, wasting precious mental and emotional energy on hostility? Certainly, she'd managed to wound Bramble by refusing to see her, but who was hurting the most?

At last Lowenna had had enough of the roundabout, and she didn't seem to want to go on anything else, so Robert strapped her back in her pushchair. He and Liz were silent as they strolled home, but she didn't need to ask what he was thinking.

The truth, she reflected as she watched him open the front door and lift their daughter indoors, was that she felt locked in a prison for a crime that someone else had committed, and no matter what he did or said, she wasn't at all sure that she could find a way out.

'I'm nervous, Katie. What if something goes wrong? What if it's a huge flop?'

Bramble was staring out of her bedroom window with Katie, watching the steady stream of visitors filtering through the temporary ticket gate and fanning out across the manor grounds before making their way towards the giant purple tent, in the shape of a cow, in which music was already blasting out from high-tech speakers.

'Don't worry, it'll be great,' Katie replied, giving Bramble a hug. 'I'm *sooo* proud of you.'

Bramble had collected Katie from the railway station the evening before, and they'd spent the morning walking around the site, chatting to the musicians, the sound and lighting people, the St John Ambulance staff, the security guards and the elderly man in a bright-red cagoule who was hoping to sell his helium balloons shaped like golden unicorns.

The ground had been damp underfoot and Bramble fully expected a mud bath later, but at least no more rain had been forecast and the temperature was mild for the time of year, which meant, with luck, that people would want to stay outside where most of the action would be taking place.

'Don't you think we should go down?' Katie asked, picking her pink bobble hat and coat with the fake-fur collar off the bed. She hadn't altered... well, only a little. Perhaps she did look slightly older now that she'd found herself a decent job in the finance department of a large City of London legal firm and started dating one of the trainee lawyers, who'd helped her to recover from the Danny trauma. She'd toned down the make-up and got herself a grown-up manicure, but she was still the same underneath. The naughty, wild laugh hadn't changed, and of course it was the weekend and she was up for some serious fun.

Bramble noticed a bit of an altercation going on between the gatekeepers and a man hoping to bring a large, hairy dog on a chain into the grounds. There was a good deal of shaking of heads and gesticulating while the crowd behind shuffled impatiently, until the man eventually gave up and walked off in a huff.

Taking a deep breath, she turned back to Katie. 'OK,' she said, giving a brave thumbs-up. 'On with the show!'

As they strolled slowly along the landing and down the sweeping staircase, passing by the stiff portraits of long-dead ancestors, Bramble found herself wishing that Matt were here. She could imagine them walking hand in hand around the gardens, admiring the fabulous sights, sounds and smells, pointing out and commenting on things that one or the other had spotted.

Once it got colder, he'd check that she was wearing enough clothes and ask if she wanted to borrow his scarf or gloves. They'd have hot drinks and dance, and then later, when it was all over, they'd retire to bed and laugh like drains at the day's events before making love. It mightn't be wild and passionate, not tonight; they'd probably be too tired. Instead, they'd go for the shortcut, both knowing exactly what they were doing and how to get it done quickly and to their mutual satisfaction.

That giddy, butterflies-in-the-stomach feeling that she'd briefly experienced with Piers seemed hateful to her now. After all, hadn't it always felt less like a joy and more a period of mental instability and exhaustion, even before he'd dumped her? And Fergus... well, the memory of their last encounter made her face burn; she couldn't quite believe how badly she'd misread him, and herself, too, for it would never have worked, not in a million years.

Now she thought that she'd happily trade everything she possessed for the solid comfort and safety of Matt, for the kindness, intimacy and respect of a man whom she knew like the back of her hand and who'd really, really cared about her. She believed that she could even be happy in that house around the corner from Bill and Cassie with a bit of garden, a carport and a utility room. But Matt was sharing his scarf and gloves with Lois, as well as his dreams and his bed.

'I think we need a drink,' she told Katie quickly. 'Let's go and find some scrumpy to get us in the mood.'

Barbara had brought her own tent, complete with a temporary bar, chairs and tables covered in red-and-white-checked tablecloths, several outdoor heaters and a barrel of warm rugs for customers to put on their knees or wrap around their shoulders. It was positively cosy in there. When the girls strolled in, she and her son, Aiden, were polishing glasses behind the bar and issuing orders to the bar staff, two slightly dopey-looking youths in black trousers and white shirts buttoned up to the neck.

Barbara, especially, seemed quite stressed, perhaps because she'd be rushing back and forth between her pub and the venue, keeping a beady eye on both. Her blonde hair, normally immaculate, was a little dishevelled, and her cheeks were rather pink, owing to too much blusher, hastily applied.

'Which cider do you recommend?' Bramble asked, eyeing the line-up of strange names: Apple Slayer, Cornish Rattler, Deep Purple, Beast of Bodmin, Spotty Dog.

'Depends whether you want sweet or dry,' Barbara replied, signalling to one of the youths to stand up straight. 'To tell you the truth, I'm more of a wine girl myself. Aiden's the expert.'

'I should try the Apple Slayer first.' He winked at the girls. 'You've got plenty of time to taste 'em all by the end of the evening.'

Katie nodded enthusiastically. 'Two halves, please.' She reached for some money in the back pocket of her jeans. 'And a bag of pork scratchings.'

They took their drinks and wandered into the purple tent, where a crowd had already gathered to hear the first act, a mixed group of young musicians from Newquay who'd been recommended by Danny. They looked pretty nervous, fiddling with their guitars and keyboard and checking the sound levels.

'Hello, Cornwall!' one of them shouted at last through his microphone, and the crowd roared back. 'Are you ready for a good time?' he went on, to cries of, 'Yes! Yes!' and, 'Hurry up, we're waiting!'

The microphone squeaked a few times and a little girl on her father's shoulders burst into tears and was escorted swiftly from the tent, while an older woman in a green puffer jacket next to Bramble and Katie put fingers in her ears and scowled.

'What did she expect? Silent music?' Katie whispered.

Bramble shrugged. 'She's in the wrong place. Wait till she hears the punk band later on.'

They stood for a few minutes enjoying the first number, which was quite catchy, before deciding to check out some of the other attractions. There was a small crowd of children outside Esme's pottery tent, a few proudly brandishing golden unicorn balloons, while others were munching on pasties and thick French-bread sandwiches from the food marquee. Bramble spotted Felipe and Tony, in matching dark-navy pea coats and stripy scarves, and some way off, Liz's daughter, Rosie, laughing gaily with a group of youngsters who were passing around what looked suspiciously like a pint of lager.

Bramble frowned. It wasn't as if she hadn't tried alcohol at their age. In fact, she'd sampled the lot by about fifteen – beer, wine, spirits; fags, too, which had made her violently sick. Not exactly saintly. But she couldn't have the police turning up and accusing her of flogging alcohol to minors. She'd have to warn Barbara and Aiden to check IDs.

Loveday bowled up in a purple fake-fur coat with bare legs and silver wedge sandals that were so high she could hardly walk, while her muddy toes, the nails painted black, peeped out from the ends.

'I'm so relieved I don't have to work today,' she told Bramble breathlessly. 'Jesse's off, too.'

She pointed at the girls' drinks in their hands. 'Where's the bar? I've been looking all over.'

Katie waved her in the right direction.

'Cheers!' said Loveday, almost tripping on a loose bit of turf and grabbing at Bramble's arm to steady herself. 'Look at me!' she giggled. 'What am I like? And I haven't even got started on the booze yet!'

The place was rapidly filling up with families, groups

of young people and older types with sensible haircuts in unflattering slacks and good, strong walking boots who'd clearly come more to have a nose around the manor and grounds than to hear the music. But the mix of ages and styles seemed only to enhance the gaiety of the occasion, and there was a great atmosphere, with folk talking and laughing, lovers strolling arm in arm, children chasing each other around the tents and grannies and grandpas hobbling after them.

As the sky started to darken and the shadows lengthened, stallholders lit decorative fairy lights around the entrances to their tents and braziers, on which they roasted chestnuts and marshmallows dipped in chocolate. The scent of damp earth, canvas and mulled wine mingled with the other smells, creating a sort of sensory overload, so that Bramble felt quite dizzy, although she'd still only had one glass of cider. Katie, on the other hand, who'd returned to the bar several times for a top-up, was already giggly.

'I think I just saw the fishmonger,' she whispered, nudging Bramble in the ribs. 'I won't know what to say.'

'You're quite safe. He's got a new girlfriend,' Bramble replied drily.

Katie saw Kieron, one of the part-time bar staff from The Hole in the Wall, and dashed off for a chat. 'I'll catch up with you,' she trilled, heading purposefully towards the 'Poetry Gazebo', where a number of local writers had banded together to erect a makeshift stage from which they could recite their work and, with luck, flog a few books at the same time.

Kieron – who was tall, fair and very handsome, if rather young for Katie – had been her second choice after Danny, until she'd discovered that he'd be off on his gap-year travels shortly before starting medical school.

'I can't be doing with all that studying,' she'd informed

Bramble soon after they'd moved to the manor. 'Never mind the travelling. He might come back with a nasty tropical disease. Besides, he keeps mentioning his mum.'

Dressed in jeans, wellies and her thick green sweater and with a red scarf pulled up under her nose, Bramble managed to amble almost incognito around the site for a while longer before venturing into the manor through the open French windows. She stood for a moment at the entrance to her large drawing room, gazing at the strangers milling around, some with children making for the soft-play areas, others looking up at the ornate ceiling and admiring the architecture and paintings.

The lamps were blazing, and Bramble and her helpers had pushed back the furniture and laid dust cloths over everything, including the wooden floor, but she had insisted on leaving the artwork, wanting visitors to enjoy it and get a real feel for what the place had been like when Lord Penrose had lived here. The paintings weren't particularly valuable, and besides, it would have been difficult to wander out with an enormous canvas under your arm without being seen.

'It's so grand, isn't it?' she heard one woman comment to her companion. 'What an incredible place to live!'

A shiver of pride ran up Bramble's spine, and she sensed that her manor was glad to be filled with noise, appreciation and laughter, with the shouts of children and the patter of numerous feet. Today it didn't feel austere at all but warm and welcoming, despite the dust cloths and mud. Whole families and children must have lived in Polgarry at some point in its history; perhaps its walls and floors, its very foundations, remembered. Perhaps they recalled her grandfather's famous parties, too, because echoes from that time seemed to pervade the air.

A tap on the shoulder jogged her out of her reverie.

'Miss Bramble, there is a call for you. I thought you would prefer to take it in the morning room.'

She stared at the housekeeper for a moment, because she'd forgotten all about her. In fact, she'd rather assumed that Maria would hide in her room for the entire time.

'Who is it?' she asked. 'Don't they know it's the festival today? Can't they call back?'

Maria shook her head. Her hair was brushed and shiny and she was in a rather pretty floral dress that Bramble had never seen before. What was going on?

'They said it is urgent,' the housekeeper insisted. 'They said it cannot wait.'

Bramble frowned. 'How inconvenient!' But she followed Maria out of the drawing room, across the marble hallway, through the door to the east wing, which had been firmly locked, and along the narrow corridor that led to the hexagonal room with the desk and corded Bakelite telephone.

The receiver lay on its side, waiting to be picked up.

'Hello?' said Bramble tentatively, aware that Maria was hovering right behind.

'Is that Bramble Challoner?' said a female voice with a cut-glass accent. She went on to explain that she was Dr Maura Levy, senior director in valuations at the auction house Bramble had contacted.

Bramble listened, spellbound, while the woman explained that they'd been consulting a number of worldwide experts about the painting she'd found in Lord Penrose's desk, and after rigorous checks they could now confirm, beyond any doubt, that the work was genuine. After the invasion of France by Germany in 1939, it had been requisitioned by the Nazis from a Jewish collector and sold cheaply at auction in

Paris to an anonymous collector. There were some references to its having then been sent to a secure location in the south of France, but in the chaos of post-war Europe it appeared to have gone missing and was feared lost.

'We now know that anonymous collector was your grandfather,' the woman went on. 'How he smuggled the work to Britain, we don't know; nor do we know why he kept it hidden in the desk. Perhaps for a while after the war it hung in Polgarry Manor until he decided that it was too precious to display. Maybe he simply didn't like it any more. In any case,' she continued, 'your painting is extremely valuable. It's worth a great deal of money, several million at least. You are a very rich woman, Miss Challoner. Congratulations.'

For a moment Bramble couldn't speak; she just stared out of the window, only dimly hearing the thud of music in the distance, the roar of the crowd.

'Several million?' she said at last, scarcely aware of Maria pulling back a chair and gently pushing her on to it. 'Are you sure?'

'Quite sure,' said the woman, before going on to suggest that Bramble should take a while to decide what she'd like to do next. 'If you wish to sell, we shall of course be delighted to represent you.'

Sell? Keep? Run away and hide? Bramble was all at sea, until a voice in her ear whispered, 'I told you that your grandfather was a good man.'

Startled, she swung around, still clutching the phone in one hand, and gawped at the housekeeper.

'You knew about this? You knew about the painting?'

Maria shrugged. 'He told me only that he would take care of you, that you – and Polgarry – would be properly provided for. He did not say how.'

Bramble's mind was racing, her thoughts flying hither and thither. 'You mean he intended me to find the painting? But if that's the case, why didn't he mention it in his will?'

Maria shrugged again. 'Lord Penrose was a strange man; he had his own ways of doing things. Maybe he wanted to give you a little test – I don't know – to see if you were clever enough to find his special hiding place.'

'What if I'd never found it? I might have sold the desk with the painting in it; someone else might have discovered it.'

'Clearly, it was a risk he was prepared to take.'

'Hello? Are you still there? Miss Challoner?'

Bramble had forgotten about the woman from the auction house, who'd been waiting patiently all this time.

'I'm sorry,' she said, struggling to make sense of what was happening. 'I'm in shock, to be honest. I hardly know what to think. Would it be all right if I called you back in the morning?'

They agreed to speak again the next day, and after she'd hung up Bramble sat for a while, trying to regulate her breathing. When at last she rose, Maria was standing with her back to the door waiting for some instruction, perhaps an idea of what this might mean and of what she was supposed to do now.

In two paces Bramble was alongside her, and before she knew it she'd opened her arms wide and Maria had walked right in. She felt surprisingly small and light, almost fragile, crushed against Bramble's chest.

'I'll look after you, too,' she said firmly.

'I know.'

'You were a good friend to my grandfather. You cared for him for all those years.'

'I wanted to,' Maria said simply.

When at last they separated, there was a slightly awkward pause during which the housekeeper straightened her dress and adjusted her collar and hair.

'Will you go back to the party now, Miss Bramble?' she asked at last, and Bramble took a deep breath and straightened her shoulders.

'I suppose I must.'

Chapter Twenty-Four

BACK OUTSIDE, AMIDST the hustle and bustle of festival-goers, beneath a sky, now black, that seemed to be lit by a thousand flickering fires, Bramble felt quite dazed and unable to focus.

'Where were you?' Katie asked breathlessly, running to her side and slopping cider from her ever-present plastic glass down Bramble's leg. 'I've been looking for you everywhere!'

Bramble hesitated. For some reason she didn't want to tell her friend about the painting; in fact, she didn't feel like telling anyone right now. The news seemed too big and portentous, too unreal to blurt out in a few sentences, and besides, she hadn't even begun to imagine what it would mean for her or for the future of Polgarry.

'I think Tabitha's up next,' Katie said, knowing that Bramble wouldn't want to miss her. 'I suppose Danny will be there.' She pulled a face but brightened again just as quickly. 'He's not as hot as Kieron.'

'Mm?' Bramble muttered, hardly hearing. 'That's nice.'

Katie looked at her oddly before taking her by the arm and leading her rather solicitously towards the main tent, which was packed tight, with barely an inch between one person and the next. At first they thought they'd have to stay outside, but then they spied a narrow opening and managed to weave their way towards the centre. They couldn't avoid treading on a few toes, but by and large it was a good-natured gathering and no one complained.

Bramble spotted Danny to her right, with Oscar on his shoulders wearing a pair of big, serious-looking ear defenders, but they were both focusing on the stage and didn't see her. When Tabitha walked on clutching her guitar in a pair of frayed jeans, cowboy boots and a silky cream top with billowing sleeves, her long black hair parted in the middle and loose around her shoulders, she looked as if she'd stepped straight off the set of a seventies' movie.

'How are you today? I hope you're having a good time!' she yelled, to a cacophony of claps, shouts and stamping feet. You'd never know that she was a bag of nerves – she looked like the Queen of Cool – but Bramble recognised the way she licked her lips and that nervous little laugh. It was all an act.

'I'm going to start with a song I wrote a very long time ago, when I was a teenager,' she began, settling on a stool with the guitar on her lap and adjusting the mike. 'I was going through a difficult time, living away from home...'

Bramble found herself drawn into the story, relieved to be distracted from her swirling thoughts, but as she listened she became aware of something behind her. Call it instinct or a sixth sense: she knew, without a shadow of a doubt, that someone was staring at her. Spinning around just as Tabitha started to sing, she scanned the sea of faces until she fell on one that brought goosebumps to her skin: Liz. The older woman was standing several rows back, near the entrance to the tent, balancing Lowenna on her hip and wearing a red woolly hat and a navy jumper. When Liz's huge dark-brown eyes met Bramble's they seemed to grow even rounder and wider, and she gave a tentative smile that was hard to interpret.

What was she doing here? Tabitha's voice started in a haunting minor key before rising to an urgent higher pitch. Bramble would have turned back to the front, glad for the excuse to look away, but Liz mouthed something that she couldn't understand and beckoned to her urgently.

Mesmerised by the act, Katie was totally unaware of Bramble's dilemma.

'It's Liz,' she hissed, digging her friend sharply in the ribs. 'What shall I do?'

Finally, Katie swivelled around and examined Liz from afar. 'It looks like it might be important. You'd better go and speak to her.'

'Really?' Bramble was aghast.

'Do you want me to come, too?'

'It's OK,' Bramble replied, and she weaved her way back through the crowd. If there were to be a nasty scene, she'd rather deal with it on her own. There was no need to spoil Katie's evening, too.

As she reached the entrance Liz moved a few steps outside, still clutching Lowenna – who, blind to any hostility, flashed a row of pearly-white baby teeth and beamed joyously, thrilled, no doubt, to be out and about at such a late hour.

'What –?' Bramble started to say, but Liz held up a hand.

'I'm sorry to drag you out but I need to speak to you.' She paused and swallowed while Bramble waited on tenterhooks for what was coming next.

'I was furious with you for what happened,' Liz went on in a faltering voice. 'I thought it was so irresponsible to take Lowenna into the water. She nearly died—'

'I know, and I'm so sorry. I realise you hate me and I wish I could put it right, but I can't.'

Inside, Tabitha's singing reached a climax before fading

out, and the audience broke into rapturous applause. The women, however, scarcely blinked.

'I didn't come here to rake up the past,' Liz explained gently.

'Then why did you come?' It seemed a reasonable enough question.

Lowenna made a lunge for the small gold chain around Liz's neck and she unlaced it carefully from her daughter's chubby fingers.

'I want to apologise for my part, for bearing a grudge and refusing to speak to you,' she blurted. 'I've been childish and vindictive and I'm ashamed of myself. Tabitha says you're in pieces, but everyone knows it was a freak accident and you weren't to blame. The sea wasn't particularly rough that day; you couldn't have seen it coming. And you did your very best to save Lowenna. You were incredibly brave. You could have died yourself.'

Liz took a tissue out of her trouser pocket and blew her nose, and for the first time Bramble noticed how pale she looked in the shadows, how drawn and pinched, with dark circles under her eyes that were almost blue they were so black.

'I'm so sorry,' Bramble whispered again hoarsely. 'I—'

Liz interrupted: 'Shush. Lowenna loves you, everyone here loves you. It was just me who couldn't move on.'

She touched Bramble on the shoulder so softly that she could hardly feel it, but it seemed to her like the warmest of warm embraces.

'Can we be friends again – please?'

A wave of relief and gratitude enveloped Bramble – and surprise, too, for she wasn't sure that she would have been able to forgive if it had been her child. She seemed suddenly lighter, as if the force of gravity itself had changed.

'Of course,' she managed to choke out in reply.

At that moment Lowenna struggled violently and made a bid for freedom. Without a second's hesitation, Liz passed her into Bramble's outstretched arms.

'Hello, gorgeous. I've missed you!' she said, hugging the little girl close before spinning her around and stroking her silky hair. 'Do you know? I think you've grown!'

'There must be magic, magic in the air,' Tabitha crooned in the background, and although Bramble hadn't heard the song before, the words seemed uniquely appropriate, as if they'd been written especially for her.

'Shall we go back inside?' Liz said at last, and Bramble followed her into the tent, still carrying her charge. She was thinking that life could throw up the most unexpected of surprises, and that all in all this was turning into a truly extraordinary day.

Most of the parents and children, including Liz and Lowenna, left at about ten p.m., and the stallholders packed up and the bands stopped playing at midnight, but the party didn't end there. The speakers were turned off outside the main tent so as not to annoy the locals, but inside they continued to blast out disco music and a gaggle of hardy revellers took to the dance floor, soon to be joined by scores more.

At last Bramble was beginning to feel that she could relax a little and pat herself on the back for what had undoubtedly been a wild success. There had been no accidents or nasty brawls, the manor seemed to be undamaged and feedback from festival-goers had so far been one hundred per cent positive. Right now, however, the most glorious thing of all was that Liz had forgiven her, which seemed to be worth more than any triumphant event or fabulously precious work of art currently hidden away in some high-security vault in London.

'You should make this an annual do!' someone shouted as Katie grabbed Bramble's hand and led her reluctantly into the mêlée. She wasn't in the mood for dancing – in fact, emotion had left her exhausted – but it would have been churlish to refuse and risk dampening her friend's high spirits.

Looking over her shoulder as she began to move in time to the beat, Bramble spotted a grinning Rick Kane, in a pink shirt open almost to the waist and revealing a good deal of grey chest hair, twirling a glamorous blonde companion around in a circle. Bramble managed to give him a thumbs-up before he spun in the opposite direction.

Close by, Audrey was doing a rather impressive twist, and to her right, Tony and Felipe were pogo-ing with Rafael and his gang of teenage friends as Rosie, with her bad leg, performed a more sedate jiggle. Nearer the stage, Loveday and Jesse were locked in a steamy clinch, unaware, it seemed, of the musicians packing up their equipment or the fact that a different huddle of youngsters, including Shannon, was staring and giggling at them.

Barbara and her team of staff had stopped serving alcohol, and as no one could get any tipsier than they already were Bramble felt that she must, surely, be largely off the hook.

Katie seemed to read her mind. 'You can let your hair down now!' she yelled, her eyes shining very brightly. 'The night's still young!'

Ryan sidled up with his pretty girlfriend and tapped Katie on the shoulder, and she grinned and waved. No more hard feelings there then. Meanwhile the handsome young former barman who'd been Katie's second choice of beau signalled to her to join his crowd.

'Come on!' she told Bramble, but she shook her head.

'You go. I want a break.'

Needing no more persuasion, Katie shimmied off, while Bramble headed for the exit, relieved to get away from the hot, sticky atmosphere. She'd tied her sweater around her waist but she put it on again quickly as the chilly night air crept up her T-shirt and coiled around her bare neck and arms, making her shiver. It was surprisingly dark now that the stallholders had taken down their artificial lights and put out their fires and, glancing up, she saw that the sky was awash with twinkling stars.

'Beautiful, eh?' came a voice, and soon Tabitha was by her side, wrapped in a dark overcoat and carrying her guitar in a case over one shoulder.

'You were fantastic,' Bramble said, meaning it. Her breath formed little puffs of smoke as she spoke. 'Everyone loved you. You should have seen their faces, and the applause was deafening. I had to put my hands over my ears!'

Tabitha smiled. 'They were a great crowd, and it's all thanks to you. It was an unbelievable atmosphere. You should be proud of yourself.'

'It was a team effort. Everyone worked so hard. I really hope you get lots more offers now.'

Tabitha tipped her head to one side and looked at Bramble earnestly.

'And what about you? What have you got from it?'

'We-ell, I hope people have had a really good time and we've made some decent money for charity. I hope they'll remember the night Polgarry Manor threw open its doors. I hope they'll see it now as a welcoming place that means something to them, rather than just a crumbling old ruin stuck up on the cliff.'

'I'm sure they will, but you must feel that you've learned

something from all of this, you personally?' Tabitha persisted. 'I mean, you've proved you're brilliant at organising big events. This could be the start of something amazing, a whole new career!'

'I couldn't do anything like it again. It's nearly killed me!'

'Not now, of course; you must be knackered. But you'll feel quite different once you've had time to recover. You'll start itching for a new project to get your teeth into. You wait and see!'

Bramble considered this for a moment. She supposed that she had learned a lot, not just about the practical side of putting on a festival but also about how to capture the public's imagination and galvanise local people. It had given her real joy to stroll around Polgarry, watching folk admire the artefacts and soak up their surroundings, and low as she'd felt about life in general, there had been moments of great satisfaction. Plus she'd grown much closer to Tabitha and the other villagers.

If only... She stared up at the stars again and wondered if Matt were looking at the same constellation from a window of his flat. Was he relieved to be away from Cornwall – and her? Perhaps he had Lois at his side. Perhaps at this very moment she was leaning against his shoulder, breathing in the faint scent of his aftershave and skin.

'Are you all right?' Tabitha asked, concerned. 'You look a bit strange.'

'I'm fine, honestly. I was a million miles away.' Bramble linked arms with her friend. 'Come on, let's go back to the manor. We'll give them another half an hour, then surely it'll be time to pack up and send everyone home to bed?'

*

Despite their weariness, neither Bramble nor Katie could sleep that night, their minds were so full of music and dancing – and in Bramble's case, that conversation with the lady from the auction house and Liz's heartfelt apology. Somehow in just a few short hours the whole world seemed to have tipped on its axis so that everything looked different; nothing was the same as before.

Katie had insisted on sharing the four-poster, and as she lay on her back, staring into the darkness, she let out a long sigh.

'That was sooo much fun. It's made me wonder if I did the right thing, going back to London. I mean, I missed the city and my family so much, and the trainee lawyer's great – we get on really well. But maybe I was a bit hasty, running off like that just because Danny wasn't interested. Maybe I should have hung around a bit longer and things would have got better? It's so lovely here.'

She sat up, propping herself on her elbows. 'Do you think I was hasty? Should I have waited a few more months?'

Bramble, who'd been on her back, too, rolled on to her side so that she could see her friend's outline in the dark, the white of her pyjama top, her pale face and glinting eyes.

'I don't know. I suppose I *was* surprised as well as sad,' she replied. 'I missed London and my parents – I still do – but I've learned to appreciate the different rhythm of life here and the amazing scenery. I love looking out on fields, trees, cliffs and sea. The air smells different; even the food tastes different. London seems so cramped and claustrophobic in comparison.' She gave a small laugh. 'I never thought I'd hear myself say that.'

Even as she spoke, Bramble realised that ever since the rescue, she'd been so focused on making the festival a success that she'd barely given any thought to how her life would be afterwards. She'd been aware that the day was fast approaching when she'd pack up her things and return to Chessington, but she hadn't considered how she'd feel: back in her old bedroom, looking out on rows and rows of identical houses and cars whizzing past; trundling in buses along roads with hardly a blade of grass to be seen, other than in the soulless municipal parks dotted along the route where nature, choking on traffic fumes, seemed to hang on by a thread.

She'd be a rich woman, of course, and could buy a mansion if she so desired, but she wouldn't want to live in a bubble. She'd still have the same friends, who'd no doubt choose to spend weekends traipsing around concrete shopping malls, then go to the same overcrowded pubs, cinemas and clubs. The only difference would be that this time there'd be no Matt by her side.

Was this really what she wanted? Surely, thanks to the painting, there was another way? Perhaps Tabitha was right and Bramble did have a talent for organising. She couldn't put on a rock concert at Polgarry every weekend, but maybe she could pour cash into renovating the place properly and then lay on other events to fund the upkeep and bring the manor back into the heart of the community. Weddings perhaps, book festivals, open-garden activities, dinners and barbecues, venue hire for corporate dos. She could build an adventure playground for children and, as Liz had once suggested, let out certain rooms on a B and B basis. Bramble had pooh-poohed the idea then, fancying herself too elevated in status, but her views had altered.

Staying was an exciting prospect, but scary, too. Even with all the money in the world, she wasn't sure that she could do this on her own. Maria had suggested that perhaps Lord Penrose had hidden the painting as a 'test' to see if

Bramble were clever enough to find it. Was she smart enough to upgrade a stately home all by herself and turn it into a going concern? Did she even fancy such a challenge?

Her mind flitted back to Matt and she knew without a shadow of doubt that she would have done it if he'd been here. Was she really the sort of girl who couldn't achieve anything without a man's help? Back in London, when she'd been working in her dead-end job, she'd wanted adventure so badly that she'd upped sticks and left him. Now, with the prospect of more cash in her pocket than she'd imagined in her wildest dreams, surely it was time to prove to herself as much as anyone else that she was worthy of her grandfather's legacy?

Katie prodded her with a finger. 'I thought you were going to come home now the concert's over? Don't tell me you're doing yet another U-turn?'

Bramble sat bolt upright, making her friend start, and hugged her arms around herself. She could feel the winds of change whistling through the manor walls, rattling the old windows. Better to have tried and failed, as the saying went, than never to have tried at all.

'Do you know,' she said, seeming far bolder than she felt, 'I believe I am.'

Chapter Twenty-Five

THIS TIME SHE wouldn't take any chances. The painting
was sold at auction for a grand sum amid much excitement
from the art world, and once the cash was safely in the bank
Bramble set about finding the very best architect around.
Together, they drew up plans to turn Polgarry Manor, room
by room, wing by wing, into a comfortable, modern home-
cum-business, without losing any of its original charm.

Tony was right: Rome wasn't built in a day, and the trans-
formation would take some years to complete. But as a new
team of highly recommended builders moved in and started
to rip out bathrooms, knock bedrooms together or divide
them and turn whole areas into temporary construction sites,
Bramble found that if she shifted her stuff around and kept to
the more habitable sections, the noise and disruption weren't
so great that she couldn't set to work on her commercial ideas.

Maria, of course, was delighted when Bramble broke the
news that she was to stay at Polgarry after all. The housekeeper made it quite clear that she, too, wished to remain,
and although she grumbled frequently about the chaos and
scowled at the builders whenever they passed, there was
generally a lightness to her features that hadn't been there
before. She was becoming physically frailer, however, and

Bramble insisted that she take more rest. Even so there was a cooked breakfast, lunch and dinner on the dining table at the exact same hour each day. It was as if the housekeeper had an inbuilt clock reminding her to heat the oven and lay the table, whatever madness was going on around her. She'd have been a tremendous asset during the Blitz.

Liz came to see Bramble often and took it upon herself to do some cleaning and help keep the dust at bay. Shannon would sometimes arrive after school to assist, and Bramble always paid her for her trouble, but Liz wouldn't take a penny.

'I like cleaning. I used to do it for a living,' she'd explain. 'I find it therapeutic.'

Both she and Bramble were delighted that Shannon seemed happier these days. Her father was on a new type of medication that eased his depression and she was even talking about pursuing a career in landscape gardening when she left school. Bramble had already said she could use her help when it came to redesigning parts of the estate, though she was anxious that the grounds should retain some of their wild, untamed beauty. If the public were to come in, however, paths would have to be cleared, signs put up, steps repaired and a certain amount of order restored. You couldn't have people slipping on broken paving stones, losing their way or falling into ditches.

She spent Christmas and New Year with Bill and Cassie in Chessington, and though she longed to see Matt, she didn't try to contact him. Her fingers frequently scrolled for his number on her phone, but she managed to stop herself just in time. She returned to the manor in early January to crack on with her plans, and she was so busy and focused that she scarcely noticed the days lengthening, and when the first newborn lambs appeared in the fields and golden daffodils sprang up on roadside and hill, she was quite surprised and wondered where winter had gone.

Several postcards arrived from Wilf, written in his uneven, childish hand, telling her about their village in the mountain region of central Spain, his new friends and their kitten called Alvaro. He sounded increasingly happy and settled, and she was pleased in a way when the cards stopped coming, because she took it as a sign that Fergus had done the right thing for them both.

One afternoon in late April she offered to pick Oscar up from school and look after him until Tabitha returned from a meeting with her new music manager, a man named Guy who was busy pushing for a record deal. On the way back they decided to pop into Tremarnock for a sticky bun, and whom should they see coming out of the bakery but Piers, with a French loaf under his arm.

He was much the same, Bramble thought: slim, suave and immaculately dressed in a well-fitting suit and shiny black shoes. But somehow today his features seemed weaselly, rather than handsome, and his greying hair made him look tired, not sophisticated. She wasn't sure who was more surprised by the unexpected encounter – him or her.

'I, um...' she started to say before clamping her mouth shut. There was no reason on earth for her to feel awkward and apologetic; he was the one who'd behaved so badly, after all.

'Bramble, how are you?' he said, gathering himself together and stepping forward to kiss her on both cheeks. She was tempted to dodge aside, but Oscar was right behind.

'Well, thanks,' she said curtly, pulling back as soon as she could and taking Oscar firmly by the hand. 'We're in a bit of a rush—'

'I heard your marvellous news!' Piers gushed, and for a moment she didn't know what he was talking about.

'The painting,' he explained. 'What a discovery! It couldn't have happened to a lovelier person!' His voice oozed sycophantic smarm. 'I was planning to give you a call actually, because I hear you're doing renovations. I thought you might like—'

'No,' Bramble said quickly. 'I don't need anything at all.'

His eyes widened and the corner of his mouth twitched, but it didn't take him long to rally.

'Of course you're sorted, clever girl.' He ran a hand through his silvery hair and grinned, revealing small, white teeth. 'How about dinner? Can I take you out one evening? We've got so much to catch up on.'

'Actually, I'm fully booked for the next, ooh, thirty years at least,' Bramble replied, smiling sweetly. 'Thanks for the offer, though. I'm sure some other gullible maiden will be thrilled to take you up on it.'

Then she looked at Oscar. 'Come on, young man. Let's get you a bun before they're all sold out.'

As she went into the shop, Oscar trotting by her side, she couldn't resist glancing back over her shoulder to see Piers staring after them, open-mouthed, as if he couldn't quite believe what had just taken place.

On a sunny Sunday afternoon in late July, when she'd been at the manor for a full year, she decided to have a small tea party to mark the occasion. The builders had almost completed the east and west wings, but the central section of the house, including the kitchen, remained untouched, so that it was possible, with Maria's help, to prepare sandwiches and bake some biscuits and cakes.

The guests were Liz, Robert, Rosie and Lowenna, Tabitha, Danny and Oscar, Loveday and Jesse, Ryan and his girlfriend, and Shannon and her brothers, which meant there were almost as many children as adults. Bramble would have liked to invite more villagers, but with Polgarry in its present state she'd felt it would be unwise.

It was glorious weather and they sat on picnic blankets in the orchard, well away from the scaffolding and mess, balancing plates on their laps and drinking tea from a thermos and glasses of fizz. With Shannon's help Bramble had managed to mow a section of grass big enough for them all.

Even Maria joined them, though she insisted on having a chair because her knees weren't up to resting on the ground. Perched stiffly beside them, her back ramrod straight and with a characteristically severe expression on her face, she reminded Bramble of an old-fashioned nanny, ready at any minute to rap her charges on the knuckles if they stepped out of line. Fortunately, however, her presence seemed to do nothing to dampen spirits but, rather, added to the general air of hilarity. After all, it wasn't every day you picnicked in the rundown gardens of a stately home with a bizarre housekeeper breathing down your neck.

'When do you think you'll be ready for your first B and B guests?' Liz asked Bramble, watching Lowenna out of the corner of an eye, who was trying her best to follow Oscar up a tree and not succeeding.

'I'll start advertising in September,' Bramble replied, munching on a slice of chocolate cake. 'But I'll have to warn people the place is still under construction so I don't suppose there'll be much interest. By next spring, though, we'll have finished all the guest rooms and bathrooms, and we'll have a brand-new kitchen, too. After that, we're going to redecorate the hall, dining room and drawing room and repave the terrace, then I'm hoping we'll get some weddings.'

'It's an ideal spot for them,' Robert commented, stretching out his long legs and helping himself to a second slice of walnut cake. 'We'd definitely have got married here if it had been possible then, wouldn't we, Lizzie?'

His wife nodded. 'The building's so unusual, and I love the fact that the garden's wild and overgrown. It's very romantic.'

Loveday, who was sitting extremely close to Jesse, nudged him in the shoulder so hard that he nearly toppled over.

'We could get married here?' she suggested with a cheeky grin. She was wearing a short, tight black PVC skirt and unsuitable wedges.

'Woah, slow down, babe. I haven't even proposed yet!' Jesse exclaimed, but he looked quite pleased all the same.

'You'd better hurry or she might go off the idea,' Liz teased. 'Besides, I'm dying to buy myself a big hat!'

'Get down on your knees, man. What are you waiting for?' Robert joked, and Jesse blushed furiously.

'Leave us alone, will you?'

'Maybe I'm not the marrying sort anyway,' Loveday sniffed. She glanced at Jesse slyly. 'Maybe I'm a lesbian!'

'What's a lesbian?' came a child's voice. It was Oscar, hidden in the branches above and listening to every word.

Maria rattled her cup and saucer loudly.

'It's a—' Shannon's brother Liam piped up.

'How about a flapjack?' Tabitha said quickly, passing him the plate. 'Have you tried one yet?'

The sun peeped through the overhanging trees and a shaft of light fell on Bramble's face. Resting on her hands, she leaned back and closed her eyes for a moment, enjoying the warmth, the low sound of happy chatter, the occasional higher-pitched shout from the children, the buzzing bees in the lavender bushes nearby.

'How Pat would have adored it here!' she heard Liz say, and a shadow seemed to pass over Bramble, for she, too, was feeling the absence of someone she'd loved and lost.

Often, she managed to blot Matt out, or at least to pack him carefully away in her bottom drawer, but at times like this, when everything was otherwise so perfect, she seemed to miss him more keenly – and worry about him a little, too. Was Lois looking after him? Did she know how to make his steak and chips just how he liked them, and was she familiar with his allergy to biological washing powder?

'Why did your grandfather never marry?' Danny asked, returning to the subject of weddings and bringing Bramble back to the present.

'He was very much in love once,' she said carefully, 'but unfortunately the woman didn't feel the same.'

She glanced at Maria, who nodded almost imperceptibly.

'It was my grandmother he loved actually,' Bramble went on, emboldened. She hadn't told anyone else the story up to now. 'He wanted to marry her after she got pregnant with me, but she turned him down. He never really recovered and he became a hermit after that.'

'How sad,' Liz commented. 'Everyone said he was strange and reclusive, but I never knew what lay behind it. I just thought he wasn't the marrying type.'

'I thought he was more than strange,' Bramble replied. 'I thought he was a horrible person until I found out otherwise.' She sighed. 'My mother had an unhappy life, too. I'm afraid it's in my genes.'

'But you're not unhappy!' Shannon cried, sitting bolt upright. She seemed quite upset, and the others looked at Bramble expectantly.

'Of course not,' she said quickly, not wishing to dampen

the occasion. 'I'm incredibly lucky. The past year has been amazing.'

'And I'm sure the next one will be even more so,' said Robert, raising his glass. 'Happy first birthday at Polgarry!'

'Yes, Happy Birthday!' the others chorused. 'Thank you for inviting us.'

They didn't leave until nearly eight, having taken almost everything into the kitchen first. Maria was tired and wanted to rest, so Bramble watched the guests drive away, the gravel crunching beneath their tyres, before padding alone across the grass to fetch the last plates, reflecting on everything that had been said.

The air was much cooler now and the setting sun had turned the sky a vivid shade of orangey-red as if someone had taken a paintbrush to it. As she wandered back towards the manor, flooded with rosy light, she almost gasped; it was so beautiful, like something out of a fairytale. Tonight, far from looking gloomy and forbidding, Polgarry's windows were flung open, the breeze catching the curtains so that they seemed to dance, as if they were having a party all by themselves. She fancied that she could hear music and laughter coming from within and a whisper in the encroaching dusk: thank you.

Despite her pleasure, she hated to think of her grandfather watching Polgarry deteriorate before his very eyes. He'd loved this place enough to wish to pass it on to her, yet not so much to nurture it himself, so that it would have been a constant reminder of his own despair and decrepitude.

'The last time I came it seemed so sad and neglected. You've worked wonders already. It's quite different now.'

That voice, at once familiar and strange... Her heart leaped. Her pulse started to race, and she felt her legs buckle as she spun around. His fair hair, receding at the temples, was slightly shorter, his face perhaps a little thinner, but the soft grey eyes were the same, the broad shoulders, that gentle, stoic expression.

'It's you!' she gasped, blinking a few times in case she'd been out in the sun too long. 'Why—?'

'Come with me,' he interrupted, taking from her the small pile of plates and the picnic rug that she was carrying and laying them on the ground. 'We'll fetch them later.'

Too stunned to protest, she slipped her hand in his and he started to pull her back through the orchard and over the fields towards the cliffs. She was wearing only shorts and flip-flops and the long grass prickled her legs and feet, but she didn't complain.

'Where are we going?' she asked in something between a laugh and a cry, but still he didn't explain. He was walking very fast, her hand felt hot in his and she could hear his breath coming in short, sharp bursts, or was it her own? She wasn't sure.

'Quick!' he said. 'Or we'll miss it.'

Now he broke into a proper trot. His legs were longer than hers and it was a struggle to keep up, but she sensed his urgency and upped her pace accordingly. Soon they were in the wooded area beyond the fields and they followed the track in the direction of Fergus's old cottage, which had remained empty since he'd gone.

'This had better be worth it,' she gasped, trying to ignore the nagging stitch in her side.

Once out in the open again, it was just a few paces to the edge of the cliff, where he stopped short and released her hand, leaving it dangling at her side.

'Look,' he said, pointing. 'I stood here once before, when I came to say goodbye.'

Together they watched the sky fade to pink and then purple,

darker and darker, until the sun shrank to a glittering dot and threw out an orange flame across the black sea, lighting a path between land and horizon.

'I feel as if I could walk across the water,' Bramble whispered, awestruck, 'right to the very edge of the world.'

'Me, too,' Matt whispered back hoarsely.

Soon they were engulfed in velvety dusk, while in the distance the twinkling lights of Tremarnock started to shine as the moon rose slowly and majestically, sprinkling her silvery magic around them like stardust.

'I hear you're quite the businesswoman now?' Matt murmured, still staring at the spectacle. His voice echoed in the stillness and his words seemed to bear no relevance to their real meaning, though she wasn't sure what that was.

'I guess so.' She was merely being polite. 'I hope I can make it work.'

'I've been doing a lot of thinking since I saw you last,' he went on, and now her ears pricked up. 'I was cut to pieces when you finished with me, but I picked myself up and tried to get on with things. I even dated someone for a while. She wasn't really my type...'

He paused and Bramble forced herself to wait.

'I didn't want to leave London. I liked my job, our friends, our life...'

'I know.' She could barely speak.

'Everything I'd heard about your grandfather convinced me we shouldn't have anything to do with the place, but I was being stubborn and it was wrong of me not to come and look.' He shuffled from one foot to the other. 'I know there's been a lot of water under the bridge...'

Could he hear her thumping heart, the blood whooshing in her veins?

'There's a job for me in the Plymouth gym if I want it, quite a good one. I thought I might rent somewhere nearby and give it a try?'

He took a deep breath. 'What I'm trying to say is, would you consider giving us another go? If you say no, I promise I'll never bother you again. I won't even come here for holidays – I'll stick to Kent or Sussex instead.'

She ignored the joke, which seemed so out of place. Wasn't it their lives he was talking about? Weren't their whole futures at stake?

'You can move into the manor with me,' she mumbled, shocked at her own boldness.

'What did you say?'

Her face leapt into flames and she wished that she could swallow the words. She must have misunderstood. She was about to mutter that she hadn't said anything, didn't mean a thing, when she felt a hand on her shoulder, a strong arm pulling her close.

'I love you, Bramble.' His voice was thick with emotion. 'I thought I was going mad.'

There was a catch in his throat and she turned around, but before she could reply his lips were on hers, their bodies pressed tight against each other's, so that if you looked down from above it would have been difficult to tell where he ended and she began. She was shaking slightly and her face was damp with tears, but he brushed them away with his fingertips.

'No more crying,' he said softly. 'Everything's going to be all right now.'

She wanted to lay down on the grass right there and then, to smother him in kisses and wrap herself around him so tightly that they could never be separated again, but she had something to ask first.

'How did you know I was missing you so much?'

'Katie told me.'

Bramble smiled. Her friend had always been a schemer. 'We'd better phone to tell her the good news then.'

'Later.' He tried to kiss her again.

It took all her self-control to push him gently away, and then she laughed, a tinkling sound that seemed to echo around the fields and cliffs before melting gracefully into the silent sea.

'What's the hurry?' She was so full of joy that she thought she might burst like a dam and flood the surrounding hills and villages with happiness. 'We've got all the time in the world.'

He smiled, a smile so warm and passionate that it seemed to light up the night sky, and without further ado they walked slowly, hand in hand, back across the darkened fields, through the shadowy orchard, past the broken mermaid fountain, through the wrought-iron gates, along the crunchy gravel path and up the old stone steps that led to Polgarry Manor – and home.

Acknowledgments

With thanks to Andrew Kidd, solicitor at Clintons in London, for his invaluable legal advice. Also, as ever, to my very special agent, Heather Holden-Brown, my terrific editor, Rosie de Courcy, and the rest of the team at Head of Zeus. I am so lucky to have you all.

Not forgetting my husband, Kevin, and our beloved children, Georgia, Harry and Freddie. Always in my heart.